Crossing the River

short fiction by
Nguyen Huy Thiep

edited by
Nguyen Nguyet Cam & Dana Sachs

translated by
Bac Hoai Tran, Birgit Hussfeld,
Linh Dinh, Viviane Lowe,
Rosemary Nguyen, Nguyen Nguyet Cam,
Nguyen Qui Duc, Nguyen Van Khang,
Courtney Norris, Dana Sachs,
Peter Saidel, Peter Zinoman

CURBSTONE PRESS

Printed in Canada on acid-free paper by Transcontinental /
Best Book
Cover design: Susan Shapiro
Front cover art: "Seeds of Life," oil on canvas, by Nguyen Trong Khoi

This book was published with the support of the
Connecticut Commission on the Arts, the
National Endowment for the Arts, and
donations from many individuals. We
are very grateful for this support.

NATIONAL
ENDOWMENT
FOR THE ARTS

Connecticut Commission
on the Arts

Library of Congress Cataloging-in-Publication Data

Nguyen, Huy Thiep.
   [Short stories. English Selections]
Crossing the river : short fiction / by Nguyen Huy Thiep; edited by
Nguyen Nguyet Cam and Dana Sachs.—1st ed.
      p. cm. — (Voices from Vietnam ; #5)
   ISBN 1-880684-92-6 (pbk. : alk. paper)
1. Nguyen, Huy Thiep—Translations into English. 2.Vietnam—
Social life and customs—Fiction. I. Nguyen, Nguyet Cam.
II. Sachs, Dana. III. Title. IV. Series.
   PL4378.9.N5168A2 2003
   895.9'2334—dc21

                                        2003001576

published by
   CURBSTONE PRESS 321 Jackson St. Willimantic, CT 06226
      phone: 860-423-5110   e-mail: info@curbstone.org
                    www.curbstone.org

Acknowledgments

I would like to thank the translators and editors for their work on this book. I also would like to thank all of my friends in the United States for their support, especially Le Thi Tham Van, Peter Zinoman, and Dan Duffy.

—Nguyen Huy Thiep

We thank the translators who contributed enormously to this book. We thank the people at Curbstone Press, especially Alexander Taylor, for their patience and encouragement. We also thank our families—Peter, Alexander, and Isaac; Todd, Jesse, and Samuel—for their love and support. Finally, we are very honored that Thiep allowed us to put together this collection.

—Nguyen Nguyet Cam and Dana Sachs

Contents

Introduction

In the history of modern Vietnamese literature, no writer has provoked more debate than Nguyen Huy Thiep. Since his short stories first began to appear in *Van Nghe* [Literature and Art] magazine in 1986, hundreds of articles, essays, and academic theses have focused on his work. As Pham Xuan Nguyen, an influential literary critic, puts it, "The more [Thiep] writes, the more controversy he creates. The publication of a new story is typically preceded by a flurry of rumors and followed by intense discussion inside offices and out on the streets."[1] Devoted fans praise Thiep for his precise and poetic prose style and for "the humanity in his short stories."[2] Those who deplore Thiep's work condemn him for his "brutal, gloomy and cold view"[3] of his fellow human beings, for his ruthless debunking of national heroes, and for "observing the past in a deformed mirror."[4] Such passionate reactions from all sides suggest that something original and provocative is going on in Thiep's writing.

Born in 1950 in Thai Nguyen Province, 50 kilometers northeast of Hanoi, Nguyen Huy Thiep moved to the capital with his family in 1960. After graduating from the Hanoi Teachers Training College in 1970, Thiep taught middle school for ten years in a small mountain village in the Northwest. The influence of this long period in the remote countryside may be seen in such Thiep stories as "The Winds of Hua Tat" and "Love Story Told on a Rainy Night," in which the author employs the oral traditions of the Thai and Muong minority communities to powerful, and somewhat eery, effect. In 1980, Thiep moved back to Hanoi, where he lives today. He has worked as a teacher, clerk, painter, potter, merchant, restaurant owner, and writer. Thiep's body of work includes seven full-length plays, a dozen essays and more than fifty short stories, a number of which have been translated into French, Russian, German, Chinese, and

Japanese, as well as English. Three of his stories have been made into films.

Thiep first began to publish during a transitional moment in Vietnam's recent history. In the mid-1980s, the ruling Vietnamese Communist Party [VCP] faced grave problems that threatened to undermine its authority. A nation devastated by years of war and a misguided post-war economic policy had become one of the poorest countries in the world. The fall of communism in the Eastern bloc eliminated Vietnam's most important source of outside aid. With crisis looming, the VCP launched a new policy known as *doi moi,* or renovation, along the lines of similar policy shifts then occurring in China and the USSR. While the main purpose of renovation lay in reorienting the country's collective economy to put it more in line with market forces, this re-alignment also loosened the Party's tight grip on literature and art during the late 1980s. It is no coincidence that Nguyen Huy Thiep appeared during this era. Not only did Thiep take advantage of the more relaxed environment to publish work that, for political reasons, would have been forbidden earlier, but the subjects of his stories also reflect the extraordinary changes that were taking place in Vietnam at that time. Readers were stunned that the government would allow Thiep to express himself so freely, and they were also shocked by what he had to say.

Nguyen Huy Thiep's image of Vietnam is seldom flattering, particularly in the way it depicts relationships between ordinary people. Defying the currently fashionable notions of "Asian values," in which the community takes precedence over the individual, Thiep presents a modern society in which each individual exists separately, in loneliness, unrelated in any fundamental way to anyone else. In his stories, Thiep highlights this sense of separation through his narrative style. For example, in "The General Retires," when characters speak, their conversation sounds forced, almost artificial. At one point, the narrator describes the discussion when a young mother, Kim Chi, complains to her extended family about the pain of childbirth. After Kim Chi's initial remark, the dialogue proceeds in a number of different, seemingly unrelated directions:

> Kim Chi cried, "Brother, it's humiliating to be a woman. Giving birth to a daughter tore my whole insides out."
> My wife said, "And, I even have two daughters."
> I said, "So you people don't think it's humiliating to be a man?"
> My father said, "For men, the ones who have hearts are humiliated. The bigger the heart, the bigger the humiliation."
> My wife said, "We all talk like crazy people in this household. Let's eat..."

Most of the time, Thiep describes his characters' speech using the word "said"—"I said." "He said." "She said."—rather than "I asked" or "She replied." Consequently, individuals seem to exist in the same world but without any sort of emotional connection to one another.

Moreover, while "Asian values" stress such qualities as loyalty, filial piety, and community identity, in Thiep's world, money has come to dominate family life. "Money's king," the butcher Khiem declares in the story "Without a King," and many of Thiep's characters seem to agree. In "The General Retires," one man's hunger for money even threatens to disturb the dead. When the story's narrator buries his mother, his ne'er-do-well uncle asks for permission to re-use the coffin after the ceremonial reburial: "There goes a damn sofa," the uncle, Bong, says. "Who else would have made a coffin with such good wood? When you rebury her, make sure you give this wood to me."

In these stories, greed and alienation have not simply emerged out of the breakdown of Vietnam's traditional values. Rather, people seem to have always existed in this way. Even in the countryside, far from the economic and social revolutions taking place in the city, Thiep depicts a world of misery and dissatisfaction:

> The resentful, stagnant atmosphere of these country villages left me numb with emptiness and bitterness. Life was a constant, frantic search for food. Prejudices and tradition weighed heavily upon these folk. I saw countless people ruined by the old patriarchal practices. ["The Water Nymph: Story Two"]

Far from polarizing urban and rural life, Thiep's stories reveal a dynamic relationship between the countryside and the city. In "The General Retires," city people still maintain many of the customs and habits of the village, while, in "The Water Nymph: Story Three," peasants leave the village to search for opportunity in the city. In "Lessons from the Countryside" and "Remembrance of the Countryside," Hieu and Nham, the two main characters, respectively, comment upon a countryside intruded upon by urban civilization. But the intrusion of the outside world can also serve as a refreshing and needed antidote to the stark monotony of rural life. In "Uncle Hoat," the narrator describes the night a travelling cheo opera troupe came to his village when he was a child:

> "We were enthralled, almost crazed over the words and the singing, the spectacular lights, and even the charged atmosphere of so many people in one place. Have you ever heard the collective sigh of ten thousand people at the same moment? No? Oh, it's wonderful, truly wonderful!"

As this moment at the cheo performance demonstrates, Thiep's stories are not unrelentingly grim. In fact, they're often funny, though usually in a dry and very understated way. In the story "Crossing the River," a robber becomes a hero, earning the adulation of everyone around him, except the ferrywoman, who knows his true career:

The teacher was stunned. What had happened amazed him. "Heavens! He dared to break the pot! What a hero! A revolutionary! A reformer!"

The ferrywoman hid a smile. She knew the misfortune of anyone who happened to meet that man alone at night.

Often, too, the stories provide delight in the fact that they continually shift, evolving in ways that are fresh and unexpected. At the end of "The Woodcutters," a story that is almost cinematic in its use of action and drama, the narrator concludes with a few terse sentences that, given the context, seem ridiculously matter-of-fact: "After that trip, my fate turned in a different direction. I no longer went off to make lumber. I got a different job."

Again and again, Thiep takes his stories in surprising directions, playing not only with a reader's narrative expectations but with literary convention as well. In "Remembrance of the Countryside," for example, Nham, a 16-year-old boy, narrates a sequence of events that take place over the course of a few days in his tiny village. Most of the time, Nham's manner of recounting the story is plain and unsophisticated, perfectly reflecting his circumstances as a poor, badly educated teenager. After a morning of exhausting labor in the fields, he describes his meal: "Lunch is rice with boiled vegetables, salted eggplant, and stir-fried small shrimp. I eat six bowls of rice without stopping. Now, I'm tired. If not, I would eat a lot more." Nham comes across as thoughtful and intelligent, and he offers a vivid picture of Vietnamese rural life, but there's nothing exceptional about his speech. He's only 16.

Then something remarkable happens. Suddenly, and regularly throughout the story, the narrative breaks out of Nham's simple prose and leaps into unidentified short passages of highly sophisticated lyrical poetry:

Who's there?
Who plays the plaintive flute at night?
And which bright souls, which dark souls are
                              searching for the way
Which faint breath
Which faint laughter
Emerges screeching out of white teeth?

These are clearly not the words of a 16-year-old farm boy. And for readers, Vietnamese as well as foreign, such inconsistency of voice will seem incongruous. But we also get used to it quickly. In the same way that Thiep plays with the dynamic relationship between the country and the city, he creates an artistic dynamism by mixing images of traditional life with breathtakingly original, thoroughly contemporary styles of writing.

Because Thiep consistently experiments with form, the stories themselves reject predictable conventions. The series of ten interconnected fables "The Winds of Hua Tat" read like magical realism, where a tiger's heart is as "small as a pebble", where a poor woman, digging for tubers, discovers an urn full of silver and gold, and where "one year, without warning, strange black worms appeared in the forest." In striking contrast, stories like "Without a King" and "The General Retires" offer acutely realistic, caustic portraits of contemporary urban Vietnam. And then there are the pseudo-historical narratives, the trilogy "A Sharp Sword," "Fired Gold," and "Chastity," which recount episodes in the country's past that might—or might not—have actually taken place.

These historical narratives, in particular, deserve a closer look. Sometimes confounding to a Western audience unfamiliar with Vietnamese history, they take a sharp—and often arch—look at the relationships between political power, intellectual life, and art. In these stories, Thiep appropriates well-known figures from Vietnamese history and turns them into fictional characters, often characters who bear little or no resemblance to the historical record. For example, in the story "Fired Gold," Thiep introduces as characters both Nguyen Du (1766-1820), the author of the masterpiece *The Tale of Kieu* and the most talented and beloved Vietnamese writer of all time, and Nguyen Anh (1762-1802), later known as King Gia Long, who founded the last Vietnamese dynasty, the Nguyen (1802-1945), and whom the current regime considers a reactionary leader because of his cooperation with foreigners. Vietnamese readers find it surprising to read a story in which such eminent figures appear as ordinary human beings, but the shock becomes even greater when these figures begin to interact with and comment upon one another, as when Gia Long regards the writer Nguyen Du as merely "one well-bred horse among many in the herds of horses, pigs, cows, and chickens."

Such surprises have a political as well as an artistic function. By describing relationships among such prominent figures, Thiep takes aim at a system in which political leaders have frequently demanded that art serve the needs of the government, compromising the quality of the art. In the story "Chastity," for example, an astute Vietnamese audience will read between the lines and see the beautiful singer Ngo Thi Vinh Hoa as symbolizing art while King Quang Trung represents political authority. When Ngo Thi Vinh Hoa places her little finger on the eyelid of King Quang Trung, the finger immediately "turned an ashen black and no amount of cleansing would wash out the stain." In other words, art has sullied itself by coming too close to political authority. Vietnamese readers, acutely aware of such subtle messages, will recognize the point: art and political power must maintain a distance from one another. Consequently, the historical trilogy's "unorthodox reworking of Vietnamese history and implicit indictment of contemporary political culture"[5] has for years provoked hot-headed debate. Some readers condemn Thiep for destroying images of national heroes while others defend the author by saying that one cannot read a short story the way one reads history, or even that Thiep's historical fiction may be more historically accurate, on a deeper level, than official history.[6]

While Thiep deals with national heroes directly in his historical stories, he plays with the idea of heroes and myths throughout his work. It's no coincidence that the plots of many of Thiep's stories involve the loss or absence of a hero or a myth: a general *retires* ["The General Retires"], there is no *king* ["Without a King"], the water nymph turns out to be a scam ["Water Nymph: Story One"]. In "The Woodcutters," the organizer of the group, Buong, likes to present himself as a strong leader, but the narrator of the story sees him quite differently: "I knew Buong. Whenever he explained about life in general, he was always wise and tried to hold his dignity high. But his real life was like dog shit: too stinky to sniff at." It's not merely the lack of great leaders that interests Thiep. Rather, the author wants to raise a question about the fate of individuals in the modern age: what happens to human beings when there is no father figure, no king, no myth?

In the more than 18 years that have passed since Nguyen Huy Thiep first emerged on the Vietnamese literary scene, he has continually occupied the highest position in contemporary Vietnamese literature. Old writers have admitted that, after reading Thiep, they couldn't continue to write as they had in the past. Young writers talk about how his writing has both inspired and influenced them. Le Minh Ha, a Vietnamese writer who lives abroad, has written that Thiep "created a new stream for contemporary Vietnamese writers to swim in and a huge shade for them to seek shelter under."[7]

For *Crossing the River,* we have put together the most comprehensive collection of Thiep's work ever published in English. We hope that these stories will introduce to an American audience an author who constantly presses against, and moves beyond, the limits of literary tradition. Even more important, Thiep does so without losing—but, rather, by enhancing—the work's power and meaning. Thiep's stories, from the most straightforward narrative to the most peculiar twisting of form, give us characters who are complicated, infuriating, hilarious, ridiculous, pathetic, and human. His stories offer intimate explorations of loss and heartbreak, envy, desire, and familial love, cut time and again with sharp challenges to social conventions and the politics of contemporary Vietnam. Nguyen Huy Thiep's writing often mystifies his readers, but it just as often dazzles them.

—Nguyen Nguyet Cam and Dana Sachs

1. Pham Xuan Nguyen, "Introduction" in Pham Xuan Nguyen, ed., *Di Tim Nguyen Huy Thiep* [*Searching for Nguyen Huy Thiep*]. Published by Nha Xuat Ban Van Hoa Thong Tin [Culture and Information Publishing House], Hanoi, 2001. p. 6.

2. Greg Lockhart, "Tai Sao Toi Dich Truyen Ngan Nguyen Huy Thiep Ra Tieng Anh" ["Why I Translated Nguyen Huy Thiep's Short Stories into English?], in Pham Xuan Nguyen, ed., *Di Tim Nguyen Huy Thiep*. p. 111.

3. Hong Dieu, "Xung Quanh Sang Tac Nguyen Huy Thiep" ["Revolving Around Nguyen Huy Thiep's Works"], in Pham Xuan Nguyen, ed., *Di Tim Nguyen Huy Thiep*. p. 453.

4. Nguyen Thuy Ai, " Viet Nhu The Cung La Mot Cach Ban Sung Luc Vao Qua Khu" ["Writing Like That Is Also a Way of Shooting the Past"], in Pham Xuan Nguyen, ed., *Di Tim Nguyen Huy Thiep*. p. 204.

5. Peter Zinoman, "Nguyen Huy Thiep's 'Vang Lua' and the Nature of Intellectual Dissent in Contemporary Vietnam" in *The Vietnam Forum: a Review of Vietnamese Culture and Society*, No. 14, 1994. p. 37.

6. For more information about this debate, see various essays and articles published in Pham Xuan Nguyen, ed., *Di Tim Nguyen Huy Thiep*.

7. Le Minh Ha, "Chan Dung Nha Van, Tu Mot The Nhin" ["Portrait of a Writer, Viewed from One Angle"] in Pham Xuan Nguyen, ed., *Di Tim Nguyen Huy Thiep*. p. 495.

Crossing the River

Crossing the River

At the Wharf:

Getting onto the ferry were a monk, a poet, a teacher, a robber, two antique dealers, a woman and her child, a couple, and the ferrywoman.

The ferrywoman laid down a plank so that the two antique dealers could push their motorbike onto the ferry.

The tall skinny guy said to the guy in the checkered shirt, "Careful!"

He was telling his friend to be careful with the bundle of fabric in his arms. There was an antique pot wrapped in it.

"Help!" The tall skinny guy called to the man behind him. That man was the poet.

They busied themselves pushing the motorbike onto the plank. The poet ineptly pulled the motorbike over on its side. He fell to his knees in the water.

The couple on the shore burst out laughing. The girl said to her lover, "Give them a hand!"

The young man took off his jacket and gave it to the girl. He went over to where the motorbike had fallen.

The motorbike was lifted and pushed onto the ferry next to the woman and her child, who were traveling back from the city to visit their home village. The woman was thirty-two years old, beautiful and aristocratic. The son was nine and looked very cute.

They adjusted the motorbike on the ferry, bumping the woman. She frowned. The tall skinny guy quickly said, "Sorry, Lady."

The tall skinny guy bent down, brushing the dirty spot off the woman's knee. She pushed his hand off, and turned her face away. Behind them, the monk was telling the teacher a story about Bodhidharma:

"When the Venerable Master sat in meditation facing Tung Mountain, Hui-k'o came to him, cut off his own hand,

and asked for the spiritual sign. He said, 'Venerable Master, my heart is not at peace.' The Venerable Master said, 'Show me your heart.' Hui-k'o replied, 'Teacher, I have searched for my heart unceasingly, and yet I can't find it.' The Venerable Master said, 'There! I've set your heart at peace already.' Then Hui-k'o found enlightenment....'"

The guy in the checkered shirt, holding the bundle of fabric in his lap, sat down next to the monk. This was the safest place in the boat. The teacher was not pleased.

"Hey! Why are you elbowing your way in here?"

The guy in the checkered shirt was bashful. "Please forgive me, Grandfather. I'm carrying a precious treasure in my arms. If this pot breaks, I'm ruined."

"What kind of pot is it?"

The guy in the checkered shirt shrank back a bit.

The couple got onto the ferry. They sat down in the front, behind the ferrywoman. The young man put his hand out to grab the jacket on the girl's thigh. His hand touched the warm flesh of her belly. He was quiet, and he didn't pull his hand out again. The girl blushed and put the jacket over his hand.

The poet sat unsteadily on the edge of the ferry. He dipped his hand into the water, making the ferry tip. The tall skinny guy scowled and nudged the poet's shoulder. "Don't fool around!" he said. "We might all die if you do that."

The poet was astonished.

"The water is so transparent!" he said. "Look at the fairy fish down there."

The tall skinny guy burst out laughing. "Really! I only see carp!"

The boy interrupted, siding with the poet. "They are fairy fish!"

The tall skinny guy glanced at the woman's belly. "Hey kid, ask your mother whether those are carp or fairy fish."

The woman got embarrassed, pushed her thighs together, and grabbed the boy's hand.

The ferrywoman pushed on the pole. The ferry moved

away from the wharf. Late afternoon, gray clouds. A bird
flew toward the mountain. The ferry set out on its course.

"Ferry!"

The sharp cry rose from the shore.

The tall skinny guy waved his hand. "Ignore it!"

The ferrywoman hesitated.

"Ferry!"

This time the cry was sharper. The ferry turned and
headed back to the shore.

Descending from the bank was a big tall guy with a bag
draped over his shoulder. He had a look of wind and dust. In
one leap he was in the ferry. River water splashed all over the
monk.

The monk was startled. "Amitabha!" he cried.

The teacher grumbled, "Man or devil! He looks like a
robber."

The guy really was a robber. He smiled politely as if to
apologize to everyone and then carelessly picked up an oar.
Hanging his cloth bag over one end of the oar, he tucked the
oar under his armpit to light a cigarette; then gave the
ferrywoman a wink.

"It isn't sunny. It isn't rainy. It's late afternoon already."

The ferrywoman responded aimlessly, "There's no storm,
so why is the raven coming down off the mountain?"

The robber said cheerfully, "I've been invited to a
wedding. A sixty-year-old man is marrying a seventeen-year-
old girl."

Everyone on the ferry was completely silent. Nobody
was fond of this kind of talk. Only the lovers weren't paying
any attention. The young man slipped four fingers through
the elastic of the girl's trousers. The girl was about to make
some gesture of resistance, but, fearing everyone would
notice, she sat still.

The sound of the oars was very soft.

The guy in the checkered shirt dozed.

The teacher continued with the conversation. "Oh,

Venerable Master! The nature of human life is cruelty. People run after sexual passion, money, and vain glory."

The monk looked into the palm of his hand.

"Oh Venerable Master! I see beasts everywhere. Everything is a beast. Even faithfulness is a beast. Even the sense of goodness is a beast, too."

The poet recited softly, "Only myself, lonely among the herd..."

The woman peeled an orange and handed it to the boy. The boy shook his head.

The tall skinny guy pulled out a pack of cigarettes and offered it to the poet. The poet noticed a beauty mark on the tip of the guy's nose. He shook his head. "What a frightening beauty mark!"

The tall skinny guy stared. "Why is that?" he asked.

"You could suddenly just kill somebody." The poet raised his hand and gestured as if to slit his own neck, "Just like that!"

The tall skinny guy burst out laughing. "How do you know?"

The poet stammered, no longer sure of what he said. "I'm a prophet of the future."

The boy pulled at his hand. "Then what about me, Uncle?"

The poet looked with concentration into the boy's eyes and saw, together with those tiny red veins, an anxious and numb sadness that the boy seemed to have inherited from our ancestors.

He asked hesitantly. "Do you dare to dream?"

The boy nodded his head resolutely. "Yes!"

The poet smiled. "Then you're unlucky."

The woman sighed.

The teacher grumbled, "There are liars everywhere."

The girl sitting in the front of the ferry stirred. Her lover slipped his four fingers a bit deeper into her underpants. The gesture did not slip past the eyes of the woman. Through her own female experience, the woman knew that the lovers were getting into monkey business.

The teacher recited:

> *Heels muddied in the pursuit of wealth and fame*
> *Weather-beaten faces revealing life's cataclysms*
> *Thoughts of helping the world bring pain*
> *Bubbles in the ocean of misery, duckweed at the*
> *edge of the dark shore*
> *The taste of the world's troubles numbs the tongue,*
> *fills the body with misery*
> *The journey through this world is bruising, full of*
> *obstacles*
> *Waves in the mouth of the river rise and fall*
> *The boat of illusion pitches and rolls at the edge of*
> *the waterfall...*

The poet exclaimed softly, "How wonderful! Whose poem is that?"

The teacher answered, "That's Nguyen Gia Thieu."

The poet sighed, "What a pity. The interesting ones die. Literature always dies so young."

The girl sitting at the front of the ferry uttered a soft moan.

The woman looked deep into the eyes of the girl and cursed under her breath, "Whore!"

The girl recognized the curse and turned her face away, but she was still followed by the woman's gaze. Unable to bear it, she shamelessly looked directly into the mother's eyes and admitted, "Okay, I'm a whore!"

The boy burst out laughing because he saw a drop of saliva running out of the corner of the mouth of the antique dealer in the checkered shirt. His eyes were shut, and his head fell repeatedly into the face of the monk.

The bundle in the hands of the guy in the checkered shirt was resting on the teacher's thigh. The teacher was irritated and snatched the bundle, causing a cord to slip and expose the pot. The guy in the checkered shirt woke up, startled:

"I'm sorry, Grandfather!"

The teacher lifted the pot in his hands to carefully admire it. "This pot is really beautiful!"

The teacher turned to his side. "Oh Venerable Master! Which period does this pot belong to?"

The monk looked up. In his eyes there was a gleam of light, almost like a ray of desire. "It's a ceramic pot from the time of the Northern Domination, the time of Ly Bi or Khuc Thua Du."

Hesitating for a moment, the monk lifted his hand to touch the mouth of the pot. "If Tuong Pagoda had a pot like this and sold it, the money would be enough to rebuild the three gates."

"Then, that would be five ounces of gold!"

The tall skinny guy proudly took the pot from the hands of the teacher. The robber stopped rowing. Nothing on the boat escaped his notice.

The girl sitting at the front of the ferry turned away to avoid an impetuous and careless gesture from her lover. The irritated young man pulled his fingers out of the girl. He stealthily wiped his hand on the boat's bottom plank, but he could not scrape one sticky curly hair off his finger. At that moment, an idea occurred to him which made him suddenly angry. He moved far away from the girl. "Women...devils... completely worthless...dirty..."

The girl stretched out her legs. Her look of disappointment caught the woman's attention. The woman smiled, unable to hide the look of satisfaction in her eyes.

The poet examined the pot with admiration. "Thousands of years of history. It's really amazing! In the past, a princess used this pot to hold hair-washing water!"

The tall skinny guy smiled. "I thought it contained liquor."

The poet nodded his head. "That's right! In the 13th

century, when the Mongolian Chinese army came through, a soldier used this pot to hold liquor. It was buried in the 15th century."

"Really?" The tall skinny guy was interested. "There are probably many legends about this pot, don't you think?"

The poet nodded firmly. "Naturally." He narrowed his eyes. "There are fifty legends about it."

The teacher dropped his bag. The guy in the checkered shirt stooped to pick up a piece of paper and saw that it had words written on it. He glanced at it and read, "'Humanity has a duty to work without stopping to create lofty people: That's humanity's mission and there's nothing else.'— Nietzsche. 'I often speak with artists—and I'll speak forever—the ultimate goal of all conflicts in the universe and among human beings is drama, because conflict serves no other purpose.' —Goethe."

The guy in the checkered shirt returned the paper to the teacher. He said politely, "Your handwriting is so beautiful!"

The teacher took the paper and said bitterly, "Handwriting? What's the point of good literature and beautiful handwriting?"

The boy leaned against the poet and thrust his hand into the mouth of the pot. The woman panicked. "Son! Be careful! If you can't get your hand out there'll be trouble!"

Maybe the exhortations of the woman were really the curses of the Creator, containing all the hatred of the past.

The tall skinny guy jumped. He told the boy, "Pull your hand out!"

The poet joked, "When you put your hand into history, it will be stuck there for a long time!"

The boy struggled. It seemed like the mouth of the pot got smaller.

The boy cried, "Mama! Help me!"

Everybody in the ferry jumped. The boy couldn't get his hand out of the mouth of the pot.

The woman was frightened. "What will we do?"

The guy in the checkered shirt sat down to help hold on to the pot. He turned the pot and grumbled, "You devil! You're so bad!"

The boy burst into tears. The tall skinny guy began to get angry. The robber didn't row anymore. He moved closer to investigate. He advised the boy, "Jerk your hand out."

The tall skinny guy wrinkled his face and said in a harsh voice, "Careful not to break the pot!"

There was only a little distance left to be rowed before the ferry reached the shore. The river was as calm as a sheet. Blue smoke rose from the direction of a far off village.

The couple also left their seats to go closer to the boy. Everyone was searching for a way to disengage the pot. Tears filled the boy's eyes.

The poet joked, clearly inappropriately, "All you have to do is cut off the boy's hand to save the pot, and then break the pot to retrieve the boy's hand."

The woman wept and groaned, "Oh God! I'm so miserable!"

The tall skinny guy held onto the pot. He jerked hard. That was the final effort. The boy's wrist got red and scratched.

"Impossible!" the tall skinny guy said.

He stood up and thrust his hand inside his shirt. The guy in the checkered shirt understood his friend's idea.

The ferry reached the dock. On the shore there wasn't a soul in sight.

A cold wind blew.

The tall skinny guy and the guy in the checkered shirt drew two sharp daggers.

The tall skinny guy said to the woman, coldly and precisely, "This pot is worth five ounces of gold. You solve the problem!"

The woman, holding the boy tightly, was frightened. "Oh God! I didn't bring any money."

Suddenly remembering, the woman, holding the boy tightly hurriedly pulled a ring off her finger.

The tall skinny guy turned his head toward the guy in the checkered shirt, who immediately took the ring and put it into his shirt pocket.

The tall skinny guy pressed his dagger into the boy's neck. A drop of blood flowed out onto the tip of the knife. The drop of blood ran slowly across the boy's splotchy skin.

"Why do that?"

The teacher shivered and dropped his glasses. The tip of the dagger pressed even deeper. A small ray of blood spurted out and onto the teacher's hand.

The girl standing next to the young man covered her face and screamed. She fell against the side of the boat. The young man pushed the poet out of the way, pulled a ring off his hand and offered it to the guy in the checkered shirt. He spoke, as if it were an order. "Let the boy go!"

The woman stopped crying. She was rather surprised by the young man's behavior.

The tall skinny guy turned his eyes. The dagger's tip gradually sunk deeper into the neck of the boy. The guy in the checkered shirt took the ring out of the young man's hand.

The robber pushed his way through, trampling on the boy's foot. The boy screamed. The robber leaned in, pushing against the teacher. The fabric bag hanging on his shoulder fell off, spilling out the tools of a profession which was clearly not at all honest: A fighting stick, as many as fifty different types of keys, a bayonet, a pair of figure-eight curved handcuffs, a crushed and tattered yellow calendar foretelling the good and bad days...

The robber hurriedly stuffed the tools back into his bag. He held up the fighting stick and tapped it in his hand. He said, "It happened already. Take it as bad luck. A lost investment."

The tall skinny guy glared up at him. The robber was

half-joking, half serious. "Stop it! Children are the future! Whatever you do, it has to be humane."

The tall skinny guy hesitated, easing up the tip of the dagger. At that moment, the stick in the robber's hand struck the mouth of the pot.

The ceramic pot shattered.

The poet let out his breath and said appreciatively, "That did it!"

The boy collapsed onto his mother. The mother and child held each other crying. The tall skinny guy and the guy in the checkered shirt were speechless. They turned and pointed their daggers in the direction of the robber.

The robber stepped back little by little, then jumped onto the shore. He rotated the stick in his hand.

"It's useless," he said calmly.

It really was useless. Obviously.

The young man helped the girl get up. The girl smiled. She knew. She would love him forever.

The poet mumbled, "Love makes people noble."

The two antique dealers put their daggers away, then pushed the motorbike up onto the shore. They grumbled and cursed until they got on the motorbike.

The teacher was stunned. What had happened amazed him. "Heavens! He dared to break the pot! What a hero! A revolutionary! A reformer!"

The ferrywoman hid a smile. She knew the misfortune of anyone who happened to meet that man alone at night.

The poet picked up a few ceramic pieces and gave them to the woman. He explained, "A souvenir."

He bent down to lift up the boy. One by one everyone went up to the shore.

Dusk was gathering. The monk remained motionless on the ferry.

The ferrywoman said cautiously, "Venerable Master! Please go on up to the shore."

The monk shook his head. "No, I've thought about it.

Take me back." Vacillating a moment longer, he hesitantly said, "I'll go later."

Not knowing what to say, the ferrywoman looked at the stars at the edge of the sky.

"Venerable Master, after returning to the other side of the river, I don't come back again."

The monk was cheerful, smiling. "It doesn't matter. One can go if one wants. In the past, the virtuous Bodhidharma crossed the river on a blade of grass..."

The ferry headed back toward the wharf. The shadows of the ferrywoman and the monk were clear on the peaceful river. The moon rose and the bell sounded sweetly.

The monk whispered the invocation:

"Gate gate! Para gate! Para para san gate!"

Translated by Dana Sachs and Nguyen Nguyet Cam

Lessons from the Countryside

My mother is a peasant,
and I was born in the countryside
—a storyteller

When I was seventeen, after graduating from high school, I spent my summer vacation at the home of a classmate named Lam in the hamlet of Nhai, in the village of Thach Dao, in the province of N.

The hamlet of Nhai lay on the Canh River, a small river that people could wade across during the dry season, the deepest spot only coming up to your chest. Lam's house was at the end of the hamlet, deep in a small alley with a hedge of cud weeds. The house had a thatched roof, mud walls, and consisted of three rooms and two outbuildings. There wasn't much furniture in the house. In the middle was a bin for rice, on both sides of which were four bamboo beds. Clothes were hung on a pole fastened to the wall. The single decoration in the house was an ancient silk painting depicting the three old men, Happiness, Prosperity, and Longevity, being offered peaches by some children. The painting was framed in glass and covered with cobwebs. With the passage of time, the surface of the glass had glazed over and become covered with fly droppings.

Lam's family wasn't large. His grandmother was old and his parents worked in the fields. His older brother, who was in the army, had married a young woman named Hien and she had been living as a daughter-in-law in the household for half a year. Lam had two younger siblings, his sister Khanh, who was thirteen, and his little brother Tien, who was four.

My house was in the city. Because I seldom had the opportunity to go into the countryside, I was delighted to go to Lam's house. My father taught school, and my mother (who came from a feudal mandarin family of long lineage)

12

was a housewife, a "teacher's aide" to my father. My parents wanted me to continue in school. "If you study, your life will be less difficult," my mother said.

I had never been away from home before. My mother told Lam, "He's very young, so you should look after him." I looked at Lam and smiled. He was actually four months younger than I was, although outwardly he was bigger and taller.

Lam's family greeted me warmly and Hien set up two food trays. The one she placed on the porch was for Lam's father, Lam, and me. The one in the courtyard was for Lam's grandmother, Lam's mother, Hien, Khanh, and Tien. The meal included crab meat broth with rau dut, pickled eggplant, and fried shrimp. Our tray also had some peanuts and two green guavas to accompany the rice whiskey for Lam's father.

Hien invited us to eat by saying, "Will the elders please make themselves at home?"

Little Tien declared, "Let me be one of the elders!" but Lam's mother dismissed his plea.

"That's disrespectful!" she said. "Your penis is only as big as a chili pepper, so how could you be an elder?"

Khanh covered her mouth, laughing. I blushed. Lam's grandmother sighed, "All of you elders sure do have big ones." Everyone rolled with laughter, except for Lam's father. His face was dark, and though it spoke of hardship he wasn't sad at all, but rather placid and unconcerned.

Tien wept and Hien comforted him. "Please stop crying! Sister-in-law will give you this crab claw."

Tien shook his head. "No way. The crab claw is so small."

Hien offered, "Tomorrow when I go to the market, I'll buy you a set of tam cuc cards."

Lam's mother said, "Gambling is the uncle of poverty. Don't buy tam cuc for him. When he grows up he'll be addicted to it, and that will be the death of him. Maybe he needs us to get out the rod."

Tien cried more. "Buy me the tam cuc cards."

Hien turned her eyes to Lam's mother, hiding their conspiratorial look. "Okay, I'll buy you the tam cuc."

Lam's grandmother chimed in, "A long, long time ago, there was a Mr. Hai Chep, a ferryman who loved playing tam cuc for money. At first he lost his money, then he lost his field, then he lost his house, and finally his wife left him. So when night came, he went out to his boat, sat, and cried. Angry at life, but wanting to redeem himself, Mr. Hai Chep took out his knife, cut off his two testicles and threw them into the river. But his wife didn't go back to him."

Lam's mother replied, "That's an unfaithful woman."

Lam's grandmother said, "Unfaithful? He only had those two testicles and now he'd lost those, too."

Hien laughed. "That's terrible. Your stories give me the creeps."

The meal was over quickly. Khanh scraped the pot noisily. "Hieu, are you full?" Hien asked me.

I nodded. "I ate four bowls. In Hanoi, I only eat three."

Lam's mother said, "Young people eating four bowls is nothing. My other half has to eat nine bowls of rice packed tightly. I myself need to eat six bowls to be full."

Hien said, "You beat me there. I can only eat three bowls at most."

Lam's grandmother said, "You should eat more, since men really don't love us at all. When they drink, they sit at the better food tray. When they sleep, they lie on top of us."

Lam's father barked, "Old woman, how dare you!"

"How dare I?" she muttered. "Damn you! I'm eighty years old, how could I be wrong?"

Afternoon. "Do you and Lam want to see a kite?" Lam's father asked.

Lam's mother said to him, "I beg you, grind a few baskets of paddy for me."

Hien replied, "Just let Father be. Let me do it. It's not often that we have guests." From a corner of the kitchen, Lam's father took down a kite as big as a one-person basket-

14

boat layered with strips of rice paper. The string of the kite was rolled rattan as thick as my index finger. Lam used sand to polish the set of copper kite flutes until they shone brightly. Lam's father dipped the roll of rattan string in the pond. We waited until the sun went down and went out into the field, which had already been harvested, leaving only stubble. Toward the horizon, rolling clouds glowed a fiery red. The cracked surface of the field exuded a rich, earthy scent. Children from the hamlet flocked after us. A few old men drying hay at the edge of the pond paused in their work to look. One of them said, "Old Ba Dinh's at it again." Someone else added, "There's a lot of wind today, so the kite will sing loud and clear."

Lam's father wore shorts and was naked from the waist up. His muscles rippled. On his shoulder he carried the huge roll of rattan string. Lam and I carried the kite with some effort. Lam's father said, "Let's go up to the Dam Tien termite mound to fly the kite."

Lam directed me, "You stand and watch." He walked to the top of the termite mound, then stood there testing the direction of the wind, his hand pushing up the kite, looking like a dancer.

I ran after Lam's father, who was leaning backwards while pulling hard on the kite string. The kite teetered and winged down. He sprinted to the right, jumping over the embankment. The kite darted across the sky. Now he ran to the left. The kite darted again, wavering for just a minute and then floating straight up. He released the roll of rattan. Beads of sweat covered his naked back and he breathed heavily. He ran. He fell down. He ran again. He fell down again.

I ran after him, almost completely out of breath. He ran across fields that were being harvested, waded through canals, silently, forcefully, straining himself, suffering like a person who knows clearly that the work he is doing is very difficult and requires intense concentration. The roll of rattan was released gradually and the kite reached its highest point, where there were no more treacherous winds, dangerous and filled with unexpected possibilities; up there, it was a different kind of wind—nice, noble, forgiving, generous, and stable. The kite tilted once, as if either to scorn the earth or to greet it, then it remained still, blowing its flutes all alone in the sky.

> *This is the sound of the flute*
> *Does anyone know what singing a song is like?*
> *Only a fragile thread connecting it to the earth*
> *It could break unexpectedly at any moment*
> *But it dares to wing and teeter freely*
> *Because only you, kite,*
> *Can feel the lightness of life*
> *Without harming anyone*
> *Amidst the precarious blue*
> *Is the little flute*
> *Let them look at the sky*
> *All the pain, even glory*
> *Can only make you more perceptive*
> *Go ahead and sing*
> *To your heart's content*
> *Because your fate has been determined*
> *What kite doesn't have its string broken once?*

The kite was swaying steadily and the rattan string was slack and gently curved. Lam's father got up on the dike to walk the kite back to the village. One hand holding the string, he lumbered in silence like a person who had just returned from herding water buffalo, not even turning back to look behind him. The whole sky was filled with the sound of the flutes. In admiration, I looked at his body covered with sweat and stained with mud. I estimated the distance he had traversed, perhaps nine or ten kilometers.

When he reached the entrance to the village, Lam's father tied the end of the rattan string to a bamboo pole that had been pushed into the ground for that very purpose. Only then did he turn his eyes to look at the sky, gazing in contentment at the motionless kite, up high. A few minutes later, he left and went down to the river. He stripped down and tied his shorts around his neck, one hand clutching his private parts, then waded into the water, dove deep, and swam to the middle of the river before finally surfacing. He paused for a moment, and I was certain that he looked at the kite and shouted something. This time, he dove underwater and disappeared. The surface of the river became blurred, and dusk began to settle over the landscape.

Alone, I walked along the unfamiliar road into the village in the twilight. The air was filled with a kind of tender and mysterious feeling. The trees swayed along the sides of the road. I lost track of the present. In me, there was no image of the city where I had always lived. I had forgotten the loving faces of my parents. Even the train ride that had taken Lam and me from the city to the village that morning had left my mind. And yet this was the first time I had been away from home. I even forgot the kite.

> *Let me forget, forget*
> *Nightfall—the great eraser of time*
> *Erasing first the accident that gave me birth*
> *Erasing the ties I have with things*
> *Erasing all the futility*
> *and shame of a shameless day*
> *Please erase, please erase*
> *Please rebind the threads in the heart*
> *Because surely you must travel in the night*
> *In sleep, the soul has to wander by itself*
> *No baggage*
> *No body even*
> *What cycles of life are waiting?*
> *And what open spaces will hold us?*

At home, Lam's mother was sifting rice in the courtyard. His grandmother lay in a hammock lulling Tien to sleep while Khanh slept on a low bamboo bed. Lam's father was already there, splitting bamboo strips. Lam's mother said, "Lam waited forever for you to go catch shrimp with the scoop net. He's gone."

Hien was pounding the rice down in the outbuilding. "Hieu, if you're not busy, come down here and help me," she called.

I entered the outbuilding. It was rather dark. Inside there was only a tiny oil lamp. The rice mortar was made of heavy wood two-and-a-half meters long, and the end was covered with iron. In the middle was a hook so that the person pounding the rice could put all of his or her strength into it. "Hieu, have you ever pounded rice?" Hien asked.

"Never," I replied.

"Step on this thing and hold on to the rope."

"Pounding rice is pretty easy, isn't it?" I asked.

Hien smiled. "How old are you Hieu?"

"I'm seventeen, same age as Lam."

She sighed. "I'm three years older than you. And that's old. Women have only one time in their lives. I'm so afraid. Hieu, change places with me. Men should never stand in front of women when pounding the rice, right?" She laughed. I was startled by the smell of sweat so near and the soft feeling of her breasts against my back.

She confided, "It's so depressing in the countryside. I've only been to Hanoi once. At that time, I wasn't married yet and it was fun, but I was nervous. Hanoians all looked mean. That day at the bus station, a man my father's age wearing glasses and a thin mustache said to me, 'Darling, come with me.' I was frightened and said, 'How dare you?' He laughed and said, 'I'm sorry, I thought you were a lost cow.' I didn't understand what a lost cow meant. Afterwards, Tan (my husband now) came up, and the man got lost. I told Tan and a cloud came over his face. 'City people are all scoundrels,' he told me. I don't know, they're all so eloquent and they're always ready to say they're sorry."

Hien confided in me some more. "In the countryside, I'm afraid of boredom the most. I'm not afraid of work, though. There are times when you're so bored, you become listless. When Tan joined the army, I almost committed suicide out of boredom. I lay by myself in the cornfield, in the middle of a colony of yellow ants. I thought that if you were bitten by yellow ants, you'd surely die, but I didn't die. Maybe they pitied me? Perhaps they found me too young, such a waste to die." She laughed.

My heart was numbed with pain. I recalled my father, wearing a thin mustache and usually wearing glasses. As for my mother, if she lay in a colony of ants, she would surely die. My mother fidgeted a lot and that species of yellow ant doesn't like people who fidget.

Hien continued, "In the countryside, sometimes it's fun. When there's cheo or tuong performances, then it's a lot of fun. I remember once there was a performance of "Tan Huong Lien Holds a Trial." I fried a bag of grasshoppers to bring along. They're so delicious. There was me, a girl named Luoc, and a girl named Thu. The three of us stood watching the play, eating. The old man Tran Si My was unfaithful, and after he became a mandarin, he treated his wife badly. Luckily the world still had Bao Cong. Without Bao Cong, people would still be suffering from injustice in their lives, right?" She stopped for a moment, then burst out laughing. "There were a few young men from Due Dong standing behind us. One of them pressed his penis against Luoc's rear. 'What are you doing?' she asked. This guy was shameless, and coolly said, 'I'm the head of a cooperative.' Luoc reprimanded him. 'Stop it.' The guy said, 'As long as the people still have faith in me, I'll keep doing it.' There were loud guffaws all around them. Luoc ran outside, with the seat of her pants all wet. She was frightened that she would become pregnant, so when she got home, she threw her pants into the pond. So that's all there was of Tan Huong Lien and Tran Si My."

Hien said, "Hieu, don't breathe like that. Inhale deeply, then breathe out slowly. You should breathe like the Major practicing Coc Dai Phong in my home village. His name is Ba. He's already retired and very fat. Every morning he runs around the village wearing shorts and shouting out loud: '1,2,3,4...Healthy!' Once, Thu and I went out to transplant rice seedlings. It was only four o'clock in the morning, but we saw Mr. Ba jogging on the road. The elastic band of his shorts broke, so he had to hold them up as he ran. Thu said, 'Sir, at sixty why do you still want to be healthy?' Mr. Ba replied, 'I need to be healthy to protect my family. Don't you know that my wife is only forty years old?' But he's very nice. He loves helping people. I'm told that he retired not because of old age but because of his stupidity. I hear that the state now only gives official positions to young, educated people."

Hien continued. "Why do women have to get married? Just like me here, my husband is away, so it's like I'm married, but I'm not. To get married and then to leave your husband, is that okay, Hieu?"

"No."

Hien said, "Sure, I understand how it works. They say, 'Bamboo floating in the river, if not bruised, will break. A girl who disparages her husband surely will indulge in certain vices.'"

"What does that mean?" I asked.

"It's talking about an immoral woman, but a lot of men are also like that. Marrying a man who is poor and untalented, but noble, could be scary. It could destroy a woman's life so easily."

"Why do you think like this?" I asked.

Hien answered, "These aren't my ideas. They're Teacher Trieu's. He teaches night school and says that women don't need nobility. Women need understanding and caresses, and they need help with money. That's love. Being noble is for politicians. And politics without nobility is frightening, since politics is something people look to for reassurance in their lives."

I was so sleepy. I don't remember when I went to bed. When I woke up I panicked from the wonderful stillness of the empty house. Nobody was home. I washed my face and went looking everywhere. In the outbuilding, several baskets of white rice were piled on top of one another next to the mortar. The kite had been thrown down carelessly, its wings in tatters. I couldn't find the flutes or the roll of rattan string. In the kitchen there was a plate of boiled sweet potatoes and four or five eggplants, maybe saved for me. I ate the potatoes and the eggplants and went up to sit in the house. The painting depicting the three old men, Happiness, Prosperity and Longevity, and four or five children offering peaches, was a mass-produced watercolor with a caption in Chinese characters. I liked Old Man Prosperity the most, with his black beard, full cheeks, strong build, and eyes that could speak. If he could have spoken, Old Man Prosperity would have said, "Hold it, I know everything. You guys have to keep calm. We have to reach a consensus, so don't cheat me."

Outside in the yard, a few chickens were pecking at the paddy. Stillness. Not a sound.

> *Stop, stop everything*
> *Brush aside the sound of a chaotic life*
> *Stop for a minute*
> *To listen to the absolute stillness*
> *You will see how small you are*
> *I am only a tiny grain of goodness*
> *With a little bit of goodness, how could I profit?*
> *With a little bit of goodness, how could I fight?*
> *The inheritance my mother has saved for me is*
> *so insignificant*

Hiding itself in a dark corner
That dark corner of conscience
Day and night become hoarse with silent tears.

It was about ten o'clock when Lam's grandmother, Khanh and Tien came home. Lam's grandmother said, "The three of us went to the temple and the old monk gave us rice cones from the altar to eat." She turned to Khanh and said, "Why don't you give one to Hieu so he can have a taste of it?"

"Grandma, you eat it," I responded. "I've already had some sweet potatoes."

She said, "I won't eat it. I've been eating those things forever. At eighty, if I'm greedy for food, it makes it hard to die. For the past four years, I haven't dared eat anything healthy, but I still haven't been able to die." The old woman sighed. "As they say, 'When you're too old, you turn into a devil.' I'm terrified of old age. Every morning I go to the temple and pray to Buddha Nhu Lai for death, but he keeps shaking his head, not granting me my wish. All because I've been working so diligently. In my younger days I should have been more of a hedonist, then things wouldn't have been this bad. Among all the girls my age in the village, whoever indulged herself has been allowed by him to go to heaven early, not having to wait until she was in her seventies. That way, you live happily and you die happily. As for me, all my life I've known only one cock. I've always been known for being faithful and virtuous. I don't know who it's good for, but I know that when you keep on living into your old age, it becomes a burden on your descendants."

I smiled but felt pained by what she'd said. "Grandma, don't talk like that," I said.

She shook her head. "You're too young; wait until you've reached the age of eighty. In this life, Lord Buddha provides each of us a little property, and everyone gets the same, equally divided. Health and virtue are also property, and if you have property, then you must know how to spend it. When you have a lot of it, then it turns into a monster. In Due Dong, there was a wealthy man who had dozens of kilos of gold, and his wife went crazy, his children, too. None of his grandchildren lived past thirty."

Lam and his father came home from plowing. "It's noon already, and you and your grandchildren haven't made lunch?" he asked.

From the kitchen, Khanh replied, "I'm making it."

Lam's father went up to the house and poured tea into a bowl for me. "You didn't go anywhere? If you listen to my mother's conversation, young man, you'll go mad."

Lam's grandmother jumped in, "You're right. I'm an idiot."

"Not an idiot, but wicked."

She replied, "A wicked heart is scary, but a wicked mouth isn't."

Lam's father said, "Young people are like a clear well, and you keep releasing turtles and octopuses into it. That's terrible."

The grandmother sulked, "Well, Son, if your mother had ten joints, eight of them would be demons, one and a half would be ghosts, and only half a joint would be human. Try to listen a little bit, and if you can't, then don't pay any attention."

When lunch was over, Teacher Trieu paid a visit. He was still young, just over thirty, with a thin body and the gestures of a person tired of life. Fleetingly, I saw Hien shrink into herself before Trieu's calm gaze. Trieu asked me, "Do you like it here in the countryside?"

"I do."

Trieu laughed. "I asked a really dumb question, since you're the guest, and if you said you didn't like it then Uncle Ba Dinh would ask you to hit the road."

"I wouldn't dare," Lam's father said.

"Uncle Ba Dinh, your guest is as shy as a girl. I look at

his face and I know that he's intelligent, but he'll meet with much misfortune. Listen to me, when you grow up, don't follow the path of a writer. You'll be beaten up. People will curse you. You can't fight against the ignorance of the educated. Look at me here, I understand profoundly how harmful, reactionary, dangerous and uncultured the ignorance of the educated can be. The ignorance of the educated is thousands of times more despicable than that of ordinary people."

"Why?" I asked.

"Because they can disguise themselves. They claim conscience, ethics, aesthetics, and social order, speaking even on behalf of the whole nation." Then he added, "If politics isn't lofty, it will make mistakes."

"Then people don't need knowledge?" I asked.

Trieu said, "Children need it. But when people grow up they need something that's more important than knowledge; they need stability in order to live naturally and harmoniously. Old people also need knowledge, but in a different form, which is religion. My concept of 'the people' doesn't include children and old people. During the adult years, life itself is knowledge."

Trieu turned to Hien, "The school year is over. You've passed and can move up to eighth grade. You got eight points for math, and three for composition, but I raised it to five arbitrarily."

Hien blushed. "I'm very bad at composition," she said.

"It doesn't matter," he replied. "Our people are good at being warriors, and that's enough. I'm sad because our literature doesn't have much value. It lacks real religion and aesthetics."

Trieu went home. "He's interesting, isn't he?" I asked.

Lam's father replied, "Very good, too. Children in this village all learn from him. We ourselves learned from his maternal grandfather, old teacher Dat."

It suddenly grew dark and a moment later, it rained. It

rained so hard that rainwater flooded the yard. Khanh shouted merrily, "There's a perch! A perch!" She rushed out into the yard to catch the fish. I followed her out into the rain. Khanh called, "Hien! Get me the basket trap."

Hien stood on the porch, looked up at the sky, then said to Lam's father, "The weather is changing. Father, take the cast net out to the river."

Khanh shouted gleefully, "Out to the river, out to the river!"

Lam's father carried the fishing net, while I carried the basket trap. Hien carried a basket and Khanh carried the crab creel. We all went out to the river, rain coming down in sheets. Fish floated on the surface of the water. Hien said, "Father, look there, a lot of fish, right?"

Lam's father waded into the water, casting his net when he was immersed to his waist. There were lots of tiny shrimp and fish as big as your hand. Hien, Khanh, and I untied the fishing net. Fish came pouring out onto the sand bank. Lam's father cast his net again and again, as many as ten times. And each time we got fish, even mudfish the size of a person's calf, slippery and slimy because they don't have scales.

It was still raining heavily and I started to feel cold. Hien and Khanh's teeth chattered. We were tired and cold, but it was still great fun.

Lam's father cast his net twice in a row but didn't catch any fish. He shook the net and told us, "I'll go home first because I need to let the water out of the seedling plot. You guys come home later."

Hien squeezed the fish into the basket until it was full and said to Khanh, "Go down and take a swim." Both of them swam well. I hesitated for a moment, then followed suit. The water was very warm. I was still learning how to swim, so I didn't dare go out far. "Hieu, you're so bad!" Hien teased.

We swam for about ten minutes and got out. The wet clothes clung tightly to Hien and Khanh's bodies. I became hard when I saw their bodies, so beautiful. Their well-proportioned curves were extraordinarily stirring, and hot blood filled my chest. "Hieu, come here and help me." Hien called. Her eyes met mine. Fleetingly, I caught a radiant taunting in her eyes. I went, stooped over, and was about to lift the basket full of fish when Hien seemed to casually sidle up to me, allowing her thigh to brush against my body. I felt weak and my jaw locked. For a moment, I found Hien looking deeply into my eyes and then she blushed. I couldn't breathe anymore and fell onto my knees on the sand bank. My whole body trembled violently. Hien put her hand on my head, then her face grew pale and she mumbled something that didn't have much meaning. Suddenly she ran very fast to catch up with Khanh who was carrying the basket trap ahead. I heard the two of them squealing with laughter.

I was panting and lay writhing on the wet sand bank. My testicles and penis were so heavy, very painful. The basket of fish spilled all over. I lay on my stomach among the fish and shrimp and ejaculated, my mouth snapping and taking in a mouthful of sand. I don't know whether I swallowed any sand. My heart was filled with a mix of fear and elation. I knew on this day that I had become an adult.

> *Farewell, childhood*
> *I have grown up*
> *From now on I must shoulder*
> *   responsibility for myself, for everyone*
> *I'm embarking on a string of slipups, one after*
> *   another*
> *Oh, childhood*
> *While in me there's still an intact masculinity*
> *Wealth, fame, law all fly over me*
> *Covering me is a pair of diaphanous wings,*
> *   my mother's*
> *Oh, childhood*
> *Where is the unprejudiced smile*
> *The strange folk tales*

26

The small road leading to school
And the fear of being abandoned...
I have grown up
In front of me is endless infatuation
My soul muddies over
I hunt for fame
Hunt for wealth
Happiness and duty torture me
Death, smiling, waits for me at the end of the road
There, there is a path leading down to hell
Oh, childhood
Innocent and pure childhood
Poor, lonely, gloomy childhood
Wretched childhood
I don't know whether I should laugh or cry with you
Farewell!

When I got back to the house, Lam's mother announced, "Let me go in time to sell the fish at the evening market." She left a few of the biggest fish and said a few words to Khanh, then carried the basket to the market in a hurry. Khanh brought the knife and cutting board out to the bridge over the pond to prepare the fish. Now it had stopped raining, but the sky was still dark and overcast. I was so sleepy that I went to bed.

I had been napping for a long while when I suddenly woke to the sound of giggles out in the yard. Khanh and Tien were sitting on the porch playing chuyen the. Khanh spread the sticks on the ground and tossed up a pebble while she sang. Tien kneeled at his sister's feet and mumbled, mimicking his sister. Khanh's voice was loud and shrill:

Pass, pass one
A pair
Pass, pass the potatoes
Two pairs

Pass, pass the eggplants
Three pairs
Pass, pass the yams
Four pairs
Pass, pass the silkworms
Five pairs
Onto the wobbly table..."

Lam's grandmother sat on the bed, tears streaming down her wrinkled cheeks. Khanh's voice was still loud and shrill:

Going into the village
Beg for meat
Going out of the village
Beg for sticky rice
Go by the river
Return by the river
Plant the mustard greens
Row the ferry across
One ferry across
Two across ferries...

I went out to the alley. The whole sky had suddenly brightened up, turning the color of chicken fat. It was strangely beautiful. Everything—the sky, the earth, the trees—it all appeared so clearly beneath this magical, bright color. The color enveloped everything. Even the crimson red hibiscus flowers now faded into a different color, as rosy as a person's lips. My heart skipped a beat out of fear. A different world, terribly concrete and horribly detailed, materialized in front of me.

A few minutes later, the sky grew cloudy. Everything returned to its former landscape. I shivered in pain, recognizing that the world around me was so pale and pitiful. I had to stand still for a long time before I recovered.

High in the sky, a few storks flew by, their hoarse cackling rather terrifying. The raindrops resting on the leaves suddenly showered down on me all at once. I followed a path filled with bamboo leaves, walking around in circles for a little while in the village, lost. Several young children darted here and there. Someone had lost some chickens and was loudly cursing the neighbors, the swear words sounding brazenly vulgar. I made a detour up to the dike. In the distance, a brown sail slowly went upstream, completely unconcerned.

Trieu was sitting on the dike reading a book. I approached him, noticing that the place where he sat had clusters of violet flowers, the petals of which, when open, looked like a person's lips. I picked one and brought it up to smell it, finding it sweetly fragrant.

Trieu laughed. "Do you know this flower?"

I shook my head.

"It's a very strange flower," he said. "It looks exactly like a smiling mouth, but if a mosquito accidentally falls into it, it closes its petals immediately. It's strange because if we leave it alone, nothing happens, but if we touch it then it exudes a fragrant scent. People call it the slutty flower. That's because it's exactly like women: If you leave them alone they're extraordinarily virtuous, but if you touch them, you may be destroyed completely. First, it's your money, then your soul, then your family falls apart, and your career is destroyed."

I laughed. "Are you married yet?"

"Not yet," he replied. "When a woman is someone else's, she's beautiful, but when she's your wife, she's just kind. It's too bad!"

Trieu lay down on the green grass and said, "Lie down here. Being from the city, do you look down on country people?"

"No," I said.

"That's right, don't look down on them. To country

29

people, all of us urban and educated people are guilty of serious crimes. We destroy them with our hedonistic pleasures, education, and bogus science, tormenting them with laws, cheating them with sentiments, exploiting them to the bone. We weigh down the countryside with a super-structure consisting of a whole lot of paperwork and notions of civilization. Do you understand? My heart bleeds for them. I always say, 'My mother is a peasant, and I was born in the countryside.'" Trieu fell silent. A moment later, he suddenly sat up and said sadly, "You'll never understand what I say."

"You don't trust me, do you?" I asked.

"It's not that. Only, you're still young. It's the fault of nature, not your own."

I was stung by an ant, and sat up. At my feet, black ants crowded around the corpse of a red dragonfly. "So many ants!" I said.

Trieu answered, "See? People are also crowded like that. They live like ants, busy, rushing about, not quite able to make a living. Take that dragonfly and put it somewhere else to see what happens." I did as he asked and then he continued, "Do you see the ants swarming that spot? People are also naive and gullible like those ants. The politicians and the talented men are the only ones who have the ability to push people in any direction they choose. Most people are only looking for profit. Promise them a little profit and they'll flock to it. They don't know that that's the very thing that's responsible for the meaninglessness in their lives. They are born, act, make a living, flock to this place and that place, never being able to set a clear direction for themselves. Perhaps someday they'll finally understand that they can't merely search for profit, because even if they do, no one will give it to them. Others only make empty promises in order to deceive, and if there's any profit in the whole enterprise, it's very little. Moreover, the profit never outweighs the harm. The profit must be produced by the people themselves, by their own labor. They need to understand that, and should look for something loftier, something that has genuine value in life: the right to be allowed to determine their lives for themselves—in one word, freedom."

Trieu sighed, thought for a moment, then said unhurriedly, "There's one more thing. Since I've started, I might as well finish. In wartime, there definitely must be despotic rule. But in peacetime, the policy of despotic rule will lead the nation to disaster. Only through benevolent rule—democracy, trust and high morals—can the country become prosperous."

We were silent for a while, then Trieu spoke again. "Hieu, don't listen to me. I'm shallow and very wrong. My mother is a peasant, and I was born in the countryside." I looked at him with pity, and suddenly my eyes welled up. I put my face down on the bank of grass, so he wouldn't see me crying.

Trieu stood up and started walking down the side of the dike. At that moment there suddenly came a loud roaring from the field. A water buffalo stained with mud was charging madly in our direction. Just then, I heard someone call to me, "Hieu, come home and eat!" Looking over, I saw little Tien standing at the base of the dike looking around. The water buffalo was charging straight toward him. I panicked, and before I could recover I saw Trieu jump out to stand in front of Tien. I only heard a terrible, agonizing scream. The buffalo charged into Trieu with a tremendous force and I saw him being lifted high by the buffalo's horns.

Trieu died instantly. His head had twisted to one side, blood spurting from his mouth and his innards spilling out. The crazy buffalo went back to grazing nearby, indifferently. Tien, who had been pushed aside by Trieu, had fallen off the embankment into the field and now, pale as a ghost, was struggling on all fours to stand up.

Many people came running, some carrying guns. A man in the local militia fired shots like mad into the head of the animal.

People from the hamlet turned out in great numbers. Lam's grandmother, taking Tien by the hand, cried and prostrated herself before Trieu. Lam's father and mother also cried, kneeling down by the side of the field and prostrating themselves over and over again. A few old men from the hamlet had a discussion and finally asked everyone to carry Trieu's body to the base of the banyan tree that had lived over nine hundred years. From a distance, its canopy spread out like a tray piled with sticky rice, with a base that took four people to encircle it.

Night fell and the sky filled with stars. Suddenly, I felt a panic like I had felt when the chicken-fat-colored glow reflected on everything. I recognized the infinite immensity of the world, in which I, myself, life and even death were so small and meaningless.

People made a coffin for Trieu right at the base of the banyan. Lam and a few young people from the hamlet brought an altar to set up, on which there was placed a picture, a bowl of incense, some fruit, areca nuts and betel leaves. The entire village gathered together by the banyan tree. Someone brought a patterned mat and spread it on the ground for the old women to sit and prepare the betel. The militia came to stand guard, carrying guns. An atmosphere simultaneously somber, sorrowful, and apprehensive enveloped everything.

People laid Trieu in the coffin at midnight, torches brightly illuminating the entire area. Everyone tied mourning bands around their heads. Lam's mother gave me one, too. I guessed the band, on which lines were sewn with black thread, had been torn from an old curtain in the house. Cymbals and drums sounded loudly, while children and women, both young and old, sobbed. I also wept.

Once Trieu had been laid out in the coffin, Lam and a few young people went home to catch pigs, and then cooked the sticky rice and pork next to the banyan tree. When it grew completely light, everything was ready.

Trieu's funeral began at eight o'clock in the morning. Now the sun shone brightly, high in the sky, and the field was bathed in its rays. The elders and people from the hamlet crowded around the casket, with the students lining up in front of them. Principal Mieu read a eulogy, his body trembling violently. I listened, completely astonished upon learning that Trieu was not from this village. His parents lived in Hanoi. His father was a government minister and his mother had been born into a well-known family of intellectuals. He'd lived a bachelor's life, staying in this village for nine years and never going back to visit his family in the city. It was said that his parents had disowned him. Trieu was only an ordinary elementary school teacher.

They buried Trieu in the village cemetery.

On the grave there was only a wreath of white flowers. In later years, I attended many more funerals, but only this funeral left an impression on me that would never fade.

> *People must thank him*
> > *the village teacher*
> *He was the great illuminator of my people*
> *Here was pure knowledge*
> *Even if it was rudimentary, erroneous,*
> > *and childish*
> *It was a, b, c*
> *Oh, the village teacher*
> *He had to work with the snot-nosed brats*
> *They didn't know which was the right hand, which*
> > *the left*
> *He will teach them, right,*
> > *he will teach them:*
> *The right hand is flung up*
> *And the left is placed over the heart...*
> *He will teach them, right, he will teach them:*
> *This is zero, this is one*
> *And their mothers, they should never forget*
> *Ahead there is truth*

There could be the Great Flood
And outside the earth, is the galaxy
This is letter a...

That afternoon only Lam took the water buffalo out to rake the fields; everyone else stayed home. Lam's mother cooked a meal to offer to Trieu. Hien wept as she plucked a chicken. The mourning band was still tied around her head. Lam's mother admonished her, "Hien, you should take it off. We mourn him in our hearts. People see you wearing it, and with your husband so far away, well, I think it looks horrible."

Hien took it off and cried, "I prostrate myself to you, teacher, who lived wise and died sacred, please bestow blessings on my family."

Lam's grandmother added, "The teacher died in Tien's place. Even though he's unrelated, now he's become a saint in our household. What a great person."

Mr. Mieu sat drinking tea with Lam's father. Mr. Mieu said, "He was the grandson of teacher Dat, who was a member of an old scholarly group, from Ninh Xa. That clan had many outstanding people."

Lam's grandmother said, "It's a pity for the girls in this village. Didn't any of them love the teacher? A person like that dying without having anyone to carry on the bloodline is such a waste, don't you think?"

Hien replied, "I heard that he used to pay attention to Thu, but she rejected him as too cold, always philosophizing, with no emotions."

"Damn that hussy," Lam's grandmother said. "I'll give her a talking to when she comes here. Young girls nowadays only like a flashy coat of paint. Serves them right if they fall for a So Khanh lady-killer type."

Mr. Mieu added, "The outstanding bloodlines in our country are drying up because beautiful women all fall for people like So Khanh, Khuyen, and Ung. What a great pity!"

Lam's father said, "Well, I don't like philosophizing, either."

Mr. Mieu replied, "People who philosophize to death should be forgiven. In our country, accidental deaths are so scary. Everyone has to hurry—'Hurry as if it's already too late.' And that was Trieu's fate."

Late in the evening the feast had just been set out when Mrs. Hop from the neighborhood came, bringing with her the women and girls from the seedling planting team. From out in the alley, she yelled for Lam's father, "Mr. Ba Dinh, come out here and see how your son has plowed and raked the field. He only put on a show of it. We've brought your seedlings back."

Lam ran out from the house, his face flushed red.

Lam's father asked Mrs. Hop, "You couldn't plant them?"

"If we could, we wouldn't be here. We wouldn't have brought them back."

Lam said, "I'm sorry. I hurried home because I really wanted to eat the food from the ceremony."

His father shouted, "Lie down here! I'm going to cane you three times to teach you a lesson. Mrs. Hop, let me order him to go out there and rake it again for you." Lam's father took down the rattan string from the rafters. Lam lay down in the yard and everyone crowded to intervene. His father said, "Please leave and let me teach my son. When he does things carelessly, he must be caned in order to learn a lesson. He still has to go out to make a living, and if he picks up the habit of cheating, then what will happen to him?"

Lam's mother pulled at her husband's arm. "I beg you, if you have to cane him, please do it lightly."

Lam's father held the cane, telling Lam, "I have to cane you three times to teach you a lesson. Two for you to remember that you have to do things carefully, and one for you to remember that you are the son of Ba Dinh, and you shouldn't let your father be ridiculed by others."

He flung the cane high into the air. Lam's body jumped

three times. His mother grabbed the cane out of his father's hand and swore, "You brute!"

Lam crawled on all fours and stood up, putting his hands together, and said, "I beg you, Father."

Without a word, Lam's father went to untie the buffalo, then carried the rake out to the alley.

At dusk, Khanh ran back to the house and said, "Brother Lam, Hieu got a letter." I was surprised, especially because it turned out to be from my father, who wrote:

> *Dear Son,*
>
> *I was very upset because your mother decided on her own to let you go into the countryside when I was away. I want to let you know that your dog, your house is in the city, your future is here....*
>
> *Son, listen to me, you have to come back at once. Your parents will open the door wide to welcome you, like welcoming home a gullible son, too gullible....*
>
> *Your Father*

I was petrified. I showed Lam the letter and he said, "Hieu, you should go back. Your father won't only cane you three times like mine did. If he's using words like these, he means to kill you. Tomorrow morning there's a five o'clock train."

Early the next morning, Hien got up to cook some sticky rice, wrapped it in a banana leaf and put it in my bag. Lam asked, "Will you be all right alone?" I nodded. Everyone in the house seemed to be busy, and no one seemed to pay attention to me. I know, what right did I have to ask for any affectionate sentiments from them—from Lam's grandmother, his father, his mother, Hien, Khanh, Tien.

I left the hamlet and the village. It was still very dark

and the field was misted over. I wondered, why did my father regard me as a gullible person?

> *Human gullibility*
> *I am gullible; you, brother, are gullible; you, sister,*
> > *are gullible*
>
> *And even you, my dear*
> *You are so gullible*
> *We are all gullible in this world*
> *I was gullible enough to believe in my father*
> *I am gullible to believe in you*
> *And even you, my dear*
> *You are so gullible*
> *Your heart is innocent*
> *And your lips are pure*
> *Your eyes are so sorrowful*
> *That faith...*
> *Faith without assumptions, without conditions*
> *What if I'm a demon?*
> *What if you, brother, are a demon? What if you, sister,*
> > *are a demon?*
>
> *What if my parents are demons?*
> *Human gullibility*
> *Will it give us wings so that we can fly up to Heaven?*

I kept on walking, crossing the field, the river, with the sun always in front of me.

I still remember...That year I was seventeen. The Hamlet of Nhai, the village of Thach Dao, the Province of N.

Translated by Bac Hoai Tran and Courtney Norris

The General Retires

In writing the following lines, I've reawakened in some of my acquaintances feelings that time had diluted, and I've also violated the sanctity of my own father's grave. I had to force myself to do this, and I beg the reader, out of respect for the strong emotion that compelled me, to judge lightly my weak pen. This emotion, I will state from the beginning, is the need for me to protect my father's name.

My father, Thuan, was the oldest son of the Nguyen family. In our village, the Nguyens are a very large family, with more male descendants than just about anyone except for maybe the Vus. My grandfather was a Confucian scholar who, later in life, taught school. He had two wives. His first wife died a few days after giving birth to my father, forcing my grandfather to take another step. His second wife was a cloth dyer. Although I never saw her face, I was told that she was extremely bad-tempered. Living with a stepmother, my father went through many bitter experiences during his youth. At twelve, he ran away from home. He joined the army and rarely came back.

Around the year 19_, my father went back to his village to marry. Love was certainly not involved in this arrangement. He had a ten-day leave, with much to do. Love has its prerequisites, and one of them is time.

Growing up, I knew nothing about my father. I'm sure my mother also knew very little about him. His whole life was linked to bullets, guns, and war.

When I grew up, I went to work, married, had children. My mother aged. My father was far away. Although occasionally he would return, each visit was short. Even his letters were short. Within those few lines, however, I recognized a great deal of love and concern.

I'm the only child, and am indebted to my father for everything I have. Because of him, I was able to study and travel abroad. He even provided for the assets of my own family. My house, on the outskirts of Hanoi, was built eight years before my father retired. It is a beautiful villa but rather uncomfortable. I had it built according to the plan of a famous architect, a friend of my father's, a colonel only adept at building barracks. At seventy, my father retired with the rank of major-general.

Although I knew about it beforehand, I still felt startled when my father returned. My mother had already grown senile (she was six years older than my father), so I was really the only one in the household who felt special emotions on this occasion. My children were small. My wife knew little about my father because we had gotten married during the war, when we had no news of him. In our household, however, we always thought of my father with feelings of glory and pride. Even in our extended family, in our village, his name was held in tremendous esteem.

My father came home carrying simple luggage. He was healthy. He said, "I've already completed the big task in my life!"

I said, "Yes."

My father smiled. Strong feelings spread throughout the house. For half a month we celebrated, with routines disrupted and nights when dinner wasn't served until twelve. Visitors arrived in throngs. My wife said, "It can't go on like this." I had a pig killed and invited relatives and neighbors to come take part in the festivities. Although my village was near the city, we still kept to rural ways.

Not until exactly a month later did I have a chance to sit down and talk with my father about family matters.

II.

Before I continue, I want to talk about my family.

I was thirty-seven years old, an engineer. I worked at the Institute of Physics. Thuy, my wife, was a doctor working in a maternity ward. We had two daughters, who were twelve and fourteen years old. My mother was senile. All day long she sat in one place.

Aside from the people I mentioned above, our household also included Co and his slow-witted daughter, Lai.

Co was sixty years old, from Thanh Hoa. My wife met him and his daughter when their house burnt down, a disaster that wiped out all their possessions. Seeing that they were decent people, deserving of pity, my wife arranged for them to live with us. They lived separately, in a house in the back, but my wife took care of all their needs. Without a residency permit, they couldn't buy subsidized food like the other residents of the city.

Co was kind and hard-working. He was responsible for the garden, the pigs, the chickens, and the dogs. We raised German Shepherds. I never suspected that it would be such a profitable business. It accounted for our greatest income. Although Lai was slow-witted, she was exceptionally strong and good at housework. My wife taught her how to cook pork rinds, mushrooms, and chicken stew. Lai said, "I never eat like that." And she really didn't.

My wife, my daughters, and I did not have to worry about housework. From the meals to laundry, everything was relegated to the help. My wife kept a tight grip on our expenses. As for me, I was preoccupied with many things. At that point, my head was buried in the application of electrolysis.

There is one other point that needs to be stated: The relationship between myself and my wife was warm. Thuy was educated and lived a modern life. We thought independently and held rather simple views on social issues.

Thuy was in charge of our finances as well as the children's education. As for me, I'm perhaps a little old-fashioned, clumsy, and loaded with anxieties.

III.

Now I'll return to the discussion I had with my father about family matters. My father said, "Now that I'm retired, what should I do?"

I said, "Write a memoir."

My father said, "No!"

My wife said, "Father should raise parrots." Nowadays, a lot of people in the city raise nightingales and parrots.

My father said, "To make money?"

My wife didn't answer him. My father said, "I'll think about it."

My father gave each person in the household four meters of military cloth. He gave Co and Lai the same. I laughed. "You're very egalitarian, Father!"

My father said, "It's a way of life."

My wife said, "With everyone in a uniform this house will turn into a barracks." Everyone burst out laughing.

My father wanted to live in a room in the back of my house, like my mother did. My wife wouldn't allow it. My father was sad. The fact that my mother ate separately and lived separately made him uneasy. My wife said, "It's because she's senile." My father brooded.

I couldn't understand why my two daughters were not closer to their grandfather. I had them study foreign languages and music. They were always busy. My father said to them, "You girls give Grandfather some books to read."

Mi smiled. Vi said, "What do you like to read, Grandfather?"

My father said, "Whatever's easy."

The two of them said, "We don't have anything like that."

I subscribed to the daily newspaper for him. My father

didn't like literature. These days, it's hard to digest the new writing.

When I came home from work one day, I found my father standing near where my wife kept the dogs and chickens. He didn't look happy. I said, "What's going on?"

He said, "Co and Lai work too hard. They can't finish all their tasks. Can I help them?"

I said, "Let me ask Thuy."

When I asked her, my wife said, "Father is a general. He may be retired, but he's still a general. He's the commander. If he acts like a common soldier, there'll be chaos."

My father said nothing.

Although retired, my father still had many visitors. This fact surprised me, and I was pleased. My wife said, "Don't be so happy about it. They only want favors. Father, don't exert yourself."

My father smiled. "It's nothing major. I'm only writing letters. For example, I write, 'Dear N., commander of Military District X. I'm writing this letter to you, and so on. In over fifty years, this is the first time I've celebrated the Floating Cake Festival under my own roof. In the war zone, we used to dream, and so on. Do you remember the little village on the side of the road, where Miss Hue made floating cakes with moldy flour? She had flour all over her back, and so on. By the way, M. is an acquaintance of mine, and wants to work under you, and so on.' Is it all right for me to write like that?"

I said, "It's all right."

My wife said, "It's not all right."

My father scratched his chin. "They've asked me."

Normally, my father inserted his letters into official hardpaper envelopes, measuring 20 x 30 centimeters, with the words "Department of Defense" printed on them. Then he would give them to the person who had asked him for the favor. After three months, all these envelopes were gone. For a while, he made his own with students' construction paper, also measuring 20 x 30 centimeters. A year later, he put his letters into ordinary envelopes, the kind they sell at the post office at five dong for ten.

That July, three months after my father retired, one of my uncles, Bong, had a wedding for his son.

IV.

Bong and my father had the same father but different mothers. Tuan, Bong's son, drove an ox cart. Both father and son were grotesque characters, as big as giants and extremely foul-mouthed. It was the second marriage for Tuan. He hit the first one too hard and she left him. At court, he testified that she had a lover, so the judge had to let him go. The wife this time was named Kim Chi. She worked as a babysitter and came from an educated family. Tuan and Kim Chi messed around and he got her pregnant, or so we were told. Kim Chi was a beautiful girl, and as Tuan's wife, it was truly a case of "planting a sprig of jasmine on a pile of buffalo shit." Honestly speaking, we were fond of neither Bong nor his son, but, since "a drop of blood is worth more than a pond of water," we unfortunately still had to see them on holidays. We often heard Bong say of us, "Damn those intellectuals! They look down on working people. If I didn't respect his father, I'd never knock on their door." Having said that, he'd still come by to borrow money. My wife would be tough, and always made him sign a promissory note. Bong was bitter. He said, "I'm their uncle, and I only borrow from them as a last resort, but they act as if they were my landlords." Most of his debts to us he never paid back.

For his son's wedding, Bong said to my father, "You have to be the master of ceremonies. Kim Chi's father is a deputy. You are a general. You two are compatible in status. My son and his wife will need your blessings. As a cart driver, I'm trash!" My father agreed to do it.

The wedding in our suburb was a ridiculous and quite

43

obscene affair. Three cars. The filtered cigarettes ran out near the end, and we had to switch to rolled cigarettes. There were fifty trays of food, but twelve of them went untouched. The groom wore a black suit with a red tie. I had to lend him the best tie in my closet. The word is "lend," but I doubt I'll ever see it again. The groomsmen were six youths, all dressed alike, in jeans, with wild facial hair. At the start of the party, a live band played "Ave Maria." A guy from the same ox cart collective as Tuan jumped up and did a monstrous number:

> *"Ooh...eh...the roasted chicken*
> *I wade through lakes and streams*
> *Trying to find my fortune*
> *Oh, money, fall quickly into my pocket*
> *Ooh...eh...the sick chicken..."*

After that, it was my father's turn. He was uncomfortable and awkward. His carefully prepared speech became irrelevant. A clarinet provided sloppy accompaniments after each pause. Loud fireworks. Inane discussions between children. My father skipped entire sections. While holding the paper, his whole body trembled. The unruliness of the event—quite ordinary, natural, rustic, and a little unclean—pained and disgusted him. The bride's father, the deputy, was also bewildered and awkward, and he even spilled wine on the bride's dress. No one could hear a thing. The live band drowned out everything with the upbeat and familiar songs of Abba and the Beatles.

After that, the first trouble came to my father because only ten days after the wedding Kim Chi gave birth to a child. Bong's family was irresponsible. Drunk, Bong threw his daughter-in-law out of the house. Tuan tried to stab his father, but missed, fortunately.

With no other possible solution, my father had to take Kim Chi into our house. That meant two more mouths to feed in our household. My wife said nothing. Lai had one more responsibility. Luckily, Lai was scatterbrained. Moreover, she was fond of children.

V.

One night, as I was reading *Sputnik*, my father quietly walked in. He said, "I want to talk to you." I made coffee. He didn't drink it. He said, "Have you been paying attention to Thuy's business? It's very creepy."

My wife worked in the maternity ward, doing abortions. Every day she carried home an ice-chest with fetuses in it. Co cooked them for the dogs and the pigs. To be honest, I already knew about it, but I chose to ignore it since it wasn't all that important. My father led me to the kitchen and pointed to the slop bucket, which had little bits of fetus in it. I didn't know what to say. My father picked up the ice-chest and threw it at the German Shepherds. "Damn it!" he began to cry. "I don't need this kind of wealth!" The dogs barked. My father went into the other room.

A moment later, my wife came in and said to Co, "Why didn't you put this through the grinder? Why did you let Father find out?"

Co said, "I forgot. I'm very sorry."

In December, my wife sold all of our German Shepherds. She told me, "You'd better stop smoking those 'Gallant' cigarettes. This year our income is down by twenty-seven thousand, and our expenses are up by eighteen thousand, which adds up to forty-five thousand."

Kim Chi finished her maternity leave and had to go back to work. She said, "Thank you, Brother and Sister. I'll take my baby home now."

I said, "What home?" Tuan had been locked up for disturbing the peace. Kim Chi took her baby home to her parents. My father escorted her right to the door in a hired taxi. He stayed at the deputy's house for a day. This man had just returned from an assignment in India. As presents, he gave my father a piece of silk with a flower design and fifty grams of ointment. My father gave the silk to Lai and the ointment to Co.

VI.

Before New Year's, Co said to my wife and me, "I need a favor from you."

My wife said, "What favor?"

Co talked in a roundabout way and made very little sense. Basically, he wanted to go back to his village for a visit. Having lived with us for six years, he had saved a little money, and now he wanted to rebury his wife's remains. After so long, the coffin must have caved in, for sure, but, as they say, "Loyalty to the dead is the ultimate loyalty." Co talked about living in the city and wanting to go back to the old village to see relatives and friends. Of course, he'd been away for so long, but, as they say, "Even the fox, dead for three years, still looks back toward the mountain."

My wife cut him off, "When do you want to go?"

Co scratched his head. "I'll be gone for ten days, and will be back in Hanoi before the ceremonies marking the 23rd of the final month."

My wife calculated. "All right. Thuan (Thuan is my name), can you take time off from work?"

"Yes."

Co said, "We want to invite Grandfather to visit our village."

My wife said, "I don't like that idea. What did he say?"

"He wants to come. Without him, I wouldn't have remembered this business about transferring my wife's grave."

My wife said, "How much money do you and your daughter have?"

Co said, "I had three thousand, but Grandfather gave me another two thousand."

My wife said, "Good. Don't take the two thousand from Grandfather. I'll make it up to you, plus another five thousand. That's ten thousand for you and your daughter. It's enough for a trip."

The day before the trip, my wife cooked. Everyone sat down to eat, including Co and Lai. Wearing her new clothes made from the military fabric my father had given her when he came home, Lai was very happy. Mi and Vi teased, "Lai is the most beautiful."

Lai giggled. "That's not true. Your mother is the most beautiful."

My wife said, "Lai, remember to look after Grandfather on buses."

My father said, "Do you think I shouldn't go?"

Co protested. "No! Please come. I already sent the telegram. It would give me a bad reputation!"

My father sighed. "What reputation do I have?"

VII.

My father went to Thanh Hoa with Co and Lai on a Sunday morning. On Monday night, as I was watching TV, I heard a "whoosh." I rushed outside and saw my mother collapsed in a corner of the garden. My mother had been senile for four years, could eat and drink when fed, and had to be led to the toilet. Normally, with Lai taking care of her, we had no problems. That day, I had fed her but forgot to take her to the toilet. When I helped her back inside, her head slumped on her chest. I didn't see any injuries, but when I woke up in the middle of the night I noticed that my mother's body was very cold and her eyes were wild. I was scared and called my wife. Thuy said, "Mother is very old." The next day mother didn't eat. And the day after that she didn't eat and couldn't control her bowels. I washed everything, changed the mat. Some days twelve times. Knowing that Thuy and the children liked cleanliness, I did mother's laundry all the time, and not in the house but down at the canal. Whatever medicine we poured down her throat she threw up.

On Saturday she was suddenly able to sit up. She trudged alone to the garden. She was able to eat. I said, "She's fine now."

My wife said nothing, but came back that evening with ten meters of white cloth, and even called the carpenter. I said, "You're preparing for her death?"

My wife said, "No."

Two days later, my mother was bedridden, and, like before, could neither eat nor control her bowels. She declined rapidly and excreted a sort of brown, pasty, very strong-smelling liquid. I gave her ginseng. My wife said, "Don't give her ginseng. It's bad for her." I burst into loud sobs. It had been a long time since I'd sobbed like that. My wife stayed silent, then said, "It's up to you."

Bong came to visit. He said, "The way she's tossing and turning on that bed is very bad." Then he turned to my mother and asked, "Sister, do you recognize me?"

My mother said, "Yes."

"Then who am I?"

My mother said, "A human being."

Bong burst into loud sobs. "Then you must love me the most, Sister," he said. "The whole village calls me a dog. My wife calls me a fraud. Tuan calls me a bastard. Only you, Sister, call me a human being."

For the first time, my ox-cart-driving uncle, who's hot-tempered, vulgar, and immoral, turned into a child before my very eyes.

VIII.

My father had been home for six hours when my mother died. Co and Lai said, "It's all our fault. If we had been home, Grandmother wouldn't have died."

My wife said, "Nonsense."

Lai cried, "Grandmother, why did you play a trick on me like this? Why didn't you allow me to come with you so I could serve you?"

Bong laughed. "If you want to go with Grandmother, go ahead. I'll tell them to make another coffin."

During the enshroudment of my mother's corpse, my father cried and asked Bong, "Why did her body decline so quickly? Does every old person die in such pain?"

Bong said, "You're being silly. Every single day, thousands of people in our country die a painful and humiliating death. The only exceptions are soldiers like you. One sweet 'Bang!' and that's it."

I had a shelter built and hired a carpenter to make the coffin. Co was always hovering around the pile of wood my wife had brought home. The carpenter barked, "Are you afraid I'm going to steal the wood?"

Bong asked, "How thick is that wood?"

"Four centimeters," I told him.

Bong said, "There goes a damn sofa. Who else would have made a coffin with such good wood? When you rebury her, make sure you give this wood to me."

My father sat in silence, and appeared to be in deep agony.

Bong said, "Thuy, boil a chicken and prepare a pot of sticky rice for me."

My wife said, "How many kilograms of rice, Uncle?"

Bong said, "Your damned mother! Why are you so sweet today? Three kilograms."

My wife said to me, "Your relatives are disgusting."

Bong asked me, "Who's in charge of the finances in this household?"

I said, "My wife."

Mr. Bong said, "That's normal. What I mean is, who's in charge of the finances for this funeral?"

"My wife."

Bong said, "That won't do, my boy! Different blood stinks up the intestines. I'll talk to your father, all right?"

"No, I'll take care of it."

Bong said, "Give me four thousand. How many trays of food were you thinking of preparing?"

"Ten trays."

"That won't even be enough to flush out the coffin bearers' bellies. You talk to your wife. I'd say you need forty trays."

I gave him four thousand dong, then went inside. My wife said, "I heard the whole conversation. I was thinking thirty trays, at eight hundred dong per tray. Three times eight is twenty-four. Twenty-four thousand. For miscellaneous costs, add six thousand. I'll take care of the shopping. Lai will cook. Don't listen to Bong. He's a shifty old man."

"I already gave him four thousand."

My wife said, "I'm really disappointed in you."

"I'll ask for it back."

"Forget about it. We'll consider it a payment for his service. He's nice, but poor."

We hired four traditional musicians for the funeral. My father went out to greet them. My mother's body was placed in the coffin at four in the afternoon. Bong pried open her mouth to place nine Khai Dinh and aluminum coins inside. He said, "For the ferry." He also placed inside the coffin an incomplete set of to tom cards mixed together with some tam cuc cards. "It's all right," he said. "She always used to play tam cuc."

That night, I stayed up to watch over my mother's coffin, and aimlessly pondered many things. Death will come to all of us, sparing none.

In the courtyard, Bong and the coffin bearers were playing tam cuc for money. Whenever he had a good hand, Bong ran to the coffin, bowed down and said, "Dearest Sister, please help me so I can clean out their pockets."

Mi and Vi stayed up with me. Mi asked, "Why do you still have to pay for the ferry after you've died? Why were coins put in Grandmother's mouth?"

Vi said, "Father, does it have to do with the saying, 'Shut your mouth, keep the money'?"

I was crying. "You kids won't understand," I said. "I don't understand myself. It's all superstition."

Vi said, "I understand. You need a lot of money in this life. Even when you're dead."

I felt very lonely. My children also seemed lonely. And so did the gamblers. And so did my father.

IX.

My house was only five hundred meters from the cemetery, but if you took the main road through the village gate it would be two kilometers. On the small road it wasn't possible to push a hearse so the coffin had to be carried on the pallbearers' shoulders. There were thirty of them taking turns, with many men my wife and I didn't recognize. They carried the coffin casually, as if it were a most natural thing to do, as if they were carrying a house-pillar. They chewed betel nuts, smoked, and chattered as they walked. When they rested, they stood and sat carelessly next to the coffin. One man, who was all sprawled out, said, "It's so cool here. If I weren't busy, I'd sleep here until nightfall."

Bong said, "I beg you guys. Hurry up so we can all go home and eat."

We continued on. I walked backward with a cane in front of the coffin, according to the custom: 'Escort your father; Greet your mother.'

Bong said, "When I die, all of my pall bearers will be hard-core gamblers, and instead of pork at the banquet, there'll be dog meat."

My father said, "Please, Brother, how can you joke at a time like this?"

Bong shut up; then he cried, "Sister, why did you trick me and leave like this...You've abandoned me..."

I wondered why he said "trick." Had all the dead people tricked the ones who were still alive? Were there only tricksters in this cemetery?

After the burial, everyone went back to the house. Twenty-eight trays of food were laid out simultaneously. Looking at the banquet, I felt nothing but respect for Lai. At each table, people were yelling: "Where's Lai?" And she accommodated them all, fluttering about with whiskey and meat. Not until after dark, after she had washed up and changed into new clothes, did Lai go in front of the altar and cry, "Grandmother, I apologize. I didn't take you out to the field...And on that day you craved crab soup and I didn't feel like making it, you didn't get any...Now when I go to the market, who will I buy a present for?"

I felt very remorseful when I heard that. I realized that I hadn't bought my mother a cake or a bag of candy in ten years. Lai continued to cry, "If I had been here, then would you have died, Grandmother?"

My wife said, "Don't cry."

I got cranky. "Let her cry," I said. "It's very sad if there are no sounds of crying at a funeral. In this house, who else could grieve for Mother like that?"

My wife said, "Thirty-two trays. Aren't you in awe of how close my estimate was?"

I said, "It was pretty close."

Bong said, "I checked her burying hour on the horoscope. Your mother has 'one grave invasion, two overlapping deaths, and a migration.' Should we invoke a talisman?"

My father said, "Talisman, my ass. In my life, I've buried three thousand men and it's never been like this."

Bong said, "That's happiness. 'Bang!' and it's over." He stuck out an index finger and pretended to pull a trigger.

X.

That New Year we neither bought peach blossoms nor wrapped square rice cakes. On the evening of January 2nd, my father's old unit sent people over to pay homage to my mother. They gave five hundred dong. Chuong, my father's old deputy who was now a general, went to the gravesite to light incense sticks. Thanh, a captain who accompanied him, pulled out his pistol and fired three shots into the air. Later, the children in the village would say that soldiers fired twenty-one cannon shots in honor of Mrs. Thuan. General Chuong asked my father, "Would you like to pay a last visit to the old unit? There'll be maneuvers in May. We can send a car down to get you."

My father said, "Fine."

General Chuong took a tour of our house, with Co as his guide. General Chuong said to my father, "Damn nice place you've got here. A garden, a fish pond, a pig sty, a chicken coop, a villa. No worries at all."

My father said, "My son built all this."

I said, "It was my wife."

My wife said, "Actually, it was Lai."

Lai giggled. Lately, her head would bob nonstop, as if she were having a seizure. "That's not true," she said.

My father joked, "It's the product of the Garden-Fish Pond-Pen Campaign."

January 3rd. Kim Chi and her baby rode a cyclo by for a visit. My wife gave the baby one thousand dong for good luck. My father asked, "Does Tuan write?"

Kim Chi said, "No."

My father said, "It's my fault. I didn't know you were pregnant."

My wife said, "These things are common. There are no virgins these days. I work in a maternity ward, so I know."

Kim Chi looked embarrassed. I said, "Don't talk like that. Although, admittedly, it is tough to be a virgin."

Kim Chi cried, "Brother, it's humiliating to be a woman. Giving birth to a daughter tore my whole insides out."

My wife said, "And, I even have two daughters."

I said, "So you people don't think it's humiliating to be a man?"

My father said, "For men, the ones who have hearts are humiliated. The bigger the heart, the bigger the humiliation."

My wife said, "We all talk like crazy people in this household. Let's eat. Today, with Miss Kim Chi, I'll serve each person a chicken stewed with lotus hearts. Now that's 'heart' for you. Eating comes before everything else."

XI.

Near my house lived a young man, Khong, whom the children called Confucius. Khong worked at the fish sauce factory but liked poetry, which he wrote and sent to the magazine *Literature and Art*. Khong came by often. Khong said, "Poetry is most superior." He read me Lorca, Whitman, etc. I didn't like Khong, and half-suspected he came by for something even more adventurous than poetry. Once, I noticed a handwritten poetry manuscript on my wife's bed. My wife said, "These are Khong's poems. Would you like to read them?" I shook my head. My wife said, "You're already old." I shuddered.

One day I was busy at work and had to come home late. My father greeted me at the gate. He said, "Khong came over at dusk. He and your wife have been tittering away, and he hasn't left yet. It's very annoying."

I said, "You should go to bed, Father. Why pay attention to this?" My father shook his head and went upstairs. I walked the motorbike to the street, and rode aimlessly around town until I ran out of gas. I walked the motorbike to a corner of a park and sat down like some vagabond. A woman with a powdered face walked by and asked, "Brother, do you want some fun?" I shook my head.

Khong was trying to avoid me. Co hated him. One day, Co said, "Will you let me beat him up?"

I almost nodded. Then I thought, "Don't."

I went to the library to borrow some books as an experiment. I read Lorca, Whitman, etc. I vaguely felt that exceptional artists are frighteningly lonely. Suddenly, I saw that Khong was right. I was only pissed off that he was so ill-bred. Why didn't he show his poems to somebody else besides my wife?

My father said, "You're meek. And that's because you can't stand to live alone."

I said, "That's not true. There are many jokes in life."

My father said, "You think this is a joke?"

I said, "It's neither a joke nor something serious."

My father said, "Why do I feel like I belong to a different species?"

The institute wanted to send me on assignment to the south. I said to my wife, "I'll go, all right?"

My wife said, "Don't go. Tomorrow, you can fix the bathroom door. It's broken. The other day, when Mi was taking a shower, Khong walked by and tried something obscene. He scared her out of her wits. I've forbidden that bastard from ever walking through the door of this house again." Then she burst into tears, saying, "I really owe you and the children an apology."

I was uncomfortable and turned away. If Vi had been around, she would have asked me, "Father, are those crocodile tears?"

XII.

In May, my father's old unit sent a car down to pick him up. Thanh, the captain, carried a letter from General Chuong. My father trembled while holding the letter, which said,

"...We need you and are waiting for you...If you can come, then come. There's no pressure." I didn't think my father should go, but it would have been awkward to say so. Although my father had aged noticeably since his retirement, holding the letter that day, he appeared vivacious and considerably younger. I felt happy for him. My wife wanted to pack his travel things in a tourist bag. He wouldn't hear of it. He said, "Stuff them in my rucksack."

My father made the rounds to say goodbye to the entire village. He even went to my mother's grave and told Thanh to fire three shots into the air again. That night, my father called for Co and gave him two thousand dong. He instructed him to have a stone marker made to be sent to Thanh Hoa and placed over his wife's grave. My father called Lai over and said, "You should find yourself a husband, my child."

Lai burst out crying. "I'm so ugly, no one will marry me," she said. "I'm also very naive."

My father became choked up. "My dear child," he told her. "Don't you understand that naiveté is the strength that allows one to live?"

I didn't recognize all of these preparations as signs that my father would not come back from his trip.

Before he stepped into the car, my father pulled a student's notebook from his rucksack. He gave it to me. He said, "I've jotted down a few things in this book. Read it and see what you think."

Mi and Vi said goodbye to their grandfather. Mi said, "Are you going to the battlefield, Grandfather?"

My father said, "Yes."

Vi quoted from a song: "'The road to the battlefield is beautiful at this time of year.' Right, Grandfather?"

My father cursed. "Your mother! Know-it-all!"

56

XIII.

A hilarious incident occurred a few days after my father left. It so happened that, as Co and Bong were dredging mud from the pond (my wife paid Bong two hundred dong a day plus meals), they suddenly saw the bottom of an earthen jar appear above the surface. Both of them dug on enthusiastically and discovered the bottom of a second jar. Bong was sure that people in the old days had used these jars to hide their valuables. The two men reported the news to my wife. Thuy went for a look and proceeded to wade into the pond to join them, digging. Then Lai went in, then Mi, then Vi and I. We were all smeared with mud. My wife ordered that the pond be blocked off, and even rented a Kohler pump to siphon the water. The atmosphere grew deadly serious. Bong loved it. "I saw it first," he said. "I'll get to keep one of those jars for myself." After a day of digging, and finding two cracked jars with nothing inside, Bong said, "There's got to be more." More digging. One more jar was discovered. It was also cracked. Everyone was exhausted and starving. My wife sent for some bread so we could regain our strength to continue digging. At the depth of nearly ten meters we found a porcelain jar. Everyone was ecstatic and assumed there had to be gold inside. We opened it up only to find a string of rusty, bronze Bao Dai coins and the shreds of a fabric medal. Bong said, "Damn it! I remember now. A long time ago, after I robbed Han Tin's house with that hoodlum Nhan, we were being chased and Nhan threw this jar into the pond." Everyone had a good round of laughs. This hoodlum was a very famous thief on the outskirts of town. Han Tin was a soldier in the Colonial army. He had participated in a movement called "Coin-Spitting Southern Dragon to Expel the German Bandits" during World War I. Both Han Tin and Nhan had been rotting in their graves for years already. Bong said, "It doesn't matter. Should this entire village die, I'll have enough ferry money to stuff into everyone's mouth."

The next morning, I woke up and heard someone calling at the gate. I went outside and saw Khong. I thought, "What a pain. This son of a bitch is the biggest curse in my entire life."

Khong said, "Brother Thuan, you have a telegram. Your father died."

XIV.

The telegram from General Chuong said, "Major-General Nguyen Thuan sacrificed his life in the line of duty at ___ on ___. Services at the military cemetery will be at on ___." I was stunned. My wife quickly made all the arrangements. I went out to hire a car and when I came back everything was ready. My wife said, "Lock the main house. Co will stay behind."

The car went to Cao Bang on Highway One. When we got there, the funeral had already been over for two hours.

General Chuong said, "We owe your family an apology."

I said, "That's not necessary. Each life has its destiny."

General Chuong said, "Your father was someone deserving of respect."

"Was the ceremony conducted according to military rites?" I asked.

"Yes."

"Thank you," I told him.

General Chuong said, "He went to the battlefield and insisted on staying near the front."

I said, "I understand, Sir. You don't have to explain."

I cried. I had never cried like that before. Now I understood what it means to grieve the death of one's father. Perhaps it is the biggest grief in a person's lifetime.

My father's grave lay in the military cemetery. My wife took a camera along and had pictures taken in different poses.

The next day, we declined General Chuong's invitation to stay and took our leave.

On the way home, my wife suggested we go slowly. It was Bong's first long trip, and he loved it. He said, "Our country is as beautiful as a painting. Now I understand why one must love one's country. Back home, even though Hanoi is so modern, I see nothing at all to love."

My wife said, "That's because you're used to it. Elsewhere, people are the same. They're the ones who love Hanoi."

Bong said, "Then one place loves the other place, and people here love people there. It's still one country, one people. Long live our country! Long live our people! Hurrah for the spinning lantern!"

XV.

Perhaps my story ends here. After that, our lives reverted to what they were before my father retired. My wife continued her work as usual. I finished my electrolysis research. Co turned quiet, partly because Lai's condition had worsened. When I had time, I read over what my father had written. Now I understand him better.

I've recorded here the confusing events that occurred during the year or so of my father's retirement. I consider these lines as sticks of incense lit in his remembrance. If you have had the patience to read what I've written, I beg you to forgive my indulgences. Thank you.

Translated by Linh Dinh

Without a King

1. The Household

Sinh had been a daughter-in-law in Old Kien's household for several years now. When she arrived, she brought with her four sets of summer clothes, a winter shirt, two sweaters, a flower-patterned blanket cover, four aluminum pots, a skillet, a two-and-a-half-liter thermos, a basin for bathing, a dozen towels—in short, a degree of wealth, according to her mother, a rice-dealer in Xanh Market.

Sinh's husband, Can, was a disabled vet. They met by coincidence, while both were hiding under the same eaves during a rainstorm. This story has already been recorded. (It just goes to show how inquisitive our writers are!) As told, it is a simple love scene, pure, without calculation. Life is dialectical, materialistic, harmonious, beautiful and lovely, etc.

Can was the oldest of five brothers, with intervals between them of one or two years each. Doai worked for the Education Department, Khiem was a butcher for a food supplier, Kham was a student at the university. Ton, the youngest, was half-witted, with a puny, weird-looking body.

There were six people in Old Kien's family. All men. Mrs. Nhon, Old Kien's wife, had died eleven years before, when Old Kien was fifty-three, an awkward age to marry again or to not marry again. Old Kien chose the lesser inconvenience, and did nothing.

Old Kien's house looked into the street. He fixed bicycles for a living. Can cut hair (when he first met Sinh, he told her he "provided services"). Having received the education of the masses (her father taught school, her mother sold rice), Sinh was not a person with narrow ideas. Moreover, she could be quite liberal in her views. Her limited education (she had only finished junior high school) didn't matter. With women, learning contributes little to their supernatural strength, a fact that does not need to be proven.

As a new bride, Sinh was at first a little startled by the house's liberal climate. There was absolutely no decorum at the dinner table. Six men, all bare-chested and in shorts, chattered away, gulping and slurping like dragons. Sinh took care of the three daily meals. The heavy jobs she did not have to do because she had Ton to help out. All day long, Ton did the laundry and washed the floor. He couldn't do anything else. Always holding a plastic bucket and a rag, he'd wash the floor every few hours. He hated dirt. Whenever anyone changed clothes, he did the laundry, and did it extremely well, including the drying. He spoke little, and only giggled when addressed, with clunky, terse answers. Often, as he worked, he'd sing a song he learned, God knows when, from the drinking crowd:

> *Aha! Without a king*
> *Drunk from morning 'til evening*
> *The days and months are nothing*
> *Me and you together*
> *Love and character: Aren't they a great pair?*

With absolute devotion, Ton always tried to help Sinh out. All her little needs he'd try to fulfill. In the middle of the night, if Sinh said, "Some dried and salted prunes would be good," there would be prunes immediately. Where he got the money, or when he bought them, no one knew.

In the house, Sinh dreaded Old Kien the most, then Khiem. Old Kien was cantankerous all day long. No one liked him. He made money. He argued with everyone out of habit, in the meanest language. With Doai, for example, he'd say: "Is that you? The civil servant? You're lazier than a leper, and illiterate. You're only good at taking bribes." Or to Kham, who was in his second year at the university, he'd say, "Parasites! What's learning? It's a waste of good rice!" With

Can, he was not so belligerent, occasionally even giving him a compliment, although the old man's compliments were worse than insults. "Amazing, this job of shaving whiskers and cleaning out ear wax," he would say. "It's humiliating, to be sure, but still it's a good source of money!" Khiem was the only one he left alone.

Khiem was a big guy, aloof, with a short temper. Each day when he came home (he worked the night shift), he'd bring either meat or intestines. Rarely did he come home empty-handed. Doai often said (behind Khiem's back, of course), "That guy will end up in jail sooner or later. I can foresee his future. He'll get six years, at least. It's weird how they've left him alone so far, stealing half a ton of meat annually!"

It appeared that Khiem did not respect his two older brothers. With Can, he'd always pay for his haircuts, saying, "Don't treat me differently, Brother. If I make you work, I have the right to pay."

Can cringed, saying, "You act as if we're not family."

Khiem said, "Family's not the issue here. If you don't want my money, I'll go somewhere else and make some other guy clean out my ear wax. Hey, be careful with that knife. Don't shave off my moustache."

Can didn't know what to say, and had to accept Khiem's money. Sinh told her husband, "If you take his money, he'll look down on you."

Can replied, "I'm still the oldest. He can't look down on me."

Doai, Khiem considered an enemy. But Doai was too smooth, and Khiem couldn't pick fights with him. Before work, Doai always put some rice and a few pieces of meat into his lunchbox. He said, "This little bit of protein means two thousand calories, enough to last me all day, thanks to Khiem, who is both clever and quick."

"What do you mean, clever and quick?" asked Khiem.

Doai said, "I meant, you're clever in dealing with people and quick in dealing with pigs!"

Khiem, choking with anger, foamed at the mouth.

Sinh's appearance in this household had an effect like rain falling on parched earth. The atmosphere softened. During the first few months, Old Kien stopped arguing with his children. Can was the happiest. He was fast with the scissors, and always very cordial to the customers. He decided to increase the fees for a haircut from thirty to fifty dong, an ear job from ten to twenty dong, a shampoo from twenty to thirty dong, and a shave from ten to twenty dong. Profits increased. The family budget, which Can controlled, became more relaxed. Doai, noticing the jump in daily expenditures, was alarmed at first, but calmed down when no one said anything about his own contributions. As for Khiem, his contribution remained just as before, never a dime, only intestines or one or two kilograms of meat per day. After ten days of intestines, Sinh would lose it and say to her husband, "If Khiem brings back more intestines tomorrow, I'm taking them to the market and exchanging them for something else."

Can smiled, stroked his wife's soft body with his eyes, and said, "According to your wishes, Madame."

2. In The Morning

Normally, Khiem was the first to get up in the morning. He set the alarm for one o'clock. When it went off, Khiem got up immediately, brushed his teeth, then left on his bicycle. Ton locked the door behind him. Doai, disrupted from sleep, muttered, "Truly, those are the working hours of a criminal."

At three o'clock, Old Kien got up and plugged in the electric stove to boil water for tea. The outlet was faulty and, though it had been fixed several times, every few days someone still got a good jolt. Old Kien got a good jolt. He blurted, "Your ancestors! You guys want to get rid of me, but there's a God above, with eyes, and I'll be around for a long time!"

From his bed, Doai said, "I don't know about elsewhere, but in this household, it would be normal if the green leaves fell down before the yellow ones."

Old Kien replied, "Your mother! Is that any way to talk to your father? Who hired you to work for the Education Department, anyway?"

Doai laughed. "They checked our family history for three generations back. It was spotless, as clear as a mirror."

Old Kien mumbled, "Of course it was. I don't know about you guys, but starting with me and going backward, no one has ever done anything uncharitable in this household."

"Oh, that's for sure," Doai said. "To jack up the price of patching a tire to thirty dong when it's really worth ten is very charitable."

"Your mother! What thoughts go through your mind when you lift that bowl of rice to your lips every day?" Old Kien demanded.

From his bed, Kham moaned, "Spare me, Doai. Can't you have a little pity? I've got a big oral in philosophy today."

Doai said, "Philosophy is a luxury for bookworms. Did you ever notice the plastic rosary on Sinh's neck? That's philosophy." Kham didn't answer. The house quieted down for about an hour before becoming noisy again. It was four-thirty in the morning, the time when Sinh got up to cook.

Sinh measured six and a half cans of rice. Can stooped to clean the vegetables. Watching them, Kham said, "A beautiful pair. Anything I can do?"

Sinh said, "The pork fat from yesterday is covered with ants. See if you can get rid of those ants."

Kham said, "In our country, we must be the leading family in terms of the amount of pig intestines consumed per head. I've done a rough estimate. In a single year, Khiem has brought back two hundred sixty sets of intestines."

Doai said, "Little Brother, that guy is a godsend for our family. Correct me if I'm wrong, but that butcher job is worth ten of our college degrees."

Old Kien opened shop. A woman carrying a pot of sticky rice stuck her head inside. "Breakfast for you, sir?"

Old Kien waved his hands frantically. "My God, I'm trying to run a business here. Now a woman shows up first thing in the morning to bring me bad luck. How can I make any money?"

The woman selling sticky rice muttered, "I've never sold a dime's-worth of sticky rice to that old guy."

Can stroked his blade against the calfskin, mumbling, "It would be good if I could cut ten heads today."

Sinh brought in the food. Kham sat near the rice pot, serving the rice. Sinh said, "It's still too hot. No one will be able to eat very much yet."

Kham said, "Don't worry, Sister. The Nguyen Sis all have mouths of steel."

Sinh said, "After you, Father. And after you, Can, and all my brothers."

Doai said, "Customs vary according to the household, and in this one there's no need for ceremony. Serve me another bowl, Kham."

Kham said, "Such speed! I've only gotten through two mouthfuls."

Doai replied, "I've been eating group meals since I was fourteen. I'm used to eating fast. In college, there was a guy who could eat six bowls in a minute and a half. Scary, huh?"

Old Kien said, "Intellectuals these days are only a bunch of mediocre bores."

Kham smiled. "Isn't there a saying, 'Food before virtue'?"

Old Kien said, "What virtues have you guys attained?"

Doai finished eating, stood up, arched his back, and said, "This is a topic for debate. I suspect that whoever made up that saying in the old days didn't know shit about virtue. The guy should have said, 'Food before love.' As in human love, my fellow countrymen."

Can chuckled, "You've got a lot of love, my brother."

Doai stared at his sister-in-law's cleavage, where a button had come open on her shirt, and pondered, "Love, love, revealed love is making me dreamy."

Sinh turned red and discretely buttoned herself a moment later.

Sinh cleaned up. Old Kien sat and drank tea. Kham put on a pair of jeans and a T-shirt with the inscription "Walt Disney Productions" on it. Then he turned to Can and said, "Brother Can, give me a fifty."

Can said, "I don't have any money."

Kham looked at Old Kien. "Father, give me a fifty."

Old Kien said, "Sit down and patch that tire over there; then I'll give you some money."

Kham cringed. "But I'll be late for class."

Without answering, Old Kien opened his tool box and started busying himself. Kham walked his bicycle to the door, paused to think for a moment, then walked back into the house. He went into the back room, looked around to make sure no one was looking, then shoveled a can and a half of uncooked rice into his bag before sneaking out again.

Sinh put the pots away in the kitchen. Doai followed behind her to pack a lunch for work. His hand touched Sinh's back and he said, "My sister-in-law's body is as soft as a noodle."

Sinh stepped back, startled. "Hell, Doai! What are you doing?"

Doai said, "Boy, one little joke and such a reaction." He walked out of the kitchen.

Ton lugged the water bucket, assiduously washing the floor and singing, "Aha! Without a king..."

A man walked in for a haircut. Can asked, "What style would you like, Uncle?"

The customer said, "Cut it close. But be careful. I've got a lump near the top of my head."

Doai finished dressing and walked his bicycle out. At the door, he turned to address Can. "The day after tomorrow is mother's death anniversary. Tell Khiem to get a good cut of meat. I already gave Sinh a hundred."

Can said, "I know already."

3. The Death Anniversary

For his wife's death anniversary, Old Kien had five trays of food prepared. From her family, Mr. Vy arrived from Phuc Yen. Mr. Vy was a retired civil servant whose retirement checks were that of a government employee of the third rank. Mr. Vy had many children, was poor, and brought only ten sour mushrooms and a bottle of rice wine as presents. From the city came Old Kien's sister, Mrs. Hien, and her family. She sold dry goods and her husband, Mr. Hien, was a tinsmith. They had five children, both boys and girls. Other guests included Mr. Minh, a manager in Doai's office, and three of Kham's classmates—a girl named My Lan, a girl named My Trinh, and a boy named Viet Hung, who wore silver glasses and had lips as red as a woman's.

All the guests had arrived by about ten in the morning. Can brought a tray of food to the altar, lit three incense sticks, turned around and said to Old Kien, "You pray, Father."

Old Kien, who was wearing a pair of work pants and a white short-sleeved shirt with three pockets, had slicked his hair back with sprayed water. He walked in front of the altar and muttered, "The Socialist People's Republic Of Vietnam, in the year 19__. To God, to Buddha, to my ancestors, to the angels, to my wife, whose name is Ngo Thi Nhon. I invite you all to share this modest meal with me. I am Nguyen Si Kien, sixty-four years old, a resident of 129 __ Street. My sons are Can, Doai, Khiem, Kham, Ton. My daughter-in-law is Sinh. We all beg you to protect us, to give us health, and to assist us in our business endeavors." After saying his prayer, Old Kien turned to Mr. Vy and said, "Now you go and bow once to your sister."

Mr. Vy wore a political cadre outfit in the Sun Yat Sen style, buttoned right to the neck and very dignified. He said, "We cadres have no gods. After forty years of following the Revolution, I have no altars in my house, and I don't even know how to say a prayer." Old Kien was silent, his eyes red. Mr. Vy walked to the altar, stood still, and bowed his head.

Old Kien wiped his eyes and said, "Now, one after another, whoever wants to bow can go ahead and bow."

Mrs. Hien, after arranging on the altar some hell money, fake gold, and a paper suit, kneeled and prostrated herself three times, with her forehead touching the floor. Mr. Hien bowed three times. Can also bowed three times. Can said, "You do it, Doai."

Doai was chopping chicken and his hands were all greasy. He left them like that and hurried to the altar, where he bowed furiously, saying, "Dearest mother, help me to go study abroad and to get a Cub motorcycle."

Mr. Vy smiled. "Which country are you going to, my nephew?" he asked.

Doai said, "That will depend on the guy with the moustache wearing the checkered shirt over there."

Hearing Doai's response, Mr. Minh asked, "How am I responsible for you going anywhere?"

"That's how it is. You're my boss. If you turn your back on me, I'm dead."

Mr. Minh said, "Keep up the good work. I'll support you."

Doai said, "How can you tell what's good or bad when you're working for the government? Just remember that Doai here has always been good to you."

Sinh was busy in the kitchen. In her room, Kham was showing his three friends a photo album that contained pictures of himself, including his baby pictures. My Lan said, "You were a cute baby, Kham."

Kham said, "My kid will be just as cute, maybe even cuter, with a beauty mark right on the chin."

My Lan turned red, rubbed the beauty mark on her chin, and rained punches down on Kham's back.

Viet Hung looked at another picture of Kham. "This one was taken when you went for training, right?"

"Yeah."

"Real sharp," Viet Hung said.

My Lan said, "That was the time you stole sweet potatoes, and the self-defense force caught you, right?"

Kham turned red. "Stop talking trash," he replied. "You're guilty of slandering a comrade. I'll make sure you pay a penalty."

"What penalty?" asked My Lan.

Kham said, "You'll know later on tonight." They all laughed.

Doai looked in, gestured toward Kham, and said, "Go set the table."

"Is it time to eat already?" Kham asked.

Doai didn't answer. Kham followed him into the kitchen. Doai asked, "Is the one with the beauty mark your girlfriend?"

"Yeah."

"And who's that sweet-smelling heroine who came with her?"

Kham laughed. "That's My Trinh. Her father is Mr. Daylight, the guy who owns the electric store."

"Has that other guy gotten any action from her?"

"Not yet."

Doai said, "I'll prick her."

Kham picked up the tray. Sinh said, "Yell if something's missing."

Kham left the kitchen and Doai turned to Sinh and said, "A little love's missing. Please give me a little love, Sinh."

Sinh said, "Devil. Go ask Kham's two girlfriends."

"How can those two sluts equal you?"

Sinh said, "Get out of here!"

Doai said, "Your old man, Can, is weak as a soft-shell crab, but he's so bossy."

Sinh said, "I'm going to tell him about you."

"Go ahead. I'm not afraid." Then he nudged closer and kissed Sinh slightly on the cheek. Sinh pushed him away. Doai breathed heavily. "I'll say it ahead of time. Sooner or later, I'll sleep with you at least once." After saying that, he walked out. Sinh burst into sobs.

Can came in, saw that his wife's eyes were all red, and asked, "What's wrong?"

Sinh said, "It's because of this lousy kitchen."

Can said, "Bring some hot water into the house. There's none left."

Sinh said, "Do I have six hands and three heads?"

Can stared at her. "Is that a way to talk? This house is not like that! And how come these dishes aren't washed?" After saying that, he knocked over the stack of bowls and walked out. The bowls crashed. Sinh burst out crying.

There were three trays during the first sitting. Some guests went home after they'd eaten. Then there were two more trays for the second sitting. By then it was two in the afternoon. In the middle of eating, Khiem came in, very sullen, and greeted no one. Kham said, "Sit down with us and enjoy yourself, Brother Khiem." The two girls, My Lan and My Trinh, chirped their invitations. Everyone held their chopsticks.

Old Kien, drunk, dozed off in bed and drooled onto the rattan mat. Doai excused himself to take Mr. Vy to the bus station for the Phu Yen evening departure.

"Where's Ton?" Khiem asked.

Kham said, "He's around somewhere. Come and eat, Brother. We're waiting."

Khiem said. "You guys go ahead."

Kham lowered his voice. "We'll go ahead all right. That guy has such an attitude."

My Trinh said, "He looks like Tarzan."

Khiem went into the kitchen and asked Sinh, "Where's Ton?"

Sinh said, "I've been busy since early this morning. I totally forgot about him. I don't know where he is."

Khiem dumped a heavy sack onto the counter. "More intestines?" Sinh asked.

Khiem didn't answer. He walked out, peered into Sinh's room and saw Can snoring. Khiem shoved the door open and asked Can, "Where's Ton?"

Can sat up. "What time is it?"

"Where's Ton?"

"We had guests," Can said. "It wouldn't have been a good idea to have him running around, so I locked him up in the shed next to the toilet."

Khiem picked an ashtray off the table and threw it at Can's face. Can gasped, "Oi!" once and keeled over. Khiem lunged forward and kicked him repeatedly. Kham ran in and pushed Khiem away. Sinh rushed in, panic-stricken, screaming, "What was that?" Khiem brushed her aside.

The shed, which sat next to the toilet, had once been a pigsty and was now used to store firewood. Someone had put a new lock on the wooden door. Khiem yanked on the lock. No good. He used a crow bar to break it open. Inside, Ton, with a black face, black arms, and black legs, bared his teeth in a smile. Khiem yelled, "Get out!"

Ton dragged his lame legs into the house. Seeing the dirty floor, he immediately fetched the water bucket and the rag.

Kham's friends tittered their goodbyes, then left. Kham walked his bicycle out after them. Before he left, he grabbed a few cigarettes from the table and put them in his shirt pocket.

Old Kien sobered up, noticed the empty house, and asked, "Where did everybody go?"

Sinh brought some beanthreads for Ton to eat. He was hungry and ate three or four bowls in a row, spilling beanthreads onto the floor. Khiem walked his bicycle out, having eaten nothing. Can clutched his chest, coughed furiously, and spat out a broken tooth. A corner of his mouth was smeared with blood. He waved a fist in front of his father's face. "You'd better throw that guy out of the house before I kill him!"

Old Kien said, "You guys go ahead and kill each other. It will only make me happy." After saying that, he held the broken lock in his hands, mumbling, "It took all morning to put this lock on. A waste of a hundred dong."

4. Afternoon

By the time Sinh finished the dishes, it was three o'clock in the afternoon. She went into her room to fetch a change of clothes before taking a shower. Suddenly, she panicked and called her husband.

"What is it?" he asked, coming into the room.

"I left a ring in the needle box this morning. Did you take it?"

"No."

"Did anyone come into this room?"

"No."

Doai walked his bicycle into the house and, noticing the mess everywhere, asked, "What's going on?"

Can grimaced. "Did you come into this room? Sinh's missing a ring."

Doai said, "Ask father about it."

Old Kien cursed, "Your mother! You think I stole that ring?"

Doai stood silently for a moment, then said, "This morning Kham and his three friends were sitting in here. I suspect the guy with the glasses and the lipstick lips. He had extremely cunning eyes."

72

At that moment, Kham happened to come back. Can said, "Your friend stole Sinh's ring."

Kham turned ashen. "Who said?"

"I saw him do it myself."

"Then why didn't you catch him in the act? When we were out just now, he insisted on going home. Now we have to go to his house to get it back. If he doesn't want to return it, we'll beat the shit out of him."

Can said, "Let's go."

The two of them walked their bicycles out. Old Kien said, "Take the hammer with you. But don't hit him on the head. If the guy dies, you'll go to jail for life."

Doai climbed into bed to read the paper. Sinh cleaned up a little then got ready for her shower. She carried two buckets of water into the shower stall and closed the door.

Old Kien was wandering around in the kitchen. When he heard water splashing inside the shower, he sighed, then walked out. After a few steps, he turned around, re-entered the kitchen, grabbed a stool, stepped up on it, held his breath, and peered into the shower. Inside the shower stall, Sinh stood naked.

Doai, drifting off to sleep, noticed Ton tugging on his shirt. He sat up. "What?"

Ton rubbed his hands together, took Doai into the kitchen, and pointed to Old Kien standing on tiptoes on the stool. Doai grimaced and gave Ton a hard slap on the face. Ton fell, face first, onto a water bucket that had a rag lying across it. Old Kien hopped quickly from his stool and hid near the door. A moment later he said, "Why did you hit him?"

Doai said, "I hit him because he has no manners."

Old Kien raised his voice. "Then I suppose you have manners?"

Doai gritted his teeth and whispered, "I have no manners either, but I don't peek at naked women." Old Kien said nothing.

Doai went into the living room and poured himself a cup of rice whiskey. Old Kien helped Ton get up. Ton fetched the water bucket and squatted down to wash the floor. Old Kien went into the house and said to Doai, "Pour me a cup." After emptying his cup, Old Kien said, "You're educated but still stupid. Now I'll talk to you man-to-man."

Doai said, "I won't forgive you."

Old Kien said, "I don't need your forgiveness. A man needn't be ashamed for having a prick."

Doai sat in silence, drank another cup of whiskey. After a while, he sighed. "True enough."

Old Kien said, "It's humiliating to be human."

"Then why didn't you remarry?" Doai asked.

Old Kien cursed, "Your mother! If I'd only been thinking about myself, would you guys have all this?"

Doai poured another cup. "More whiskey, Father?"

Old Kien turned his face into the shadows and shook his head.

"I'm sorry, Father," Doai said.

Old Kien said, "Now you're behaving like a melodramatic actor on TV."

Ton washed the floor, noticed the ring beneath the cabinet and gave it to Sinh, who was elated. Doai held the ring up to the light and said, "Half a karat, maximum."

Sinh said, "It's an heirloom from my mother. It represents her entire life's savings."

Old Kien said, "Shit, with Can picking a fight at that guy's house, we'll all look ridiculous."

Can and Kham came back right before dark. Both looked as if they had just crawled out of the gutter, all slimy and pathetic.

Doai laughed. "Got a good beating?"

Can didn't answer. Kham said, "They keep two German Shepherds in that house. There's no way to get in."

Doai said, "That'll teach you a lesson for acting like gangsters."

Old Kien said, "We found the ring."

"Where?" Can asked.

Old Kien said, "Your wife kept it inside the hem of her pants, that's where."

Can said, "You bitch!" Then he slapped Sinh across the face so hard that she saw stars. He was about to hit her again when Doai shoved him out of the way. He stood in front of Sinh, shielding her, his hand poised on a knife, and hissed, "Go away! If you touch her again, I'll stab you immediately."

Sinh pressed her face against the bedpost and cried out, "Oh, God! Why am I humiliated like this?"

Old Kien asked Kham, "Did you bring the hammer back?"

Kham got testy. "I almost lost my life to two German Shepherds. Who cares about hammers?"

Old Kien said, "There goes another hundred."

5. New Year's Day

Soon it would be Lunar New Year's Day. On the 15th of the final month, Old Kien went to the bank to withdraw eight thousand dong, the interest from his savings. He bought a shirt for Ton and a pair of socks for Sinh. He gave the rest of the money to Can. Kham said, "Father only dotes on his daughter-in-law and his youngest son."

Khiem had to travel to different towns to buy pigs and would be gone for long stretches. It must have been hard work. Most days he left at eleven at night and didn't return until the next afternoon, his entire body reeking of pig manure. Although he'd fall asleep as soon as he got home, his eyes remained bloodshot and sunken.

Can was busy, too. From six in the morning until ten at night, there would always be a customer waiting to get a haircut. When Can napped in the afternoon, Kham filled in for him. The first day, he wasn't used to it. He nicked a customer's ear, drawing blood. The man got angry and, instead of seventy, only paid twenty. Can used a pencil to jot down the daily intake in a notebook, a plus sign for one hundred, a circle for two hundred. Then he'd draw triangles with a dot in the middle for who knew what. Doai said, "Your accounting book is like espionage."

December 23rd was Mr. Tao's Ascension Day. Sinh cooked beanthreads, and everyone ate until their bellies were taut. Kham asked, "Why is he called Mr. Tao?"

Doai said, "The story's like this. Mr. Tao represents 'three hearth stones.' Once upon a time there were two brothers who married the same wife. She would sleep with one brother one night and the other brother the other night. The King of Heaven was moved by their close relationship and turned each one into a hearth stone so that they could always be near each other. We call them the Patron Saints of the Kitchen, or Mr. Tao." Sinh carried the tray into the kitchen.

Kham said, "It was easy to become a saint in the old days."

Old Kien said, "Don't listen to him."

Doai said, "Then there's another story. In this particular household, a father-in-law grabbed his daughter-in-law's breasts. The son said, 'Why did you grab my wife's breasts?' The father said, 'To settle an old score. Why did you used to grab my wife's breasts?' It's said that these people also became saints."

Can said, "Your stories, I don't get them."

Old Kien said, "Don't listen to him."

On the 27th, Old Kien wrapped rice cakes. A vat and a half of sticky rice means twenty-eight cakes. There were two kinds of cakes, ones stuffed with peanuts, and ones stuffed with sugar. They marked the sugar ones with a red string. While Sinh boiled the cakes, Doai hovered around the kitchen.

"Do you know, Sinh, where the future of this house lies?"

"No."

Doai laughed. "With me," he said.

"How's that?"

"Father's old. He'll die. Khiem will go to jail sooner or later. Kham, when he graduates, will be sent to either Tay Bac or Tay Nguyen. Ton we don't have to talk about. He's useless."

Sinh asked, "What about Can?"

Doai said, "That depends on you. If you love me, I can pick a fight with him and throw him out into the street."

Sinh said, "As easy as that?"

"Why are you hesitating?" Doai asked. "Old Can is both stupid and cowardly. And he's weak. The doctor said he has chilly semen. He's been married to you for two years now, and where are the children?"

Sinh sat still. The pot of rice cakes boiled furiously.

Doai said, "I'll come into your room tonight, all right?"

Sinh grabbed the knife. "Go away. If you come near me, I'll kill you!"

Doai smiled wanly, stepped back, and went into the house, muttering as he walked, "Women are evil."

On the 29th, Old Kien went to the market to buy a branch of peach flowers. On the evening of the 30th, Khiem brought home a large potted mandarin-orange tree with three tiers of fruit and a string of firecrackers measuring six meters.

Kham said, "Getting extravagant here."

"He's showing off," said Doai.

Kham said to Doai, "We're the two educated ones. But, come New Year's Day, we don't even have decent suits to wear."

Doai said, "The only way out is to marry a rich wife. Tonight, you take me to the daughter of Mr. Daylight, all right?"

"Easy enough. If you can seduce her, what's my reward?"

"A watch."

"Sounds good. Write it down so I can prove you said it."

"You don't trust me?"

"No."

Doai wrote on a piece of paper: "To sleep with My Trinh, the reward is a watch worth three thousand dong. To marry My Trinh, the reward is five percent of the dowry. Dated and signed, Nguyen Si Doai."

Kham put the scrap of paper into his pocket, then said, "Thank you."

A few minutes later, Kham said, "I heard Khiem telling that story yesterday, then I had a really scary dream last night."

"What story?" Doai asked.

"When Khiem was talking about killing pigs. Each hand holding an electric node to the pig's temples. 'Eeech' and it's over. During a power failure, Khiem had to use a sledge hammer to hit each pig on the back of the neck. With one strong pig, ten blows weren't even enough to kill it, and the pig's neck got all messed up. And when Khiem got tired he hit one pig in the leg. In a single shift, Khiem killed over a thousand pigs and was awarded a citation."

"What does this have to do with your dream?"

Kham said, "I dreamed I had to kill a pig, but it wouldn't die. It only smiled at me. As a punishment, I had to clean up an entire cesspool. The cesspool was made of cement, measuring 10 x 6 x 1.5 meters, 90 cubic meters capacity. A rainstorm came, flooding the cesspool with me in it. There was shit in my mouth and in my ears."

Doai said, "That's a good dream. You shouldn't worry about it. Buy a lottery ticket and you're sure to win. Old people say that stepping on shit means good luck. You were drowning in it, so you'll probably hit the jack pot."

Kham said, "That's so true. If you hadn't told me I wouldn't have known." After that, he ran excitedly into town.

On New Year's Eve, only Khiem, Ton, and Sinh were in the house. Mr. and Mrs. Hien had sent their son-in-law over at dusk to invite Old Kien and Can to town. They were probably drunk and unable to make it home yet. Doai and Kham took My Trinh and My Lan to Ngoc Son Temple to pick branches from the trees for good luck.

Khiem arranged on the altar a young hen that Sinh had cooked earlier that evening. It had a rose in its beak. He also opened a box of candied fruits, poured three cups of wine, and laid out a pot of tea. Khiem said, "You handle the ceremony, Sister Sinh." Sinh had put on a little lipstick, a pair of tight pants, a long-sleeved sweater, and an unbuttoned vest, then tied a canary-yellow scarf around her neck. She looked entirely different from her usual self.

Sinh told Khiem, "You take care of the ceremony. I'm a woman. I know nothing about such things."

"But you're older. Just bow three times and I'll take care of the prayer part."

Sinh said, "Good enough." Then she stepped in front of the altar, bowed three times, mumbled something, then bowed three more times, clearly not a person who was ignorant of ceremonial procedures.

Khiem said to Ton, "I hung the string of firecrackers near the door. After my prayer, you light it." With that, he stuck a lit filtered cigarette into Ton's mouth and said, "Light it with this." Ton nodded.

Khiem turned to the altar, bowed three times, and said, "The Socialist People's Republic of Vietnam, in the year 19__." Ton lit the firecrackers. Earth and sky became harmonious; human emotions stirred.

Khiem said: "It's a New Year. I wish you health and luck. Here's a thousand for good fortune."

Sinh's eyes watered. "You're giving me this much? I also wish you a healthy New Year—five, ten times better than last year. Can keeps all the money, though, so I have nothing to wish you luck with. Ton, take a hundred for luck. It's from Khiem."

Ton held the bill up to the light and asked, "Is it money?"

Khiem said, "Yes."

Ton asked, "What's money?"

Khiem said, "Money's king."

Old Kien and Can came home at one in the morning. A little later Doai and Kham also showed up. The whole house feasted until three, closed their eyes for half an hour, got up again, cursorily bowed and prayed, then feasted some more. By eight, Old Kien said, "I'll go and visit the neighbors. Can and Sinh, come with me. Khiem, give your father some money so he can wish people luck."

Old Kien and Can and his wife made the rounds. Old Kien had on a pair of workpants, a wool shirt, and a knit cap. Can wore a military-style uniform of the rank of major, a suit purchased at the flea market with a cigarette burn in one sleeve. Sinh wore a pair of corduroy jeans and a German-made fur jacket. Kham said, "Sister Sinh looks like a queen."

Some neighbors paid the customary visit. Doai came out to greet them. After wishing each other good luck, everybody sat down to drink tea and chat. Doai said to one old man, "I'm sorry, Uncle, but I don't know how many people are in your household or what their names are."

The neighbor smiled. "Same here."

"In the old days," Doai said, "burglars had four categories of houses they wouldn't rob. The first was neighbors' houses. The second was friends' houses. The third was houses in mourning. And the fourth was houses in the middle of a celebration. These days, if I were a burglar, I'd break those rules."

The neighbor laughed. "My sons are the same."

After tea, everyone went home. The neighbor's son said, "That Doai is educated but talks a lot of trash."

The neighbor said, "Chaos."

After three days of celebration, the streets were littered with spent firecrackers. Everyone felt that New Year's Day had passed too quickly. But, my God, which day doesn't pass too quickly?

6. Night

By the end of March, Sinh's period had stopped, she craved sour foods, retched every so often, and her body stiffened: symptoms of pregnancy.

Old Kien got sick in May. Initially thought to be minor, his condition gradually worsened. At first, his eyesight merely blurred, then he saw double, missing the door and walking into the wall. The whole household grew worried, and they took him to the Western hospital. The doctor came up with a wild diagnosis of nerve disorder and prescribed vitamin B6. The doctor said, "Look here, these nerves are like this: when they clash, one becomes two, a chicken turns into a moor hen."

Can asked, "What can we do, Doctor?"

The doctor said, "Medical Science is investigating."

Bedridden at the hospital for a week, Old Kien's eyesight worsened.

Doai said, "I suspect a misdiagnosis." He went to see someone he knew at the Eastern hospital.

The man at the Eastern hospital said, "Western medicine is nonsense. You can bring the old man here."

Doai asked for a discharge for Old Kien. The doctor said, "Once you leave here, don't come back."

Old Kien stayed at the Eastern hospital but didn't get any better. His body was wasting away. His head hurt. By October, a brain tumor was detected. The doctor said, "If we leave him like this, he'll die, but an operation may save him."

Can gathered the family together for a meeting. "What should we do?" he asked. "Since father's been sick, we've spent a lot of money." He opened the account book and read from it. "Brother Khiem gave a thousand one time, eight thousand another time, five thousand another time. Brother Doai gave a hundred one time, sixty another time, one thousand one hundred another time. Brother Kham gave three hundred one time, but when I gave him a thousand to buy medicine from Mr. Toai, the herbalist, it only cost five hundred, and he kept the remaining five hundred and hasn't given it back to me. Food cost is this much, then this much. I've written down all the expenses."

Doai said, "I think he's too old. An operation won't change a thing. Better to let him die."

Ton sobbed out loud. Can asked, "What's your opinion, Kham?"

Kham said, "Whatever you all decide, I'll go along."

Can turned to Khiem. "Why are you so silent?"

Khiem asked, "What have you decided?"

"I'm thinking."

Doai said, "What a waste of time. If you agree that father should die raise your hand. I'll count the votes."

The day Old Kien had his brain operation, everyone went to the hospital except Sinh and Ton. The procedure lasted forty-two minutes. Sitting in the waiting room, Doai said to Kham, "It's bad that the old man never wrote a will. How are we going to divide his assets later?"

Kham replied, "And Can is so greedy that the rest of us will end up on the street."

Doai said, "I'm going to marry My Trinh next year. Mr. Daylight promised me a stick of gold. You think one stick's enough to buy a house?"

Kham said, "In my hands, I could multiply it into several sticks."

Doai said, "Business skills are the best. The other skills— art, literature, etc.—all of them are useless."

Can had a meeting with the doctor. Later, he walked out shaking his head. "The doctor said we should just take father home in about a month."

The day Old Kien came home, his head was bandaged, he couldn't respond to questions, and his eyesight was bad. Inside the house, Sinh unwrapped his bandage. Old Kien's head was bald, with a lump the size of an egg. Within two weeks, this lump had increased to the size of a grapefruit. Nudged with a finger, it felt like it had bean paste inside. A big indentation would result from a big nudge, a little indentation from a little nudge. Sinh had to tend to the old man, a terrible job.

Kham asked Doai, "Is this illness contagious?"

"It's better to be careful. Can and his wife have money. Khiem has money. But if either one of us gets sick, where do we get money for treatment?"

Soon after that, Old Kien went into delirium. He was always moaning, "Please let me die. It hurts too much." The atmosphere in the house turned morbid, depressing everyone. Even Ton stopped washing the floor. All day long he'd sit by himself in the woodshed next to the toilet.

Mrs. Hien came down from the city, saw her brother in writhing pain, and cried, "My brother, what debts haven't you paid to be tortured like this?" She said to the family, "You guys figure something out, or are you just going to leave him like that?"

"What should we do?" Can asked.

Mrs. Hien said, "I have a friend who has a text of the Special Mantra. We could copy it and bring it back here to read. Maybe then he'll go peacefully."

Doai said, "Now it comes to this."

Mrs. Hien made Khiem go to town, to her friend's house to copy the Special Mantra. Khiem brought it back and said to Doai, "You're good with words. You read it."

Doai turned the piece of paper every which way and said, "I can't deal with your handwriting. It's worse than Can's accounting book."

Khiem read the mantra. It was dusk. Mrs. Hien lit incense and sat next to him. Old Kien was writhing at first, then lay still. At eleven o'clock, everyone else went to bed. Khiem continued reading the mantra. Over and over. Basically, the mantra asked Buddha to forgive the dying person's sins and to leave his debts to be repaid by the ones who are left behind, all in difficult-to-understand language. Khiem read all night, his voice distorted. At four in the morning, Old Kien stopped breathing. A faint smile was on his lips. He looked very benign, serene. Khiem closed his father's eyes then went to tell Can. Everyone woke up.

Doai said, "The old man's gone. How fortunate. I'll go buy a coffin."

7. A Normal Day

A hundred days after Old Kien's funeral, Sinh gave birth to a baby girl. A party was planned to welcome her back from the hospital. Can and Kham went to the market. Khiem cooked. Doai and Ton cleaned up. The two girls, My Lan and My Trinh, came by, with flowers even.

At the table, Sinh sat in the middle, with My Lan and My Trinh on either side. Sinh was radiantly beautiful. Doai poured rice whiskey into a cup, stood up, and said, "With this cup of whiskey, I toast to life. This whiskey is both sweet and sour. Whoever accepts life should toast with me. Life is trouble, but it's also very beautiful. To the newborn and to her future!" Everyone raised their cups. Doai said, "Hold on a second. What's the baby's name?" Everyone laughed.

Buoyant with whiskey, Khiem said, "Sister Sinh, is it rough being a daughter-in-law in the Nguyen Si household?"

Kham said, "Sister, answer in such a way as not to scare off My Lan and My Trinh."

Sinh smiled. "If it's like this, then it's not rough."

Can asked, "Then it's rough, normally?"

Sinh said: "Of course it's rough. And very humiliating. A lot of pain and a lot of anguish. But I also love it."

Ton grinned and repeated innocently, "Also love it!"

The mailman came up to the door and looked in. "Is this house number 129? I've got a telegram for you."

Can went out to accept it. When he came back inside, he said, "Uncle Vy in Phuc Yen died at eight yesterday morning."

Doai said, "We can deal with that later. What's so unusual about old people dying? Let's get on with this party. After you, Generals!"

Translated by Linh Dinh

My Uncle Hoat

My home village is in a poor area of rolling hills, just a bit before you get to Chu. Yes, indeed, people call that place "a land where dogs eat rocks, and chickens eat pebbles." You ask what people eat there? Well, you eat whatever you can, just so you're not hungry. The staple at our house was mashed manioc. You pick them up in the hills, boil them, grind them, and then you fry them up with a bit of pork fat to make it easier to swallow. Now, if you tried it once, you'd like it because it's different. But try eating this stuff for a week, then a month, then year after year. You'd get sick of it, and you'd get feverish! Later, when I was older, to tell you the truth I couldn't eat it at all. I couldn't even look at a manioc. I don't know who came up with the phrase "to live to eat manioc." I don't even know how you would use it, or what the meaning would be, but whoever thought of that phrase must be someone whose experience with manioc couldn't have been too pleasant, just like mine.

Yes, my father was an elementary school teacher. As for my mother, when she filled out her identity papers, she wrote down "homemaker" in the space for "occupation." But what did my family have that required a "homemaker?" My mother worked the land, planted vegetables, went to the market, collected firewood. She did everything that she could to earn some money to feed my sisters and me.

Both of my older sisters only finished elementary school, then stayed home to help my mother be a "homemaker." My father's younger brother, Uncle Hoat, was a cripple. One of his legs was tiny, like a small manioc plant. Every day he looked after the cows. Uncle Hoat knew how to carve a flute, and he played the flute extremely well. My mother said that when my grandfather was still alive, Uncle Hoat received a proper education and read a lot of books and magazines. Later, my grandfather went into decline. Because of the times and because Uncle Hoat got sick with his leg, he had to stop attending school.

My father taught in the village, and his students were an uneven lot. He didn't appear to be such a good teacher anyway. He'd dictate the lessons while coughing loudly: "In the pond—Ahem!—what's more beautiful—Ahem!—than lotus—Ahem!" The students called him "The Crow." He had a wooden ruler, a meter long, always ready in his hand. Bad luck for any rowdy kid who got a whack on the head with the ruler. That would be something to remember until old age.

Our family was always short of money. One time, when the government devalued the currency, my family had only about a single dong. That's equal to about a thousand dong today. To change the currency, we had to go to the provincial capital, which meant walking for more than five kilometers. That's no small deal! I'm telling you the truth, for such a small sum these days I'd just as soon throw it all away. Why bother with exchanges? I'm not saying that I'm disdainful of money—that would be stupid; who can afford to be disdainful of money?—but what the hell can you actually buy with one thousand dong? Even so, back then, my mother insisted on making her way down to change that miserly amount. When she came back with the new bill, the whole family passed it around and examined it, and everyone admired how the drawings on it were so beautiful and detailed. When Uncle Hoat remarked that the human figure in the drawing seemed slightly too well-fed, too rotund, my mother yanked the bill away, giving him a scowl that shocked him into silence.

In our family, since my mother had tight control of all our spending, she was forever miserable and difficult because of the lack of money. She always complained, grumbling about Heaven, about ill fate, about how useless my father was, and she considered Uncle Hoat and my sisters and me to be "open-mouthed boats." My mother could not have really known what an "open-mouthed boat" was, but she repeated what she'd heard from others. My guess is that she decided that "open-mouthed" meant capable of consuming a vast amount of food. My father was always ashamed to hear my mother complain; he'd sit quietly in some spot, sighing and fidgeting with the tobacco pipe in his hands, repeating over and over the old saying, "Even mountains would crumble if one just sat and ate without working." I thought he was so powerless, absolutely powerless. If only I could have dug up a pot of gold! I knew that in ancient fables, miracles and turns of luck often happened to poor and decent voiceless folks like us.

By the time my sisters and I grew up, the need for money had become even more urgent. It didn't matter to me, but my sisters were miserable because they didn't have enough clothes. Cold seasons are most terrible for the poor. My mother often griped or alluded to Uncle Hoat's uselessness. Clearly, he was a burden, a hopeless appendage to the wreck that was our family. Naturally, my mother never griped about Uncle Hoat in front of my father. But whenever he heard my mother speak, even indirectly, Uncle Hoat's face would turn pale, and he'd head up to the hills. My mother said, "Vuong, you go after him. Make sure he doesn't jump into the river, or into an abyss, to kill himself. People would call us a cruel family. But then, people like Hoat have a strong will to live. Who knows what for—*live to eat manioc*! It's just one more bit of predetermined bad luck for this family."

Once, when a traditional cheo opera troupe came to the province for a performance, my father allowed my uncle, my sisters, and me to go see the show. It was freezing cold. Between my sisters Nhu and Nha there was just the one tattered, short-sleeved green sweater, and they kept passing it back and forth, each wanting to give it to the other. In the end, each wore nothing but a simple thin shirt, and, to keep warm, they shouted as they ran. Uncle Hoat hobbled behind them. You find this touching? Sir, what's so damn touching about poor people? Your way of thinking is that of people with a full belly, looking down at the bottom of society. That day, the cheo troupe performed "The Story of Quan Yin," and there were as many people as you'd find at a traditional fair. We'd never seen a live performance before. We were enthralled, almost crazed over the words and the singing, the spectacular lights, and even the charged atmosphere of so many people in one place. Have you ever heard the collective sigh of ten thousand people at the same moment? No? Oh, it's wonderful, truly wonderful! I don't know how to describe it. I just feel it's terribly good. And so, that's how we came to see the cheo performance. It was a different world compared to our mundane daily life. Afterward, the lyrics stayed in our minds. We couldn't escape them. You want to know whether I remember any of the lines? Sure I do: *"The woman Thi Kinh wrote: 'The debt I owe to the land I could never repay. Neither can I stay nor leave. This woman's fate, even multiplied by ten, would still amount to nothing* [a reference to the saying, "Ten women still amount to zero"]. *To live is to live with shame. Even in death, there's shame. The one who stays suffers; the one who leaves suffers, too. Who should face this sudden calamity?"*

I remember those lines because they reflected our family's situation. After that night of watching the cheo performance, my sister Nha left home. Nha was the most intelligent in the family. She recognized a different world, a different horizon, beneath the performers' colorful costumes. My parents were stunned. They had never imagined that this could happen. After that, my father actually withered. My mother cursed him as a useless person, complaining that he didn't care about looking for his daughter. Maybe my father knew that if my sister Nha had stayed her life would have been even more dismal. That year, Nha turned eighteen. When she left home, she left behind the short-sleeved green sweater for our oldest sister, Nhu.

Please give me a glass of water. Damn! How did I get so sentimental? It's been more than thirty years, and I have no

89

idea where my sister Nha might be right now. It reminds me of that line, "To live is to live with shame. Even in death, there's shame."

All of the misery in my family from then on was blamed on Uncle Hoat. My mother no longer cared, and she would yell at him or tell him off right in front of my father. To tell the truth, Uncle Hoat was in fact a clumsy, helpless person, and he was always breaking the family's bowls, plates, and bottles. Others would have thought those things were fit for the recyclers, but we considered them heirlooms.

Sometimes, after that time at the cheo performance, Uncle Hoat would ask me for pen and paper, though I didn't know why. Then some months later, I saw him holding a stack of paper with writing on it. He approached my father, saying nervously, "Brother, I'd like to read this to you." Uncle Hoat read to my father several verses about skies and rivers and mountains. My father turned red. I'd never seen him lose so much control. He cursed, "Ah, so it turns out you're a poet and a writer. Heavens! You damn dog. So, my family has produced an artist after all. We're clearly blessed. Who did you think you'd teach with your writing and your poetry?"

Uncle Hoat twisted his hands together miserably, tears in his eyes. He said, "Brother, you're mistaken. I had no intention of teaching anyone. I only meant to express myself."

"Oh, to *express* yourself?" My father sneered. "You want to complain about us? You're blaming us? Heavens, this is certainly a case of feeding a stinging bee right inside your own shirt, of keeping a fox in your own den. It's bad luck! It's bad luck for this house!" My father tore up the pages, threw them on the ground, then picked up the pieces to throw them into Uncle Hoat's face. From the time I was a kid, I'd never seen my father so angry. Uncle Hoat's foolish act seemed to have touched something deep inside my father, something so deep that people would say, "It came from the roots of one's life," from the place that contains the original hatred between night and day, between water and fire, the place that contains the offense and suspicion, even despair, shame, suffering, and, above all, fear—yes, to be exact, a terrible fear—of an abnormal world, an abnormal adversary that had sent Hoat's poetry as an initial message of war and death. My father taught school, all day long repeating words like a person reciting some mantra, and he never questioned this existence. Now Uncle Hoat, the cripple, the cow herder, the good-for-nothing, was making rhymes about the skies and rivers and mountains, questioning his entire existence, and his entire family! Like they say, this was "an overflowing cup," and so my father coldly chased Uncle Hoat away.

My mother was terrified. Even though she had always complained about Uncle Hoat, now she defended him, begging my father to think again, asking him not to be so cruel, to think of the blood ties between two brothers. My father refused absolutely. And so Uncle Hoat turned around to leave, kneeling in the front yard and bowing toward the house. My father threw the tobacco pipe at him. My mother cried and rushed after him, giving him her hand and screaming, "Hoat, Brother, I didn't do anything to you. Please don't be angry with me. Don't leave like this." Uncle Hoat put aside my mother's hand, tears welling in his eyes, then turned and limped away into the night.

That was a first day of the month, like today. The crescent moon was dangling in the open sky like a gloomy brush stroke. You think that's beautiful? Why are you always preoccupied with such senseless and unreal beauty? You are someone of the upper class. You're used to being comfortable, which is why you can have such sentiments. With poor people, beauty must be something akin to actual riches. The moon has to be round, the trees full of fruits, pockets lined with money. In other words, everything must be as full as this glass of beer. Hey, Mister, drink up. One hundred percent!

After Nha and Uncle Hoat left, our family practically went into mourning. Those left behind felt guilty. Everyone avoided talking too loud, and we even avoided looking at each other. My sister Nhu seemed to shrink, my father's back became stooped, and my mother, who was never sick, who could never afford to be ill, was now dazed and befuddled. My father talked to my mother about moving somewhere "closer to civilization and humanity," which he saw as the only chance to get me educated and to allow me to develop a career and a decent life for the future. We ended up moving to this town of X, and here we are, talking to each other. My family sold rice and vegetables in the market and managed to build a house right next to it. I was able to go to school and my sister Nhu married an old widower. My brother-in-law, Phuc, though old, was a golden toad who had money and wasn't too stingy with it, so everything fell into place. My sister Nhu was able to build herself a nest, a place to rest in her old age. Our lives changed in the city, but, I'll admit to you, I still prefer the old and poor hill country. My parents were quite mistaken when they moved here. This is not the place that is "closer to civilization and humanity" that my father imagined. But that's a different matter, nothing to do with the story I'm telling you. I'm telling Uncle Hoat's story.

No one really knew where my Uncle Hoat went and what he did. Many years later, my father happened upon a newspaper with a picture of him and a poem he'd written, accompanied by some comments as well. The poem talked about fertilizers and insects, which I found trivial, laughable, even worthless, but my father shouted over it as if he had discovered gold: "Heavens, young Hoat did become a poet. Right here! There's even a commentary in italics."

My parents were thrilled. My mother said, "See! You used to always say he was useless. Now he must be really rich. He probably has so much money he couldn't even spend it all!"

My father read the poem over and over again, then said with surprise, "Great! It's so great! I can't believe it, really. It turns out he had hidden talents. Literature is the most difficult thing in life, but he's succeeded at it. I truly admire him." My father stroked and caressed the newspaper, then asked Phuc, my brother-in-law the golden toad, to come have a drink so he could show off the poem. Phuc was bald, a mere few strands of hair on his scalp, and he kept nodding. Then he said, "Not bad. Quite good. Actually, if the word *rare* had been switched to *well-done*, the poem would be more profound."

My father seemed to view Phuc merely as a wealthy but average and vulgar man. My father said, "The word *rare* is good there because it is not yet *well-done*. It only suggests *well-done*. If there wasn't the word *rare*, then let me ask you, would you have thought of *well-done*?"

Phuc agreed. "Indeed, had it not been for *rare*, someone of my level wouldn't have thought of *well-done*."

My father laughed. "That's it! The magic of literature is right there. That's why people see literature as the top in all of the arts!"

In fact, I don't believe in literature and its fake glories. In the old days, people who studied literature were linked with exams and being appointed to posts as mandarins. Pass a minor exam, you're a junior mandarin; pass a major exam, you're a senior mandarin. Because of that link to the mandarinate, literature in those days was something quite important. Later, when the Romanized language replaced the Han and Nom scripts, people began to write according to the Western methods. To tell you the truth, these days I see only a bunch of inept people in bed with con artists. There are a few intellectuals with some ideas, but they're all social revolutionaries. The rest are worthless. These days, many people still consider literature as a means to an end, like a fishing pole used to reel in fame and fortune. Yes, fame and fortune. There's nothing bad about that. You should aim for it, but make it worth your while. Anyway, I don't want to talk about that. I was talking about Uncle Hoat and his poems about fertilizers and insects. My father was mistaken, because he really didn't know anything about literature.

Please don't laugh. Literature is something no one really understands, don't you agree? To quote Homer, "There must be a God."

And so, every few months, my father would dig up a poem, a little ditty, by Uncle Hoat in some odd newspaper. My father scoured all the newspapers. The cost for these newspapers became a considerable expenditure in our family, but thankfully, my brother-in-law the golden toad took care of it. Phuc said to me, "Let him stay involved with that because it's harmless. Otherwise, he might get involved in something else, and we'd be dead." I didn't like my brother-in-law's practical way of thinking very much, but he was nearly my father's age, and frequently gave me money, so I remained courteous.

I don't know how, but as time went by my father truly came to believe that Uncle Hoat was a very successful man in society, while my mother was quite sure he would be very rich by now. Both my parents couldn't stop talking about him all day long. My mother said to my father, "Dear! Maybe you should go to Hanoi once and visit him. We owe him an apology. These days, he's a man of fame and position. I feel so bad! Then there's the issue of the future of our Vuong. Who knows, maybe he can say just a word and Vuong could go on to become a decent man. He would know plenty of places to ask for help. Otherwise, how can we allow Vuong to just hang around and do nothing?"

My father nodded. "You're right. I should apologize. Only then could I close my eyes and die peacefully. And we should also ask for his help with Vuong's future."

After my parents talked over their plan, they discussed it with Phuc, who said, "It's up to you, Father. If you ask me, I think you should go. But I've been to Hanoi; poor people get eaten there. It's a very cruel place and has no pity for anyone."

My father said, "I was thinking of selling the twenty-kilo pig to have some money in my pocket for safety. I'll let Vuong come with me."

Phuc said, "That's fine. But when you go to Hanoi the money from selling the pig will only be enough to buy some simple snack. All right! I'll loan Vuong my American jackknife. He can take it with him to feel safe. A long time ago, when I was his age and first started making money, I only had a dart!" Phuc gave me a heavy jackknife. He said, "This knife has nine functions. The blade has an automatic spring. If you have to stab someone, all you have to do is push this button once. The blade will automatically shoot out with a force of about five kilos—enough to kill a strong man. Just slice across the wrist like this and blood will immediately gush out."

My mother sighed. "Forget it, forget it. It's horrible to hear you talk like that. If you have to kill someone in Hanoi, why go?"

My father said, "That's only to be prepared. He just means to tell us not to let anyone humiliate us."

My father and I went to the station to buy tickets for the train trip to Hanoi. When we arrived in the city, we went directly to a newspaper that had published Uncle Hoat's writing and asked where he lived, but they didn't know much. "Yes!" someone told us. "There is a man with a beard and long hair who walks with a limp. Sometimes he'll come by to submit something and give his name as Hoat, and sometimes he'll use the pen name, Sharp Kick. He's often drinking beer in the afternoon in the stalls around the Hoan Kiem Lake."

My father sighed. The rather liberal information made him hesitate. He was a country teacher and, to him, anything to do with words was divine, not a joking matter. He and I walked around the lake three times, carefully looking at all the men. The security guards around the lake grew suspicious and asked us for our identity papers. My father explained about looking for Uncle Hoat. They said, "If your relative is frequently here drinking beer, then the vagabonds, newspaper vendors, and shoeshine boys would know." The head of the security unit, wearing a red armband, stopped a man in glasses and a checkered shirt who was passing by and asked, "Hey, Wolf, do you know a man named Hoat with a limp, often drinking beer in the afternoon somewhere around here?"

The man trembled, nodded his head in greeting, then fearfully replied, "Sir, that man left about a month ago. He went bust, and I heard he's drifted down to Nam Dinh."

The security unit chief waved an arm to dismiss the man and told my father, "Your relative is no longer around. He must have been afraid of getting caught by the police, so he left for Nam Dinh at least a month ago."

My father's eyes bulged out. He was frightened and said to the unit chief, "You must be mistaken. My brother is a decent man, and he's very nice. He even writes for magazines and newspapers!"

The security unit chief smiled, "Goes to show! In Hanoi, anything is possible. If Wolf said so, then it is so. You'd better go home and rest."

We said goodbye to the security guards, then walked around for a while, almost getting lost. Suddenly, a bunch of shiny cars drove by. Someone stuck his head out and waved. My father cried out, "Hoat! That was Hoat!" I, too, felt that the person in the car was Uncle Hoat, and he didn't look that different from when he was young. My father kept looking at the cars with a mournful air.

At the end of the afternoon, we went into a small pagoda. A monk was giving a lecture to some thirty or forty people, including students taking notes and some foreigners. The monk was saying something about literature and religion. He said, "Literature is close to religion, you see. Yes but no. No but yes. 'The Being' and 'The Void' are two realms of consciousness. Those who are too concerned with 'The Being' will have evil thoughts: 'Could *this* person write literature?' 'Could *that* person have religion?' Those who are too concerned with 'The Void' will criticize the scriptures and literature. According to them, Buddhist teaching should use only the direct spoken word, not complicated scriptures—in other words, they don't need the literature of the scripture. But if human beings don't need the literature of the scripture, then that would mean they don't even need spoken words because spoken words are the outward form of the scriptures. Nature made it that way. If we're ignorant within ourselves, well, so be it, but it's an offense to criticize the scriptures. As for literature, we need to distinguish between literature of the mediocre and literature of the divine. Don't make the distinctions too hastily, but do make them in order to decide what's worth reading and studying. Neither those people who are too concerned with 'The Being'—and, therefore, are always searching for 'The Truth'—nor those who are too concerned with 'The Void'—and therefore reject even great masterpieces—will ever attain understanding. If you see literature as another form of religious, then you won't be too confused."

After listening for a while, my father said to me, "It turns out that when Uncle Hoat pursued a career in literature, he was pursuing a spiritual discipline. If you're talking about spiritual education, then abandoning this earthly life is normal. We don't need to be too concerned with finding him, then. Let's just hope he's at peace, with a clear mind to see, pursuing his own chosen truth." After we left the pagoda, my father and I bought a few things and then went home. Since then, no one in our family has mentioned Uncle Hoat very often. All of this happened more than ten years ago.

Drink your beer! See? You asked about the faded portrait up there. Well, that's just my Uncle Hoat. All right! One hundred percent! Bottoms up!

* * *

I heard this story once when I was passing through Bac Giang. It was raining. I stopped at a restaurant by the side of the road. The owner was a warm man, rather talkative. On the wall hung a few family pictures. I only paid attention to the photo of a man with bright eyes and a rather concentrated look, both tense and pained. That gaze obsessed me. I asked the restaurant owner about the man.

He told me, "Oh, that's my Uncle Hoat. Do you want to hear a story? Order some beer and some snacks and I'll tell you the story. Anyway, you can't really go anywhere in this weather."

I have faithfully recorded the restaurant owner's words. In my notes, I have changed the names of a few characters, and added some punctuation to make it easier to read.

Since it's New Year's Day, I offer it to you, dear reader, as a token gift to celebrate the new year.

Translated by Nguyen Qui Duc

The Winds of Hua Tat:
Ten Stories in a Small Mountain Village

For Nguyen Hong Hung
— N. H. T.

In the northwest mountains, about a mile from the foot of Chieng Dong pass, there is a small village of Black Thai people. Its name is Hua Tat.

Hua Tat lies in a long, narrow valley, surrounded on all sides by tall peaks. At the end of the valley is a small pond that never seems to run dry. Around the pond, when autumn arrives, wild daisies bloom so golden they sting the eyes.

There are many paths out of the valley of Hua Tat. The main path is paved with stone and is wide enough for a buffalo. Both sides of the path are thick with bamboo, reeds, fig trees and mango trees, and rows of hundreds of kinds of vines with unknown names. Many people have left their footprints on this path, even an emperor, it is said.

The valley of Hua Tat gets little sun. All year long a blinding silver mist lingers in the valley. Only the hazy outlines of people and creatures are visible, nothing more. These are the mists of legends.

In Hua Tat there are many old stories. Those stories are like golden wildflowers, small as buttons, growing on fences in narrow lanes. Men holding these flowers in their mouths can drink and never get drunk. They are also like white stones with red veins as slender as thread, hidden deep in the hearts of streams. Women like these stones. They each choose one and wrap it inside their undershirts for a hundred days. They make mattresses for their husbands and sew the stones inside. According to tradition, the husband who lies on that mattress will never even think about another woman.

Hua Tat is a small, lonesome village. People there live

simply, and simple-heartedly. Work in the steep mountain fields is laborious and exhausting. Hunting is like that, too. However, the people there still treasure their guests. When you arrive in Hua Tat, you will be invited to sit by the fire, drink rice wine from an urn, and eat the dried meat of a forest animal. If you are respectable and honest, the man of the house will invite you to hear some old stories. Maybe these old stories will dwell on the miseries of human beings, but when we understand those miseries, then wisdom, morality, nobility, and humanity will bloom within us.

The people who live in these old stories are no more. In Hua Tat, they have turned to ashes and dust. And so, their souls still flutter above the rooftop woodcarvings on village houses.

Like the winds.

The First Story: A Tiger's Heart

In those days in Hua Tat there was a young girl named Pua. There was no one as beautiful as she in all the provinces, her skin as white as a peeled egg, her long, smooth hair, her pure red lips. Pua's only flaw was her legs: they were paralyzed. Every day and every month she lay in one place.

When this story occurred, Pua was sixteen. Sixteen is the age of springtime, the age of love. Of loves there can be many, but a woman has only one spring. Spring begins in the sixteenth year; by nineteen, autumn might have already arrived.

In springtime Hua Tat was filled with the sound of bamboo flutes. The sound of flutes swirled around the houses of unmarried girls. No grass could grow there, and the faded earth was flat and smooth.

No flutes played at Pua's house. No one would marry a girl with paralyzed legs. The men pitied her, the women pitied her, even the children pitied Pua. People made offerings to the spirits for her, and looked for medicine. But nothing came of it. The girl's legs didn't move.

That year, Hua Tat endured a terrible winter. The sky was in chaos. Vegetation withered, water froze, and in the forest of Hua Tat a terrible tiger appeared. All day and all night the tiger prowled near the village. The village pathways were deserted, and no one dared venture out to the fields. In the evenings, every stairway was fenced and barred with thorns, and doors were sealed tight. When morning came, the footprints of the tiger could be seen around each and every house. The entire village lived in fear.

It was rumored that the tiger had a heart that was not normal, a translucent heart as small as a pebble. The heart was a charm; it could also be used for sacred medicine. Whoever could possess the tiger's heart would be lucky and wealthy for his entire life. The heart, steeped in alcohol, could heal the most serious illnesses. Even paralyzed legs, like Pua's, could be healed with a drink of that medicine.

Rumors are like swallows, flitting here and there. In the kitchen, out in the courtyard, by the stream, up in the fields, everywhere people were talking about the tiger's heart. The rumor drifted down to the plains where the Vietnamese lived. It flew up to the highest mountaintops of the Hmong people. Rumors are like that: as they pass across the lips of the ignorant they become extraordinary. Rumors are far less interesting in the mouths of experienced men.

Many people came to hunt the tiger. There were Thai, Vietnamese, Hmong. Some wanted to shoot the tiger to take the heart as a charm; others wanted to make medicine with it. Who could blame them? In life, who has not chased after such fleeting things?

Among the crowd of hunters, the largest band was made up of the boys of Hua Tat, who wanted to capture the tiger's heart to heal Pua's illness. The hunt lasted the entire winter. As if possessing supernatural power, the clever tiger knew to avoid the places where the hunters were waiting. The hunters became the hunted. More than a dozen people were killed by the wild tiger. The sound of weeping floated in the howling wind that blew through the village. People gradually gave up, and the number of hunters dropped as fast as ripe figs from a tree. In the end there was only one person left. That person was Kho.

Kho was from Hua Tat. He was an orphan, and he lived like a porcupine. Porcupines live solitary lives; they follow their own paths, and nobody knows how they eat and drink. Kho never took part in a single village gathering, not even a festival. He did this in part because he was poor, and in part because he was ugly. He had suffered from smallpox, and his face was pitted and pockmarked. Kho was deformed—his arms dangled down to his knees, his feet were bony, and he always looked like he was running. Do porcupines ever walk?

The sight of Kho going to hunt the tiger surprised many people, especially when they learned that Kho was hunting not to use the heart as a charm, but to make medicine for Pua. Night after night they saw Kho outside Pua's house, like a prowler, as dumbstruck as any suitor.

The people of Hua Tat didn't know what path Kho took to track down the tiger. Not even a tiger knows the porcupine's trail. The tiger sensed danger. It shifted its lair, it changed the trails it took. Hour by hour, Kho and the tiger hunted one another.

One night, while people sat in Pua's house telling stories, they heard a gunshot. The sound of the gun exploded like a thunderclap. The tiger's desperate roar reverberated through the mountains.

The tiger is dead! Kho shot the tiger! The entire village was shocked into motion as if the monsoon had hit the forest. They applauded. People wept as they cheered. The village men lit torches and headed up into the forest to find Kho.

Near morning, they found Kho and the body of the dead tiger. The two had rolled down into the deepest abyss in the valley. Kho's back was broken, and his face was covered with claw marks. The tiger's skull had been split open by the shot. The bullet had pierced its forehead and plowed deep into its brain.

But the most extraordinary thing was that the breast of the tiger had been cut open, and its heart was gone. The knife-slit was still fresh, and blood flowed from the wound, foaming into bubbles. Someone had stolen the tiger's heart!

The men of Hua Tat were silent, and they looked down at their feet. They felt ashamed, angry, anguished.

More than a dozen people had died that winter because of the tiger. Two more died after that: Kho and Pua.

The villagers of Hua Tat buried the tiger where it had died. No one repeated the myth of the magic powers in a tiger's heart. People forgot it the way they forget all the bitter things that happen in this world. It is necessary to do so.

Of those who remember this story, very few remain.

The Second Story: The Largest Animal

In those days, there was a family of strangers living in Hua Tat. Nobody knew where they had come from. They built a house at the edge of the village near the haunted forest. Only an old husband and wife lived in that house, and they were both getting on in years. Wherever they went, they were together. The old woman was always gloomy and quiet; no one ever heard her make a sound. The old man was tall and skinny, stonefaced, with a nose like a bird's beak. His eyes were deep and cloudy; they looked like cold, cold rays of phosphorous.

The husband was a celebrated hunter. Guns had eyes in his hands. When his gun went off, birds and beasts of the forest rarely escaped death. Behind the couple's house, bird feathers and animal bones were piled into small hills. The mounds of stripped quills were as black as ink, and the piled bones were the color of limestone with rotting, yellow streaks of marrow. The piles were as large as tombs. The old hunter was like the incarnation of Death in the forest. Birds and animals were terrified of him. The other hunters of Hua Tat were envious and indignant. The old man didn't let a single creature within firing range escape. One person said he saw with his own eyes the old man shoot a dancing peacock. A dancing peacock: its head arched like a rice stalk, its tail unfurled in an arc of color, a bright ray of sunshine flashing off it like gold as it pranced about on two spindly legs. Only love steps so delicately. A dancing peacock, so very...Boom! The gun recoiled in the old man's hands, a sudden lick of red flame. The peacock fell, its iridescent rainbow wing smudged with blood. The man's wife stepped forward, bony, dark and somber, picked up the peacock, and put it in her straw backpack.

Even though the old man spent his life hunting, he could only shoot birds and common creatures. He was never able to shoot large animals, anything weighing three or four hundred kilos. His gun could shoot only insipid little creatures. And this was what tormented and shamed him.

All the villagers of Hua Tat avoided the old couple. No one spoke or spent time with them. When people saw them, they quickly turned away. And so, the old hunter lived a lonely existence by the side of his gloomy wife.

At the end of that year, the forest of Hua Tat was barren; all the animals had fled and the birds seemed to have flown away. Not even a footprint remained. The people of Hua Tat had never had such a difficult time. People said that Heaven was punishing them.

The strange old hunter also found it hard to find food. The couple roamed the forest. They traveled to remote areas for the first time in their lives. For three barren months, the hunter never fired his gun. Every day he rose at cockcrow, hoisted his gun onto his shoulder, and went hunting until the night was pitch dark. Soon his emaciated wife no longer had the energy to follow her husband. She stayed at home and kindled the fire, waiting. The flame seemed haunted: it was not red, but piercing green like the eyes of a wolf.

One time the old man was out for a week. He was exhausted. His knees drooped and his muscles had atrophied so much they could be squeezed like leeches bloated with blood. He dragged himself everywhere but found nothing. Not even a hummingbird; not even a butterfly. He stopped, terrified. Was Heaven punishing the earth, as people said?

At last, exhausted, he dragged himself home. When he got to the edge of the village, he stopped and looked at his house. There was firelight, a green flame; surely his wife was up waiting for him. He shut his deep, cloudy eyes. After a moment's thought, he turned again to the forest. With his nose he picked up the scent of a beast...A stroke of true luck! He saw it. A peacock, dancing. The peacock's feet moved lightly to the right; its tail unfurled into a circle and shifted to the left. A brilliant green light burned in the cluster of feathers around its head. The old man raised his gun: Boom! He shot it. He heard a dying scream and ran to the creature he had shot. It was his wife. She had gone into the forest to wait for him. She still held the peacock feathers in her hands.

The old hunter lay down and buried his face in the blood and the fetid, rotten leaves that reeked like rats. From his mouth came the grunt of a wild boar. He lay like that for a long time. A dark cloud descended, and the forest turned pitch black. The heat was stifling, like a fever.

Near morning, the old man leapt to his feet like a gibbon. He had an inspiration: he would use his wife's corpse as bait to hunt the animal, the largest animal in his life. He lay in the bushes an arm's length from the rotting corpse of his wife, his gun ready. He waited anxiously. But Heaven punished him. No animal came to the old man; only death came to him.

Three days later, the villagers dragged his crooked corpse

out of the bushes. There was a bullet hole in his forehead. He had shot the largest animal in his life.

The Third Story: Bua

In Hua Tat there was a woman who was unlike any other. Her name was Lo Thi Bua. No one would greet her on the village pathways. "An evil spirit! Stay away from it!" That was what mothers warned their children. That was what wives warned their husbands.

Bua was a graceful young woman. She was tall, with big, strong hips, a solid and meaty body, and sturdy, supple breasts. She was always cheerful; she radiated a light that encircled the hearts of others and drew them to her.

Bua lived alone with her nine children. None of them knew who their father was. Not even Bua could name the father of any one of them. Many, many men had come to her and then abandoned her. Young men with the smell of milk still on their breath and hardly enough experience to be fathers, old and experienced men, brave hunters, misers. Each came to Bua in his own way and left in a way unlike any other. In love stories, men are admired for being wise yet irresponsible, while women are frivolous yet overly devoted. Bua was ardent with all the men who came to her and equally cold with those who had left her behind. Bua herself looked after all the fatherless children she had borne. She had no attachment to any man in Hua Tat. She lived unshaken and ashamed of nothing. Who knows if she cared at all about the opinions of others?

Bua's populous family lived happily, in harmony, and in poverty. But the women in the village flew into tantrums and screamed hateful words through the gaps in their teeth. They were, in truth, frightened. The men quipped and lusted. They sat side by side around the fire, spittle dribbling from the corners of their mouths, eyes twinkling and slippery.

In Hua Tat everyone had a proper family of their own. Everyone lived in accordance with traditional customs: wives had husbands, children had fathers. How could there be such an appalling family? A wife without a husband! Children without fathers! Nine children! Nine of them and none look alike! Ridicule spread like an epidemic through the village. Among the women, it was like an epidemic of lice; among the men, it was fever. But it was the women who were most afflicted. They cornered their men and demanded the matter be resolved: Either send Bua away, or find the fathers of her children. How could such a family remain among the community of Hua Tat? When those children grew up, they would be village men and women. They would destroy every proper tradition.

The men of the village planned many meetings, but none took place. Many men felt themselves to blame for the situation. Their consciences were tormented. As for standing up and acknowledging their children, they didn't dare. They were afraid of the tongues of their impulsive, faithful wives. They were afraid of what people would say. But, above all, they were afraid of a life of poverty.

That year, for some reason, the forest of Hua Tat produced innumerable tubers. People effortlessly dug up the enormous roots. They were porous, fragrant, and rich. After boiling, the roots crumbled, and people delighted in eating them when they were still hot enough to burn the roof of one's mouth. Even Bua and her band of children dragged each other out to dig them up. The forest was tolerant and generous with everyone.

One day, while probing the earth for tubers, Bua and her children dug up a cracked urn, its glaze tarnished like blackened eelskin. Bua dug away the dirt surrounding the urn, and to her surprise saw that the jar was filled with sparkling bars of silver and gold. Bua's entire body began to tremble, and she fell to her knees, tears of happiness streaming down her face. Her band of children gathered around and stared at their mother in fright.

In an instant, a poor, troubled, scorned woman had become the wealthiest person in the village, in the entire province.

Now the men no longer needed to hold their meeting. People came to Bua's house in turns to identify their children. The faithful and impulsive wives hurried their husbands to Bua's house to name their children. It turned out that there were not only nine fathers, nor merely twenty: the number climbed to fifty men. However, Bua did not acknowledge any of those men as the fathers of her children. But still they came to her, and each one received a gift to please his proper wife.

At the end of that year, Bua married a hunter, a kind man, widowed and childless. Perhaps she was in love at last, for on her wedding night she shed many tears of happiness. She had never wept with any of the men who had come before.

After that, Bua should have borne and raised one more child with her acknowledged husband: the tenth child; but the woman was not accustomed to delivering a baby in the proper and traditional way. She died in labor, under a pile of warm quilts.

Everyone took part in her funeral. Every man, every woman, every child. People forgave her, and perhaps she forgave them, too.

The Fourth Story: The Happiest Celebration

Ha Thi E was the daughter of village chief Ha Van No. There had never been a girl as beautiful as E. She had a waist like the waist of a golden ant, a melodious voice, and eyes that twinkled like the morning and evening stars. The sound of her laughter was clear and carefree. Not only was E naturally beautiful, but few were as virtuous as she. E was the pride of Hua Tat. It was the hope of the entire village that E find a worthy husband. Village chief Ha Van No hoped for this; the village elders hoped for this. To entrust a girl as beautiful as E to an unworthy husband would be an insult to Heaven, because E was Heaven's gift to the people of Hua Tat. Who should be chosen? The entire village met to discuss the issue. Many people—boys from Hua Tat and boys who lived elsewhere—wanted to be the son-in-law of village chief Ha Van No.

One night the village elders stayed awake until dawn. After drinking five full urns of rice wine, they decided they would hold a contest to choose the person with *the virtue that was most precious and most rare* as a husband for E. What virtue was most precious and most rare? Who had that virtue? The young men crowded in debate around the kitchen fires. It's hard to imagine how much alcohol and meat vanished at those meetings. Nowadays, of course, the young cannot think on plain water alone.

A couple of days later a young man with a courageous demeanor came to speak with the village chief and elders.

"Courage is the virtue that is most precious and most rare! I have that virtue!" he said.

"Go ahead and show us!" the village chief responded.

The young man went into the forest. In the afternoon he returned: across his shoulders he carried a wild boar he had shot. There were over one hundred kilograms of meat on that boar; its hair was bristly like a hedgehog's, and although it was already dead, its staring eyes were still bloodshot.

The young man dumped the animal in the courtyard. His eyes twinkled brightly, and there seemed to be a halo around him. Everyone praised him.

The district chief called his daughter: "Child, look, a truly courageous young man. He has proven his bravery."

E smiled, and her heart leapt when she saw the brave eyes of her suitor. A flame burned in those eyes. But E, who was intelligent by nature, knew that brave people become infatuated with their own accomplishments.

"You are right, dear father," E replied. "The young man has proven his virtue. Bravery is truly precious. But dear father, it is a virtue that is precious but certainly not rare. It took him just from morning until afternoon to prove it."

All the elders nodded. They agreed with E. The boar was carved into meat. The entire village danced all night in celebration of the virtue of bravery, a virtue that is precious but not rare. Many exemplary young men of the forest share that virtue.

Some time later, a young man with an intelligent face came to speak with the village chief and elders.

"Wisdom is the virtue that is most precious and most rare. I have that virtue!" he said.

"Go ahead and show us!" the village elders responded.

The young man went into the forest. In the afternoon he carried back a pair of otters, both unharmed. The otter is the wisest creature in the forest; it is infinitely wary, and to trap it is almost beyond the ability of men. The young man smiled. His eyes twinkled brightly, and there seemed to be a halo around him. Everyone praised him.

The village chief spoke to his daughter: "Child, look, a truly wise young man. He has proven his wisdom."

E smiled, and once again her heart leapt. A flame burned and a storm raged in the eyes of her suitor. But wise people will always be miserable, and even cursed with an unlucky fate. They know too much.

E replied: "Father, the young man has proven his virtue. But dear father, it is a virtue that is precious but certainly not rare. It took him just from morning until afternoon to prove it."

The elders all nodded. The people cooked the meat of the two otters. The entire village once again danced all night in celebration of a virtue that is precious but not rare. All exemplary young men of the forest must have that virtue.

Then there was the time a fat young man rode into the village on horseback. The fat boy said: "Wealth is the virtue that is most precious and most rare. I am a wealthy person."

The fat boy filled the courtyard with countless gold and silver coins. Everyone was dazzled. The village chief and all the elders were silent. They had never seen such a wealthy man.

"Wealth is something a person does not need to prove!" the fat boy said.

The elders all nodded. The village chief nodded. The fat boy smiled, and a flame burned and a storm raged in his eyes, and the darkness of night was there within them as well. There seemed to be a halo around him.

The village chief asked E: "So, my child, is wealth the virtue that is most precious and most rare?"

"Rare, yes," E replied. "But wealth is not a virtue. Now, mendacity, that is a virtue. One cannot be wealthy without telling lies."

The elders burst out laughing. And once again the people danced all night, in celebration of the wealthy boy.

At last, a young man from within the village of Hua Tat sought an audience with the village chief and elders. It was Hac, an orphan, the most exceptional hunter in the village.

Hac told everyone: "Sincerity is the virtue that is most precious and most rare!"

"Go ahead and show us!" the others replied.

"Sincerity is not a silver necklace to be displayed for everyone to see and touch," Hac said.

There was a great clamor among the people. The elders debated the matter. The village chief was enraged, and his face turned red as fire. "It must be proven!" he yelled at the top of his lungs. Then he saw his daughter's eyes gazing lovingly upon Hac. "Who believes this boy? Who says he has the virtue of sincerity?" the village chief asked.

"Heaven knows," Hac replied.

"And I know it, too," E said solemnly.

"Madness!" the village chief howled. He looked at the elders for support. He knew that old men always find the simplest way out of life's complications.

"Go pray to Heaven!" one of the elders instructed Hac. "The skies are parched and all the streams have run dry to the source. If you are sincere, go pray to Heaven for rain!"

At noon the following day, the villagers erected an altar. The heat was suffocating. Hac stepped up to the altar and raised his eyes solemnly to Heaven. He said, "Your child is living with sincerity, although everyone knows that sincerity always brings suffering and loss. If a sincere heart deserves forgiveness and can bring love into the world, then please, Heaven, let it rain."

The sky was silent. Suddenly, from somewhere far away, a faint wind came blowing. The trees in the forest began to rustle. Dust rose from the earth into small whirlwinds.

In the afternoon, the skies filled with thick, turbulent clouds, and when night fell a torrential downpour began.

This time everyone danced for an entire month to celebrate the wedding of Hac to the village chief's daughter. It was the happiest celebration in Hua Tat. The whole village was drunk. Every pillar of every house and every tree in every garden was invited to drink a great hornful of rice wine.

The Fifth Story: A Wolf's Revenge

In Hua Tat there was a family of hunters by the name of Hoang. By the time Hoang Van Nhan was born, the family's reputation had spread to all the villages in the district. Nhan was an excellent shot, and he was the leader of the hunt every season. Nhan didn't know what fear was. His father, his grandfather, and his great-grandfather before him had all been the same.

Nhan had two wives but neither of them bore any children. When he was past fifty, Nhan married a third wife, and with great luck she delivered to Nhan a baby as beautiful as an angel. Nhan named the boy Hoang Van San.

From age five, San followed his father into the forest. Nhan was determined to train San to become a veteran hunter. But the village elders advised him: "Wait until San is thirteen. That is the age to begin. You must teach him to fear the forest! To let him enter the forest at such an early age is not good!"

"When I was five my father had already taken me into the forest!" Nhan responded.

"Those days were one thing, but today is different," the elders replied. "Your father had four children; you have only one."

Nhan laughed with scorn. We young folks often laugh with scorn at old people. We don't realize that the words of old people are sometimes prophetic. Old people know fear; they also know that fear is not something to be enjoyed.

Day by day San grew older. At eight he could trap pheasant; at ten he could hit a target on seven out of ten shots. Nhan decided the time had come to teach his child to hunt wild animals. Nhan took his child, now twelve years old, to hunt wolf.

The hunters of Hua Tat followed Nhan into the forest. There were at least thirty people. Wolves are proud, wise animals. They are tricky and cruel. When hunters attack a pack of wolves, the animals scatter, allowing some cubs to be sacrificed as decoys in order to save the rest of the pack. Nhan was a man of experience; this time he sent several hunters after the decoy while he and the others made sure the rest of the pack didn't get away. Nhan wasn't tricked by the wolf, an old bitch with reddish fur. When she ran, she hugged the earth and sped along a twisting, elusive path. Nhan was determined to follow and corner her in her lair.

San stuck close behind his father. He was already familiar with the shrill yelping of the wolf pack. Nhan had taught his child to distinguish the different signals that wolves make:

the sound of a command, the sound of a summons, a yelp of fear, even the meaning of each different wag of the tail.

By day's end, the wolf pack had been nearly destroyed by the hunters. The hunters closed in on the leader in her lair, a deep cave with mossy stone pillars. The wolf was old, and clumps of fur on her back were speckled with gray. Cornered in her cave, she fought back fiercely, her eyes red and bloodshot. Who knew what she was thinking? She stared at Nhan as if she recognized him, and then fled into the deepest corner of the cave, where her brood clustered together. As she snatched up a cub in her teeth, a gun went off. Nhan sent a burst of pellets into the wolf's back. The wolf collapsed on top of the tiny cub and sank her teeth into the top of its head. The hunters converged. They dragged the body of the wolf away and captured the cubs. San pried the tiny cub out of its mother's mouth and carried it home. It was the most handsome cub of the brood.

The wolf cub grew up among domesticated dogs. It still had toothmarks in the crown of its head; a scar had formed, and no fur could grow there. The cub was raised in Nhan's house. It grew accustomed to people, and it almost had the disposition of a house dog. Only its eyes and its posture set it apart. Its eyes were vicious and angry, and it moved furtively. Nhan and San didn't like the wolf cub. However, it never went against the will of the humans or other animals in the house. It kept its distance from everybody; it was mild in temperament, so mild it was bizarre. It didn't vie for food with the rest of the dogs; it didn't provoke the horses, goats, pigs or chickens. It lived alone, and sensibly, as if it knew that everyone in the house disliked it.

Time drifted by, and San turned thirteen. Nhan arranged a celebration for his son. He told the workers to slaughter two pigs and, while they were at it, to kill the wolf, to provide a feast for the village.

As the workers were sharpening their cleavers to slaughter the pigs, a terrible thing happened. San sat beside his father, wearing his most handsome cotton outfit. He had the air of an old boss. Nhan told his child to check on the workers. San nodded, jumped up and with three strides bounded down the wooden stairs, but unluckily his pant leg got caught on a bolt on the stairs. He fell to the ground where the wolf was chained. The wolf, lying half asleep, sprang to its feet in surprise. San's head crashed into a rock beside the wolf, and the boy's mouth hit the metal chain that was tied around the wolf's neck. Blood flowed from San's mouth. The trail of blood awakened something within the hazy subconscious of the beast. Baring its sharp white fangs it sprang forward, and it snapped at the splotchy skin on San's neck. Nhan's workers jumped back in terror. The crazed wolf did not release the child. It bit at San's neck; it clawed; it nibbled; it chewed; it tore off bits of flesh, tendons and ligaments soiled with blood. San's eyes rolled back into his head and he died at once. His neck had been hollowed into a red emptiness from which blood erupted, frothing and bubbling. Spurting blood filled the eyes of the wolf and dyed its ruffled fur red.

The workers tried frantically to pull off the animal. Nhan crept towards it with an axe in his hand, tears streaming down his face. The others stood aside to make room for him. Nhan's entire body shuddered. The wolf cringed and scurried beneath the stairs. Nhan stopped for a moment, then swung the axe down onto the metal chain. The axe blade bent as it shattered the chain. The wolf howled and ran towards the forest, a short section of chain dangling from its neck. The people stood around Nhan, stunned. Nhan dropped the axe and fell to his knees by the corpse of his only child, and he plowed his stiff bony fingers deep into the bloodstained earth.

The Sixth Story: Forgotten Land

Lo Van Panh was an old man famous in Hua Tat. Over eighty years old, he still had the perfect teeth of a seventeen-year-old boy. He could pound rice effortlessly on the millstone with a single hand. He did the work of three men. He had a great tolerance for alcohol, and could out-drink a team of men. Even the strongest youth of Hua Tat held Panh in great regard.

Panh had three wives, eight children and about three dozen grandchildren. They lived in harmony and prosperity. The family was like a charcoal stove: the lumps of coal shared their warmth and then set each other aflame. What family is not like that?

Nothing would have happened if Panh had just stayed in Hua Tat, wandering about the valley. But the old man suddenly got the idea to go to Muong Lum to buy some buffalo. And as it happened, if he had gone only to buy some buffalo, then the trip need not have been so rigorous; he could have simply headed over to Chi or Mat village to buy plowing buffalo of the highest class. But Muong Lum was where Panh had spent his youth. Memories from long ago had reawakened within him.

Muong Lum was far off, in a remote territory at the farthest border of Chau Yen. In the language of the Thai, "Muong Lum" means "forgotten land." In Muong Lum there were primeval forests, towering trees, and countless birds and animals.

Panh made the journey by horse. He was not far from Muong Lum when the sky turned dark and a violent hailstorm came crashing down. Panh searched for a place to take shelter, but the entire hillside where he stood was an expanse of reeds as sharp as knives. The hail rattled down in waves from above. Panh's horse refused to move; terrified, it whinnied and pawed at the earth with its hooves.

Panh, cursing, quickly dismounted. He had never seen such a terrible storm. The wind was overpowering, and the hailstones pounded the old man painfully. Night fell quickly, and thunder and lightning shook the earth. Panh's horse snapped free of its bridle and bolted down the hillside. Panh was about to chase after it when, suddenly, he saw a dark form moving in his direction. He regained his composure. It was a girl returning from work on the rice terraces. The storm had taken her by surprise, and she had fled, frightened, stumbling as she ran, and yelling at the heavens. When she reached Panh she collapsed into his arms.

It was pouring, and the hailstones hurtled down like shotgun pellets. Panh leaned over the girl and shielded her. She covered her face with her hands and her entire body trembled. She leaned with trust against Panh's strong, bare chest. He spoke soothingly, "Don't be scared. Don't be scared. Heaven's tantrum will pass."

They stood that way in the middle of the reed-covered hill as the hail and thunder roared around them. Panh grew dizzy with enchantment. In his long life, Panh had never had that feeling. He knew it was exactly what he had always thirsted for and yearned to find. More than love, more than the feelings with all the women Panh had met, this was like happiness.

When the hail stopped, a dreamy reddish light flickered in the sky above. The girl, feeling awkward, pulled her hands from between Panh's palms. The old man had never seen anyone so beautiful. The girl fled. Panh, bewildered, took off after her; he stumbled, but at last he caught her by the arm.

"What is your name?" he asked. "Tomorrow I will come to propose. Will you marry me?"

The girl seemed embarrassed. At last she stuttered, "I'm Muon...from Muong Lum village..."

She pushed Panh away and ran off down the hill, her calves looking white and soft. Panh fell to his knees. Sweat poured off him. He was exhausted. A feeling of joy flooded his heart. He collapsed among the wet dripping reeds, ignoring the enormous black ants that crawled across his bare chest. He slept there until his clever horse found him and woke him with its warm, rank mouth, nibbling at clumps of black curly hair in the old man's big ears.

At noon the following day, Panh guided his horse into the village and found Muon's house. He knelt before Muon's father and made a pile of all the silver coins he had brought to buy buffalo.

Muon's father laughed loudly when he heard his guest's proposal. He called for his wife and children and the other villagers. Everyone made jokes and chattered with one another. Panh waited, unbroken among words of ridicule as sharp as knives. Muon peeked out from her hiding place behind the door of the house. She was amused, thinking what was going on was rather humorous. In truth, she had already forgotten the hailstorm of the previous night, as well as her tears, and the meeting on the hill.

Panh, single-minded and obstinate, repeated his proposal. He was so excessive that the villagers could laugh no more. Muon's father was forced to declare his conditions. "All right, if you wish to be my son-in-law, then while you are here, you must cut down the tallest ironwood tree on Phu Luong peak, and carry it back to the village. The timber from that tree will make a house for you and my child."

The villagers burst out laughing again. They all knew of the ironwood tree: eight people linking hands could not circle its base. It grew on the summit of a limestone mountain so high that looking down from its peak Muong Lum village appeared as small as a single rooftop.

"Agreed! Please sir, keep your word!" Panh replied like a knife cutting stone.

The next day, so it is said, Panh climbed to the summit of the mountain, swung his axe one time into the base of the ironwood tree, and lost his strength. He died of a broken heart.

Muon didn't go to Panh's funeral. That day she went to the market in Yen Chau to see the cockfights. On her way home that afternoon it rained once again, but this time it didn't hail.

The Seventh Story: The Abandoned Horn

In Village Chief Ha Van No's garret there was a horn that had been left behind from another era. Made from the horn of a buffalo, with silver inlay, the instrument was cracked and covered with cobwebs, and some bees had built a hive inside it. Nobody noticed it. It lay there unprotected and got banged around.

One year, without warning, strange black worms appeared in the forest of Hua Tat. They were small as toothpicks, and they clung in thick masses to the leaves of every tree. If you entered the forest or climbed to the rice terraces, you would hear the sudden clattering of the worms as they gnawed at the leaves, and the sound would make you tremble with fright. There was no leaf that these worms couldn't eat. The leaves of the rice plant, bamboo leaves, even rattan, even thorny cane trees—all were gobbled up by the chewing mass.

Village Chief Ha Van No grew thin. He and the villagers searched for a way to destroy the infernal worms. They shook the trees to make the worms fall, lit fires to smoke them out, poured hot water and poison onto the branches to destroy the worms. Nothing worked. The worms reproduced even faster.

The village of Hua Tat was desolate, as if a plague had hit. People debated whether they should flee the village. The village elders called a meeting to decide what to do, and they invited the sorcerer to join them.

Village Chief Ha Van No told the people to sacrifice buffalo and pigs to beg heaven and earth and all the devils and spirits to assist them. And then the sorcerer spoke. "The beehive bone of the Ha family is rotting and turning into worms. Take the bone out into the sun and wash it, and only then will we be finished with the worms."

The village chief shivered. The Ha family's custom was to cremate people when they died. After the cremation, the bones were put into a small urn and hidden away. In the entire clan there was only one man at any time who knew this hiding place. Before dying, that man would pass the secret on to a clan member of his choice. According to tradition, if one clan hates another they must simply find the bones of their enemy's ancestors, grind them up and mix them with gunpowder, and explode it, thereby annihilating the entire enemy clan. The Ha clan had more than a few enemies. And now, if the bones were exposed for cleaning, the hiding place would be revealed, a good opportunity for their enemies.

The village chief thought about it. He knew his clan's enemies were watching his every step; but was that reason enough to let the plague of worms destroy his native land?

One night, at the end of the month, the village chief awoke and told his son, Ha Van Mao, to follow him. Mao was eighteen years old, a gifted, intelligent boy with a mind superior to that of other men.

The village chief and his son slipped stealthily out of their house. The secret burial place of the Ha clan's bones was deep in a cave near the peak of a mountain. The roots of an old fig tree spread downward to conceal the mouth of the cave. Only after chopping through the dense knotted roots could you slip inside. It was tough work, and not until the sun began to shine did the village chief and his son finally carry the small urn out of the cave.

The village chief opened the lid of the urn, set the bones on the ground, and prepared to wash them with alcohol. The bones were well preserved; they were not at all decayed as the sorcerer had said. Among the jumble of bones there was a silver cord of exceptional workmanship.

"What is this cord for?" Mao asked his father.

"I don't know." The village chief was pensive. "Maybe it's to secure or carry weapons or something."

"I like it!" the boy told his father, and he stuffed the silver cord into his pocket.

The father and son left the cave and headed back down the mountain trail. When they came to a switchback only a short distance from the cave, they saw a band of strange men waiting in ambush. The village chief recognized one of his enemies. He told his son to run down to the village and find help, while the chief remained to block the trail.

The village chief devised a plan. He searched for a way to lure his enemies far from the secret cave. So clearly outnumbered, his life seemed to be hanging by a single hair.

Mao made it back to the village. He immediately summoned the best marksmen in the village to help his father. The intermittent sound of guns from the forest set Mao's heart on fire.

At noon, they found the village chief. He was tied to a tree at least a dozen miles from the secret cave. A rifle, its bullets spent, had been tossed on the ground at his feet. The enemies had cut out his tongue for refusing to reveal where his family's bones were hidden.

Mao helped his father back to the village. The village chief didn't die, but from that time on he could no longer speak.

The destructive plague of worms continued to spread, becoming more severe every day. Mao's anger grew, and he ordered that the sorcerer's tongue be cut out in revenge for his father's. Afterward Mao told everyone to prepare to flee the village to new territory.

On the day he cleared out his family's furniture, Mao discovered the horn in the garret. It had a small hole for a cord. Mao suddenly remembered the silver cord he had taken from among his ancestors' bones. He found the cord and tied it onto the horn. The old horn suddenly appeared much more beautiful. Mao carried the horn outside and blew into it. How extraordinary! At the very first sound, the black worms in the trees began to writhe and squirm and fall to the ground.

Surprised, Mao lifted the horn and blew it several times. The black worms trickled down like rain. Mao was overjoyed. He hurried to stop everyone from clearing out their homes. The entire village, cheering, followed Mao into the forest.

The extraordinary tone of the old horn didn't falter once that morning. The black worms poured off the trees, leaving the people simply to gather them together and kill them. In only one day, the entire plague of worms was annihilated.

Once the worms had been destroyed, the people of Hua Tat held a celebration. The old horn was placed in a prominent position on the altar.

From then on in Hua Tat, at first light of every day a horn blast was sounded. The sound of the ancient horn reminded everyone of their ancestors and signaled a peaceful life free from the harmful worms.

The horn was always hung by the side of old, mute Ha Van No. The horn looked rather plain and had little to distinguish it from other ordinary horns. Even as ugly as it was, the sound of its call was no louder than the rest.

The Eighth Story: Sa

The craziest person in the village of Hua Tat was Sa. Sa was the youngest child of old Panh—an old man, famous throughout all the villages of the province, who had established a populous family of eight children and three dozen grandchildren.

From the time he was little, Sa had always liked to roam about and cause mischief. Through all his years he dreamed of accomplishing extraordinary things. Ignoring each and every word of advice, he obstinately followed his own desires. Drink wine? Whoever can guzzle twenty horns full of alcohol at one go, come challenge Sa! Hunt deer? Whoever can chase a deer for more than three days until the tormented animal collapses, come challenge Sa! Who can hit the shuttlecock faster and more skillfully than Sa? Who can make the pan-pipes sing more alluringly than Sa? Furthermore, who can conquer the hearts of women as deftly as Sa?

On one occasion the villagers had netted a large haul of

fish and with a great struggle raised them from the depths of the pond and into their boat. When the time came to divide the fish into shares, Sa suddenly overturned the boat into the water. Ignoring curses and laughing hysterically, Sa dove into the mass of flopping silver fish he had just set free.

Sa was so crazy he would jump straight into a fire, just on a dare. To Sa, praise from a child or woman was more precious than a heap of gold. But—and this is a fact as cruel as any other worldly custom—not one of the villagers in Hua Tat ever praised him. People didn't even call him by name. "Crazy Guy," "Nut Case," "Mad Dog" was how they addressed him. He was like a strange beast living among the people. With a life like that, Sa suffered miserably. He doubted his own intelligence and abilities. In the middle of a festival he was happy, but the moment it was over, he grew silent as stone. He sat all day, all month, making toys or some weapon or another, but as soon as he finished, he threw them away. No one dared put their faith in him or entrust any task to someone so full of surprises. A terrible loneliness trampled his heart to pieces. Fierce longing and a passion for life lured Sa away from any normal routine. And so, when he was thirty years old, after hearing the exhortations of a salt-seller from downriver, Sa left Hua Tat, with the intention of achieving extraordinary accomplishments in new territory.

After Sa had left, life in Hua Tat seemed much drearier. Fights weren't as fierce as before. Women had fewer affairs. There were no more parties that went on all night and into the day. There were fewer smiles. Even the birds that flew across the sky over Hua Tat flapped their wings lifelessly. People became sullen, and their work weighed heavier on their shoulders than before. That was when people first began to miss Sa, and regret his departure.

News of Sa, carried back from time to time by the salt-seller, astonished everyone. It was said he was collaborating with the Royalists somewhere far downstream. One time, people said he had left to be a diplomat in some country terribly far away. Another time it was said he had been sent into exile for taking part in a conspiracy against the Imperial Court.

The women began to hold Sa up as an example with which to teach their husbands. The villagers in Hua Tat used him as a standard of comparison with people of other villages. People even recalled past deeds of Sa's that he had had no part in. His reputation became the pride of the village.

And so the years passed. People assumed Sa had died somewhere far from his native land. And then one day he returned.

It was no longer the same youthful and exuberant Sa. He was a decrepit old man. He was like a savage from the forest. He had lost one of his legs, and the fluid in his eyes had begun to stagnate.

When asked about the glorious life he had experienced, Sa replied with reticence. The magnificent rumors that the salt-seller had recounted were true, in part.

The people of Hua Tat built a house for Sa. He lived normally, like everyone else. If anyone repeated an old story, Sa changed the subject.

Sa got married. A boy was born to the old couple. Sa lived until he was seventy years old, and then he died. It is said that before he died, he declared: "With these final years, living an ordinary life like everyone else in Hua Tat, I have now truly accomplished extraordinary things."

Was that possible? No one in Hua Tat ever disputed his statement. And at Sa's funeral, people participated with the solemnity of a funeral for a great man.

The Ninth Story: The Epidemic

In Hua Tat there was a couple, Lu and Henh. From the time they were small they were close to each other. When they grew up they loved each other, married, and gave birth to several children. They knew each other's gestures, moods, and thoughts. They were never far apart. By the time of the cholera epidemic in Hua Tat, the couple had been by each other's side for fifty long years.

The cholera spread to Hua Tat from Muong La and Mai Son on a day of extreme weather. The sun was strong and bright, and, at the same time, the rain came down in torrents. Steam curled oppressively upwards from the surface of the earth and chilled the people with fever. The youngest died first, and then the old. The poor died first, and then the rich. Kindhearted people died first and then came the turn for the mean-spirited. In just two weeks, thirty people died in Hua Tat. People dug graves as fast as they could dig them, sprinkling lime on top when they had finished. At night, Death held a party under the dark red moon.

The villagers of Hua Tat fought off the epidemic with a mixture of powerful liquor and finely ground ginger with garlic and chili. People poured the potion by the bowlful into the mouths of infants still feeding on mothers' milk. The babies wailed as it raked and tore through their insides. No matter: whatever happens in life, mustn't one's insides be raked and torn many times?

When the epidemic came, Lu was far from home. His great obsession, to wander and gamble, had taken its toll many times since he was small, and now his payment would be his life. All this time, Lu was absorbed in a gambling party far away, in Muong Lum. For ten days running, luck did not desert him; even when he went to piss he found some lost coins. All the other gamblers suspected the man had surely used sorcery. On the last day, with a handbag full of silver coins, Lu bowed out, leaving behind only bitter despair for the other players.

Passing through Yen Chau market, Lu bought a horse without even bothering to bargain. The Vietnamese horse merchant was so stunned he pounded his chest repeatedly in regret for the missed opportunity, went into a tavern feeling sorry for himself, guzzled alcohol until he was nearly unconscious, and lost all the money Lu had given him. Lu, tottering, rode the horse all the way home with an uplifted heart.

When he arrived at the village, Lu was stunned to see a thatched fence blocking his way. White lime had been spread everywhere. Flocks of fat ravens perched on the roof-carvings of every house.

People warned Lu not to enter the village. They pointed the way out of the village into the haunted forest, where Lu's children had buried their mother just that morning. Henh had died; the grave freshly sprinkled with lime powder was hers.

Insane with misery, Lu galloped his horse to the burial place of his wife. Prostrate before the grave, he wailed and he sobbed. "Oh Henh, how will I live without you? When I come back from the rice terraces, who will I find to heat water for me to wash my face? When I shoot a deer, who will cook it for me? Who will I find to share my happiness, my sorrow?"

Lu cried for a long, long time. His memories awakened and made him even more miserable. His love for his wife was bottomless. He realized how ungrateful and unloving he had been, and he saw his wife had been generous and tolerant. The more he reflected, the more remorseful and grief-stricken he became. All the bits of food Henh had passed on to others, all the pieces of beautiful cloth she had set aside. All for him, for the children. Living with him, Henh had been like an older sister, a mother, a servant. And in over fifty years, what had he done for her?

Hanging his head before the grave, Lu suddenly heard a moan echoing upwards from beneath the earth. It was Henh's moan! Lu knew by heart the sound of his wife's breathing, and he recognized it at once. Setting aside his fright, Lu frantically scooped away the earth with his hands, hoping in his heart that there had been a mistake.

The deeper he dug, the clearer the moaning sound became. Lu was crazed and elated. His fingers bled but he felt no pain. At last he struck the lid of the coffin, and found Henh at the very edge of death.

He pulled his wife out of the coffin. He hurriedly lifted her onto the saddle of his horse, and carrying his bag of silver he sped to Chi village in search of medicine. But the people would not let him enter their village. Lu poured out half of his silver to persuade them. At last the people allowed the couple to enter, on condition that Lu leave two-thirds of his silver.

Once inside the village, Lu searched out the house of the druggist. Piling up all his remaining silver coins, Lu pleaded with the druggist to do everything he could to save Henh.

Lu had not calculated the disasters he had caused. He had caught the illness. Both of them died that night. The druggist took Lu's silver to organize a funeral for the couple.

They were buried together in one grave. As the earth was shoveled in, people sprinkled lime and tossed down a handful of white silver coins.

Six feet under, Lu's soul must be pleased. Not long after the funeral, the epidemic ended in Hua Tat. Feelings of terror from that epidemic lingered for several generations. Today, the tomb where Lu and Henh are buried is a raised mound of earth; some thorny rattan trees grow on its summit. The old people of the village have named it the tomb of faithfulness; the young children call it the tomb of two people killed by an epidemic.

The Tenth Story: Sinh

Sinh was an orphan girl in Hua Tat. It was said that once upon a time her mother fell under the spell of a ghost and left her child in the forest. Sinh was tiny and thin, rather pitiful. She never had the chance to eat good food or wear nice clothing. With an untouchable's fate, she lived like a quail, avoiding everyone.

In Hua Tat, on the path into the haunted forest, there was

a small shrine. The shrine was for Kho, who had killed a terrible tiger in another time. In the shrine there was a small stone, as wide as a hand, set upon a brick altar. The stone was smooth and polished; deep within its layers were tiny red lines like human blood vessels. If someone wanted to make a wish, they would touch the stone and then, with their lips up close, talk to it at length. The stone had rested on its altar for many lifetimes; it had witnessed many lives, many destinies. It had become a sacred fetish, and some nights it was seen giving off light like a flame. Everyone's miseries and hopes were gathered within the small stone.

Once, a strange visitor came to the village from downriver. He was large and tall and rode a strong black horse. He turned into the home of the village chief, visited all the village elders, and lingered here and there. He understood the customs of the village very well. The villagers guessed that he was a merchant of ointments or the fur of rare creatures. He had a great deal of money, and conducted himself nobly, like a gentleman.

One day the visitor passed the shrine to Kho, and upon seeing the stone he tried to pick it up. But oddly, he was unable to lift it from the altar. Surprised, he called the villagers to come look. People gathered around the small shrine. The visitor told everyone to enter the shrine one by one and try to lift the stone, but no one was able to do it. The stone was so heavy it was frightening.

"Is there a secret here?" the visitor asked everyone. "Is there anyone in this village who has never tried to lift this stone?"

The villagers looked around for Sinh. They had completely forgotten about her.

The visitor told the others to find Sinh and bring her to the shrine. She had left a long time before to dig for tubers by the upper reaches of the stream.

Sinh came to the shrine. Everyone stepped aside to let her pass. The visitor told her to try to lift the stone. As if with some strange dispensation, Sinh effortlessly lifted the stone in her hands. The people were stunned, and they cheered in amazement.

Sinh carried the stone to the visitor. The light of the sun shone down on the girl's hands, her two callused hands, her deformed fingers. Sinh lightly rubbed the sacred fetish. The stone suddenly turned to water before everyone's eyes. Droplets clear as tears slipped through the girl's fingers and fell to the earth, leaving impressions shaped like stars.

The visitor was stunned, and he cried. He asked the villagers if he could take Sinh away with him. He had a new skirt and a new blouse made for her. Sinh suddenly became exceptionally beautiful.

The following day, the visitor departed from the village of Hua Tat. It was rumored that from that time on, Sinh was very happy. The visitor was an emperor traveling in disguise.

From Hua Tat, a road paved with stones leads out of the valley. It is a small road, just a path, both sides thick with bamboo, reeds, mango trees and rows of hundreds of kinds of vines with unknown names. That road is called Sinh's Road.

That very road still passes there today.

Translated by Peter Saidel

The Salt of the Jungle

The month after Tet is the most pleasant time in the jungle. Plants and trees begin to bud and the jungle is deep green and damp. Nature is both dignified and sentimental, partly a result of the spring rain.

If one goes into the jungle during this time, it's extremely delightful: stepping into a layer of rotten leaves, breathing the pure air, being startled when a drop of water falls from a tree onto one's bare shoulder. All the absurd and ignoble things that one has to encounter every day can be completely dismissed at the sight of a small squirrel leaping onto the branch of a rambai tree.

It was during this time that Old Dieu went hunting.

He thought of the idea of hunting after his son, who was studying abroad, sent him a double-barreled rifle. The rifle was magnificent, light as a feather, exactly like a toy. Even in his dreams, he could not have imagined such a rifle. At the age of sixty, Old Dieu felt that hunting in the jungle on a spring day with a brand-new rifle would really make life worth living.

Old Dieu put on his belt, warm clothes, fur hat, and boots. To be on the safe side, he also brought along a ball of sticky rice. He followed the shallow stream upward toward its source, which lay about a mile beyond a group of limestone caverns.

Old Dieu turned onto a well-worn, winding trail. Great numbers of bluebirds nested in the gam trees lining both sides of the trail, but he didn't shoot them. Shooting bluebirds with this gun would have been a waste of ammunition, since he had eaten his fill of them already. Although delicious, they had a rather strong taste. And there was no lack of birds at home, with pigeons everywhere.

At a bend in the trail, Old Dieu was startled by a rustling in a thornbush. A bundle of garish colors appeared before his eyes. He held his breath and saw a pair of wild chickens dart ahead, heads bent low, squawking. Old Dieu put them in the sights of his gun, then thought, "I'm going to miss them." He sat motionless in the same posture for a long time, wanting to wait until the jungle became tranquil again. The pair of wild chickens would think they hadn't seen a human being after all. That would be good for them, he thought, and for him, too.

The rocky mountain range was towering and majestic. Old Dieu looked at it, appraising his strength. Bringing down a monkey or a mountain goat would be quite satisfying. Mountain goats were difficult and Old Dieu knew it. Shooting this species happened only by chance, and he didn't believe that luck was on his side.

Weighing this decision carefully, Old Dieu reckoned that he would follow the foot of the limestone mountain over to the forest of rambai trees and hunt monkeys instead. That way, his chances would improve without his having to exert himself. The kingdom of the monkeys was in this valley. In the rambai forest, the monkeys moved in packs, so shooting one shouldn't be difficult for him.

When he reached the rambai forest, Old Dieu paused at a mound covered by creeping vines. He didn't know what kind of vine it was. Its leaves were a fading silver, like nhot leaves, and the flowers, which cascaded to the ground, were as yellow as earring studs. He sat there, silently observing. He needed to determine whether monkeys lived here. These animals were as smart as humans, and when they looked for food one of them always acted as a guard. The guard monkey had a very sharp ear, and if Old Dieu didn't spot it first, the hunt wouldn't be victorious. Shooting the leader would be impossible. Of course, the leader was just a monkey. But it was his monkey, that monkey, and no other. So he had to wait, had to find a way to shoot it.

Old Dieu sat quietly for half an hour. The spring rain was thin and soft, and the weather was warm. It had been a long time since he had had occasion to sit still like this, without thinking about anything, without being sad or happy, without any worries, and also without any calculations. The stillness and tranquility of the forest penetrated him thoroughly.

Quite unexpectedly, a sudden commotion came out of the rambai forest, apparently caused by a gigantic animal. Old Dieu knew that the leader had arrived. This monkey was very smart, making his appearance with a ceremony suitable for royalty, full of self-confidence verging on brazenness. Old Dieu smiled to himself and watched attentively.

A few minutes after the commotion, the leader did appear, swinging its body so fast that its movements were fluid, without pause. Old Dieu admired it for its quick agility, and then, in a flash, it disappeared. A feeling of self-pity pierced Old Dieu's heart. His destiny was not to coincide with that of royalty. The joy he had felt since he left home was reduced by half.

As soon as the lead monkey disappeared, a pack of about twenty more monkeys rushed out from all different directions. Some were hanging high above, some swinging below, and still others jumping onto the ground. Old Dieu saw three monkeys sticking together. A male, a female, and their baby.

The notion that the male monkey would become his prey clung to Old Dieu immediately. What an immoral father it was! Decadent lecher! Crude patriarch! Dirty legislator! Wretched despot!

Old Dieu felt the heat rising within him. He took off his hat and cotton-padded jacket and put them under a thicket. He also laid down his ball of sticky rice. Slowly, he moved toward a depression in the ground. Looking carefully, he saw that the guard monkey was a female. How convenient. Females got distracted so easily. There, see? What could be more irresponsible than searching for fleas on her body while supposedly keeping watch? For females, their bodies were the most important things. That fact was so simple and beautiful, but so pitiful, too.

Old Dieu estimated the distance, then wove his way against the wind toward the female guard. He had to come within twenty meters of the pack before he could shoot. He crawled fast and very nimbly. When he had identified his prey, then he could be guaranteed success. Nature had saved that very monkey for him and no one else. He knew that even if he stepped a bit heavily, and was rather careless, it wouldn't affect the outcome. It seemed irrational, but was actually quite normal.

But even with this thought in mind, Old Dieu still approached the pack carefully. He knew that nature was full of unforeseen circumstances. You could never be too careful.

Old Dieu rested the rifle in the fork of a tree. The family of three had no idea that disaster was imminent. The father was precariously sprawled in a tree, picking fruit and throwing it down to the mother and baby on the ground. Before throwing anything, it always chose a good piece to eat first, an act that was truly despicable. Old Dieu pulled the trigger. The sound was so terrible that the pack fell silent for a whole minute. The male monkey lost his grip and hit the ground with a thud.

The chaos in the pack made Old Dieu tremble with fear. He had just done something evil. His limbs went limp, as if he had just completed some heavy labor. The pack quickly disappeared into the jungle, with the mother and young monkey running alongside. But after covering some distance, the mother suddenly turned back. The male monkey had been shot in the shoulder. He tried to get up but was forced to lie back down again.

Looking around, the female approached the male carefully, suspicious of the silence. The male called out, and the sound of his cry was painfully sad. The female stopped to listen, frantic with terror.

"Run away!" Old Dieu moaned softly. But the female monkey, apparently bent on risking her own life, went to prop up the male.

Angry now, Old Dieu raised his gun. The female monkey's act of self-sacrifice filled him with hatred. Villain! You're trying to prove you have a noble heart, just like any other female bourgeois! It's because of melodramas like this that morals start to break down. How can you even try to deceive me?

As Old Dieu was about to pull the trigger, the female monkey turned to look at him, her eyes filled with terror. She dropped the male monkey and fled. Old Dieu sighed with relief and chuckled, rising from his hiding place.

As soon as he revealed himself, the female monkey came back.

"I've blown it!"

Old Dieu cursed silently. "If she knows that I'm human, she'll ruin everything!" Exactly as he'd predicted, the female monkey threw him a glance and rushed to the male monkey, tightly hugging him very quickly and deftly. Both monkeys rolled on the ground. Surely, the female would now become as frenzied as someone who had lost her mind. She would passionately sacrifice herself, her noble heart standing in judgment before Mother Nature. And he had shown himself to be an assassin! Even in death the female monkey would wear her toothy grin. Whatever the outcome, Old Dieu himself would be in pain, lying awake at night, and he might even die two years before his time if he went ahead and shot at this moment. All because he had stepped out of his hiding place two minutes early.

"Oh, Dieu," he thought sadly. "With your rheumatic legs how can you keep pace with the devotion and fidelity of monkeys?"

As if to taunt him, the two monkeys ran away supporting each other, with the female occasionally swinging her bowed legs in a way that seemed both funny and vile. Upset, Old

Dieu heaved his rifle forward, hoping that the animal would panic and drop the prey.

From behind the rock, the young monkey suddenly appeared, grabbed the shoulder strap of the rifle, and dragged it away. The three monkeys crawled and ran away wildly. Old Dieu was only dumbfounded for a moment. Then he burst out laughing: What an outrageous situation!

Picking up clods of earth and rocks to fling at the monkeys, Old Dieu chased after them, shouting. The monkeys were horrified, and two of them ran toward the mountain, while the young monkey ran toward a precipice. "Losing the gun will ruin me!" Old Dieu thought, chasing after the young monkey. He gained on it so quickly that, if not for the rocky terrain, he could have flung himself forward and grabbed the gun.

Old Dieu had not foreseen the consequences of pushing the young monkey to the edge of the precipice. Because of its lack of experience, it couldn't figure out any other solution under these circumstances. Without any hesitation, it went right over the edge, gripping tightly the shoulder strap of the gun.

Old Dieu turned pale, his body soaked with sweat. He stood at the edge of the precipice looking down and shivering. From the bottomless abyss echoed the horrible screams of the young monkey. He had never before heard such a scream, and he stepped back in horror. From out of the precipice, a terrifying mist billowed up, filled with the air of death. The mist crept through the underbrush and quickly enveloped the entire scene. Old Dieu turned back, running. It had been such a long time, perhaps since his childhood, that he had run this way, as if chased by a ghost.

Reaching the foot of the rocky mountain, Old Dieu felt exhausted. He slumped down and looked back up toward the precipice. By now, the mist had enshrouded it completely. Suddenly, he recalled that this was the most fear-provoking area of the valley, one that hunters had named the Ravine of

Death. Every year, almost regularly, someone became trapped by the mist in this deep ravine and died.

"Could it be ghosts?" Old Dieu thought. "Could it be the lonely souls of unmarried dead people that are often transformed into white monkeys?"

This monkey had been white. The fact that it had taken away his gun was so unusual that he doubted whether reality could be as simple as it appeared.

"Am I dreaming?" Old Dieu looked around. "Everything seems like a dream." He rose to his feet and looked up at the cliff face with bewilderment. In the direction of the rocky mountain opposite the Ravine of Death, the sky was clear without even a trace of mist, revealing every last detail of the landscape.

Old Dieu heard a panicked cry. He looked up and instantly saw the wounded male monkey lying sprawled on a rocky promontory above him. The female monkey was nowhere to be seen. He felt overjoyed and tried to find a way to climb up.

The rocky mountainside was steep and slippery. Climbing was dangerous and extremely laborious. Old Dieu gauged his strength and thought, "Whatever it takes, I will catch you!" He coolly clung to the crevices and climbed up.

About ten meters up, Old Dieu felt hot all over. Choosing a convenient place to stand, he took off his shoes and his outer clothing and put them in the fork of a duoi tree. Stripped to his briefs, he felt more comfortable. He climbed quickly and sure-footedly, surprised that he could be so fast and agile.

The wounded monkey lay rather precariously on a flat outcropping. Beneath the outcropping, a crack the size of the span between his thumb and forefinger separated it from the cliff. Old Dieu shivered, terrified by the feeling that at any moment the large rock could break off from its precarious position. Nature, capricious, seemed to want to test his bravery.

Old Dieu used his elbows to hoist himself up. The

monkey was so beautiful, with soft, yellow fur. He lay on his stomach, his two hands scratching the outcropping as if trying to edge upward. Red blood stained his shoulder.

Old Dieu put his hand on the monkey and found that the animal was feverish. "Perhaps it's over ten kilograms," he told himself. He stuck his hand beneath the monkey's chest and lifted him up to estimate his weight. From inside the monkey's chest came a soft "hum," which sounded rather frightening, as if the Grim Reaper himself were upset and bad-tempered because of Old Dieu's interference. Old Dieu withdrew his hand quickly. The monkey trembled violently, and looked at him through dazed eyes, as if pleading. Old Dieu suddenly felt pity for the creature. The bullet had shattered his shoulder, and a piece of bone four centimeters long was sticking out. Each time the bone came into contact with anything, the monkey writhed pitifully.

"Leaving it like that won't do!" Old Dieu grabbed a fistful of Lao grass and smashed it into a pulp. He put it into his mouth and chewed carefully, then applied it to the opening of the wound. The fistful of leaves would have the effect of staunching the flow of blood. The monkey curled up and turned his rather wet eyes to Old Dieu, who tried to avoid looking into them.

A moment later, the monkey pressed himself into Old Dieu's arms. The creature's mouth emitted a mumble that sounded like a noise from a child. He knew that the monkey was pleading and looking for help. Old Dieu was very uncomfortable.

"I'd rather have you fight against me," he said. He looked at the obedient head of the small creature and frowned. "I'm getting old and you know that old people feel pity easily. Now what can I find to bandage you, oh monkey?"

Old Dieu thought about it. He had no choice but to take off his briefs, using them to bandage the wound. The wound stopped bleeding and the monkey didn't moan anymore.

Naked, Old Dieu held and supported the monkey, looking

for a way to get down to the foot of the mountain. Suddenly, earth and rocks from halfway up the mountainside slid off in a rumble as if pushed by some powerful force.

Landslide!

Startled and petrified, Old Dieu clung tightly to a rock. In a single instant, the rocky path that he had climbed up a moment before became just a flat vertical surface. Old Dieu no longer saw the duoi tree where he had put his clothing and shoes. Going down that way would now be extremely dangerous. He had no choice but to go around towards the back of the mountain, farther but safe.

Old Dieu groped along for nearly two hours before he reached the foot of the mountain. Never in his life had he experienced such difficulty or been so exhausted. His body was covered with scratches. The monkey was half alive, half dead. Dragging the animal on the ground now would cause it a great deal of pain, but he didn't have the strength to hold it in his arms.

Returning to the thicket of climbing plants where he had hidden that morning to wait for the monkeys, Old Dieu paused to look for his hat, jacket and the ball of sticky rice. There, a termite mound had formed that was nearly as big as a heap of rice stubble. The sticky termite mound was made of a new kind of earth, deep red and filled with damp termite wings. What luck, getting mixed up with a termite nest: his things would be turned into bran! Sighing in despair, Old Dieu turned back and lifted the monkey into his arms.

"Do I have any choice but to go home stark naked like this? How degrading!" Old Dieu was upset. "I'll become a laughing stock."

While he walked, he thought and thought, wandering around for a little while before he could recognize the trail home.

And then he burst out laughing. "So what? Who could shoot a monkey like I did? It must be fifteen kilos of meat. And fur so yellow it looks like it was dyed. It was still worth it to be able to shoot an animal like this one, even if I do lose every shred of clothing."

Behind him, he heard a soft sound. Old Dieu turned around and was startled to see the female monkey. As soon as she saw him, she vanished into the bushes. She had followed him all the way from the mountain without his knowing it. He felt rather strange. After covering some distance, Old Dieu turned around and still saw her patiently following him. Damn it! Old Dieu put the male monkey down and picked up a rock to chase her away. She screamed shrilly and ran away. A moment later, Old Dieu looked around and saw her there again, following him determinedly.

The three of them continued through the jungle like this in silence. The female monkey was so persevering. Old Dieu suddenly felt terribly insulted, as if he were being watched, as if something had been unfairly demanded of him.

By now, even the male monkey had recognized the call of his species. He struggled, causing a lot of trouble. Old Dieu felt exhausted, lacking the strength to hold the monkey any longer. The monkey's fingers had scratched his chest until it started to bleed. In the end, unable to bear it any more, he threw the monkey down on the ground in anger.

The male monkey stretched out on the wet grass. Old Dieu sat looking down sadly. A short distance away, the female monkey peeked out now and then, spying at them from behind a tree.

Old Dieu felt sad to the depths of his soul. He looked at both monkeys and his nose filled with bitterness. He felt on the verge of tears. It turned out that in life the responsibilities weighing down on the backs of each living thing were truly heavy.

"Well, I think I'll just release you!" Old Dieu sat for a moment, then stood up and spat a glob of saliva at his feet. He hesitated for a moment, then hurriedly walked away. As if waiting for that very moment, the female monkey jumped from her hiding place and rushed to where the male monkey lay.

Old Dieu turned onto a different trail, hoping to avoid running into other people. Thornbushes blocked the way, but there were countless tu huyen flowers. Taken aback, Old Dieu paused. This species of flower blossomed only once every thirty years, and it was said that whoever saw tu huyen flowers would meet with a lot of luck. The flowers were white, salty-tasting, and as tiny as the heads of toothpicks. People called them "the salt of the jungle." When the jungle crystallized into salt, it was an omen announcing that the country would find peace, and the crops would be bountiful.

Leaving the valley, Old Dieu walked down to the fields. The spring rain was gentle but the drops came down fast. He kept on walking, naked and lonely. A moment later, his figure vanished into the curtain of rain.

In only a few more days, summer would arrive. The weather would get warmer.

Translated by Bac Hoai Tran and Courtney Norris

A Drop of Blood

"Let's discuss stories of
a hundred years ago..."
—Tran Te Xuong

I.

In the early 19th century in the village of Ke Noi, Tu Liem District, there lived a man of some fortune named Pham Ngoc Lien. He was building himself a house on the outskirts of the village, on a flat plot of land more than one thousand square meters large. One day, a passerby stopped at the spot and said, "What a splendid piece of land. It's shaped like a writing brush, a sure sign of success in literary pursuits. Alas, this success will come at a high cost: the water will run dry, the ship will be empty, and the family will be plagued by a dearth of male heirs."

Upon hearing this prophecy, Lien grabbed the stranger's sleeve and said, "My whole life I have been a simple farmer, but I dearly wish my grandsons to acquire a little learning so that we may live with our heads held high. I don't care how few boys are born to my descendants so long as they become men of virtue, and earn the respect of the world."

The stranger smiled. "Can you eat words?" he asked.

"Indeed, not!" replied Lien.

"Then what is the use of a wealth of learning?" the stranger continued.

"Say what you like, a scholar is still better than a farmer."

"Is a learned man then by necessity a virtuous man?"

"Most certainly," Lien said. Thereupon the stranger only laughed, refusing to say another word, though Lien pressed him with questions. Gathering his robes around him, he walked away. "What a lunatic!" Lien muttered angrily.

To celebrate the completion of his new house, Lien butchered two pigs and a cow which he offered in solemn rites to Heaven and Earth. Ninety platters of offerings were spread here and there throughout the house. It was truly a magnificent building. In the middle stood the ancestral hall, its three rooms decorated with a wealth of wooden sculptures depicting the four mythical animals—dragon, turtle, unicorn, and phoenix. The living quarters consisted of five rooms, each with double doors and pillars of fine hardwood. On either side of the house were annexes. The courtyard was paved with bright tiles from the famous kilns of Bat Trang and graced with a basin and an ornamental stone screen. Enclosing the compound was a ten-foot wall, spiked with glass and pottery shards and cemented with an especially strong mortar made of lime, sand, and honey.

Lien sat in the center of the courtyard and addressed his family. "From now on, we'll hold the memorial rites for our ancestors on the twelfth day of the first month. The Phams have always been the equal of the other clans in this village— the Dos, the Phans, and the Hoangs. Yet they call us vulgar and rustic because we are only farmers and merchants. Never has one of us studied the classics and sat for an imperial examination. In truth, I am sorely vexed."

Lien then called his five sons to him and told them, "Whichever one of your sons or grandsons achieves the rank of first doctor or second doctor in the imperial examinations shall be sole heir to this house and to my entire fortune. In return, he will have to demonstrate to the world how virtuous we Phams are."

Lien lived to the age of eighty. He had three wives, and, in addition to his five sons, he had six daughters. When he fell ill, his eldest son, Pham Ngoc Gia, a butcher by trade, nursed him for a full month, never once leaving his bedside. Gia's eyes were sunken from lack of sleep, and his beard grew long and tangled. Bananas, oranges, preserved meat and every delicacy were never lacking by the sickbed.

"Father, would you care to eat anything?" Gia asked.

Lien answered, "All I want is steamed rice with boiled greens and pickled eggplant."

Gia cooked fragrant rice in an earthenware pot, prepared a soup of tamarind leaves and a plate of tender greens with bean sauce, and carried the meal himself to his father. Lien sipped a single spoonful of soup and then pushed the bowl away. Gia started to cry.

"What good is food when what I crave is learning?" said Old Lien; then he drew his last breath. It was noon, the hour of the snake, on the twenty-first day of the twelfth month of the Year of the Rat (1840).

Gia spent a fortune to bury his father in strict observance of the appropriate rites. Three days after the death, he conducted the mourning-clothes ceremony, and thirty-five days later led the funeral procession to guide the dead man's soul to its final resting place in the pagoda. He prayed and made offerings on the 49th- and 100th-day anniversaries of his father's death. The villagers all praised his filial piety.

After the funeral ceremonies were completed, Gia had the ancestral hall repaired and extended by one room. The rest of the house he left as it was. And so it still stands today. Time has left its mark of wear and decay, and some parts have fallen to ruin, but the basic structure remains unchanged.

II.

Pham Ngoc Gia's first grandson, Pham Ngoc Chieu, was a remarkably bright child. From the earliest age he showed signs of a quick intelligence. One day, when the boy was eight years old, Gia took him on an excursion to Ke Cho, which Hanoi was then called, to see the sights of the city. When he returned home, the lad busied himself with clay and sand until he had built a sort of model depicting a row of buildings surrounded by a high wall. He colored chicken feathers green to make trees, and with the clay fashioned some very lifelike figures of turtles carrying tablets on their backs, which he placed in his model. Clapping his hands with delight, Gia asked, "What have you made, my boy?" Chieu beamed a gap-toothed grin. "It's the Temple of Literature, Grandpa." Old Gia was shaken—could this possibly be a sign from Heaven that this boy would be the first of the Phams to tread the Road of Learning?

The next day, Gia went to the family butcher shop in Ke Noi Market and selected a pig's head weighing a full fourteen pounds. He ordered his daughter-in-law to cook it and prepare a platter of sticky rice colored red with the seeds of a climbing gourd. He placed the pig's head atop the rice, and then set out to visit Ngoan the schoolmaster, carrying the platter of food on his head.

Schoolmaster Ngoan had red eyes, no money, and a very frank nature. He had sat for the imperial examination of 1868. When he saw Gia approaching with his platter of offerings, Ngoan jumped up, ran out of the house, and bowed low twice. Gia placed the platter at Ngoan's feet and said, "Please, sir, I've come to request that you accept my grandson Chieu as your student."

Ngoan led his visitor inside and asked him to sit down. Bowing several more times, he said, "I cannot lie to you. I'm not a very learned man. I knock a few young heads together, and by this deception I make a living. My school is little more than a children's prison. On the pretext of teaching them their letters, I keep little boys from spending their days wandering the streets, catching cicadas, falling into ponds, or being bitten by dogs. I am afraid that if you hire me as a tutor, you'll be sorely disappointed."

Half irritated, half amused, Gia said, "If such is your opinion, I won't insist. It's just that before my father passed away, he instructed me to do all I could to see that his grandsons would study and excel. Some day, he hoped, one of them would ride home with a doctor's pennant to hang in the ancestral hall."

Master Ngoan shuddered. "My dear sir, I must warn you that words are frightful creatures. They're like evil ghosts who possess weak souls and don't let go until they've brought those souls their full share of suffering and pain." He then fell into a brooding silence.

Presently, Ngoan's wife, dressed in a patched skirt, approached the men. She bowed twice to Gia, and then turned to her husband: "The children are terribly hungry. With the gentleman's permission, could you run out to our field and dig up some sweet potatoes for them to eat?"

"Have you got a crop of potatoes already? When did you plant them?" Gia asked.

"At the end of February," answered Ngoan's wife.

"But that is only fifty days ago! How can they possibly be ready yet?" exclaimed Gia.

"We finished the last of our rice eight days ago already," she replied. "We have to eat the potatoes."

Gia sighed. "Take out the rice and meat that I brought and give it to the children. Bring us a plate, too, and we'll have some wine with our meal." Gia pulled out of his bag a small gourd of rice wine in which a gecko was marinating.

Ngoan's wife carried the platter to the kitchen and doled out two portions. Gia and Ngoan sat inside drinking while in the courtyard the eight children pressed around their mother, excitedly waiting for her to dole out their share.

Master Ngoan said, "I know of a certain Mr. Binh Chi, in Ke Lu, who was once prefect of the province of Son Nam, but he was demoted, and returned home to start a school. He is a man of great knowledge and high moral stature. If your grandson studies with Mr. Binh Chi, he will certainly win a doctor's pennant to hang in the Pham family hall."

Gia nodded. Later, as he trudged home with the empty platter under his arm, he told himself, "I must go to Ke Lu."

Not long after this visit, Gia chose an auspicious day and, leading Chieu by the hand, set out in the direction of Ke Lu in search of Mr. Binh Chi. The teacher's house stood on the bank of the To Lich River and looked well-to-do. When Gia and his grandson entered, Binh Chi was in the middle of discussing a text with his pupils. A dozen boys sat on mats in a semicircle before their master. They appeared to be about sixteen years old, and every one of them looked intelligent and quick-witted. In front of each boy lay a notebook made of rice paper, and to his right an inkwell.

Binh Chi dismissed the class and sent the boys out to play in the yard. Chieu leaned against a pillar and watched them with obvious pleasure. Binh Chi invited Gia inside and asked him the purpose of his visit. Gia introduced himself in the most deferential terms he could muster. "What is Chieu's purpose in studying?" asked Binh Chi. Gia had no idea how to answer this question, but then he said, "I get the impression that learning is something like reason. That is why I'd like my grandson to study your letters."

Binh Chi replied, "There are many different kinds of learning. One kind is useful for earning a living. Another aims at self-improvement. Yet another serves its owner as a means of escaping reality and avoiding work. Finally, there is a brand of learning that causes confusion and destruction."

"I see what you mean," said Gia. "I am a butcher by trade. I guess literature is very much like meat: you have the ham, the head, the ribs and the bacon. Different cuts, but it's all meat just the same."

"Exactly. Now, which kind of learning would you like your grandson to acquire?"

"Well," replied Gia, "it seems to me that bacon is about right. It's a cut that has both lean and fat. It's always in demand. It sells well. If there's a kind of learning that's something like bacon, which suits everyone well and enjoys a wide following, that's what I'd like him to study."

"I understand," said Binh Chi. "What you desire is the course of learning one pursues to become an imperial official."

"That's it!" Gia exclaimed and clapped his hands with delight.

Gia called Chieu inside and told him to bow three times to his new teacher. He presented Binh Chi with a roll of Ha Dong silk and five strings of copper coins, which would serve as Chieu's enrollment fee.

After lunch, Gia gave his grandson a few final instructions and turned to leave. Chieu ran after him crying and calling out, "Grandpa, I don't want to study at all! What's the use, if it means being so far from home, from you, from my mother and father?" Gia wiped tears from his eyes, turned around, and almost broke into a run. Binh Chi led Chieu back inside. At that moment, it dawned vaguely on the boy that, in learning letters, he was entering a world in which he could rely on no one nor anything but himself.

III.

On the first and the sixteenth day of each month, Gia traveled to Ke Lu to deliver his grandson's school fees and the rice for his board. Chieu advanced rapidly in his studies. By the age of ten he had read the Four Classics and the Five Sutras. By the age of twelve he had mastered the art of literary criticism and was fluent in all the classical rhetorical forms. Binh Chi said, "The boy truly has a gift. He's like parched earth that absorbs as much water as I can pour onto it." This pleased Gia immensely. "No one in my family for many generations has learned to read or write even half a character. All we know is plowing and planting, and butchering pigs. This boy will bring glory to the Pham family," he said.

Chieu was therefore refused nothing he wanted, and no expense was spared in his education.

Binh Chi had a daughter named Dieu who was about the same age as Chieu. The two children often played together and in time grew very close. Chieu liked to tell Dieu, "When

I grow up I will take you to be my first wife." Dieu said nothing, only blushed deeply. Once, after Chieu had been playing in the fields with some buffalo herders his own age, his genitals became infected and painfully swollen. At first, Chieu felt merely uncomfortable and could not sit at his lessons, but no matter how many times Binh Chi asked him what was wrong, he refused to answer. After a few days, the swelling increased, and the pain became more intense. Giving in to Dieu's repeated entreaties, Chieu consented to lower his pants and let her inspect his private parts. Dieu took a piece of straw the length of Chieu's penis, folded it in three, spread the pieces open like a fan, and chopped them in half with a knife. She then told Chieu to wash himself with salt water. The infection healed; Chieu remained deeply grateful to Dieu for it.

In 1888, the Year of the Rat, Chieu passed the baccalaureate. Gia invited the entire village to a banquet celebration. The guests were treated to a feast composed of seven soups and seven dishes. There was bamboo shoot soup, glass noodle soup, taro soup, two soups of pork rind and fish bladder, and two of tofu dumplings stuffed with minced pork. The seven dishes included boiled chicken, glazed duck, boiled pork, pickled meat, pickled green papaya with shredded dried beef, pickled cucumber, and a dish of almonds. Binh Chi came and outdid himself in eloquent admiration of his host's house and gardens.

One year later, Gia died. At the same time, the imperial examinations, which Chieu was to attend, were being held in Nam Dinh. Gia died with his eyes wide open, and try as they might, no one could close them. "He's waiting for news of Chieu," said the relatives. They finally resorted to pressing on the eyelids with a red-hot chopstick. No one dared inform Chieu of his grandfather's death for fear the news would make him fail.

In Nam Dinh, a fine rain was falling, and the streets had turned to sticky mud. Chieu was pursuing his studies in the house of a songstress in Hang Thao Street. He spent the day studying, and at night the courtesan, Miss Tham, taught him many delightful games. Chieu graduated in third place, but he also caught syphilis, which made his penis very inflamed and his genitals chronically sore.

As soon as the mourning period for his grandfather was over, Chieu took up his post as chief of the district of Tien Du. It was a large district, rich in rice, and famous for quan ho, a style of singing in which the girls of Lim and Biu villages excelled. For a mandarin, this district was a paradise on earth.

As he embarked upon his new career, Chieu recalled his teacher's words: "Becoming a mandarin is but a means of earning a living, and only a fool would fail to earn it well." He therefore set to the task of extorting that living with the greatest zeal. In the courtyard of the district offices he built massive stocks weighted with a millstone. The few people who were punished by this means returned home with their ankles crushed. The wounds soon became infected, the worms set in, and the victims were carried away by tetanus in less than a fortnight. The people of the district feared Chieu. During the three years of his administration, not a single lawsuit was pressed, nor did a single theft occur. As a result, the district was considered peaceful. The governor of Bac Ninh province often invited Chieu to dine.

Chieu had by then taken two wives. Dieu was aware of her husband's dishonest behavior, which worried her all the more because although she and the second wife had given birth to a number of daughters, neither had managed to bear a son. Dieu prayed daily to the Lord of Heaven and to Buddha for a son and kept incense burning day and night in the ancestral hall in Ke Noi.

The venereal disease soured Chieu's temper and kept his subordinates in constant fear of his unpredictable moods. One day a former schoolmate by the name of Am Sac, who lived in Tu Son, came to thank Chieu for his help in a lawsuit. The dispute had been over land, and Chieu had settled in Am Sac's favor. Am Sac brought him two baskets each of ordinary rice and sticky rice, a basket of dried beans, and five pairs of ducks. "You've gone to far too much trouble on my account," said Chieu, looking over the gifts.

"No trouble at all," replied Am Sac. "All this comes from my land and gardens." Chieu invited Am Sac to stay for dinner.

During dinner, Am Sac noticed that Chieu appeared to be in discomfort, and asked, "Do you suffer from boils?"

"I'm afflicted with a venereal disease," Chieu replied.

"I know of a healer called Vong who is very skilled in his art," said Am Sac.

"I don't believe in healers," said Chieu. "They're all charlatans. They take your money and leave you as sick as ever."

"Ah, but Vong is no ordinary healer," Am Sac replied. "A schoolmaster, Thong by name, caught a chill that caused him to curl up like a shrimp. None of the usual remedies seemed to do any good, so his relatives carried him in a hammock to the healer's house. Vong asked Thong to sit down. He couldn't. Vong asked Thong to stand up. He couldn't. Vong then angrily banged the table and yelled, 'You dirty old scoundrel! This is the reward for all your whoring, gluttony, and immorality!' Thong turned red. He had always practiced moderation, hardly ever indulged in a good meal, and never so much as glanced at a pretty girl. To be accused of such sins! He was speechless with rage. Suddenly, Vong stood up and kicked his patient hard in the back. Thong fell forward, his back cracked, and he was healed. Thong then understood that Vong had tricked him in order to cure him. He fell to his knees and thanked the healer profusely." Am Sac then recounted another cure. "There was a young woman in town who suffered from a stiff neck that kept her head permanently twisted to one side. She consulted Vong, who asked her to go behind a screen, take off all her clothes and look at herself in a small mirror that hung in front of her. Suddenly Vong pushed aside the screen and walked in. The woman, who was much alarmed, crouched down, attempting to cover her nakedness, while at the same time turning her head to look at the intruder. And so she was cured."

Chieu smiled. "What you have related are simple cases: ill-winds, chills, and the like. The illness that plagues me is from sex. Can Vong do anything for me?"

"Don't worry," Am Sac answered. "Vong can cure anything."

Chieu acquiesced, asked for the customary gifts to be readied, and set off with Am Sac to visit Vong the healer.

Vong's house was in the village of Diem. When he heard that the district chief was coming, Vong laid out his finest mat, printed with a pattern of flowers, between the gate and the door. Chieu sent his guards in, laden with munificent gifts. Vong prepared some tea and asked the visitors to enter. Chieu noticed that, although Vong was a young man, his hair was completely white. His eyes were uncommonly bright and his earlobes were long like the Buddha's. Chieu saw in these traits the signs of an exceptional nature, and was much reassured by it. He proceeded to describe his symptoms honestly and in detail. Vong felt Chieu's pulse and said, "There are four stages to this disease. In the first stage, the glans develops cracks which emit a whitish and foul-smelling liquid. Urination is painful. This stage can be successfully treated in two months. In the second stage, the glans is covered in blisters, and the patient is feverish, suffering from sore limbs, loss of appetite, and constant restlessness. Treatment lasts three months. In the third stage, there is pus in the glans, blood in the urine, a discharge several times a day, and the patient can no longer stand up. At this stage the treatment lasts three years, but it is difficult to achieve a full cure. In the fourth stage, the hands tremble, the eyes become dull and the blisters spread to the abdomen and the legs. At this stage you should go ahead and build a coffin."

"Well, which stage have I reached?" Chieu inquired anxiously.

"The second stage," Vong replied.

Chieu sighed with relief.

"Don't worry, Excellency," Vong continued. "The first two stages are quite common."

Chieu was indeed cured, and his temper softened somewhat. That year he arranged for the Lim festival to be especially large and he invited Vong as his guest of honor. The day after the festival, the weather was beautiful. Chieu had a table set up in the courtyard. No one dared walk past the gate of the district offices while he sat there, drinking until he could barely sit up. Two servants fanned him. Chieu said, "I am the first of the Pham to have studied. My only regret is that I am posted so far from home. I haven't yet been able to contribute anything to my ancestral village."

At that moment, a palanquin passed on the road in front of the house. Chieu went into a rage. "What impudence! Who dares pass the district chief's gate without dismounting? Guards! Find out who that is, and bring him in here immediately!" The guards ran out of the gate and stopped the palanquin. It turned out that the passenger was a French missionary. Chieu was drunk. He ordered the guards to give the foreigner thirty lashes. The missionary was very angry at the beating. This incident cost Chieu his position. He was demoted and sent home to pasture. He was just forty-two years old.

IV.

The missionary whom Chieu had beaten, Father Jean Puginier, was an influential man. And so it happened that Chieu's glorious career was arrested in mid-flight. Chieu returned to the family mansion in Ke Noi, where, depressed, he spent his days idly lying on his bed. The village folk soon began to circulate rumors about him. They said Chieu had been a member of the group of loyal mandarins who had rallied behind King Ham Nghi to oppose the French. They said he was the commander of the famous rebels De Nam and De Tham who ruled the mountains of Yen The, up north. They said that Chieu was a loyal mandarin who had been dismissed only because he refused to collaborate with the Nguyen emperors when they sold out to the French. One rumor spawned ten others, and ten spawned a hundred, until Chieu's fame had spread far and wide. He never denied any of it and even came to see the beating of the missionary as the most meaningful act of his career.

Around this time, the villagers of Ke Noi took up a collection to build a brick road through the village, and Chieu, who felt he had not yet contributed anything to his native village, donated a large sum of money to repair the assembly hall and to build gates at the entrances to the village. People now spoke of him with the reverence usually reserved for saints. The village notables and the scholars of the province held him in high esteem. Yet Chieu was downcast. From time to time, he would look at the ivory tablets on which his former title was inscribed, and sigh deeply.

As Dieu had still not borne a son, she persuaded her husband to accompany her to the Perfume Pagoda to pray at the sanctuary there for a male heir. Chieu agreed and chose the first day of the second month for the pilgrimage. That morning, husband and wife rose at cockcrow, breakfasted, dressed, and set out on their way. When they reached the town of Ha Dong, Dieu bought fifty small rice cakes, joss sticks, sheets of gold leaf, and a sheaf of printed prayers, then rented a horse-drawn carriage. A fine rain was falling, and the wind was bitter cold. The coachman was a vulgar-looking man about fifty years old, with a low forehead. He bargained with Dieu as vociferously as a fishmonger. The road from Van Dinh was crowded with people headed to the Perfume Pagoda. The pilgrims were mostly elderly women, in groups as large as thirty, dressed in long tunics and capes of palm leaves to keep off the rain. Here and there were also small bands of elegant young mandarins' sons wearing black silk turbans and narrow black trousers. Trudging in an endless stream along the dike through the driving wind and rain, they looked like the wandering souls of the dead in a cheo opera. The carriage passed a roadside tavern, and Chieu told the coachman to stop.

Chieu walked into the shop and ordered rice wine and dog meat. Dieu warned him that he should abstain from such rich food while on a pilgrimage, but Chieu only laughed, saying, "I have always been told to look for Buddha in my heart. Since when has he moved to my stomach? Van Dinh is famous for its dog meat. I'd be a fool not to try it." At a loss for words, Dieu took a ball of pressed rice from her bag and began to eat her meager lunch.

The owner of the shop brought Chieu a dish each of boiled meat, tripe, stew, and grilled meat, a bowl of broth, a bowl of blood pudding, and a bottle of rice wine. Chieu ate noisily, paying no attention to his manners. Dieu soon finished her simple meal. She bought some rice dumplings stuffed with pork for the coachman, then sat in the carriage waiting for her husband.

As Chieu ate, a man richly dressed in a silk tunic and turban, and carrying a black umbrella entered the shop. When he saw Chieu, the man immediately set down his umbrella, joined his hands, and bowed. "What can I do for you, sir?" asked Chieu, waving his chopsticks in the stranger's direction.

"Don't you recognize me, Excellency?" asked the man. "My name is Han Soan. In Tien Du, you once helped me out of a very difficult situation."

"Oh?" asked Chieu, gesturing for him to sit down.

Han Soan continued, "The district police had caught a gang of thieves active around Cam Son. The thieves named me as their leader, so you ordered a search of my house. The

154

stolen goods were found in my possession, but you released me anyway."

"That's right. And to thank me you gave me ten baskets of rice and a bronze incense burner," replied Chieu. Han Soan nodded.

After chatting a while, Han Soan asked, "What is the purpose of your pilgrimage?"

"To pray for a son and heir," replied Chieu.

Han Soan smiled and said, "I observed your wife sitting in the carriage outside. I dare say, she's not as young as she once was. Buddha may grant you a son, but it would be under duress. There is a novice at the Perfume Pagoda called Hue Lien, who is as beautiful as she is virtuous. She is the daughter of the governor of Ninh Binh province. They say that disappointment in love drove her to retire from the world. She has shaved her head only these six months. The monastic rule can hardly have taken deep root in her heart in so short a time. Therefore, I suggest you pray first for love, and only second for a son."

Chieu loved courting women, so this offer delighted him. "How do you suggest I pray for love?" he asked. Han Soan gazed at the empty wine bottle. Chieu understood immediately. He ordered more food and wine.

When Han Soan had finished eating, he spoke. "I'm acquainted with Miss Hue Lien. She's an idealistic girl, and she's mad about stories of heroes and their bravery. A few years ago, at the time of the Can Vuong Rebellion, she was determined to cut her hair and disguise herself as a boy in order to join the loyal mandarins fighting the French. When her father found out, he was beside himself and beat her severely. Her betrothed fought alongside the rebel general De Tham. After he died in the battle of Phuc Yen, she resolved to become a nun. Everyone in the land has heard about the beating you gave the French missionary and people admire you for it. I think she will agree to anything a hero like you proposes."

Chieu found this plan to his liking, but after reflecting for a moment he replied, "It won't be easy. Stealing a woman from her own chamber is one thing: I've done it many times and there's nothing to it. But stealing a woman from Buddha's chamber is another game altogether. I have to admit I've never done anything of the kind."

Han Soan smiled. "The game is played in five rounds," he said. "I know the superior monk of Thien Tru Pagoda, where Hue Lien has taken her vows. When you get to this pagoda, you will pretend you have a terrible stomachache and send your wife on ahead to the inner sanctuary without you. Offer the monk an ounce of gold. If he refuses it, you should give up then and there. If he accepts the gold, you have won the first round. Then, in the evening, the Superior will give you a guest room inside the monastery. For an ounce of gold, I will stand guard. The Superior will ask you to share his vegetarian meal, and the young nun in question will pour your wine. You will urge her to drink a cup of wine in which you have poured a powerful sleeping potion. If she refuses to drink, the game is over. If she accepts, you have won the second round. As soon as the meal is over the nun will fall asleep, and the Superior will avert his eyes as you carry the unconscious girl to your bed. This is the third round. You undress her and do with her as you please—this is the fourth round. The next morning when the girl wakes up, the superior and I will burst in and scold you and the nun for profaning the pagoda. The superior will make you sign a confession accepting full responsibility for Hue Lien. You will place an ounce of gold in the collection box as expiation for your sin. You will have won the fifth and final round."

Chieu laughed. "That's all very well, but how many ounces of gold will it take? You spoke so fast I quite lost count."

"Three ounces," Han Soan replied.

"With three ounces of gold," mused Chieu, "I could buy myself six wives."

"As you like, Excellency," said Han Soan. "But remember, there is only one Hue Lien."

"That's true," said Chieu.

The discussion over, Chieu paid for the meal and led Han Soan out to the carriage. "Who is he?" Dieu asked her husband.

"A friend of mine," he replied.

Han Soan greeted Dieu respectfully and took a place in a corner of the carriage. He laid his umbrella on his lap and spent the rest of the trip staring straight ahead without uttering a word.

V.

Exactly at noon, the hour of the horse, they arrived at the Duc Pier from whence they would continue by boat up the river. The crowd of pilgrims was very large. Two dozen boats of all kinds were moored on the Yen River below. For the trip to the sanctuary and back, Dieu rented a small rowboat seating six for the modest price of five measures of rice. A pretty, talkative girl plied the oars. Through the beautiful countryside, the boat glided as gently as a lullaby. Water lilies and reeds parted under the gentle nudge of the oars. Dragonflies, some long and thin as needles, others red-bellied like flying chilis, followed the boat and sometimes landed on the deck. The pilgrims stopped at Trinh Pagoda, where Dieu placed on the altar the prayers she had bought in Van Dinh. Standing some distance behind his wife, Chieu murmured, "Great Buddha, if you grant me the nun Hue Lien, I will reward you with a sumptuous vegetarian meal."

Han Soan knew this area thoroughly and could converse about every sight and monument they passed, to Dieu's great admiration. When a boat moving up river to the pagoda crossed a boat returning down river, strangers greeted each other courteously. On the river it seemed to them that they had escaped from the dreary world, and they were suddenly moved, reflecting that their lives on earth were nothing but dust.

They arrived at the Da Pier, where it had been agreed that the boat would wait for them. Han Soan led the way, with Chieu and Dieu following behind. The first temple on their route, Thien Tru Pagoda, was thick with people, and the scent of burning incense filled the air. Hawkers spread their wares on the ground. Restaurants and small inns—flimsily built of bamboo and matting but clean and tidy—had sprouted around the temple. Han Soan guided Chieu and Dieu to the superior. He was a fat man, with a rosy complexion, eyebrows that seemed drawn with a brush dipped in black ink, and eyes like those of a fish, betraying nothing of their owner, neither kindness nor cruelty, neither shallowness nor depth. Dieu laid out her offerings and the Superior nodded his acceptance. Chieu observed that he spirited the gifts away quickly and skillfully. "I am sure to get what I want from him," Chieu thought to himself. As they sat exchanging small talk, Hue Lien stepped in to greet them. Chieu stole a glance at her and saw with pleasure that Han Soan had not deceived him about her beauty.

Once they had completed their prayers, Chieu complained of terrible stomach pains. Dieu was a guileless woman, unable to imagine that this was a ruse devised by Han Soan. She panicked. It took all the persuasive powers of Han Soan and Chieu combined to convince her to leave her bags behind and pursue the pilgrimage to the upper sanctuary alone. Although she finally agreed, she felt uneasy.

Having disposed of his wife, Chieu followed Han Soan's plan to the letter. Poor Hue Lien! She had become a nun to escape the world, but the world, it seemed, would not let her escape.

Hue Lien's real name was Do Thi Ninh. She became Chieu's third wife, and one year later she gave birth to a son. He was named Pham Ngoc Phong.

VI.

When Pham Ngoc Phong was sixteen, he lost both his father and his mother. On the morning of the eleventh day of the fourth month, the village festival day, Chieu went to the village hall to pray. When he returned home, he felt faint and lay down to rest. By afternoon, he was running a fever. He sat down to dinner but could barely swallow half a bowl of rice. Dieu sent Ninh to pick pomelo, bamboo, and other medicinal leaves she needed to prepare an inhalation for Chieu. He refused to touch it. Ninh, not wanting to throw out the warm water, used it to bathe herself. Late that night, Chieu woke up and noticed that his third wife smelled unusually good, and he was seized with desire for her. After the storm passed, however, Chieu grew weaker, and by morning he was dead. At dawn the house awoke to the sound of Ninh's terrified screams. Dieu flew into a rage. "You whore!" she cursed, "You failed nun! Now you've gone and killed your husband!"

Ninh felt sorry for herself. She had been tricked into marriage. As a third wife she was worked to the bone, treated like a servant, and could not even sleep openly with her husband. Now to be accused of killing him! She walked to the top of the dike and threw herself into the river. As Chieu was being laid in his coffin, a group of fishermen ran up from the river with the news that they had found the third wife's body in their nets. Dieu beat her head on the ground, crying, "Miserable bitch! Your death must be my punishment for the sins of a former life!"

The two funerals were celebrated simultaneously. The husband's coffin led the procession, the wife's coffin followed behind. Within days the whole province had heard of it. The story made such an impression that people still talked about it thirty years later. The village elders saw an opportunity to profit from scandal and demanded an autopsy in order to determine whether Ninh had died a natural death. Dieu was forced to buy them off. It cost her five acres to bury the rumors and accusations once and for all.

Following these events Dieu fell seriously ill and began to lose her mind. She would never recover her sanity.

Unlike his father, Phong did not study the classics but received a modern education in the new romanized Vietnamese script. He was an indolent, willful boy. Although he had inherited all his father's property, amounting to a dozen acres of rice fields, he took no interest at all in farming and left the management of his property to his elder half-sister, Cam, a daughter by the second wife. She was a spinster, shy, and honest.

Phong studied in Hanoi, returning home only rarely. One day however, he appeared with a woman on his arm. She was at least ten years older than him, tall and dark-skinned. In her mouth gleamed several gold teeth, and she appeared to be in an advanced stage of pregnancy. "This is Miss Lan," Phong announced to Cam. "She's a medical student, and the niece of Mr. Tan Dan, the newspaper publisher in Hanoi. We have been living together for a year." Cam could think of nothing to say, and turned pale, while Lan turned red as a poppy, hanging her head and tugging nervously at her tunic of Bombay silk whose low-cut lines revealed the glint of a heavy gold necklace.

"What do you and the young lady plan to do?" Cam finally asked.

"Lan will stay here. I will return to Hanoi and go into the newspaper business," Phong replied.

"Brother, we have always been farmers and butchers in this family. In my experience, people who leave home to try their luck elsewhere never come to much. But what does an ignorant woman like me know about such things? If that is what you want, fine. But whatever you do, I urge you to be prudent."

Phong shoved his hands into his jacket pockets and, with a smirk, said *"Merci."*

Cam opened her eyes wide. She did not have the faintest idea what he meant.

At lunch, Lan served herself a scant half-bowl of rice and ate it one grain at a time. Cam served her sister-in-law a spoonful of a delicious star fruit and meat soup and urged her to eat it.

"Don't you dare!" Phong rebuked her. "In her condition my wife is strictly forbidden to eat onions." Cam turned red. After lunch, Phong walked all the way to the market in Ke Noi to buy rice cakes and meat dumplings for his wife.

During her first week in Ke Noi, Lan hardly emerged from her room, where she lay on the bed reading all day long. Cam was in awe of her brother, and so she did not say anything. One day, Lan asked Cam, "How much land do we own?"

"About eleven acres," said Cam. "But Phong sold eight acres to raise money for his business in Hanoi. So we have three acres left. And a butcher shop in Ke Noi Market."

"Who looks after the shop?" Lan asked.

"A relative, Binh, manages it for us," Cam replied. "We put up the capital and split the profits evenly with him."

"From now on, I will manage the shop," Lan declared.

The next day, despite her big belly, Lan went to the market and inspected the shop thoroughly. She reorganized everything, gave orders, and went over the accounts with a sharp eye. Both Cam and Binh felt anxious. Binh no longer dared steal so much as a cent from the till.

Meanwhile, day by day Dieu grew weaker and more senile. All day long she walked aimlessly around the room, defecating wherever she happened to lie down. "Why does the old bag keep on living?" Phong complained.

"Feed her some rat poison and your troubles will be over," Lan suggested.

"No need for that. Just let her go hungry for a few days," replied Phong. Turning to Cam, he said, "Sister, from now on, stop feeding our father's first wife. She's eighty-two. Why the hell does she want to live any longer?"

Cam was frightened. "Please, Brother," she said. "Think this over. Don't you want to earn a little merit in this world for the sake of your children and grandchildren?"

Phong scowled at her. "Don't you know that old witch killed my mother?"

Cam protested, but Phong locked the door to the old woman's room and dropped the key into his jacket pocket.

Locked in her room, Dieu became so thirsty and hungry that she ate her own excrement. Once a day, Phong would open the door to check whether she was dead. Two weeks passed, and still she clung to life. Phong was alarmed. "Could she really be a witch?" he wondered aloud to his wife.

Lan searched the old woman's room and found a grain of rice under the bed. "Your mother could well live much longer. Why, she might even bury us all!" said Lan with a hollow laugh. "Where did you leave the key?"

Phong pointed to the pocket of his jacket, which hung on a hook close to the door. "No wonder," said Lan. "Leave the jacket where it is. I'll put an end to this witchcraft." She took the key out of the pocket and put it in her purse.

Around midnight Lan woke Phong with a pinch. By the pale light of the moon they saw a shadowy form reach into the pocket of the jacket, which Phong had laid on the wooden platform bed in the next room. Lan grabbed a heavy wooden ruler and brought it down on the shadow's head. The figure crumpled with a weak cry. Phong lit the lantern and saw Cam, her forehead bathed in blood. "My goodness!" exclaimed Lan, "I thought you were a robber."

"What do you think you're doing, creeping around like this in the dark?" Phong scolded. Cam only moaned softly. Her face lay in a mess of cold, blood-stained rice that was strewn across the platform.

Three days later Dieu passed away. Phong gave her a respectable funeral and chose the name of Doan Thuan for her in the afterlife. As for Cam, she progressively lost her grip on the management of the household, and Lan assumed control of the entire property. Lan gave birth to a daughter, named Hue, and hired a wet-nurse to look after the baby. The child soon grew into a pretty little girl, but her mother did not love her, and left her upbringing entirely in the hands of the nurse and her Aunt Cam.

VII.

The real name of Lan's uncle, the Hanoi newspaper publisher Tan Dan, was Nguyen Anh Thuong. He was well known in literary and journalistic circles, where he had a reputation for greed and opportunism, but that fact isn't relevant to this story. Tan Dan liked to tell Phong that, "Literature must be ruthless. To plunge into the mud, wallow in filth, and, then, transform into butterflies and flowers! Now that is what I call Genius!" Phong always agreed with a nod. Tan Dan and Phong pooled their capital to start a business which they called publishing a newspaper, although they were really only selling newsprint.

One day Tan Dan told Phong, "I have just received permission from the government to trade salt. If you like, I'll let you in on the deal. You'll go to Phat Diem and finalize the purchase from Father Tat, the priest. Then we'll transport the salt to the mountains and sell it there. While you're down in Phat Diem, I'll go ahead to Son La to discuss the deal with Cam Vinh An, the district chief." Phong agreed.

When he arrived in Phat Diem, Phong went straight to the cathedral, the buildings and grounds of which spread across some three acres, forming what looked like a small town, with gardens, a cemetery, a church, and a seminary, all built of stone in a very ornate style. In front of the cathedral was a large artificial pond shaped like a half moon. Peering into the clear water, Phong saw fish swimming in lazy circles. Behind the pond lay a rockery crowned with gleaming white statues of Jesus and the Virgin Mary. Phong gazed upon all this with deep admiration. "Son of a bitch!" he said to himself. "This must be the only building in this country that was built to last forever. What sort of religion is Christianity, to be so imposing?"

Phong wandered around the grounds a while longer. Presently, an elderly servant led him to Father Tat. The priest was a youngish man with a fair complexion, high forehead, and mischievous eyes. He read the letter of introduction Phong had brought from Tan Dan and asked him to sit down. The priest then gestured toward the door behind him. A youth dressed in a black cassock appeared and served them tea. Two more youths similarly dressed appeared and started to fan them. Phong sipped his tea and noticed it was deliciously fragrant. "Father," Phong asked, "has the business we entrusted to you enjoyed success?"

Father Tat spoke softly, "The scriptures say, 'Is there anyone among you who, when his child asks for bread, will give him a stone?' Have no fear, my son. Stay here and rest and you will see that everything will go as planned."

Phong asked for permission to sleep at an inn in town instead, which Father Tat gave gladly.

Phong lay on his bed in the inn listening to the patter of the rain on the roof. Because of the large sum of money he was carrying, he didn't dare go out. The innkeeper spent the entire day sitting on his doorstep staring blankly at the road. Phong was bored. He stood up, sat down again, and thumbed through a cheap copy of the comic poem *The Catfish and the Toad,* which he had read many times already. He wondered how many people were staying at the inn. Since he had arrived he had not seen anyone go in or out of the building. Overcoming his slight embarrassment, Phong asked the landlord, "Are there any pretty whores around here?" The innkeeper nodded. "Well, then call one over for me," said Phong.

"What would you prefer—a virgin or a girl with experience?" asked the innkeeper.

Phong slapped his thigh and exclaimed, "What could be better than a virgin?"

The innkeeper disappeared into the back of the building and soon returned leading a young girl of about fifteen. "My daughter," he said. Phong almost choked on his tea.

The girl was little more than a child and seemed completely ignorant of sex. Phong felt a twinge of pity for her, but soon controlled his emotions. "What's the use of fretting?" he asked himself. "After all, everything happens sooner or later." With Phong leading the way, the girl followed, docile, crossing herself and praying as she climbed the stairs.

A couple of days later, the old servant from the cathedral came to the inn and told Phong, "Father Tat has completed the business. You can now return to Hanoi to take delivery of the merchandise." Phong took the papers from the servant and handed him the money. He was full of admiration for the priest—a man who was still so young but with such a knack for business!

Back in Hanoi, Phong went straight to Tan Dan's house. It was the first time he had been to his friend's residence. He rang the bell, and a poodle came running to the gate, followed by cries of "Loulou! Loulou!" The dog slinked back inside with its tail between its legs. The houseboy opened the gate. "How can I help you, sir?" he asked.

Phong gave his name and handed the servant his business card. The servant replied, "Mr. Tan Dan has gone to Son La, but he sent a letter to you here. Please come in. My mistress will receive you."

Phong followed the servant inside. The furniture was elegant and expensive looking, and the house was decorated with taste. "The shifty old bastard!" Phong thought to himself. "Just look at this house, and yet he claims to be poor. Why, he is constantly asking me to lend him money." Phong sat down to wait, and soon enough he heard the soft shuffle of slippers approaching. A woman of about thirty entered the room. Phong stood up to greet her and noted her air of refined beauty. "Good morning Mr. Phong," she addressed him. "My name is Thieu Hoa. I have a letter for you from my husband." They sat down and exchanged small talk about the cost of goods in the markets, about the weather. Phong was very impressed by Thieu Hoa's refined manner. She rearranged the folds of her tunic and smiled at him. "Please feel free to read your letter," she said.

"Please excuse me, madame," said Phong, then looked down at the letter, which said:

> *To Mr. Phong, my bosom friend,*
> *I have been in Son La since the sixteenth of July. I have settled everything with Mr. Cam Vinh An, and as soon as the merchandise arrives he will pay me. Would you therefore do your utmost to convey the goods as soon as possible? You may take several of my servants to help you if you deem it necessary. I know that your intelligence and zeal will ensure a smooth outcome. Unfortunately, an attack of rheumatism prevents me from returning to help you. I therefore look forward to seeing you on your arrival in Son La. I trust that both you and your family are well.*
> *Yours respectfully,*
> *Tan Dan*

Phong read through the letter and smiled sourly. Thieu Hoa asked, "Sir, what do you think of this business?"

"Please don't trouble yourself, madame," replied Phong. "Your husband is a veritable genius at such matters."

Thieu Hoa blushed. "You are too generous with your

compliments. It often seems to me that my husband is terribly selfish."

Phong laughed. "Selfishness is also an element of genius."

"My husband has nothing but praise for you, sir," said Thieu Hoa.

"What sort of praise?"

"He says that you are a 'gentleman.'"

Phong said, "Dear madame, I would like to invite you to dine with me at a restaurant in Sailmakers Street. If you refuse, I will take it to mean that you do not think me worthy of that title." After a moment of hesitation, Thieu Hoa accepted.

Back home (at a bachelor's flat he kept in town), Phong said to himself, "Tan Dan is a real scoundrel. I put up the money for this business, I did all the legwork, and he sits up there waiting to collect the profit. Well, well. We'll see how much he'll profit from this one." He sprang to his feet, called a rickshaw, and ordered the driver to head for a Chinese restaurant in Sailmakers Street. "Vuong Binh," he said to the restaurant owner. "Prepare a special meal for two, and throw in an extra measure of aphrodisiac powder." Vuong Binh nodded.

That evening, Phong went to pick up Thieu Hoa. They ate and drank merrily, at first with some reserve, and then, as the aphrodisiac took effect, with greater abandon, until they sat with their shoulders pressed languorously together. Phong took Thieu Hoa to the backroom. The restaurant owner shut the door and stood guard.

They met several times more after this first encounter. For Thieu Hoa, the young and vigorous Phong was like a rainstorm after a long drought. They vowed never to be parted.

Finally, the day came for Phong to leave. He collected the salt from a boat on the Cai River and left immediately for Son La.

VIII.

It took Phong and his caravan of horse-drawn carts a full fortnight to reach Son La. The home of Cam Vinh An, the district chief, stood on Ban Mat escarpment in a village of Thai people. Although it was a mandarin's residence, the house looked just like an ordinary Thai house: a wooden structure set up on pillars with a thatched roof, only larger and better-built than its neighbors. When Tan Dan introduced Phong to Cam Vinh An, the district chief remained absolutely expressionless. Phong noticed that Cam Vinh An had a low forehead, flushed skin, heavy eyelids and plodding movements, the look of a man who thinks slowly. Worn out by the hardships of the road, Phong's blood boiled at the sight of Tan Dan enjoying three full meals a day, with wine, and passing his time in hunting and idle chitchat. Tan Dan said, "I know how tiring this has been for you. Truly, you're more responsible than I am for the success of this business." Phong didn't reply. He merely asked Cam Vinh An for some bear-gall tonic to rub on his sore arms and legs.

"How much salt have you brought?" Cam Vinh An asked.

"Eight tons," replied Phong.

"But how can that be?" Tan Dan exclaimed. "I thought we'd agreed on twenty tons?"

"You Vietnamese often say one thing and do another," Cam Vinh An muttered.

"On this trip, I only brought eight tons. That's how much I'll charge you for, so why do you accuse me of deception?" Phong said.

"Because Mr. Tan Dan has already received payment for the full twenty tons. That's why."

"I took payment in advance in order to buy opium to take back to Hanoi," said Tan Dan.

"You can count me out," said Phong. "That's strictly

against the law. If you get caught, you'll go to prison. Use your share of the money to buy opium, not mine."

"But I've already bought it," Tan Dan admitted. "What should I do now?"

"That's not a problem, sign a promissory note for me," said Phong. Then, turning to the district chief, he asked, "Sir, will you be our witness?"

"With pleasure," said Cam Vinh An. Tan Dan turned pale.

The afternoon was oppressively hot. Tan Dan was forced to return the money for twelve tons of salt to Cam Vinh An, then sign a promissory note for Phong. The agreement specified that payment would be due a month hence, with Tan Dan's house as collateral should he fail to pay. As he had already bought the opium, Tan Dan had no choice but to agree to these terms.

The next morning, Tan Dan hastily prepared for the trip back to the plains and asked Phong to accompany him. "You go ahead," said Phong. "I need a few more days of rest before I'm fit to travel."

Cam Vinh An organized a farewell dinner. Phong said he was tired and went to his room to sleep.

The next morning, as soon as Tan Dan had gone, Phong jumped out of bed. He pulled twenty pieces of black fabric and twenty pieces of red fabric from his bags and gave them to Cam Vinh An. "I am very honored to make your acquaintance," he said. "Yesterday I was terribly tired. It seemed an inconvenient time to present you with these gifts, and so I take the opportunity to do so now." Cam Vinh An nodded, and Phong continued, "We had indeed agreed to sell you twenty tons. My word is my bond. You will receive the remaining twelve tons in three days." Cam Vinh An nodded again. Phong went on, "When the salt arrives, you will pay me for ten tons only and keep the remaining two for your own consumption." With An still nodding, Phong said, "I am in business with Mr. Tan Dan, but I consider him an enemy.

He is committing a terrible crime by smuggling opium. Sir, I urge you to inform the authorities." Cam Vinh An nodded.

The next day, Cam Vinh An started early on horseback. In the afternoon he returned and told Phong: "Tan Dan was caught before reaching Yen Chau." They laughed. Cam Vinh An pulled a bag of coins from his pocket. "This is the reward."

"Divide it into three parts," Phong suggested, "giving one to the women in your household, for new clothes."

"There are many women in my family."

"Well, then," replied Phong. "Divide it into four."

The very next day the horses arrived, loaded with the remaining salt. Phong inspected the load and saw with satisfaction that none was missing. He rewarded the drivers with a handsome tip. Cam Vinh An was pleased, and killed a buffalo in order to give Phong a large farewell dinner. During dinner An urged Phong to eat a Thai specialty called Nam Pia (which looked like chopped lungs). Phong made a show of eating, but he did not swallow the food, and when he went outside to relieve himself he spat it out on the ground.

IX.

Back in Hanoi, Phong informed Thieu Hoa of her husband's arrest. "If he goes to prison, how long will he stay there?" she asked.

"Cam Vinh An assured me he would get at least ten years," Phong replied.

Thieu Hoa said, "That means he'll get out just in time to die."

Phong returned home to Ke Noi to discuss his marriage to Thieu Hoa with his first wife, Lan. She was very angry, but she knew how ruthless and scheming her husband could be, and justly concluded that if she made any fuss she would be the first to suffer. She resolved therefore to accept the situation with a semblance of good grace. The wedding was an elegant affair. Tan Dan was sentenced to ten years in prison for opium smuggling, and judged insolvent. Phong sold Tan Dan's house soon after. Thieu Hoa had a son from her first marriage, a cripple named Hanh who had an abnormally large head and a stunted leg. Hanh moved around by small jumps, like a grasshopper.

Lan gave birth to a daughter whom she named Cuc. Phong brought his first daughter, Hue, to live in Hanoi, and there she married a man called Diem, an artist who drew illustrations for the newspaper in which Phong owned a share. Diem's parents were grocers.

One year, on the full moon of July, Phong and Thieu Hoa returned to Ke Noi where he planned to celebrate his 50th birthday. He discussed the organization of the party with both Lan and Thieu Hoa. That evening, as the moon was large and bright, Phong had a mat laid out in the courtyard where he sat drinking tea, while Cam rocked her little niece Cuc in the hammock. She sang her a lullaby that went:

> *Mr. Moon, Moon up in the sky,*
> *What do you know of life below?*
> *Life is a child's nonsense rhyme:*
> *Laugh at it with all your might.*

In the kitchen, Lan barked orders at the relatives who had come to help with the cooking for the party.

Cam sang:

> *The white crane flies through rain and storm.*
> *The night is dark, who guides him home?*
> *Home to the place where he was born,*
> *To mother and father, and the one who waits.*

Phong said, "Ten years from now, if Heaven lets me live that long, and if business is still good, I will invite the whole village to a celebration of my longevity."

"If you go on carousing like this, how do you expect to live even another five years?" retorted Thieu Hoa.

Cam sang:

> *A boy should show his worth and mettle*
> *Wander everywhere, from Phu Xuan to Dong Nai.*

"You see that girl over there—the one plucking the hen? What's her name?" Phong asked Cam. "Who are her parents?"

"That's Chiem, Mua's daughter," Cam said.

"The same Mua who used to carry me on his back to watch the kites flying?" asked Phong.

"The same," Cam answered.

"How is he getting on?"

"He has a large family, and things are hard for him. Last March he almost passed away from the fever."

Phong turned to his son-in-law Diem. "You're an artist. Don't you agree that this little Chiem is the village beauty?"

"I find her quite ordinary," replied Diem.

"You don't know how to look at a woman. All you can see are her clothes. That's because you lack experience."

"You're right, Father," Diem agreed.

"When it comes to girls, you are each as bad as the other," said Thieu Hoa.

The next day, over thirty guests arrived from Hanoi. A whole section of the dike was filled with their automobiles. Among the guests were government officials, writers, journalists, businessmen. Some brought their wives. Gifts piled up on the wooden platform in the ancestral hall. Phong greeted his guests at the gate with Thieu Hoa at his side, looking magnificent. Lan stayed in the kitchen, feverishly overseeing the cooking.

Around noon the village dignitaries came to pay their respects. They numbered twenty or more. Phong invited them to sit down. Firecrackers exploded.

To Phuong, a businessman, stood up and congratulated Phong on behalf of all his guests. Everyone clapped. Phong shook To Phuong's hand and said, "Thank you, sir. Thank you all. Here I stand in my house, in my village, surrounded by family, friends, and neighbors, drinking wine made from rice grown in my own fields. To me, this is happiness, although I know that in life nothing lasts." Everyone nodded approvingly.

The feast continued for over three hours. To crown it all, there were cakes inscribed with the words "Pham Ngoc Phong" in butter frosting. The village notables ate the cake with their hands, getting frosting on their fingers, which they wiped on their seats.

After the celebration, Phong sent Thieu Hoa back to Hanoi on her own, while he remained in Ke Noi to rest for three months. Phong took frequent walks through the village. He noted that several rich houses had been recently built, but that the larger number of villagers remained very poor. The overall impression was of dirt and squalor. Sometimes Phong walked to the dike for some fresh air and lay on the grass, gazing at the sky and flocks of cranes flying into the distance.

One day, as he was sitting on the dike, Phong noticed a crowd gathering below him. He approached and saw in their midst an old blind man playing a two-stringed lute. A child accompanied him with her singing. Phong listened, but could catch only a few words of her song—"compassion," "loyalty," "filial piety," "respect." Next to the musicians, using a winnowing basket for a table, a man was molding figures from rice dough dyed red and blue. Many of the figures depicted heroes of old, each figure quite distinct from the others. In the crowd, Phong saw Chiem. She had dropped her carrying pole with its two baskets piled high with grass. Her eyes shone like dewdrops, and she held a sap-covered stalk of green rice between her beautiful lips. Beads of sweat pearled at her temples.

Back home, Lan asked Phong, "Why do you look sad? Have you fallen in love with some young girl?"

"I have developed quite a fancy for Chiem," answered Phong.

"Then tomorrow I will ask for her," said Lan. "I like her too. She's a hard worker."

"I would be most grateful," said Phong.

"There's nothing to be grateful about," Lan replied. "You were born in the year of the Tiger. Like the tiger, once you have chosen your prey, you won't rest until you've devoured it."

The next day, Lan sent a matchmaker to Mua's house to discuss Phong's intentions. Mua responded meekly, but Chiem refused the proposal outright, even threatening to kill herself if she were made to go through with the marriage. Phong felt peeved, and confronted Mua. "Why are you so stubborn?" he asked. "This time I'm making a formal offer for your daughter. If you turn me down, I'll reduce you and your family to beggary." Mua pushed his daughter harder. The relatives pleaded with her. Chiem finally gave in.

The wedding was splendid, but Chiem was escorted to her husband's house in a stupor of misery. In the following years she bore Phong two sons. They named the elder Pham Ngoc Phuc. The younger they called Pham Ngoc Tam.

X.

During his long sojourn at Ke Noi, Phong entrusted all business dealings in Hanoi to Thieu Hoa and his son-in-law Diem. One day Thieu Hoa told Phong, "I've met a poet who has a collection of poems for sale. I find them quite good and would like to buy them and have them published under your name."

Phong shot her a look of contempt. "What nonsense!" he said. "Trust a woman to think up a scheme like that. The title 'poet' is for unlucky people. Good poetry is melancholy but impotent. Yet happier sentiment makes for bad poetry."

"Well then, what if I edited it and printed it under my name?"

"Women can't write poetry! Poetry is the expression of the most profound feelings, but women have no depth of feeling. Poetry must be sublime, but how could you possibly be sublime when you bleed every month?"

Thieu Hoa turned red in the face. She pursued the subject no further, and she never mentioned it again.

One day, Phong's newspaper ran a cartoon depicting a man wearing a pair of antlers on his head, on which a guest was hanging his hat. The horned man bore a strange resemblance to Phong. When he saw the cartoon, Phong asked at the paper whether anyone knew who drew it, but the employees all denied any knowledge of the culprit. Phong became angry, and threatened to fire the editor. The latter then admitted that a stranger had brought him the drawing and paid him to publish it. "Is there any truth to the allusion in the cartoon?" Phong asked.

The editor said, "I've heard a rumor that when you were in Ke Noi your son-in-law Diem and your wife Thieu Hoa were very intimate."

Phong laughed hollowly. "Thank you, sir," he said. "Please carry on with your work. Just remember next time to keep the interest of the owner at heart. If you can't remember this simple rule, then you shouldn't be in journalism."

The editor looked confused. "But I thought a journalist should work in the interest of freedom, equality, and fraternity," he said.

"I see that you have a good sense of humor," said Phong. "Now get out of my sight before I get angry, or you'll soon be eating shit."

At home, Phong knocked a mirror off the wall and broke it. "Are you so disgusted by the sight of your own face?" Thieu Hoa asked.

Phong didn't answer.

"You seem tired. You should take a rest," she said.

"Tomorrow I'm going back to the country," Phong replied.

The next day it rained hard. The drops formed small bubbles as they fell in the flooded courtyard. Phong sat on the veranda and folded paper into little boats which he set afloat on the puddles. Suddenly he stood up and declared that he was returning to Ke Noi immediately, in spite of the rain. Neither Diem nor Thieu Hoa could persuade him to stay.

Phong opened his umbrella and set out on foot. After a minute the umbrella was soaked through, and Phong was drenched to the bone. In a fit of anger he threw the umbrella away. The rain fell harder and harder. Phong walked in the middle of the street. A passing rickshaw driver honked at him.

Phong turned around. At the gate to his house he did not ring but let himself in with his key. Thieu Hoa and Diem were in bed together. When they saw Phong they turned as white as the sheets.

Phong ordered Thieu Hoa to sit down, then took a seat himself. "How many times have you slept together?" he asked.

"Six times," said Thieu Hoa.

"Seven, if you count the time in Paul Bert Park," said Diem.

"We were in such a hurry that time. It doesn't count," said Thieu Hoa.

"Was it really seven?" Phong asked. "Or more like seventy-seven? Diem, I fed, clothed, and taught you. Is this how you thank me? Get down on your knees and lick my feet, and my wife's feet, or I will kill you right here." Diem got down on all fours. Thieu Hoa started to pull back her foot, but she saw the furious look on Phong's face and put it forward again. Diem lifted Thieu Hoa's foot to his lips, then crawled towards Phong, who kicked him in the face with his muddy shoe. Phong said, "Get out of my sight."

The only thing Phong would say to his wife was, "How could you sleep with such a coward?" He went upstairs to his room, lay down on his bed, buried his face in a pillow, and cried. That same afternoon he ran a high fever. Thieu Hoa nursed him devotedly, watching by his bedside day and night. After a fortnight Phong recovered, but he had changed. He rarely spoke and was cold and indifferent towards everyone.

XI.

After this illness, Phong spent his days sitting idly at home in Hanoi. One day, Mrs. Van, a dry grocer from Dong Xuan Market, came to visit, bringing as a gift four pounds of candied lotus seed and several ounces of tea. "How is business these days?" Phong asked.

"Times are hard," replied Mrs. Van. "We can hardly make ends meet."

Phong commiserated. "Yes, Lady Fortune has no pity for righteous people."

"This is why I would like to borrow some money from you," said Mrs. Van. "I want to buy some benzoin powder. I know of a supplier but I don't have enough capital."

"How much would you like? And when can you pay me back?"

"In one month's time, at ten percent."

"I'm also rather short of cash these days. But, all right." Phong sighed. "I don't like to see a woman scrambling in the dirt to earn a living. Women should be pure and aloof from such concerns."

"Goodness, yes, I know what you mean," Mrs. Van said. "But if we don't scramble in the dirt with the rest of them, what will we eat? If you were running this country, Mr. Phong, we could rely on you."

"Politics is a rotten business," Phong muttered.

Mrs. Van said, "I have a lady staying with me, Mrs. Ton Nu Phuong from Hue. She is a gifted fortune-teller and physiognomist. Allow me to bring her to see you."

The next day, Mrs. Van returned with an elderly woman dressed in a pale yellow silk tunic embroidered with a pattern of flowers on the chest. "This is Mrs. Phuong," Mrs. Van announced. "She's related to the royal family." Phong called Thieu Hoa to greet their guests.

"Who will go first?" asked Mrs. Phuong.

"Tell my wife's fortune first," Phong said.

Mrs. Phuong observed Thieu Hoa's face for a while, then said, "Please pull your hair back from your face." Then she said, "Show me your right hand." Then she said, "Stand up and walk around." Mrs. Phuong observed Thieu Hoa for a several minutes and then said, "Dear lady, your carriage is elegant, your hips are large, your head is small. These traits are those of a mandarin's wife. From childhood you have been spared all toil and trouble, and you have enjoyed the respect and affection of all who meet you. You have been twice married. Your lovely smile will inspire malicious gossip, but whatever your transgressions may be, your husband will always forgive you. I see a shadow on your brow, and a crooked line over your lip. This month is very unlucky for you. I fear that your life may be in danger."

Thieu Hoa shuddered and went pale. Nervously, she asked, "Is there any way of avoiding this bad luck?"

"It's a secret of Heaven," replied Mrs. Phuong. "We have no choice but to submit to our fate."

Mrs. Phuong then turned to Phong and said, "Please show me your left hand." Then she said, "Stand up and walk around." Then she said, "You are cunning and ruthless, but generous at heart. You respect virtue and despise material possessions, yet you have never allowed yourself to lack anything. You have received both honors and riches aplenty. You act in all circumstances with subtlety and discretion. You were born under the sign of the golden tiger, and few are those who can keep up with you. This month is ill-fated for you, too. You must be careful."

Phong nodded but did not question the fortune-teller. The conversation then turned to a discussion of the Book of Changes. Phong asked, "What do you think of the way some people use the Book of Changes as an oracle?"

"It can be put to such a purpose," Mrs. Phuong replied. "Those who succeed in this art become saints. Those who fail, demons. Among ten thousand people, you may never find a saint; all are demons."

Impressed by the fortune-teller's eloquence, Phong asked, "Did you ever study the classics, madame?"

"I did indeed receive some instruction. Living in Hue, one naturally meets many men of talent. In some cases that means opportunity, but it means misfortune in most."

Phong nodded, then invited Mrs. Phuong to stay for dinner, after which he gave her a sum of money for the road.

From that day on Thieu Hoa was anxious and restless. Phong told her, "Fortune-telling is nonsense. Why fret about it?"

"I'm so scared," replied Thieu Hoa. "I've heard that Tan Dan has been released from jail. He's a very dangerous man. Please be careful."

"Who told you Tan Dan had been released?" asked Phong.

"Last night I saw him in a dream. He was calling his son, Hanh. It was the middle of the night, but I saw him pass a jerry can to Hanh through the gate."

"That was just a stupid dream," snapped Phong. Nevertheless, he went down to the side building where Hanh lived. He found the boy sitting on a chair as he did every day, dozing, his huge head nodding on his breast and his withered leg bent up under him. Reassured, Phong returned upstairs.

That night Phong was awakened from a deep sleep by the sound of screaming. He opened his eyes and saw flames licking the windows. He kicked the door, but found it locked.

In a panic, he broke the window and jumped out. He saw a shadowy figure that seemed to jump like a grasshopper, holding a can with which it sprayed the house with gasoline. Phong recognized Hanh. Throwing himself on the boy, he grabbed him by the neck with both hands. The fire raged, and Phong felt his back catch fire, but he gripped the boy's neck, throttling him until the eyes popped out of his head. Only then did he let go. Phong stood up and watched his house burn like a pile of straw. He dragged Hanh's body into the fire. As he turned to flee, a heavy object hit him on the head. He rolled to the ground and lost consciousness.

XII.

The talk of the town was the news that Tan Dan, after his release, had set fire to Phong's house in revenge. Rumor had it that Tan Dan had fled to Cambodia. Thieu Hoa, who had been sleeping upstairs, was trapped and killed. Phong's back was badly burned. He was treated for his injuries but the pain was terrible.

Meanwhile, in Ke Noi, Cam had died. Seeing that Phong came only rarely, Lan had secretly taken a lover, the elderly Truong, who like herself owned a butcher stall in the market. When she heard of Phong's misfortune, Lan didn't visit him in Hanoi, but sent servants with money and food. Later, when it appeared that Phong was gravely ill, Truong and Lan boldly walked arm in arm for the whole world to see. Chiem, who lived in one of the annexes with her two sons Tam and Phuc, didn't dare say a word about the affair.

One day, a relative from Ke Noi paid Phong a visit. The relative said, "This is the end of the Pham family. Lan and Truong have taken over the house. Truong has even moved his furniture into the ancestral hall."

Phong sat bolt upright, coughed up blood, and said, "I'm not dead yet. The Phams cannot lose the house. I still have my sons, Tam and Phuc."

A few days later Phong dragged himself out of bed and ordered a servant to take him to the house of a lawyer he knew. This lawyer had recently returned from studying overseas and knew the law inside and out.

When Phong entered, the lawyer was sitting at his desk, talking to a middle-aged woman. "Good day, Mr. Phong," said the lawyer. "Please sit down and have some tea. I won't be a minute."

Phong sat down, and while he waited, he listened to the discussion between the lawyer and the woman. Her story went more or less like this: She and her husband had a twelve-year-old son. Once, when the boy had been extremely rude, the wife gave him a whipping. Unfortunately, she had accidentally hit him in the testicles, after which he died. Her husband, who for some time had had a liaison with another woman, accused his wife of killing the child. The wife, however, pleaded not guilty on the grounds that the fatal blow had been unintentional. The husband contested. The wife believed that her husband wanted her imprisoned so that he could divorce her and take her half of the property. She had come to the lawyer for help.

Phong listened to the woman's story, and watched the lawyer searching his law books, quoting articles and bylaws to her as they spoke. Discouraged, Phong stood up to leave. "Why are you leaving?" asked the lawyer.

Phong said, "I have a house in the countryside. A couple of scoundrels want to steal it from me. I want you to stop them."

"That's quite simple," said the lawyer. "According to Article 318 of the Civil Code—"

Phong interrupted him. "Thank you, sir. I'm afraid there is no law that can resolve this issue. I will adjudicate it myself."

That same afternoon, Phong had one of his servants go out and locate the most notorious gangster in town, a man known as Tuoc the Scar. "This is what I want you to do..." Phong explained. "How much will it cost me?"

The Scar replied, "What we do, we do for the sake of justice. We don't bargain like vulgar hoodlums."

"I understand," Phong replied. "In the meantime, please accept this small sum, if only to please me. Don't worry. Money is one thing, justice is another. How could I possibly confuse the two?"

The Scar left Phong's house quite satisfied.

Not long afterwards, Truong and Lan were closing their shop when a gang of men no one had ever seen before walked in and started to pick a fight. It was early evening and the sky was already dark. These thugs beat them so savagely that Lan died on the spot. Truong was carried home, and died three days later. When the authorities came to investigate, the attackers had disappeared into thin air.

Towards the end of the year, Phong grew much weaker. He withdrew his investment from all his businesses, one after the other, and returned to Ke Noi for good.

XIII.

Chiem's two sons were born eight years apart. Phuc was almost ten, and Tam was two. Phong wanted to send Phuc to school, and he had returned to discuss the plan with Chiem.

It was early summer. For the past ten days the sky had been white hot. All of a sudden, dark clouds drifted across the sun and lightning flashed. This would be Phuc's first trip away from home, and he could not contain his excitement. "How long will the rain last?" he asked every few minutes.

Chiem did not want to send her son away to school, but she was afraid of Phong and so she said nothing. Phuc asked, "When I'm at school, will I live in Hanoi for good?"

"Yes," Phong said. "I'm sending you to stay with an old friend of mine who's a professor of literature. He'll look after you."

Phuc jumped up and ran through every room in the house, from the ancestral hall down to the kitchen, as if consigning to memory the objects and places that held his earliest memories. When he had finished, he sat down on the doorstep, turned his face to the sky, and waited for the rain.

Black clouds rolled in from the east. The air was perfectly still, without a breath of wind. Then the first huge raindrops thudded on the roof tiles. Chiem was inside, packing Phuc's clothes into a wooden chest. Phong sat on the bed fanning Tam to sleep. Phuc cried out, "Hailstorm!" and ran out into the courtyard. There was a flash of lightning and then an earth-shattering crack. The air was filled with smoke, and in the middle of the courtyard was a small black heap that reeked of burnt hair. Inside the house, Chiem and Phong had been thrown to the floor. Roof tiles crashed around them.

When Phong regained consciousness, he stood up, stiff-limbed, and saw Chiem kneeling next to what remained of Phuc, wailing. The rain was pouring down now, but the smell of burnt hair was still strong. Phuc lay curled up like a wood shaving, dry, bald, charred, as if every drop of water had been sucked from his body. All around him lay shattered Bat Trang tiles.

Phong took to his bed soon after the lightning killed Phuc. Burning with fever, he refused to eat or drink. In his feverish sleep he had a dream. He was in hell: there was a great cauldron hanging over a roaring fire, and black-faced devils and creatures with long tangled hair were busy stoking the flames. Pitiful cries rose from the chained figures in the cauldron. One of them turned to Phong and said, "I am Pham Ngoc Lien." And then another said, "I am Pham Ngoc Gia." And another said, "I am Pham Ngoc Chieu." And he heard the women say, "I am Dieu," "I am Lan," "I am Thieu Hoa." Phong awoke with a start and realized that the people in his dream had faces that he saw every day. His great-great-grandfather Lien was the man at the telegraph office. His great-grandfather Gia was the lawyer. Chieu was the man who sold the newspapers. Lan was the woman who sold rice, and Thieu Hoa the one who sold sugar.

Chiem often carried little Tam to Phong's sick bed. One day Phong said, "My wife, Tam is the last drop of blood of the Pham family. I pray only that the blood in his veins will be red, and not black like his father's and grandfather's." After speaking these words, he gasped for breath, groaned once, and died. It was the hour of the chicken, on the thirteenth day of the third month of the Year of the Dragon (1940).

XIV.

Today, if you go to Ke Noi, district of Tu Liem, you can still see the Phams' great house. It has stood still while the world runs turbulently by, and although time has left its mark of wear and decay, and some parts have fallen to ruin, the basic structure remains unchanged. I've heard that after her husband's death, Chiem continued to live there with Tam. Mother and son tended their vegetable garden, raised pigs, and made tofu which they sold in the market. Tam was self-taught, and although he read voraciously, he never sat for a single exam nor did he try to become anything.

Chiem passed away in the Year of the Tiger (1986) at the age of ninety. She was buried in a spot called Co Co Field. Her grave is under an ancient solitary flame tree, facing the Red River. Under this tree are three termite mounds that lean in towards each other very much like the clay tripods still used in many kitchens in our country. People say that in the wet season, the river god and his generals, the turtles and water snakes, gather under the tree to feast by the light of fireflies, while listening to the sweet croaking of the frogs, a sound like a person crying.

Translated by Viviane Lowe

A Sharp Sword

We all partake of woe,
our common fate
—Nguyen Du

Among the men who were close to our forefather Nguyen Phuc Anh during the years in which he was scheming to restore the fortunes of the Nguyen Dynasty, there was one of outstanding talent whose name does not appear in any history books. His name was Dang Phu Lan.

Born in Hung Hoa, Lan was the son of Dang Phu Binh, who had been a general under Lord Trinh Bong. Binh was a skilled but rather headstrong warrior. Seeing that the Trinh lord was cowardly and exhibited petty behavior unbecoming a prince, Binh left Lord Trinh Bong and moved to the Inner Region. At the outbreak of the Tay Son Rebellion, Binh joined up with Nguyen Nhac.[1] Because Nhac considered Binh to be a crafty and duplicitous Northerner, he decided to appoint him to a minor post in the mountainous regions of Tay Binh Thuan. Disappointed, Binh took to drink, spending his days inebriated, sobbing loudly and pining for his home in the North. Lan tried to console his father, but it was no use. A short time later, Binh came down with malaria. His hair and whiskers fell out, he lost weight, and his skin turned the color of turmeric. Finally, he took to his bed and awaited death.

Binh possessed an ancestral sword, as sharp as water, reinforced with a lead spine, and capable of striking horrific

---

1. Nguyen Nhac, Nguyen Hue, and Nguyen Lu were three brothers who led the peasant-based Tay Son Rebellion against the ruling Nguyen clan in southern Vietnam towards the latter part of the 18th century. Named after the area in which the three brothers were born (and today known as Kien An Province), the Tay Son Rebellion succeeded in conquering the southern, central, and northern regions, setting up a governing administration and repelling major Siamese and Chinese invasions. Internal squabbling, external pressure, and the death of Nguyen Hue, who was the movement's most brilliant leader, led to its weakening and eventual defeat by the forces of Nguyen Phuc Anh (later known as King Gia Long) in 1802.

blows. Before he died, he handed the sword to Lan and said, "My child, our homeland is in chaos. The Tay Son Rebellion is a relentless force sweeping over the country. But I fear that the power of the rebels is the power of a vulgar new stratum of wealthy men. How can they shoulder the burdens of our country? The Tay Son is not fated to last long. Today in Gia Dinh dwells the royal descendant Nguyen Phuc Anh. You must go there and find him, my child."

Lan wept tears of blood. Binh broke into an icy sweat, shook violently for several moments, and finally died. With the ancestral sword, Lan dug a grave and buried his father. He then set off on the road toward Gia Dinh to find Nguyen Phuc Anh. He was just twenty-eight.

In Gia Dinh, Nguyen Phuc Anh was plotting to overthrow the powerful Tay Son regime. A brilliant strategist, Anh was unyielding and trusted no one. He valued men who displayed gallantry and propriety, rather than those known for their benevolence, righteousness, wisdom, or truthfulness. From time to time, Anh would slip into the land of Thuan Quang swiftly like a magician. In the Inner Region where he was more feared than loved, people said that a swirling mass of black clouds preceded Anh wherever he went. Whenever it rained, people said that Nguyen Phuc Anh was passing through.

When Anh met Lan, he was impressed with the young man's intelligence, eloquence, and bold, strategic mind. He immediately invited Lan to join his entourage.

A short time later, Anh and four attendants, including Lan, took a small boat down the Tien River. During the course of their journey, they noticed a large crocodile swimming threateningly behind them. After numerous attempts to elude the beast had failed, the small crew grew progressively more frightened. Finally they decided that to save themselves and salvage their mission, one attendant would have to jump overboard to satisfy the crocodile's hunger.

"Who is willing to give his life for the country of Viet?" Anh asked.

Three of the attendants immediately volunteered; only Lan remained silent. Glaring angrily at Lan, Anh bellowed, "What kind of a hero are you who values his own life so highly?"

"My Lord, please don't be angry," said Lan. "No harm will come to the country of Viet. A life needn't be wasted just to escape the jaws of this crocodile." So saying, he grabbed a stone from the floor of the boat and flung it at a wild duck that happened to be flying overhead. Seeing something plummet down into the water, the crocodile forgot about the boat and sped away to devour the fallen duck.

"This certainly bodes well," said Anh, laughing heartily. "Heaven seems to grant me whatever I need to fulfill my ambitions."

Afterwards, Anh made sure that Lan was always at his side. He often sought Lan's advice, especially concerning evaluations of personal behavior, because Lan's suggestions were always on target.

Once, right before Tet, when Anh's power was rising like a kite in the wind, the strongest warlords and richest merchants in the region, plus scores of ordinary people from Gia Dinh, brought offerings to Anh. When Anh ordered Lan to receive the gifts, Lan personally accepted every one of them, then stored them together in a warehouse. Thus, as guests came to pay their personal respects to Anh, they entered his presence empty-handed. When the powerful noblemen Le Van Duyet, Nguyen Van Thanh, and Vo Tanh saw their gifts mixed in with the offerings of commoners, they felt slighted and complained to Anh that Lan's methods were insulting. Anh laughed and said, "Lan is upright, faithful, and skilled both in words and in the martial arts; let him settle this. He has his own way of arranging things. The men I keep by my side are never ordinary."

On the first morning of Tet, a platform was set up on

which to pray and make spiritual offerings. Anh ordered Lan to divide up the blessed offerings among the assembled guests. Lan parceled out everything exactly evenly and everyone was content. When Anh asked Lan afterward why he had been so scrupulous, Lan replied, "My Lordship's ambitions are not yet realized. Some of your subjects have contributed much to you; some only a bit. Some will expect a great deal of special consideration from you in the future; some will expect only a little. If you know the size of their offerings it will be more difficult to manage them effectively."

"You're right," said Anh.

"If we divide everything equally," Lan continued, "then everyone will feel compelled to make an equal effort on your behalf."

"That's also true," said Anh, but after a moment he added, "Somehow I fear that perhaps you are a little too thrifty."

"Extravagant servants can bring their masters great harm," Lan responded.

"You are a Northerner," said Anh. "You can't understand the people of the Inner Region as I do. You think you've considered everything, but princes love luxury more than anything else."

"You're right, my Lord," Lan said. "Thriftiness is only for the poor. But does my Lord imagine that he has greater resources than the Tay Son?"

"I have only three meters of earth in which to bury myself," replied Anh, frowning.

"That's not so," said Lan. "My Lord has both Heaven and Earth on his side, so he need only remain dedicated to his cause."

After sitting silently a moment, Anh said, "Nguyen Nhac is nothing. Nguyen Lu is nothing. How, then, is it that Nguyen Hue is so skillful?"

"Hue is skillful," said Lan, "at managing men of talent.

188

But he has no skill at managing ordinary men. My lord is different from Hue."

Anh said nothing.

After Nguyen Hue died, his son Nguyen Quang Toan took the throne, and the Tay Son regime began to splinter into factions. Anh was thrilled and ordered a feast in celebration. Lan tried to dissuade him. "Don't do this, my Lord," he said. "The people will think you are unkind."

"Hue called me a national traitor," Anh said. "He denounced me in front of everyone. He denigrated me in vile and very mean terms. He and I were locked in a death feud. Now that he is dead, am I not allowed to rejoice?"

"Hue committed no crime," Lan replied. "He was a man of talent who was tortured by his own destiny. Hue was a powerful force, just like yourself, my Lord. The two of you hated each other. But Hue's power failed to receive the support of Heaven and did not last long. If our behavior demonstrates our gratitude to Heaven for its support, both Heaven and men will see that we are righteous."

Anh followed Lan's advice, but ground his teeth angrily. "When my ambition has been fulfilled, I will disembowel Hue and bury alive three generations of his family."

"It won't be long now, my Lord," replied Lan. "Hold back your laughter, and soon you'll be able to laugh to your heart's content."

As expected, after he seized the old capital of Thang Long and unified the country, Anh brutally took vengeance upon the Tay Son.

When Anh sacked the capital Phu Xuan, he seized an exquisitely beautiful singer named Ngo Thi Vinh Hoa. Although only eighteen years old, Vinh Hoa was a skilled singer and musician with a charming appearance. One evening, Anh, in high spirits, ordered Lan to arrange a feast during which he could sit and listen to Vinh Hoa sing.

"Sing 'Ode to an Emperor,'" ordered Lan. Vinh Hoa picked up her lute and sang:

Light green over yonder
A few tender young buds
A few tender young leaves
Spring rain will nourish them
Spring wind will invigorate them
The earth will fortify them
Let no one gather them
The more they grow, the more beautiful they are
The more they grow, the more virtuous they are
The more they grow, the more bashful they are
What poetry can capture this beauty
What brush can suggest this sense
Whoever is heartbroken frowns
Sleep brings release, but awake you'll remember
                                        again

That is Heaven's gift
A perfect beauty
A precious beauty

"Great singing!" Anh said, applauding loudly.

"Now sing 'Love of the Country,'" prodded Lan. Repositioning the lute, Vinh Hoa began:

A high mountain over yonder
A green river over yonder
From where springs such a mountain?
From where springs such a river?
A hero far from home
Braves many dangers along the road
Back in your native land
Waits a gray-haired old mother
A girl tosses and turns at night
How to repay such love?
Drink a cup of sad wine
And offer the high mountain a cup

> *And offer the deep river a cup*
> *Bow three times before the emperor*
> *Forget not the sadness of the country*
> *Pity the old mother and the beautiful girl far away*

Anh furrowed his brow. "You sing well," he said, "but too sadly."

Kowtowing, Vinh Hoa replied, "Excuse me, my Lord. Your humble servant has inadvertently saddened a celestial being."

Lan helped her up and said, "Don't worry. My Lord has a generous heart. The melodramatic sentiments of ordinary people are inappropriate for him." So saying, Lan prostrated himself before Anh and said, "Tomorrow, my Lord enters battle. Enjoy yourself only slightly tonight. You need your rest."

Anh sighed and stood up. "You're correct," he said. "You have helped me restrain myself for nine years. I haven't forgotten. Since you offered your sword in my service, even my eating and sleeping have been tightly regulated. Before you arrived, it was never so."

"My Lord must bear the will of Heaven. Your burden is heavier than that of an ordinary man," replied Lan.

"I only wish to be an ordinary man," sighed Anh. However, he stood up, shook out his gown, and retired to his chamber.

Vinh Hoa took her lute and left.

The next day, Anh led his army to the North. On the way, he said to Lan, "The voice of that singer still rings in my ears. Neither the roar of the wind nor the crash of weapons can drown it out."

"My Lord will have many opportunities to listen to music, but only one to destroy the Tay Son," said Lan.

Soon after moving north, Anh met with his generals to discuss the plan for attacking Thang Long. "The North has many talented scholars," said Le Van Duyet. "If that wicked clique is induced to join us, the masses will more easily flock to our banner."

"No," said Anh. "We have Heaven's will on our side. We have no need to induce anyone. Wherever we go, we'll dig graves and bury those talented scholars. The masses will have no other choice but to follow us." Seeing that Anh was correct, the generals sat in silence.

That night Anh couldn't sleep. He called Lan and ordered him to perform a sword dance. Lan held the ancient sword and danced for Anh, the wind howling all around. Anh watched, mesmerized. When the dance ended, he ordered Lan to bring him the sword. Anh held the sword with two hands. Then he turned to a nearby frangipani tree with a trunk as thick as the pillar of a house. With one stroke, he split it down the middle. Sap spurted out like white blood.

"Why is your sword so sharp?" Anh asked.

"I don't know where this magic sword came from originally," Lan said. "It was handed down from my grandfather."

"Why is this the first time that I've seen it?' asked Anh.

"Before, my Lord only saw the heads that fell beneath the blows of this sword," said Lan. "Now you see the sword itself. Soon you will see the peace and prosperity that follow from it."

Anh clenched the sword, unwilling to release it. He asked, "Why did you turn pale this afternoon when I said that I wanted to bury the famous scholars of the North?"

"I am from the North," answered Lan. "Thus, I was simply lamenting my own fate."

"I only hate that bunch of scholarly know-it-alls," said Anh. "You are the child of a warrior clan, so you have no need to fear. Their knowledge reeks of deceptive and pretentious sophistry. They don't scare me. They're just a bunch of shit-stinking maggots."

"Most of them are as you describe and deserve to be

buried," Lan said. "But there are a few decent ones, my Lord, and you should try to add them to your entourage."

"None of them would follow me," replied Anh. "They're too caught up with their whining words and phrases. To them, I am immoral and heartless. It would be too much trouble to try to brainwash them."

"It seems that my Lord is still used to managing ordinary men. A superior person stands above the questions of morality or immorality. His heart aims at success, not simply at good intentions. If they don't understand this fact, it's their own fault. Does anyone understand why my Lord employed the services of Pigneau de Béhaine, a foreigner?[2] You will suffer a bad reputation for this single act for over three hundred years."

"Then what should I do?" Anh asked anxiously.

"My Lord can't do anything, but if you can get people like Ngo Thi Nham to join you, then everything should be all right."

Anh said, "I want you to go in advance to recruit a couple of these people. If you're successful, you'll be making a truly great contribution to the cause."

Lan kowtowed to Anh. "For me," he said, "there could be no greater honor. If I can do what you ask, I'll have no need to feel ashamed of my native region."

Anh said, "I'll keep your sword until you return. If you bring good news, I'll shower you with praise. But if you fail, I'll use the sword's magical powers to punish you."

Lan went pale, but had to consent to the terms.

Lan left in disguise and, carrying a small amount of gold and silver, headed north. At this time, the region was in great disorder and the Tay Son regime was on the verge of crumbling altogether. The Tay Son generals quarreled among themselves, oblivious to the impact such behavior would have

2. Pigneau de Béhaine was an 18th century missionary in Vietnam who dreamed of building an empire for France in Asia. He befriended Nguyen Anh and negotiated a treaty on Anh's behalf with Louis XVI in 1787.

on their future reputations. Alone and friendless, Lan wandered about, searching everywhere for men of talent, but unable to find any.

One day, Lan stopped to rest at a roadside inn. Inside, he saw a gentle-looking man sitting and drinking tea, a slightly worried look on his face. Speaking to him, Lan felt surprised by the stranger's extraordinary serenity. He seemed to possess a soul as pure as mountain water. Lan offered him some whiskey, and, after drinking only a few drops, the young man's face turned red. When the innkeeper's beautiful daughter stood to serve them, he said, "Our guest has come from a faraway place. It seems that although his empty ambitions have sapped his strength, he still doesn't know the path of life. Sing him a song, Miss Cam." Lan was surprised but quickly felt both relaxed and eager to hear the song. The innkeeper's daughter handed the young man a lute and, as he began to play in an elegant style, she sang the following song:

> *Over a hundred years*
> *What talent and fate*
> *We know only sorrow*
> *A young bud, a green leaf*
> *The rain will nourish them*
> *The wind will invigorate them*
> *The earth will fortify them*
> *Let no one pick them*
> *It would be a waste to fall into anyone's hand*
> *Beauty will vanish*
> *Virtue will fade*
> *The more they grow, the more bashful they are*
> *Try to describe such beauty*
> *Try to paint such a thought*
> *Whoever is heartbroken feels sad*
> *Sleep brings release, but awake you'll remember*
> > *again*
> *That is a destiny decided by Heaven*

Loneliness for a young girl
Go hunting, go fishing
A perfect beauty
A precious beauty
Whenever you transfer a tomb
Offer up a teardrop
Over a hundred years
What is talent and fate
We know only sorrow

Lan listened until the end and sighed, his five senses overwhelmed by the song. "My God!" he declared. "Why does it sound just like 'Ode to an Emperor?'"

The singing girl smiled. "This song has no title," she said, and then pointed toward the young man. "He composed it only for me to sing."

Lan sighed again. "The song is excellent. I truly do not know the path of life." So saying, he left the room and went to sleep. The next morning, he rose early and left. He did not say farewell to the innkeeper, nor did he ask for the young guest who had been with Miss Cam, the innkeeper's daughter.

When Lan arrived at Thang Long, Nguyen Anh had already seized the city. Anh's armies had swept in like a flood, and now Lan became like seaweed caught among the waves. He was neither happy nor sad, but deep in his heart he felt stirred by the momentousness of the occasion.

Lan explained to Anh that he had failed to complete his task and that, therefore, he must be punished. Anh listened from a throne surrounded by heavily armed guards. Lan stood on the imperial platform, had himself tied up, then kowtowed to the ruler.

Anh said to Lan. "You have served me for nine years and one hundred days," he said. "For nine years you did nothing wrong, but over the last hundred days your work has been poor, virtually useless. To climb a tree but fail to pluck the fruit is a crime worthy of death." Without a word, Lan positioned his neck for the blow that was to come. People say that Nguyen Phuc Anh had the executioner use Lan's ancestral sword to behead him. Afterwards, the blood that spurted forth wasn't red but, rather, white like the sap of a tree. A moment later, it thickened and clotted.

Conclusion

I, the writer of this short story, recently went up to Da Bac to visit the home of a Muong villager in Tu Ly. The head of the household, Mr. Quach Ngoc Minh, showed me his ancestral tablets. I was utterly surprised when Quach Ngoc Minh informed me that his forefather had been an ethnic Vietnamese. He said that his grandfather, Dang Phu Lan, had married a woman named Ngo Thi Vinh Hoa who had originally been a singer. To escape from the king, Lan and Hoa had fled to Da Bac where, posing as Muong, they set up a household and started their own family. Mr. Quach Ngoc Minh claimed that his grandfather had once met Nguyen Du, the author of *The Tale of Kieu*.[3] I was lucky to hear Quach Ngoc Minh's daughter, Quach Thi Trinh, sing an ancient ballad. It had sublime lyrics about the buds of a young tree.

I would like to dedicate this story to the family of Quach Ngoc Minh in gratitude for the kindness they have shown me. I also would like to thank several historical researchers and close friends who have helped me collect and arrange the documents that have been essential for my writing, a process that has been exhausting, complicated, and even tedious.

Translated by Peter Zinoman

3. Nguyen Du (1765-1820) is generally considered Vietnam's greatest poet and man of letters. His epic poem of an ill-fated young woman, *The Tale of Kieu*, is the most widely known piece of Vietnamese literature, both domestically and internationally.

Fired Gold

The heart feels sad, but it accepts its lot...
—Folk song

Mr. Quach Ngoc Minh from Tu Ly village in Da Bac District wrote me a letter. "I've read your short story 'A Sharp Sword,' which tells of my ancestor Dang Phu Lan. I didn't like the detail concerning Lan's meeting with Nguyen Du. The character whom you describe as the strange, pure young man at the inn with 'a soul as pure as mountain water' seems like nonsense. The song 'The Discordance of Talent and Fate,' which you attribute to Nguyen Du, while clever, is not really that clever. Please come up for a visit and I will show you some documents that should put things in a different light. My daughter, Quach Thi Trinh, will prepare some fish-and-star-fruit sour broth, which you enjoyed last time..."

After receiving this letter, I went up to visit Quach Ngoc Minh and his family. The ancient documents he possessed were truly original. I then returned to Hanoi and wrote this story. As I wrote, I freely amended and reorganized extraneous details and edited the documents so as to make them consistent with the telling of my story.

* * *

In 1802, Nguyen Phuc Anh invaded Thang Long and seized the throne, taking the royal name Gia Long. The new king was assisted by a handful of European advisors including François Poirée—a Frenchman recommended by Bishop Pigneau de Béhaine. The king called him Phang.

Phang had been a wanderer since childhood. He participated in the French Revolution of 1789 and was friends with Saint Just. After the failure of the revolution in 1794, Phang escaped to a foreign land. In 1797, he boarded a merchant ship bound for Hoi An. While no one knows anything about the meeting between Phang and Pigneau de Béhaine, the bishop definitely did write Phang a letter of introduction to King Gia Long.

In his diary, Phang wrote:

> The king is one colossal solitary mass. He performs his role in the imperial court with great skill. He moves, stands, exists, enters, issues orders, and receives homage from his clique of court officials. He is a stern father toward his selfish and dimwitted children. As a husband, he commands respect from his mediocre wives. He knows he is old, and, with the beautiful young concubines in his royal harem, he is impotent. As the founder and architect of the imperial court, he knows that it is superficial and that his nation is poor. He worries constantly because he is aware that the power that lies exclusively in his hands is far too great for the strength of a single human being...

Phang followed Gia Long on a hunting trip north of Hue, the royal capital. According to Phang:

> The king rides a horse, his back erect. He is radiant in the wild, and the anxious scowl he wears daily disappears. He is happy, thrilled by the hunt. Sitting with me in the evening, he says, "Do you see those miserable wretches over there? They take care of everything. As I pass through the hunting grounds, they actually release the prey for me." Surprised, I ask why the king (by birth a skilled military leader) tolerates this insult. He laughs and says, "You understand nothing. Is there any glory not built on dishonor and shame?" Sitting there listening to the king, I am struck by the dreadfulness of his life. He understands that his existence is essentially dependent on symbiosis. As fate has arbitrarily placed him in a paramount position, he

dares not tamper with any of society's fixed relationships, since this might upset the delicate symbiosis and weaken his throne. I ask the king about Eastern philosophers, but he shows no interest. He responds, "They are all embittered by life. They are the past. Our concern is the present." Here, the king is visibly more engrossed in finishing his tiger tendon than in continuing the conversation with me...

Phang received Gia Long's permission to travel around the realm. He met Nguyen Du, who at that time was serving as a district chief. Phang wrote:

Before me is a slight young man whose face is creased with misery. This man is a famous and talented poet. I sense that he understands absolutely nothing about politics, and yet he is an unswervingly dedicated official. His character is superior to that of others, yet what value does such character hold when his real, material life is impoverished and luckless? He lacks even the most basic conveniences. He can be neither frivolous nor magnanimous. Spiritual life suffocates him. His speech is simple and humorous; his intuition, wonderful. Like Gia Long, he is also a massive bulk of material, but lighter, less substantial, and thus besmeared with thinner layers of soot and impurities. Both men are priceless national treasures.

Nguyen Du took Phang to visit several areas under his jurisdiction. Phang wrote:

Nguyen Du displays a deep sympathy for the people. He loves his people and embodies their most lyric and melancholy characteristics, but also their most pitiable ones. Gia Long embodies nothing other than himself. Herein lies his glory, but also something horribly vile. The king perceives reality exclusively in relation to the perpetuation of his own existence. The king is aware of his own pain. But Nguyen Du is numb to his. Nguyen Du sympathizes with the odd miseries of small and isolated destinies but does not understand the immense misery of the nation. The most significant characteristics of the country are its smallness and weakness. It is like a virgin girl raped by Chinese civilization. The girl simultaneously enjoys, despises, and is humiliated by the rape. Gia Long understands this fact, and herein lies the bitterest sentiment that he and his community must endure. Nguyen Du does not understand this fact because Nguyen Du is the child of this virgin girl, and the blood that flows through his veins is laced with the qualities of the brutal man who raped his mother. Whereas Nguyen Du appears to be drowning in the mud of life, Gia Long stands tall, unencumbered, almost detached from that life. Nguyen Du's mother [the political regime of the time] has, through supreme restraint and self-control, concealed her own shame and anguish from her child. Only in another three hundred years will we understand that this gesture was meaningless.

Nguyen Du lives a simple, country life and naively endures poverty along with the people. He stands beside them and enjoys life's pleasures no more than they do, which shows he understands nothing about politics. Because his livelihood is based on unproductive activities, he can only satisfy life's minimum requirements. His kindness is consequently of the small variety and is incapable of saving anyone. Gia Long is different. He is horrible for his audacity in resisting the flow of nature and for deceptively using his people to serve his own interests. He certainly makes history more exciting. His is the immense kindness of a politician, a type of kindness concerned not only with good works for individual destinies, but also with becoming a driving force in the community, within which, according to natural laws, each element will exist, adjust, and develop. If one strong force does not exist, a community will stagnate and decay. The Vietnamese community suffers from an inferiority complex. How small it is next to Chinese civilization, a civilization equally glorious, vile, and ruthless.

Phang described to Gia Long his impression upon meeting Nguyen Du:

The king listens to me without interest. It seems he is deaf, but I know otherwise. He does not acknowledge Nguyen Du, or perhaps he simply considers him to be one well-bred horse among many in the herds of horses, pigs, cows, and chickens that he must tend. 'I know that man,' he says. 'His father is Nguyen Nghiem. His older brother is Nguyen Khan.' I see that the king realizes his helplessness in the face of his impoverished and stagnant nation. He does not believe that the scholarly arts can transform his race. Priority must be given to the material situation. Unproductive economic activities offer the people only an anxious existence. The problem at hand is how to rise up and strive to become a strong country. This will require the courage to withstand a swift clash with the broader community of nations. Decrepit Confucian practices and political masturbation will never result in pure or wholesome relations. A time will come when the worldwide political regimes will seem like an all-too-familiar mixed salad, and the very concept of purity will possess no significance.

In 1814, gold was discovered. Phang entreated Gia Long to give him permission to lead a band of Europeans on a search for gold. The king agreed. While Phang left no account of the expedition, an anonymous Portuguese participant did leave a memoir. According to that memoir:

Our band includes eleven men: four Portuguese, one Dutchman, five Frenchmen, and a Vietnamese guide. François Poirée leads us. Gia Long chooses to rely on this cruel man. We travel on horseback, carrying weapons and the kind of panning equipment used in North America. At this stage, François Poirée is unable to fathom the events that are about to unfold. For this, we ultimately pay a high price. Most of us have joined the expedition out of simple curiosity. We prepare enough provisions for one month. After snaking our way through the jungle, we arrive at our destination. Here, we find the source of a big river lying peacefully within a deserted valley. We can see no human shadow. A raven circles overhead. On his map, François Poirée names this place the Valley of the Ravens. We pitch tents along the river. That first day, the Dutchman suffers a high fever. He progresses through several frightful seizures. His body turns as hot as burning coal and his face turns gray. We suggest that someone remain behind to care for him, but François Poirée won't listen to us. He insists that everyone dig for gold on the mountain and help filter the ore. Returning that evening, we find the Dutchman dead. François Poirée orders the dead body thrown into the river. A black swarm of ravens immediately descends upon the corpse...

The gold mine is almost like a strip mine. We are overcome with elation and forget our exhaustion. On the third day, we are attacked by local natives. We cluster together in a defensive circle. The natives wield knives and sticks from a safe distance, hurling abuse and showering us with stones. Their only intention is to expel us from the valley. Seeing the attackers, our Vietnamese guide disappears. François Poirée's

Vietnamese is poor. He raises aloft King Gia Long's
royal banner, but to no effect. At that point, we should
hastily withdraw, but François Poirée will not retreat.
Instead he opens fire. A native is hit. The rest run helter-
skelter. We implore François Poirée to let us turn back,
but he refuses to listen and forces us to return to work.
Dazzled by gold, he has become blind to reason.
Returning that afternoon, we see the skull of our
Vietnamese guide skewered on a stake posted near our
camp. Against a red-hot sky, a flock of ravens circle
above the jungle, savagely shrieking as they fly.

In the middle of the night, a violent fire erupts
around our huts. Arrows soaked in deadly poison rain
down. Five members of our group are hit and die
immediately. Seizing as much gold as possible, François
Poirée attempts to beat a bloody path of escape. The fire
grows unbearably hot. Before us, behind us, overhead,
and underfoot, the entire jungle is engulfed in flames..."

The memoir of the anonymous Portuguese ends here. I,
the writer of this short story, have endeavored to search the
content of ancient texts and the memories of aged men, yet I
have uncovered neither documents nor individuals with
information on the Valley of the Ravens and the Europeans
who entered it during Gia Long's reign. Over many years, all
my attempts have been in vain. I therefore offer three
conclusions to the story, so that each reader can select the
one that he or she feels is most suitable.

CONCLUSION ONE:

Three members of the expedition survive and Phang
returns home with virtually the entire quantity of unearthed
gold. The expedition's success thrills the king. He orders an
exploration of the Valley of the Ravens and assigns Phang

the task of overseeing the further exploitation of the mine. The two other surviving Europeans are also invited to participate, but they refuse. For two years, Phang oversees the work in the mine. The king relies exclusively on Phang and bestows many generous awards on him. One day, the king sends Phang an elaborately prepared meal called Eight Jewel Bird Stew. After Phang eats, a violent ache begins to gnaw at his stomach. His eyes roll back in his head; blood pours from his mouth. He dies hunched over the dining table. Afterward, the following lines are discovered in his diary:

All human efforts to achieve goodness are painful and exhausting. Genuine goodness is as rare as gold, and ultimately it must be guaranteed with gold to have real value.

We live without meaning, poor and miserable among makeshift theories and specious reasoning, consumed with ethnic and class antagonisms. How fragile and trifling are our lives. When, I ask, when on the face of this earth, will progress appear?

CONCLUSION TWO:

Only Phang escapes the sea of fire. With the remaining gold, he arrives at the house of the district chief. Showing the royal banner that bears the seal of Gia Long, Phang asks for protection. The district chief, an elderly Confucian scholar, is skilled in medicine. Phang undergoes treatment at this secluded district capital. Vu Thi, the young widowed daughter of the district chief, falls in love with Phang. When Phang returns to the capital, Gia Long bestows upon him a generous reward. The king orders the exploitation of the gold mine.

In Europe at that time, the monarchy of Napoleon Bonaparte lies in ruins. Europe matures. It begins to understand that the beauty and glory of a people are based on neither revolution nor war, on neither ideologists nor emperors. In grasping this, people can live more simply, less intensely, and be in greater accord with nature. Phang requests Gia Long's permission to return with Vu Thi and a large store of gold to his native land. In France, he sets up a bank and lives happily for many years. To his grandchildren, he often conjures stories about the historic upheavals he witnessed in distant Annam. According to Phang, the period during which he lived in Annam marked the beginning of Vietnam as a nation. Its people determined their borders, popularized a writing system based on the Roman alphabet, gradually escaped from the frightful domination of Chinese civilization, and established a general intercourse with the rest of humanity.

CONCLUSION THREE:

All members of the gold expedition are killed. They were in fact encircled and attacked not by the ethnic minority peoples, as mistakenly reported in the memoir of the anonymous Portuguese, but by dynastic troops. The Europeans' possessions are searched for concealed gold, their clothes and written records are examined. Gia Long appoints a person of royal blood to oversee the exploitation of the mine. Toward the end of his life, Gia Long lives in his forbidden palace, seeking to avoid contact with the outside world. The king hates anyone who dares remind him of the early relations he had with Vietnamese, Chinese, or Europeans back in the days when he was poor and powerless.

The Nguyen Dynasty of King Gia Long was a horrific dynasty. Please pay attention, dear readers, for this dynasty left many mausoleums.

Translated by Peter Zinoman

Chastity

"Chastity is worth great amounts of gold..."
"What little chastity I may have saved..."
"Chastity has many paths..."
                                    —Nguyen Du

The discovery of an ancient tomb atop a lake-bed in the region of the Da River hydroelectric power station prompted me to return to the village of Tu Ly in the district of Da Bac. Mr. Quach Ngoc Minh (whom readers might recognize from my two previous stories, "A Sharp Sword" and "Fired Gold") suspected that this was the tomb of Ngo Thi Vinh Hoa who lived nearly two hundred years ago. According to an ancient legend told by the Muong inhabitants of this region, it was she who founded the Quach clan.

I arrived on the day the tomb was to be moved from the lakebed up to Tu Ly. The tomb lay within a narrow rectangular mound of smooth earth about two hundred fifty meters from the banks of the Da River. From the river surface, it measured roughly sixteen meters high. The runoff from the Da River had never submerged this place.

From outside, the ancient tomb resembled an enormous termite mound. Laborers dug three meters into the mound, revealing a wall of bricks. The corpse had been buried in the traditional fashion, set in an inner casket, which was in turn placed within an outer coffin. The coffin was made from eight-centimeter-thick planks of rare and precious wood, and in the open air it took on the color of ripe plums. The inner casket had been carved in a simple but elegant style. The casket was opened to reveal a length of pink silk stretched over the interior. From beneath this piece of pink silk, a translucent haze drifted slowly skyward, gradually taking the form of an exquisitely beautiful woman with a radiant face and wearing an elegantly embroidered dress. The tomb was enchanted. A great fear swept over us. Suddenly, a cloudy mist began flowing out over the sides of the casket. After ten minutes, the mist dissipated. The pink silk had disappeared, leaving behind only an ashen black skeleton. In the casket, bits of dried tea and pieces of precious jewelry were also found.

Quach Ngoc Minh rinsed the bones in alcohol and fragrant water, wrapped them in a square piece of white cloth, and placed them in a glazed burial urn. Never had a reinternment left such an impression on me. Quach Ngoc Minh's daughter, Quach Thi Trinh, asked me if I knew of the woman who had been buried in the tomb. I became very flustered. Surely, only those who are both romantic and serious would understand that the concept of knowing and not knowing is often quite vague; the distinction is a limited and historical one.

The following story tells of the woman who rests in that tomb.

* * *

Ngo Thi Vinh Hoa was the tenth child of Ngo Khai, a descendant of Chuong Khanh Cong Ngo Tu, who also gave birth to Ngo Thi Ngoc Dao, the mother of King Le Thanh Tong.[4] Ngo Khai was a rich and powerful silk merchant. He lived near the Tien Tich Pagoda. His treasury, as opulent as that of the Trinh Lords, was managed by hundreds of servants. Khai was well connected and possessed many close friends in high places.

The women of the Ngo clan were famous in the capital for their beauty, and for several generations many had been selected by the royal court. Of Khai's seven daughters, six had become beloved concubines in the Trinh Lords' harems.

---

4. King Le ThanhTong (1442-1497) reigned over Vietnam for almost forty years in the second half of the 15th century. His rule was marked by peace, prosperity, and a cultural revival.

The seventh and youngest, Vinh Hoa, was pampered and doted on by her father. At the moment of her birth, a mass of five-colored clouds suddenly appeared, bathing Khai's house in a shimmering light and a sweet aroma. Wrapped around the neck of the newly-born Vinh Hoa were seven strands of flowers, and a pearl was discovered in her clenched hand. Two characters, "HEAVEN'S WILL," were engraved on the pearl. Overcome by fear, Khai set up an altar to thank Heaven and Earth. He was advised, "Heaven has sent you a gem. Take good care of it."

When Vinh Hoa grew up, she was not only exquisitely beautiful and a skilled singer and musician, but she was also frighteningly clairvoyant. If on a blazing hot day she let slip, "It will rain in two days," then naturally it would. If she predicted that a person would die the next day, he would invariably drop dead, even if he had not been in the least bit sick. Nervous couples would appear before her: if she nodded, they would wed; if not, they would not.

Ngo Khai owned a silk shop near Restored Sword Lake. Whenever Vinh Hoa tended the shop, customers would flock inside and recklessly spend money as if they were at some sort of festival. Those who tried to cheat the shop would, on their way home, either be attacked by dogs or find their houses engulfed in flames.

People used to say:

> *Those with sense, avoid Vinh Hoa*
> *Steal five cents, you will lose your house*

In 1789, Nguyen Hue—known by his royal name, King Quang Trung—moved his troops northward to mop up the Chinese army and the final vestiges of the old regime and to reestablish order. Following the advice of Tran Van Ky, the king held a banquet for the heads of the great Northern families. Khai was invited.

Upon receiving the invitation, Khai consulted with Phuong, his chief attendant.

"I cannot go," said Khai. "Quang Trung is a great man and obviously very heroic, but I have long been a favorite of the deposed Le Kings and Trinh Lords. How can I accept this invitation? I'd be called an opportunist!"

"Your Excellency," Phuong responded, "it's meaningless to worry about being called an opportunist. Quang Trung is now strong, and common sense demands that we support the strong. Your Excellency must dine at the banquet. If you do not support Quang Trung, your fortune may be lost and no one will help you. The Tay Son armies will not hesitate to torch your estate and blame it on Ton Si Nghi. When they have done so, who will dare come to your aid? Needless to say, your family could be harmed and your servants, including myself, would be affected."

Khai laughed. "Your advice is very shrewd. I will follow it." So saying, Khai ordered Phuong to prepare offerings for the king.

In fact, Phuong was a scoundrel who had descended from buffalo merchants. For a long time he had intended to do in his master. To prepare gifts for the banquet, Phuong procured a large trunk, and placed inside it trinkets made from imitation gold and silver. He also packed several pieces of precious silk, but only after shredding them into tiny worthless bits. Oblivious to Phuong's machinations, Khai ordered the trunk delivered to the palace.

King Quang Trung's banquet was attended by the heads of several hundred of the richest families in the region. Khai was seated with the most honored guests.

"I am of peasant origin," said King Quang Trung. "I have risked my life to rescue and protect the four corners of the country. In war, I need strong men. In peace, I need wise men. You who have been invited here are all men of

---

5. Ton Si Nghi was the Chinese general who led the 1789 attack on Hanoi.

considerable property, which means that you must be wise. I hold this banquet for you. I ask you to develop trade and industry so as to make our country rich and our people strong."

Khai was happy to hear this. The atmosphere turned merry and all the guests pledged to make money for the good of the country.

With the food finished and the guests merry, King Quang Trung asked about the feast. Khai, who was a little tipsy, foolishly responded, "The food's not bad, but it's pathetically prepared. I feel nauseated."

The king smiled ominously but said nothing.

One after another, the guests presented gifts of pearls, gems, and exotic delicacies to the king. Quang Trung was delighted. At his turn, Khai ordered his servants to bring in the three large trunks. The trunks were opened, and everyone saw the imitation gold and silver trinkets and the tattered strips of silk. Khai went white and a panicky sensation swept over the guests. Furious, Quang Trung berated Khai, "You stupid clod. Oh, how you dishonor me! Heaven has allowed you to live up till now, and steal who knows how much of Heaven's blessings. You eat my good food, but can't keep your big mouth shut. You owe your wealth to the dumb luck of some ancestor. Go to hell! The Devil will skin you alive! I'll give you some real shit to eat, and we'll see what makes you nauseated!" So saying, the king grabbed a feather duster and lashed Khai across his mouth. He ordered Khai to lie prostrate, crammed a pile of shit into his mouth, stripped him from the waist down, and had him dragged back to his house.

Upon returning home, Khai felt great anguish and bitterness toward Phuong. But Phuong had already left. Puzzled and helpless, Khai watched as the Tay Son general, Dang Tien Dong, and his troops entered his house and confiscated all of his belongings. Khai wept and proclaimed his innocence but to no avail. Vinh Hoa, who had been listening from her chamber, came out and faced the Tay Son troops. She knelt before Dang Tien Dong and beseeched him. "Forgive us, General. This was the work of a wicked servant. My father is innocent. His insult to your authority was completely inadvertent. Please, General, be just. How can the trick of a simple buffalo merchant provoke such terrible retribution?" Struck by Vinh Hoa's unusual beauty, Dang Tien Dong dropped his sword. Worldly and educated, he understood the rarity of true beauty and heroism. He knew that to take these things for granted would be a violation of Heaven's will.

"The crime of your father should be punished with death," said Dong. "I don't have the power to pardon him. If you wish for him to be reprieved, you must go to the palace and entreat the king."

So saying, Dong ordered his troops to surround Khai's house and escorted Vinh Hoa off to the palace.

Dang Tien Dong entered the palace and consulted with King Quang Trung. Upon seeing Vinh Hoa, the king shuddered in awe and dropped a goblet of expensive wine. Vinh Hoa spoke very skillfully and the king was pleased. She responded to every question he asked. Her explanations ranged effortlessly from the past to the present, from the east to the west. The king's henchman, Tran Van Ky, and his like, sat listening, bathed in sweat. The king commanded Vinh Hoa to sing. She picked up the lute and began:

> *A five-colored cloud is a good omen,*
> *But nature's course always waxes and wanes*
> *Who knows when they will find one another?*
> *Your dreams are illusive on*
> *Your thousand-mile journey*
> *While you ride your elephant, beat drums of war,*
> > *or sack a city*
> *Do you recall how a firefly once flickered in your*
> > *small garden?*

*Do you recall the days when your decayed canine
                    tooth was treated by your mother?
Only the moon knows of your true sadness
Do you fear anything atop your high throne?
Your royal jade seal rules over the affairs of state,
But success or failure depends only on Heaven's will
In the material world of men
A wise man should not try to explain whether there is
                    a ghost or not
Time passes slowly, and he should tremble with fear*

The lute sounded cold. No one dared breathe. When Vinh Hoa finished, King Quang Trung asked softly, "The destiny of the Tay Son Dynasty will stretch over how many generations?"

Vinh Hoa responded, "Perhaps you should ask, 'Over how many days?'"

King Quang Trung kept Vinh Hoa in the palace and ordered Dang Tien Dong to withdraw his troops from Khai's house. Arriving there, Dong found that Khai had hanged himself. Quang Trung was filled with remorse, but it was too late. In the middle of the night, the king, his hair unkempt, his feet bare, hastily stumbled down to Vinh Hoa's room to tell her of Khai's death. Vinh Hoa set up an altar in the palace, burned incense, and prayed for her father's soul. "Do not fret, Your Majesty. Each person has his own destiny. Heaven gives life, but no one's parents live forever. If you have pity for me, please open your vaults and withdraw a peck of gold as a funeral offering." The king nodded in assent.

Later, the king explained himself to Tran Van Ky. "Naturally, I am hot-tempered. I have my reasons. Those rich bastards are all wicked. They care only about themselves. That's why no one stood up for Khai when he was in trouble."

"Your Majesty must understand the character of those wealthy families," Tran Van Ky said. "When have they ever pitied anyone? As it's said, 'Property-holders must be cruel; the truly wealthy must be as moral as humping dogs.'"

"If Khai were so clever and cautious, then how did he let himself be tricked by a wicked servant?" asked the king.

"Men's lives are full of misfortune," replied Ky. "Khai did not fear Heaven. He was selfish. Despite being fabulously rich, he kept his front door shut and ate alone. He helped no one, offered no charity, and was unconcerned with the happiness of others. He never shared his wealth with others and turned away from great men. How could he avoid misfortunes? Not only a buffalo merchant's trick, but even a small fly could destroy his fortune." The king nodded. To comfort Khai's soul, he ordered Phuong skinned alive and his bones fed to the dogs.

While Vinh Hoa resided in the palace, Quang Trung showed her kindness and sympathy. From mandarins down to soldiers, everyone treated her well. She spoke generously, behaved intelligently, and displayed great wisdom. The king's advisors and generals respected her. She did much to help the dynasty. The king admired and followed all of her suggestions, and they always proved correct. From time to time she would dance and sing for the enjoyment of the court. The king often said, "My Vinh Hoa is like a precious gem. She's worth thirty thousand men."

Despite the king's considerate behavior and unqualified affection towards her, Vinh Hoa refused all of his offers of marriage. Each of his proposals she would skillfully rebuff. The king felt very sad. Daily efforts brought him no closer to his objective.

With the pacification of the North complete, Quang Trung entrusted the court to his advisor Ngo Van So and moved his own troops and Vinh Hoa to Phu Xuan. Soon after the move, the king suddenly fell gravely ill. Vinh Hoa came to his deathbed. The king stared up at her without blinking. The court went into mourning. The king's son, Nguyen Quang Toan, attempted to close his father's eyes, but each time he lifted away his hands, the king's eyes would spring open. Queen Ngoc Han also tried, but to no avail. Finally, Vinh Hoa placed her little fingers on the king's eyelids and his eyes suddenly closed. Vinh Hoa's little fingers turned an ashen black and no amount of cleansing would wash out the stain.

Following Quang Trung's death, the Tay Son Dynasty fell into disarray. Nguyen Quang Toan moved his troops to Quy Nhon and attacked his uncle Nguyen Nhac. The Tay Son generals split into many factions and attacked each other. In 1801, King Gia Long (Nguyen Phuc Anh) sacked Phu Xuan, Nguyen Quang Toan fled to the North, and the Tay Son court collapsed. During the sack of Phu Xuan, Gia Long's general Truong Viet Thi entered the city, seized the royal palace and carried off the imperial harem, including Ngo Thi Vinh Hoa. Thi's soldiers broke into the vaults and gathered up the gold and silver. Originally of mixed parentage, Thi had been born in Ai Lao, where his family tended elephants. Although he served King Gia Long, Thi secretly despised him.

Arriving to oversee the pacification effort, Gia Long took careful stock of the Tay Son treasuries and saw that much was missing. He questioned Thi. "It seems that the Tay Son treasure flies, yet it has no wings."

"Since Nguyen Hue's death, the Tay Son has squandered its wealth," Thi said. "Only the rats are left."

"Are there no more imperial concubines?" asked Gia Long.

"Women are as slippery as snakes," Thi responded. "They immediately escape when their nest is disturbed. I couldn't do anything about it."

The king said nothing.

Later, it was secretly reported to King Gia Long that Thi's house was overflowing with gold, silver, and beautiful young girls. The king flew into a rage. That night, he went to Thi's house and, finding him asleep on a mat, ordered him bound and gagged. General Nguyen Van Thanh and the king surveyed the estate and saw that the secret report had been correct. The king turned to Thi, "So, you would suck from the scraps of an elephant's half-eaten sugar cane, you scoundrel. You've used my name to steal fortune and sleep with whores, haven't you?"

"Forgive me, Your Majesty," pleaded Thi. "I have served you from the very beginning, sleeping on thorn mattresses and eating gallbladder. I've endured many hardships for you. Now, with your ambition realized, I wanted to enjoy myself. I only saw it as just payment for my services."

The king smiled ominously. "You think your services are so great? You have been by my side, but you've never understood me. Don't talk of your services to me. You have merely played in my games. And what kind of games are ever just? You broke my law and now you must pay. Don't say that I am cruel!"

"Your Majesty! Your Majesty!" Thi begged again. "What are you saying? In what kind of game do tens of thousands of men die in battle?"

"War is the game of Heaven," replied the king. "I play a different game. I play the games of kings."

"Your Majesty," Thi pleaded, "have pity on me. Take back the gold and silver. Leave me only Ngo Thi Vinh Hoa!"

The king became even more furious. "You stupid fool! One foot in the grave and still you're horny! I'll slice off your balls and make you eat shit." So saying, the king ordered Thi's balls cut off, crammed a pile of shit into his mouth, and had him dragged back to his native village.

The king entered the room where Ngo Thi Vinh Hoa was kept. As the door opened, he saw that she was tied up and that not a single stitch of clothing covered her body. The servants said that Thi had planned to defile her, but that she refused to submit to him. The king pitied her. He approached and was struck by her exquisite beauty. Suddenly, a sensation of dizziness swept over him. The aroma wafting up from Vinh

Hoa's vagina was as fragrant as a milk flower. The king swooned, fell on the ground, and lost consciousness.

Vinh Hoa moved into the palace where the king adored and pampered her. She gradually recovered and became as pretty and fresh as a new leaf in the spring. He loved her singing and dancing and was greatly pleased by her prophesies. He wanted to make her his wife.

"Your Majesty," Nguyen Van Thanh counseled him, "Vinh Hoa lived with Nguyen Hue for many years, but he dared not touch her. I beg your Majesty to protect your dragon body."

"Hue was foolish," responded the king. "He respected the spirit but disdained the flesh."

"Do you want Vinh Hoa for her spirit or for her flesh?" asked Thanh.

"For a general, you're quite stupid," replied Gia Long. "A king's maintenance of the country is a spiritual matter, but his maintenance of himself is a material affair." Thanh shook his head and left the room.

The king entered the palace looking for Ngo Thi Vinh Hoa.

"I want you to be mine," he said. "I want to possess you as one possesses a duck or a chicken."

"Why does Your Majesty want to be the king of the ducks or the king of the chickens?" Vinh Hoa replied.

The king sighed. "The fate of a king is a wicked fate. He must display his power in the most exalted ways. He has no right to be vile."

Vinh Hoa responded, "It's the same for everyone." So saying, she picked up her lute and began to sing:

> *Is the country still here?*
> *Is the country still strong?*
> *The king is the great root of his people*
> *A tall tree can cast a long shadow*
> *It can shade everyone in the realm*

> *But winds and clouds can change quickly*
> *Remember deep in your heart that*
> *When attempting a great endeavor*
> *It's important to maintain one's virtue*
> *The correct way, and imperial perfection*

Transfixed by the dreamy sounds of the lute, the king hung his head down on the table and fell asleep. When he awoke, Vinh Hoa was gone. All that remained were the following words scrawled into the table:

> *Fortune comes; the wind blows it towards the*
> *Da River*

The king searched everywhere, but could not find Vinh Hoa. Not long afterwards, some people in Da Bac (in the district of Hung Hoa) discovered the corpse of an aristocratic-looking woman drifting in a river. In her arms she held a small child. Local officials reported the information to the court. Attendants sent by King Gia Long to investigate recognized that the dead woman looked identical to Ngo Thi Vinh Hoa. The king made a generous offering to her spirit and erected a shrine in her honor. Some Muong villagers took in the child and raised it as their own. The king had the following couplet hung in the shrine:

> *She served two kings yet kept a virgin heart.*
> *Through the ages her chastity remained intact.*

Translated by Peter Zinoman

Rain

*"I regard myself as the kind of person
who inexplicably becomes a victim
of his own sophistication."*
—Nguyen Du

Darling,

*I begin this story at eight o'clock in the morning in the
shabbiest coffee shop in town. There are no other guests,
nobody to bother me. It's raining.*

*I sit here writing. Your face appears to me. You are far
away. Where are you? All my thoughts are directed toward
you. You appear very clearly. You sit next to me, giving order
to these incoherent words. On that day in my memory, it is
also raining, raining cats and dogs. You and I sit in a dark
corner. In front of us are two women, a short one and a tall
one, both beautiful. I tell you to pay attention to the tall one,
the one with long, free-flowing hair, who leans back in her
chair every time she laughs.*

*You ask me her name. I say, "Does it matter what she's
called? People's names are just a kind of label. I call her N."*

You say, "So, the one sitting next to her is M then?"

I say, "Yes."

"The thing is," M said, "You don't understand at all what
he's like. He'll ruin your life. I beg you, don't love him!"

"No, I don't love him. I'm not insane." N took a flower
from the table and shredded it. "But he's so kind and
intelligent. Being around him, I can learn something, don't
you think?"

"From men, women can't learn a thing. They're only
good at throwing you on the bed and seducing you with sweet
words. We think we got lucky. We believe it's love or human
nature. In fact, life is over."

"Why are you so cynical?" N sighed. They were quiet for a moment. One could hear the sound of the falling rain.

N said, "He recites poetry in a deep voice. It's indescribably beautiful."

"Poetry, now! What guy who wants to seduce a woman doesn't write poetry? They have composed poetry without a break from the stone age until now, for four thousand years so far."

"You seem so strange today. But you yourself got married. Aren't you happy?"

"Well, I don't know. Of course I am. But this husband of mine is terribly roguish. I know he betrays everyone. I don't understand why I thought so highly of him before I got married."

N giggled. As she was laughing her hair flowed down along the side of the chair.

"Let me have one of your cigarettes. Since I got married I have to smoke in secret. If my husband finds out, he'll beat me."

"It's your own fault. Didn't I tell you that he's no good? I hate him. I've never ever heard him speak the truth."

"Well, it's all fate. What can you do? For me it's as good as over. I'll get pregnant, go to the hospital and—I don't know why I think this—afterwards I'll be paralyzed and that'll be the end of my life. But you, I beg you, do not love him!"

"No, I don't love him. I'm not insane."

"Swear it. I beg you. Do not love him."

You ask, "Why would they be like that? Why would they discourage love?"

I say, "Don't worry. No one as admirable as she is would ever pledge her word so lightly."

M sat there smoking. The tip of her cigarette glowed bright red.

"I beg you. Don't love him. Swear it!"

"No! Don't force me to swear. That's ridiculous."

"Don't you understand what a bad person he can be? He'll do whatever he likes. He can even become violent."

"I hear you."

"I used to know him. He detests people. Someone like this does not respect anybody."

"But he's very kind to me. Sweet, even."

"You don't understand a thing. He's kind to everyone. He's false! He doesn't care about anything. Have you noticed the way he spends money? If he had the wealth of an entire nation in his hands, he'd spend it all in five minutes."

"His poems are very unusual."

"Poetry again! If you keep on dreaming like this, you are doomed. He only wants to amuse himself. Have you seen him play hackeysack with that kid for six hours straight? Just think about how much work one could do in six hours."

"Pretty cute, isn't it?"

"Cute? What do you mean by cute? It's crazy!"

They sat in silence. One could hear the sound of the falling rain.

"I beg you. Be careful! Do you know what it means to be loved by a guy like that?"

"No. How could I?"

"Your heart could break in a second. You don't get it. He does whatever he wants. When he's in love, he forgets everything else. It'll make you really miserable. And it's embarrassing."

"Why embarrassing?"

"Do you live as if you're all alone? You still have friends, parents, your grandmother, and there's your work, too."

"Yeah, grandma is very difficult."

"What next? He'll push everyone else aside. Then, he'll laugh it all off. It's a hideous laugh. For him, nothing has any value. I forbid you to love him!"

"I know."

"I beg you. Don't love him."

"His poems are very unusual. They have no beginning or end. Here. Listen to this one:

> *For this reason I rise at midnight,*
> *wandering the city streets ...*

"For what reason?"

"Who knows? I asked him the same question. He laughed. He doesn't understand it all himself. He just pointed to the sky."

"See what I mean? That's crazy!"

"And it goes on like this:

> *I pluck a hair from my leg*
> *to see whether it's anything like a buffalo hair.*
> *I have signed a contract*
> *and strive to drive the wind back*
> *into that desolate room of mine ...*

M sat up straight.

"He signed a contract with the devil. For sure. I know. He doesn't interact with people, only with ghosts."

"He could die from the most trivial accident. He's extraordinarily credulous."

"Enough. I beg you. Stop dreaming. Credulous, not credulous, it doesn't make any difference."

"Really, I've never met a person as admirable. So warm, and he's as deep as the dark night. Honest as well."

"You are so weak."

They sat in silence. One could hear the sound of the falling rain.

"Again, I beg you. Do not love him."

"I hear you."

You ask, "What is love?" I say, "It's the most refined level of virtue. Not everyone understands that." You ask, "Why do people write poetry when they're in love?" I say, "Love brings out talent. Poetry is the most ordinary kind of talent." You ask, "What type of talent is not ordinary?" I say, "There's one kind that isn't." You ask, "And you know what it is?" I say, "Yes." You ask, "Do you have it?" I say, "Yes." You say, "In that case I love you."

"Again, I beg you. Don't love him."

"I hear you."

"Let me tell you a story. Once upon a time, he loved a young woman. She belonged to an educated family. Do you know what a chaste and noble young woman is like? Her lips are always a deep warm red. Her eyes shine blue like the shell of a starling's egg. This young woman was brought up on fairy tales and fragrant rice with fine pork sausages. A young woman who grows up like this has the clearest white skin."

"Enough, stop describing her. I can't stand it. A chaste and noble young woman, that's really unbearable."

"Yes, you're right. But, still, he approached her, even though he had to know that nothing could harm her more than his love. I do believe he loved her madly. A girl like this, how could he not love her madly? He probably thought that by being near her he'd grow calm, stop being restless. He would mend his ways and no longer be some ruffian loitering about."

M fell silent, she lit another cigarette. The tip of her cigarette glowed bright red. One could hear the sound of the falling rain.

"So, you can't really call him unrefined. He merely dared to get close to her. It was more than love. He admired her. He worshipped her in the way that people worship the spirit of General Tran."

"Why General Tran?"

"Because this love was platonic. Only love for a saint can be that way."

"I understand. It's kind of strange. I think he's gotten bolder now."

"Be quiet! I beg you, don't think about him any more."

"I hear you."

"The two of them were like two people in a dream. She withered because of him. Imagine it. A young girl just coming of age, learning about love for the first time. And this guy, a hairy, sweaty, greasy goat who laughs and talks like a gangster. He'd think nothing of standing on his head in front of her parents! Her father is an intellectual. He has photographs of famous people hanging on the walls. He loves classical literature, classical music, and classical politics. And that guy—he makes music by sticking two fingers in his mouth."

"It's kind of funny, don't you think?"

"What's funny about it? Once, he caught a lizard and put it on the table. He explained society by describing that creature. According to him, the head represented the superstructure, the legs were the base, and the tail was ethics. He said that when the tail of the lizard falls off, it will simply grow back all over again. Ethics, he said, can wag like a tail, disconnected from everything else."

"That's too much!"

"Right. If even you can admit it, then how could anyone else stand it?"

"It's unbearable, really."

"I beg you. Do not love him!"

"All right. So what happened to his love for that girl?"

"He seduced her. Or she seduced him. Who knows? These are passionate people. Let's say they seduced each other. If he went for only a day without seeing her, he'd start picking fights. As I tell you this, I realize that one cannot really complain about a love like that. Really, if you can't call that love, then I don't know what love is."

"I understand completely."

"There you go, thinking about him again, right? I forbid it. I beg you. Do not love him."

"I hear you. Now, go on with the story."

M continued smoking. Silence. One could hear the sound of the falling rain.

You say, "Basically, life is sad, isn't that right?" I say, "But love isn't." You ask, "Which of the two is happy?" I say, "One just let go of happiness. And the other has happiness in her hands, but if she isn't careful then she'll also lose it."

M continued telling the story.

"They loved each other. He wanted to marry her. Everyone stood in their way. He persuaded her to run away with him."

"Where to? "

"Certainly to some really backward place."

"Why backward?"

"In a civilized place, who would have him? Nothing for him is too high, or too low."

"So did they escape?"

"Right at the last minute she changed her mind and broke her promise. She didn't go with him."

"God damn!"

"Yeah."

"Did he come back?"

"A guy like that? What would he come back for? His noble feelings are those of a devil, not a human being. He knew better than to sacrifice his life for a coward, even if she was chaste, with deep warm red lips and the clearest white skin."

"He just took off?"

"Right. He took off straight away. He was gone without a trace. He is especially discerning when it comes to humiliation."

"And then?"

"She fell seriously ill. He had some medicine sent, but

she refused to take it. How could medicine help? Time passed. Her life began to waste away. She realized that she wouldn't find a second man like him."

They sat in silence. One could hear the sound of the falling rain.

"Again, I beg you. Don't love him. He doesn't have a generous heart. He doesn't forgive anyone. As for you, you mustn't love him. He's a devil."

N rummaged in her pockets, then put a small photograph on the table.

"Here's his picture."

"Really, I beg you. Don't love him. Burn this picture. Tear it up."

"You do it."

"No! You have to do it with your own hands. Tear it into pieces."

N took the photograph from the table and quietly shredded it. Lightning flared brightly. Thunder. One could hear the sound of the falling rain.

"Wicked!"

"Who are you calling wicked?"

"You don't get it. You have no idea how mean and wicked life became for her after this love affair ended."

"Is she still alive?"

"No, she's dead! Her soul has died. All that's left is her body. She turned into a despicable person. She got married. Her husband is also rotten to the bone. He's a thief. He hits her every time she smokes."

"I don't understand. What are you saying?"

"There. I'm sorry. But you've already torn up the picture. You did what I asked you to do."

They sat in silence. One could hear the sound of the falling rain. Suddenly both of them burst out crying. M said, her voice muffled in tears, "Forgive me. But do you think I will forgive you, just because you tore up the picture?"

"What do you mean? What's wrong with you?"

"You still don't understand? Do you think that I told you all this simply to put my heart at ease? To make myself feel better? Don't you understand that I have torn every single shred of meat from my heart?"

"What are you talking about?"

"Do you think that I'll forgive you for being so cruel? Never. Now do you understand? If I could, I would abandon my husband to follow this man. If he went to prison, I would bring him food every day. I'd follow him to the end of the world, only if he would come back to me. But he'll never come back."

"My God. Why are you telling me this?"

"Why? Don't you understand? Because I don't want him to fall into the hands of another woman—into your hands."

N got up and left. A moment later, M also left. One could hear the sound of the falling rain. The rain sounded indescribably sad.

You say, "Basically, life is sad, isn't that right?" I say, "No." You ask, "Who is this man the two were talking about?" I say, "I don't know." You ask, "A worker, a peasant, or a craftsman?" I say, "I don't know." You say, "Perhaps he's an artist, because she read his poem." I say, "You call that poetry? Do you want to hear my poems? Mine also talk about the plucking of hairs." You say, "No, another time. But I feel uneasy, because I don't know who he is. I noticed that the photograph she had was from a newspaper. He must be a politician." I say, "I don't know." You say, "He must be really admirable."

Rain.

It is still raining. Your face appears to me. You are far away. Where are you? All my thoughts are directed toward you. Now it is two o'clock in the afternoon. I've been writing this story for six hours. Six hours without a break.

Six hours. The principal character in this story played hackeysack for six hours. That scoundrel! That immortal fool!

Rain

Where are you?
Outside, it's raining.
When are you coming back? When, darling?

Translated by Birgit Hussfeld

Life's So Fun

A small house on the hill, thirty meters from the main road. A solitary, forlorn house. Behind the house are two thorny trees with red leaves, the kind that grow in the wild, useful only for firewood.

A small flagstone-lined footpath leads up to the house from the bottom of the hill. After twenty steps, the path opens onto a clearing; a foundation for a new house was planned for this spot, then later abandoned. From this clearing to the house are sixteen more steps.

This house was made to be temporary, with giant bamboo pillars, a thatched roof and mud walls. Foresters built it as a shelter several years ago when they were digging holes to plant sandalwood and pine.

The house is almost empty. The only noteworthy piece of furniture is a beat-up bed made of lumber from a jackfruit tree. Children have carved their wishes and sorrows into the side of the bed: the sorrows are sublime and absolute, while the wishes are bodacious. At the end of the bed is a heart pierced by an arrow, carved by a playboy perhaps.

Hanging on a wall right in the middle of the house is an altar made from a piece of bent tin. The incense bowl is the kind normally used for eating beanthread noodles. Beside the altar, on the left, hangs a mirror next to a film poster of the Hong Kong actress Mai Diem Phuong. A poem has been handwritten on Mai Diem Phuong's pure white bosom, near her neck. The words are mediocre:

> *There are no heroes in our time.*
> *One goes without a soulmate.*
> *At night, a beauty turns on her pillow,*
> *Wiping silent tears.*

An iron cooking tripod sits in one corner of the house. The charcoal beneath it is cold. Next to it lies a water bucket, a pot, a pan, and a woven basket for holding dishes.

A boy sits on the bed, leaning against the rolled-up comforter. He's about six. There are no traces of hatred or anguish on his face. Those things will come later. There are also no traces of generosity or boredom. Those things will also come later. It's an unharried face.

The boy turns his eyes to the door. His mother has locked it from the outside. She has gone to the market to buy books and pens so that he can go to school tomorrow. He's in the first grade.

The boy sits up. He gazes curiously at a wasp as it builds its nest. The wasp fetches little balls of earth from a wet corner near the water bucket and carries them back to a spot near the door latch, where it patiently shapes them into a thin vault. The wasp flies back and forth dozens of times, never varying its flight pattern.

The wasp flits by the boy's face. The boy notices the wasp's narrow waist. On it are curving wrinkles. A female wasp.

In the boy's young mind appears the image of his mother. His mother's belly is flabby, with curving wrinkles also. This morning his mother hitched a ride on Mr. Hao's coal truck.

The boy does not like Mr. Hao. Mr. Hao has a beard. The boy can remember when Mr. Hao said, "You slut! Your belly's going to burst!"

The boy's mother just laughed.

Mr. Hao then said, "A fat girl! A dogface!"

The boy's mother laughed again.

The wasp flits by his face. Yellowish traces tint its two wings. On the boy's mother's cheekbone is an indentation, with a yellowish trace of its own. The boy touched it once and noticed that his fingertips were wet.

Mr. Hao said: "A woman's tears! Cow piss!"

His mother laughed again.

"You'll leave me, Son," she has told the boy. "Just like your father did."

A wasp is raising a spider.
When the spider's grown, he'll leave.
The wasp sits by himself, sobbing,
"Spider! Spider! Where did you go?"

The boy asked his mother, "Where did Daddy go?"

His mother sighed. "Your father was a wolf. He went hunting. He ran after women."

The boy saw a wolf once. The wolf ran along the edge of the woods, nervous, impatient, his tail between his legs, his tongue hanging out. The wolf was afraid. He was alone. The boy was not afraid of him.

Mr. Hao also seems filthy, like a wolf. Mr. Hao once said, "I'm tired of life. I'm so tired of life."

Mr. Hao was lying on the bed, his feet propped on the wall.

He sang:

Girl, my lover, with your tender lips,
And your distant, dreamy eyes,
I've been chasing you all my life...

The boy feels hungry. He goes to the dish basket to find something to eat. Before leaving, his mother left a treat for him: cold rice with boiled bananas. The road to town is thirty kilometers. Mr. Hao's truck won't be back until the afternoon.

The boy squats in one corner of the house and peels his bananas. He arranges several bowls, then bites pieces of banana to place into them. The boy pretends it's a holiday feast he's prepared for his mother, himself, and the stranded traveler who once arrived at the house in the rain. The boy's mother also cooked for the guest, a tall man with a booming voice. When he walked around, the entire house shook.

The guest said, "It's all nonsense. There's no gold to be dug. I watched all those people digging for gold and I felt pity for them, and disgust. I felt like laughing. Everywhere is viciousness, lust, treachery, greed—"

The boy says, "Here, sir, you have the tastiest piece."

He eats a piece of banana. He can remember saying to the guest, "Please, eat."

The guest laughed. "This kid's all right. To be a man, and cross an ocean of deceit, an ocean of romance, it smashes up your life. If you have either cash or kindness to keep you afloat, then you're lucky. Otherwise, you suffer. Fire tests gold. Gold tests women. Women test men. Men test the demons and the angels. As it turns out, there are only demons. Very few angels..."

The boy remembers the wolf at the edge of the woods, his tail between his legs.

The guest, holding the boy in his lap, clapped in time and sang a song of the gold diggers:

> *If there's gold, then we can eat, then we can play.*
> *Life's so fun!*
> *If there's gold, then we're dead, then we're done.*
> *Life's so fun!*

The boy doesn't eat any more. The guest came and then he went.

"Goodbye, Miss. Goodbye Kuanyin, Goddess of Mercy. Goodbye Bodhisattva. I'm leaving now."

"My son and I say goodbye to you. As you go, we hope that your feet will be hard and that the rocks will be soft...But where will you go? To your home village?"

"Why would I go back there?" the guest chuckled. "I have more traveling to do. Life's still fun. Why would I go home? The human heart is black, the land is barren."

The boy knows nothing about his own home village. His mother has often promised to take him there, but she never has the money. She said they know many people there. Although the boy's grandparents have died, their graves are there so his mother hopes to go back to light incense for them. And then there are uncles and aunts and friends, like Aunt Luot, Aunt Na, Uncle Suu, Uncle Ben.

Mr. Hao also talks often about going back to his village. He's gone back three times, and each time he returns a little sadder.

Mr. Hao said, "My home village has this huge communal hall. It's fun during festivals. The women watch the men wrestle each other. When I was small, my friends would dare me to slap girls and women on the butt, a penny for each one. I made lots of money that way and could gorge myself on whatever I wanted to eat at the festival."

The boy's mother laughed, "Three years old and you were already horny."

Mr. Hao shook his head. "It's the ones with the money who were horny! Because I was destined to be poor, I had to leave my village in shame."

The boy's mother said, "I heard you left your village to chase girls."

Mr. Hao said, "Slut! Dogface! Shut up!"

Then he began to sing:

> *I leave. I leave. I'm not afraid of hardship.*
> *I surge forward, unleashing my masculinity.*
> *My determination hovers above the clouds.*

The boy's mother laughed, "Men are no mystery to me! You people are only after gold and women. That's all!"

Mr. Hao said, "Slut! Dogface! Shut up!"

Then he sang some more:

March forward, towards the red dawn,
Satisfy your male lust for adventure,
View death as nothing but a red feather,
How many will have their bones covered with
horse hide...

The boy stands up and tries to hear the sounds of the truck. He knows it's useless to do that. His mother won't come back for a while yet.

No sound can filter into the house except the sound of the wind. The wind blows quietly, in waves, like a man snoring. He can tell by the partitions of the house, knocking against one another.

The boy tilts his face to look at the hole in the roof. A small hole, only the size of a nickel. Sunlight slipping into the house through the hole creates a light beam filled with minuscule dust particles. The boy opens his hand to receive the light beam. Light fills his hand.

The boy remembers how the guest picked up a clump of dirt with his hand. The guest said to the boy's mother, "If this dirt could be turned into gold, then the game would be over. That's the wish of every ordinary man on this earth. But all of it is nonsense!"

"What do you need money for?" the boy's mother asked. "We women live for love."

Mr. Hao said, "Slut! Dogface! Shut up!"

The guest shook his head, "It takes a lot of effort to earn love. You can strive your whole life and still not succeed."

The boy's mother cried, "We women are very gullible, always empty inside, always lacking love. Whenever anyone starts to talk about love, we just dive right in and lose ourselves."

The guest laughed, "It's a pity. But that's what it's like to be a woman."

Mr. Hao said, "That's what you get! Slut! Dogface!" Then, he added, "Women are evil witches. That's why they feel a lack of love. Does a man ever feel a lack of love? Hurray for men! Hurray for the old billy goats!"

The guest crumbled the clump of dirt, then sprinkled it on the ground as if he were sowing seeds. He waved his hand, "Fly away. Fly away, hatred. Fly away, deceit. Fly away, injustice. Fly away, base desires."

The guest straightened his clothes, then stood up. When he walked, the whole house shook.

The guest pulled from his bag a bundle of cloth and gave it to the boy's mother, "Goodbye, Bodhisattva. Goodbye, Miss. Take this to feed the child. It's not much, but it may help you make it through this stretch."

The guest laughed, then waved his hand in an incomprehensible gesture, some sort of symbolism. The rain came down steadily. It was the spring rainy season.

The boy goes over to the bed. He leans his back against the spot where the arrow pierces the heart. The arrow sticks out of his shoulder.

He looks around for the wasp, but can't see it anywhere now. The nest is only half finished, with its trace of wet earth. The boy sighs. The wasp nest is built right by the door latch. When the door opens, the nest will be destroyed.

He hears a faint noise somewhere. Not outside, but inside the house. The boy listens. It sounds as if someone or something is trying to sneak into the house. The boy feels frightened. He shudders. Beads of sweat pool near the roots of his hair. He scans his surroundings. His instinct was correct: he catches a glimpse of a long shadow in the dark corner where the pots are. But what kind of a shadow? The boy begins to shake. He curls his legs onto the bed and backs his body up against the wall. It is clearly a shadow. But what kind of a shadow?

A faint, wet, and surreptitious noise. The boy's body shakes violently. He has never heard such a noise before. He clearly saw a shadow. The light in the house suddenly darkens, becomes murky and colder. What kind of a shadow?

The boy feels his heart contracting. He doesn't dare breathe. Again, a long something in the corner. He can sense such things without seeing them.

"Mama..."

The boy curls his body into a ball. He screams. Tears stream from his eyes. His fists press against his body. He slams a foot against the hard surface of the bed. Clearly, something is crawling slowly, anxiously, determinedly, coldly, beneath the bed.

Bang! The boy hears the sound of glass breaking, of something dragging across the floor, of bones being gnawed. A faint chewing sound, greedy, deliberate. Sounds of marrow being sucked. Of bones being shattered. Also, of lips smacking.

The boy feels dizzy. He feels a pain in his chest. He can't catch his breath. Tears stream from his eyes. His face turns plum red.

"Mama! Mama!"

He screams in desperation. He convulses on the bed. He has no more doubts. He can hear bones being chewed. Marrow being sucked. Lips being smacked. Gnawing.

The boy sobs. He lies with his face buried in the comforter. He loses consciousness.

The house is still, with only the shrill sound of wind from the outside. After a long time, the boy wakes up. He peeps around cautiously. Sweat drenches his face.

He listens. The house is oddly quiet. He hears nothing. Nothing.

The boy pinches his own leg. It hurts. He gets on his hands and knees, and eyes the steel rod his mother has propped at the end of the bed, a weapon against intruders. He moves stealthily toward the steel rod.

The boy holds his breath. He lifts the steel rod and holds it firmly. He listens, but can't hear a single sound. It's oddly quiet.

The boy smacks the steel rod against the bed, then listens again. It's still quiet.

He breathes quietly. He gathers his strength, then crawls stealthily towards the edge of the bed. He looks beneath it. Nothing.

The boy puts his feet on the ground, trying not to shake. He pokes the steel rod around beneath the bed. Nothing. A shapeless anger fills his chest. He pokes the steel rod into the water bucket, into the pot and the pan. He smashes the mirror. He pokes around all over the house—along the floor, across the walls, into the thatch roof. He knocks everything over. Nothing. Still silent. A frightful silence.

The boy listens. The wind outside has stopped entirely. The boy feels that all the air inside the house is stagnant and weighing upon his body. He feels compressed. He shakes violently, the steel rod falling from his hand. He collapses onto the floor. His nerves have turned to mush. He can't move.

The boy lies there curled up, his face to the floor, right where there's a puddle. His heart pounds frantically, chaotically, in panic, at times stopping its beat altogether. He has no strength left. He tries to open his eyes but simply can't.

His lips move silently. He wants to call out to his mother but cannot push out a single sound from inside his chest.

The boy lies still like that for a very long time. It is not clear how much time has passed. The wasp has finished building its nest. The boy's pudgy face has drained of all liquid, of all blood. It is washed out and dried up.

The solitary, locked house lies on the hill. The rain comes down steadily. It is the spring rainy season.

It's not until noon that the truck carrying the boy's mother returns. The bearded driver opens the door for the boy's mother to get out.

A woman with a pock-marked face, swollen perhaps because of beriberi, smiles coquettishly as she pulls from the cab two filthy reed baskets. The driver closes the cab door, then yanks the reed baskets from the woman's hands. He is cranky: "Slut! Dogface!"

The woman stops and notices a smudge of blood on her pants leg.

Embarrassed, she turns, squats down quickly, and grabs a handful of grass from the edge of the path.

The driver turns his face toward the two thorny trees with their red leaves. He sings softly:

> *Girl, my lover, with your tender lips,*
> *And your distant, dreamy eyes,*
> *I've been chasing you all my life...*

The woman, finished cleaning up the trace of blood, gets up and walks hastily toward the house. The driver walks behind her, carrying the bags. It appears he has suddenly remembered something. He says, "Listen...listen, slut!"

The woman turns around, her face worried, waiting.

The driver sighs, "Listen, that man who stayed here that rainy day is dead."

The woman seems bewildered, "How do you know?"

The driver shakes his disheveled head and seems baffled. "Gold diggers shafted the guy. They thought he had money, but it turned out he had nothing on him."

The woman, silent, turns around to resume her walk up the hill. Nine more flagstones and she'll be home.

A small house on the hill. A solitary, forlorn house. The spring rain falls steadily on the thatched roof. The spring rain falls steadily on the two thorny trees with their red leaves. The spring rain falls steadily on the hill.

The spring rain in this damp weather is bad for the rice crop and brings many worms. The spring rain from the beginning of March until now has lasted fourteen days.

Translated by Linh Dinh

Love Story Told on a Rainy Night

While in the Northwest, I knew a Thai man named Bac Ky Sinh. I met him through a chance encounter. This is what happened:

One day I went to the Muong La Market. Set alongside the mountain road, the market was bustling, with genuine and fake merchandise all tossed in together. The Thai and Xa girls sold peaches, plums, wild pears, and other fruit gathered from up in the mountains; there were stalls of printed cloth, thermoses, pots, and other Chinese imports one could find anywhere. Hmong men and women led horses bearing baskets of cardamom seeds, ginseng, and herbs, as well as their exceptional sticky rice, an incomparable variety, pink as if with dye, truly fragrant and sticky.

Muong La Market opens in the early morning when the mist is thick. People go to market as if in a dream, unable to see farther than an arm's length. The mist in the high mountains is different from the mist on the plains. It is weighty; it is like a curtain of thin milk, vast and mysterious, unfanciful, harmless; it is mountain air that has dissipated and recondensed; it is not the vapor, made of water, dust, and light rain, that is called mist down on the plains.

Around noon, when the mist had cleared, the market was most animated. The Hmong gathered around the thang co pots, drinking liquor and playing their khen pipes. The Thai and the Xa, too, drank and played their khen pipes. The Lahu played their leaf pipes. The Thai, Xa, and Dao girls stood in clusters and sang duets, love songs, and courting songs with the young men. Some people felt inspired to fire a few rounds into the air with their flintlocks, and the crowd around them scrambled like bees from a broken hive.

I went to the market with no intent to buy or sell a thing. And many others had come as I had. A mountain market is a meeting place, a gathering place, a small festival, a playground. It is a place for people to escape their bland, ordinary lives.

I walked along the market road, and when I reached the end I turned and walked back. At the center of the market an old Chinese man sat telling fortunes. Before him was a plate with three dice. Customers put their money down, placed the dice in a dry gourd, shook it hard, and rolled them into a dish. They called this "divination." From the sum of the dice the old man deduced his customers' destinies. People oohed and aahed, appreciative and terrified. Everyone was sincere and credulous. Something like a mystery, like a threat, like a daring deception, wavered over the heads of the crowd. I felt cheered, oddly excited, and I too moved forward to test my fate. At that moment someone grabbed my arm. I turned around and saw a Thai fellow in a dyed blue shirt and pants, wearing a beret and an honest face. He spoke Vietnamese fluently, shaking his head. "Don't believe a thing! It's a con! Come, look at this."

The fellow held up something blackened from a kitchen fire, dirty and unimaginably putrid. It looked like dried chicken gizzard. "Bear gall. One hundred percent. I shot the bear in Xop Cop. It weighed 137 kilos. I'll sell it to you, very cheap."

Laughing, I shook my head. I knew how people made fake bear gall from the gall of pigs. I also knew that people used a syringe to extract real bear gall from its sac, and then refill it somehow with plain water. The Thai fellow pleaded for a bit, and made a final show of great disappointment. After raising his arms to the sky and lamenting in Thai, he walked away. When I turned back to where I had been, I noticed my wristwatch was gone. I was angry and shocked. I was so young then! The feeling that someone had deceived me, tricked me, fooled me, led me by the nose because I was so gullible, made me lose all self-control. To a poor, insignificant teacher, that wristwatch had been a priceless possession; it was my treasure, it was my pride, even though it never kept the right time.

I crossed the market looking for the bear-gall salesman so I could give him the lesson he deserved. And then I saw a Thai girl leading a horse in my direction. She was young, beautiful, with shallow, remote eyes that were wise and somewhat bold. Two old men followed her, clutching gamecocks.

The girl greeted me. "Uh, sir, can I ask you to watch my horse a minute for me?"

I was flustered and didn't know what to say. She shoved the tether into my hand, and said, "Sir, stand here at the side of the road. Just a second, I'll be right back." She smiled, a smile full of promises, and then she walked away. The two men who had been following her settled immediately in the middle of the road and let go of their gamecocks. At once, the two birds went at each other in unrestrained combat. An unruly crowd gathered around, crazed and unimaginably absorbed.

A shout came to clear the road, and a jeep drove up with several police officers and a prisoner in handcuffs. The jeep had to stop because the crowd watching the cockfight was blocking the road. When several officers climbed down from the jeep the crowd hollered louder and surrounded the officers. Mud and sand clouded the air. Out of nowhere a wasp nest appeared and burst open just above the crowd. People fell and kicked each other and yelled to each other to flee. Before I could figure out what to do, the Thai girl appeared and seized the tether. The prisoner jumped quickly from the jeep onto the back of the horse. I only had time to notice his long hair and his dyed blue shirt and pants. The Thai girl leapt on behind him and at once they galloped through the stalls and booths and towards the Ta Bu forest, on the left bank of the Da River.

I was arrested and taken to the police station. At first

they thought I was involved in helping the prisoner escape, but when there wasn't enough evidence to indict me they made me a witness. I had to sign my name to an extremely sloppy, vaguely worded statement.

I learned that the prisoner was a bandit. His name was Bac Ky Sinh.

* * *

The mountain school where I lived and taught was on a bare hill known as Pine Hill, though there wasn't a single pine on it. On a level plot of land, three rows of classrooms had been built of bamboo thatch and leaves. They looked like stables. In those days the neighboring teachers' quarters had tile roofs and plaster walls, but when the rain fell, they leaked more than the thatched buildings. By nature I preferred independence, so I lived in a small house apart from the others, surrounded by its own fence. In my place I had the pleasure of a free man—which is to say I was free to let myself fall into loneliness without anyone peeking in on me—and I depended on no one. In our country, to make oneself lonely was the cheapest and safest way to create the illusion of freedom. Such an illusion didn't really change anything, but provided the discipline that was necessary in youth, when it is natural to become infatuated and corrupted.

The summer of that year I had to stay to look after and guard the school. Torrential rains and floods dragged on from early July into mid-September, making my home nothing less than an oasis. My supply of rice was nearly exhausted. I felt morose and sorry for myself. I could have become ill and died in vain in that remote and forsaken place. I had seen the graves of unnamed teachers who had died that way in Muong Hum and Chieng Co, and even in Chi Village out at the end of Route 19. After pondering my options, I decided to cross the Chieng Sa Valley and look for help in Po Mat Village. I put on my raincoat and carried at my side my rust-eaten,

241

blocked-up shotgun, which I brought for show, though in fact it was completely useless. I found the road and descended into the valley.

No matter how hard I tried I couldn't cross the flooded valley. I didn't dare risk it because I didn't know the terrain, and if I were washed into a crevasse I would clearly perish. Hopeless, with the dark approaching, I returned home, where I was surprised to see a light on in my house.

A wood fire had just been kindled in the middle of the room. A Thai man sat, at ease, grilling a grouse. When he saw me he didn't lift his eyes but looked to the side, warily judging my shotgun.

"You are the master of the house?" he asked after I had hung the gun up on the wall.

I nodded dejectedly. The Thai man said, "We'll be here three days waiting for the flood to subside."

I was a bit surprised when he used the word "We." It meant he wasn't just there by himself.

"I have nothing left to eat," I told my guest. I offered no warm welcome, but he didn't seem to care in the least.

"I know," the Thai man nodded to me. "Before you came back I searched all over the house. Miss Muon went out to get some rice."

I was a bit offended at the guest's casual attitude. He seemed to notice, and introduced himself with a smile. "My name is Bac Ky Sinh."

I was a bit shocked. Bac Ky Sinh said, "I'm with a girl. That's Muon."

Just then the Thai girl I had met at the Muong La Market walked in, wet as a drowned rat, carrying a basket over her shoulder. Bac Ky Sinh stood up and took the basket of rice. I had no clue where they got that pure white rice, out in the rain, in that deserted place surrounded by flood waters.

Bac Ky Sinh and the girl spoke together in Thai. The girl looked at me and smiled. "I've seen you before! You helped watch the horse for me at Muong La Market."

While Bac Ky Sinh prepared the rice the girl went into the inside room to change. I heard her rummaging noisily. She stuck her head out. "Mr. Teacher! Can I borrow a shirt?" I looked at Bac Ky Sinh. He seemed to approve, so I said yes.

I had been in the mountains a long time, and knew that many Thai men have terribly jealous dispositions. A man could easily be stabbed to death for even unintentionally flirting with a girl who has tang cau—that is to say, tied the knot. There had been an incident like that in Yen Chau some years earlier. A Vietnamese teacher from Hung Yen had his "family jewels" cut off with a bushwhacking machete. His "gunner" never again went to battle, and he had to "retire" at age twenty. I didn't want to end up like that. It was the beginning of my twenty-first year, and I still knew nothing about "wind, flowers, snow, and moons."

A bit later the girl stepped out in my streaked T-shirt and a new skirt. She looked beautiful, a beauty that was at once remote, ardent, and savage.

We sat and ate and chatted with one another. Bac Ky Sinh said little. His eyes were cold and bleak, as intense as the eyes of a hawk. Sometimes they would brighten as if with a spark, a flash of lightning. Only when the spark met the light of Muon's eyes did his eyes soften and come to look like the eyes of a man. Bac Ky Sinh had a cautious smile that always looked like he was mocking himself or someone else.

We sat and talked about the regional products of the Northwest, about the customs of the Thai people, about how the Vietnamese had come up there to make a living. Bac Ky Sinh appeared to dislike the fact that every day there were more Vietnamese coming up and "going deeper" into the Northwest to "civilize" and "light the lamp of culture." Muon felt differently, expressing criticism of the Thai way of life as sheltered and too close to nature. She even thought the people of the mountains were ignorant in some ways. From this discussion I saw them as two people who understood many things, who were not at all naive or narrow-minded in the way we city-folk still imagined the "ethnic minority" to be.

Finished with his meal, Bac Ky Sinh leaned back against the wall and gazed into the flickering flame. Outside in the night the rain had not let up. Bac Ky Sinh sang a song in Thai, expressing himself poignantly. Muon sang along on many of the verses. I picked up bits of it, trying to make sense of the words...

> *Po Me Oi! Oh Ma and Pa...*
> *You gave birth to me in a mountain cave*
> *So windy and cold*
> *Raining all night, so windy and cold*
> *Growling tigers, howling wolves*
> *Python and boa hunting prey*
> *A band of rank foxes lurking in wait*
> *Porcupines hiding in the cave*
> *Your bare naked child shivers*
> *Cold wind pounds my breast*
> *I light a fire, the wind blows it out*
> *I grope in the darkness*
> *And grab something soft and damp*
> *I'm terrified, what is it?*
> *It swells in my hand*
> *Oh such pain, throbbing pain*
> *That soft, damp thing*
> *Is my heart, fallen to the ground*
> *That ground, so windy and cold*
> *Oh Ma and Pa, who will love me*
> *Oh Ma and Pa, who will love you...*

Bac Ky Sinh sang simply, as if speaking. I had never heard anyone sing like that: unwavering, unforced, emphasizing words and trilling so gently that words can't describe it. His singing was full of sorrow and grief but it was not melodramatic. It conveyed a lonely, icy mood ensnarled with ardent cravings. The song pulsed, dense as honey. Every word another drop. As I listened my tears ran so naturally that I couldn't hold them back.

The song stopped. Everything went quiet. The distinct sounds of falling rain and insects suddenly poured into the house. No one uttered a word. The song wavered and flew through the air, entangled in our hair, our lips, burning and crackling in the bright red fire.

Bac Ky Sinh gave a ghastly smile, full of terror, as if all his vitality had been poured into the song. A moment later, as if she couldn't bear the silence, Muon began singing again. Her song was tormented and sorrowful, no less so than the song of Bac Ky Sinh:

> *Ing Noong, O Ing Noong*
> *If I build a house*
> *It will be a small house with big windows*
> *A stove with pink flames*
> *On the table a bouquet of red and white flowers*
> *New sweet-scented blankets*
> *And you by my side*
> *I want you by my side*
> *This is my dream*
> *My love, where have you gone?*
> *Have the forest ghosts taken you, has some flame*
> *   summoned you?*
> *Which way did you go?*
> *No one's waiting for you there*
> *My love, come back to me*
> *We'll build a small house with big windows*
> *My love, where have you gone?*
> *Dear one, where have you gone?*

While she sang I listened in silence, watching the tears spill down her cheeks. Bac Ky Sinh seemed moved. He put his arm around her and drew her toward him. When Muon had finished singing, he said something quickly in Thai that I could not hear, but I guessed it was a curse or a hex. Muon glared at him and, indignant, moved away. They spoke about someone named Ngan.

Night turned to early morning, and the rain fell heavier with each passing moment. Rain soaked into the earth, the walls, the heart. We sat for a long time without moving. Bac Ky Sinh was the first to speak. He bemoaned the miserable living conditions of one place or another, most likely his native village. I had traveled a good deal in the Northwest. The living conditions of the people there were truly severe. In many places the people had enough rice to last only three months, and so for nine months of the year they had to go into the forest to dig for yams. Hunting and gathering were still the common means of survival there, just as they had been a thousand years before. The blights of shifting cultivation and deforestation were leaving the forest terrain increasingly barren. I made a point of asking Bac Ky Sinh about his heritage.

He replied cautiously, giving very little information, "I'm a bastard child of the forest."

He whispered this sentence like a confession, a bit wearily but as if he felt a special, secret pride. I recalled what happened at the Muong La Market and he smiled. "Did that make much trouble for you?" He rubbed his hands together sheepishly and said, "I owe you a favor." Then he pointed to Muon and said, "I have to thank this hedgehog!"

Much later, after hearing many people retell the story, I finally learned about the events that led up to that troubled day.

I lay down to sleep by the stove, listening to the sound of the rain, dreaming, slumbering around the images of the soft supple heart, wet, heaving on the cold ground, and the small house with the big windows. Weren't those the images that haunted the destiny of that couple's love?

* * *

Bac Ky Sinh was a descendent of the Bac family line in Muong Vai. His was a long and distinguished lineage. It is said that his ancestor was a Vietnamese man who had held a minister's post, leaving for the Northwest when he got fed up with the way things were. That was around the 18th century, the time of the Le kings and Trinh lords: a troubled time in history. Bac Ky Sinh's forefather married a Thai woman, built a farm, and made his living trading opium with the Lao and Chinese. By Bac Ky Sinh's time, things had changed. The authority that exists among us now was becoming established. A border precinct was immediately instituted at Muong Vai. The opium trading business was outlawed. The soldiers on the border would often come down to the village to help the people, teaching the children and protecting the order and security of the forest. The head of the border post was Lo Van Ngan, a Thai man from Yen Chau, an industrious and rigid second lieutenant. Fate is precarious. In the relations between Lo Van Ngan and Bac Ky Sinh there were many ironies.

Once, at the traditional New Year, a horse race was organized for the youth of the forest. The race was rather dangerous, crossing many cliffs and streams. There would be many prizes, and first prize was a beautiful horse. Muon, the most beautiful girl in Muong Vai, was to hand the tether to the winning rider.

Seventeen riders took part in the race, Lo Van Ngan and Bac Ky Sinh among them. The two men battled for every inch, pulling ahead of all the others. In the last leg, the most dangerous section, it was necessary to leap a mudslide that covered an old underground spring said to be bigger than the Da River. The spring spouted up in many places, making the mire extremely dangerous.

Lo Van Ngan was a skilled rider. His horse was bred from the East River horses of Russia. Only six such horses had been brought to Vietnam, to be bred to the finest standards at the Ba Van Horse Farm in Thai Nguyen in hopes of propagating the breed for use by the border guards. This horse ran very fast. On a good road it could run up to 300km an hour, and it could leap up to four meters. It was twice as tall as a normal horse. Bac Ky Sinh rode a horse from the northwest mountains. It was ugly, with short legs, and looked like an old donkey. It didn't run fast, but it never tired, and it climbed mountains like an antelope. This breed of horse was especially fit for mountainous terrain. It ate little, and kept going even when thirsty.

As they crossed the pass, Ngan's East River horse and Bac Ky Sinh's horse were running side by side. They cut through a turn, squeezing together on the narrow path at the edge of a ravine. In the hard wind the stronger East River horse shoved Bac Ky Sinh's horse down into the canyon. Bac Ky Sinh escaped death thanks to the exceptional sensitivity of his rugged horse. It put its hooves together and, scrambling on the steep slope, somehow managed to hook one leg around the trunk of a wild lychee tree.

"Life was truly hanging by a hair," Bac Ky Sinh said. The horse, too, seemed to know that if it just stretched its legs the two of us would plunge 300 meters. The wind blew and the rocks scratched the horse until its hide had been scraped away. It began to shake and pour sweat. Its face seemed to ask, "Why? Why die such a meaningless death?" Struggling like that, its power seemed to multiply.

Doing everything he could, Bac Ky Sinh at last got free and coaxed the horse off the tree. Bac Ky Sinh had been badly injured, but though he had a broken femur and a dislocated ankle, a rider from the mountains never quits. He rejoined the race.

If he followed the basic, original trail to reach the finish line, defeat would then be certain. With more than twenty kilometers of forest path to go, man and horse would both expire from blood loss. So Bac Ky Sinh chose to scale a cliff to get back to the valley: the way was shorter—only two kilometers—though it would be "mountain climbing" and no longer "horse racing." The racers weren't required to follow a certain route. Since long ago, the people of the mountains set only the direction of the race, not how to reach the finish line. Racers had to fumble their way alone with only foresight and intuition to guide them through.

Bac Ky Sinh scaled the cliff—which means he held certain death in his hand, his hope for survival one in a thousand. Somehow, some way, he made it. Both man and horse were speckled and stained with blood as Bac Ky Sinh reached the finish line looking no different than a jungle phantom.

The race had come to an end. No one awarded a prize to the jungle phantom. The prize went to Lo Van Ngan and the East River thoroughbred. All Bac Ky Sinh got was the furtive praise of a few of the most taciturn mountain folk, who have their own way of assessing the value of men.

Bac Ky Sinh treated his injuries at the house of Muon's father, Sung. Sung was a physician who cured illnesses with leaves from the forest. The love between Bac Ky Sinh and Muon began during those days. But Lo Van Ngan, the second lieutenant in command at the border, was also very much in love with Muon.

Bac Ky Sinh's health improved as autumn came to an end. The leaves were changing in the forest. The row of trees behind Muon's house turned from green to red, the color of plums and the color of blood. The dinh lang is a forest flower, yellow as golden earrings, which blossoms in hedges abundant with yellow vines that look like golden rings.

Bac Ky Sinh sat by the window. Muon sat out in the side room spinning thread, singing the song she was so fond of:

Ing Noong, O Ing Noong
If I build a house
It will be a small house with big windows
A stove with pink flames...

Her father asked Bac Ky Sinh, "Now Sinh, do you think the mountain folk are happy?"

Bac Ky Sinh laughed. "Yes, as long as they remain ignorant."

Muon asked, "And what about civilization?"

A voice on the stairs outside responded, "It's not good at all!" A Thai man came inside carrying a heavy basket of goods. He was Lo Van Cuong, Sung's younger brother and Muon's uncle, who still sold opium from the Golden Triangle, brought on the road through Upper Laos to the Northwest.

Lo Van Cuong spent the night at his brother's house. He told Bac Ky Sinh, "I saw your horse race against the government men. Follow me! You're a forest phantom traveling on the narrow paths. You want Muon, then listen to me. Go move goods up in Hoang Sa Phi. Now, worry about freedom and silver; later, worry about women. That girl will kill you."

Two weeks later, Lo Van Cuong was shot dead. Border guards under Lo Van Ngan's command ambushed and killed him as he transported opium across the border. Lo Van Ngan was promoted to lieutenant. He rode his East River horse to Muon's house. He gave her a pair of silver bracelets.

Muon asked, "If you kill one man do you rise one rank?"

Ngan replied, "That depends on who is killed."

Muon said, "That man was my uncle."

Ngan replied, "I didn't know that."

When Ngan went down the stairs, his East River horse had had its hoof tendons cut and was lying slumped by the hedge. Ngan ran up the stairs, pulled out his gun and pointed it at Bac Ky Sinh. "You killed my horse! Do you know how many of you that horse was worth?"

"If I had to cut a tendon, do you think I would cut the horse's?" Bac Ky Sinh asked.

Bac Ky Sinh was arrested. Muon wailed, "He's ill!"

Ngan said, "Every day this horse ate twenty kilos of paddy rice, six liters of milk and two kilos of sugar. In the whole country there were only two horses like that one!"

Bac Ky Sinh was detained for nine months. In prison, Lo Van Cuong's friends set him up with all their customers, taught him how to travel in the forest, how to fool around with girls without catching diseases, how to elude the border guards, how to tell real money, Thai baht and Lao kip, from counterfeit—the kind of knowledge that has to do with either freedom or depravity. It's hard to know the difference.

One thief, a Dao man named Trieu Phu Dai, helped Bac Ky Sinh escape during a night of heavy rain. The two men pushed aside the metal roofing and stole out, fleeing stealthily towards the Thuan Chau Forest to hide.

Within a few days Bac Ky Sinh was on the road to Muon's house. Trieu Phu Dai grumbled, "We have to get away to Upper Laos at once. If you dawdle here you'll be dead any day now."

"What do you know about love?" asked Bac Ky Sinh.

Trieu Phu Dai sighed. "It's an unscrupulous emotion."

Muon ran out to greet Bac Ky Sinh, wearing on her wrists the two silver bracelets that Ngan had given her.

"You love him?" asked Bac Ky Sinh.

"I don't know. I only like the uniform."

Bac Ky Sinh and Trieu Phu Dai stayed at Muon's house for three days. Trieu Phu Dai told Bac Ky Sinh, "Decide. Either go to Upper Laos or stay here and snuggle with Muon while you wait for Ngan to come arrest you."

At five in the morning the border guards surrounded Muon's house. Trieu Phu Dai and Bac Ky Sinh hid in a secret room. Trieu Phu Dai said, "This time death is certain. I don't regret a thing. I'm just sorry that you're only twenty-five."

Bac Ky Sinh said, "When Ngan climbs the stairs, I'll put a knife to his neck. When the others bring the horses, we'll flee in different directions."

Bac Ky Sinh climbed up into the rafters like a bat. Lucky for him it was five in the morning, for in the mountains it was still dark as ink. At that moment it began again to rain heavily. The two men escaped to Upper Laos.

"Mr. Sung and his daughter have certainly been arrested by now," said Bac Ky Sinh.

Trieu Phu Dai smiled. "With Muon there's no need to be afraid. You never know which cat will bite."

Bac Ky Sinh traded far and wide in upper Laos, and even crossed many times into Thailand. He had money, he had many possessions, but in his inconsolable heart he thought of Muon and missed his homeland. Sometimes he dared to find the road back and visit Muong Vai. Once, he got caught, leading to the escape that I witnessed at Muong La Market.

* * *

Bac Ky Sinh and Muon stayed at my house through a second day, quarreling with each other. They both lost their tempers. I didn't understand much because they spoke very quickly in Thai. I could only make out a few words. I guessed that the two disagreed about how to escape their current predicament. Muon insisted on one thing and Bac Ky Sinh put up his hands and refused. A moment later, Bac Ky Sinh was insisting on something that Muon rejected. In the end Bac Ky Sinh stood up and howled in a terrible voice like a wolf. He looked mournful. Muon put her hands to her face and ran out into the rain. By then it was late in the night. Bac Ky Sinh ran after her. They wrangled for quite some time and then Muon ran off towards the forest. Bac Ky Sinh returned to the house and dropped himself down beside the fire.

I had sat quietly observing the two guests. In compassion, I felt a vague misery. Why must we torture ourselves? Why must we torture each other? Back then I was young, and had yet to experience the sweetness or the bitter taste of love. Oh, love! Later, I learned what it was like. Young friends, go ahead! Love! It will make you crazy and stupid, it will make you better, or worse—I don't know—but I know for certain it is the most wonderful thing in life, the most valuable of all the treasures that God has granted us. Young friends, don't believe those who tell you that love is a mistake. There is no mistaken love. Those people are jealous over love; those who have had no opportunity to love are the ones who slander and frustrate it.

That night we saw no sign that Muon would return. Bac Ky Sinh sat by the fire as if turned to stone. I tried to start a conversation. He sighed, "She won't come back. Women prefer houses with big windows so they can sneak out."

He thought for a little while, and continued, "Women are naturally inclined towards order. There's no order that can accommodate a great love."

I piled more wood on the fire. It was raining very hard. The two of us sat beside the fire until it expired and the morning dawned. Bac Ky Sinh told me about his hot burning love. He spoke about women, about life, about many other things. "No one has brought me so much happiness and pain as Muon," he said. "Have you ever loved? Love sets fire to your heart. It makes you powerful. It makes you wise and spry. And it makes you sober. Love teaches you to walk like a tiger, like a panther, and gives you the strength of a wild animal. It teaches you the wiles of a fox, of a venomous snake. It commands you to be either more humane or more cruel. The vile do not love."

I asked Bac Ky Sinh about Muon. He said, "She's just

like any other woman. I'm too insane, too dangerous with her. Sooner or later she will climb out the window and head for safer, more familiar surroundings. She'll die more slowly than me. But enough, all these things I've said are useless. Some day you'll understand."

Bac Ky Sinh stayed with me until noon the next day. Without discussion he gave me money for the lodging. A considerable sum, more than many months of my teacher's salary.

Bac Ky Sinh and I said farewell. He said he would go to Thailand that very day. Neither of us thought we would meet again. I didn't imagine that twenty-five years later I would meet Bac Ky Sinh in a uniquely strange situation.

One year I had a chance to return to Muong La. I met Lo Van Ngan. By then he had been promoted to major. Ngan's building stood right at the gate to Muong La Market. It was designed like any city house, the downstairs used for selling goods or to rent as an office, the upstairs for a residence. Ngan and Muon were married. Their two children were in college. When I greeted Ngan he received me cautiously, even somewhat coldly. We didn't discuss old affairs.

I found a convenient chance to meet Muon alone. She was still very beautiful and wore fancy clothes like the city people. When I recalled what had happened with Bac Ky Sinh, Muon was shocked, and blurted out, "I don't know what you're talking about! Don't ever repeat that story again!"

I went back to Muong La Market. It had barely changed. The Thai and Xa girls sold peaches, plums, and wild pears gathered up in the mountains; Hmong men and women led horses bearing baskets of cardamom seeds, ginseng and herbs, sticky rice. At the corner, there was still an old Chinese man telling fortunes. No crowd surrounded him. I approached and paid, rolled the dice and asked him about the fate of Bac Ky Sinh. The old man read to me a poem in Chinese:

Meeting as if not meeting
Having as if not having
Like the moon in the ocean
A person in a dream

I sighed and turned away in thought. I said to myself, "Oh fate! What creates fate? What has worth? What is worthless? What has the most meaning in the life of one man?"

* * *

A few years after I returned from Muong La, I met Bac Ky Sinh by chance when I went to America. One day, in New York, I visited a cafe where poets and artists gathered. There was a Vietnamese man very stylishly playing guitar. He sang songs in English and Vietnamese. When I heard one song I froze and couldn't believe it. It was the same song I had listened to one day years before:

Po Me Oi! Oh Ma and Pa...
You gave birth to me in a mountain cave
So windy and cold
The life of men, so windy and cold
O Freedom, love, homeland
The roads are rough and wearying
Your bare naked child shivers
And gropes in the darkness
I grab something soft and damp
I'm terrified, what is it?
It swells in my hand
Such pain, throbbing pain
I look up to heaven and ask
Where is love? Where is freedom? Where is home?
Po Me Oi!...
You gave birth to me in a mountain cave...

The man singing and playing the guitar was Bac Ky Sinh.

That night, Bac Ky Sinh brought me to his home. It was a small place with a big window, on the upper floor of an apartment building. It was rather full of comforts. Bac Ky Sinh rented the place and lived there alone. After the last time we met, he had crossed to Upper Laos, to Thailand, and then he came to reside in America.

We drank through the night. Bac Ky Sinh asked me many questions about the Northwest of Vietnam. I asked Bac Ky Sinh if he anticipated an opportunity to return to Vietnam. He shook his head wearily, pointing to his breast: "I don't know. I still feel pain in here." He smiled, the same smile that looked like he was mocking himself or someone else.

On the wall Bac Ky Sinh had hung a photograph of Muon. Despite the fact that the emulsion had turned yellow, Muon still looked very pretty. I didn't have the heart to tell Bac Ky Sinh that in Vietnam Muon was living happily.

Bac Ky Sinh pressed me to drink strong liquor. We were both dead drunk. I asked him what love was like. Bac Ky Sinh said, "Believe me! It's a ghoul."

That night in New York it rained very hard, like in the Northwest of Vietnam, a kind of prolonged tropical rain, the kind of rain that seemed like it would never subside, like it would never stop, like it would never come to an end...

Translated by Peter Saidel

Remembrance of the Countryside

I am Nham. I was born in a village and grew up in a village. If you're on Route 5 and looking toward my village, you'll only see a small green spot in the yellow fields. You can vaguely see the outline of the Dong Son mountains, which seems close but is actually fifty kilometers away. My village is near the ocean, and in the summer an ocean breeze blows through it.

The fifth month of the moon calendar is the harvest time. My mother, my brother's wife Ngu, Uncle Phung, and I are out in the fields by dawn. Those three cut and I haul the rice.

I haul the rice home, following the edge of the path by the ditch. It's very bright outside, probably forty degrees Celsius. The dry mud at the edge of the ditch is bent and broken like rice crackers.

I'm very dreamy, always thinking. My father is a major in the marines, a middle-rank technician who travels to many islands setting up radar instruments. Once a year he gets permission to come home. My father knows the names of all the islands by heart. My mother has never gone far from our village. She says, "Everywhere's the same. In every place, there's just people."

Uncle Phung is different. He's been to a lot of places, and when he and I are alone together he tells me, "Within the universe there's not just people. There are saints and there are devils." Uncle Phung's family are all women: his wife's mother, his wife, and four daughters. Uncle Phung jokes, "I am the most handsome person in the family."

Ngu is married to my older brother Ky, who works in the Tinh Tuc iron mines in Cao Bang. Ngu is the daughter of Teacher Quy, the village elementary school teacher. I used to study with him. He has a lot of books. Everybody calls him "the eccentric scholar." They also say, "He's an old goat," and "Quy the goat." Teacher Quy has two wives. The first wife gave birth to Ngu, my sister-in-law, and the second, Aunt Nhung, who sews clothes and keeps a small shop, is the mother of my friend Van. Aunt Nhung used to be a prostitute in Hai Phong. After teacher Quy married her, there was nothing left of his reputation.

I haul ten loads of rice, which fill the courtyard. Then I call Minh to pile the straw to make room for the rice. Minh is my little sister, skinny and dark, but bright-eyed and tough. She comes out of the kitchen, her face red, her clothes soaked with sweat.

I go out to the barrel of rain water, fill a coconut shell, and drink it in a few gulps. The water is cool. My mother often eats rice with rain water and salted eggplant. My mother can't eat fatty meat.

The courtyard is scorching, and it feels like the air is steaming, oppressive with the smell of rice.

Rice husks lie haphazardly across the village paths. When I walk by Aunt Luu's gate I see a crowd of people. Aunt Luu's daughter Mi calls, "Nham!" The village postman, Ba Ven, is cramming letters and newspapers into the canvas bag on the back of his bicycle. Mi tells me, "We have a telegram from Quyen, in Hanoi."

Aunt Luu is my mother's younger sister, who's been paralyzed for years. Her husband Uncle Sang is a transportation engineer working in Laos. Uncle Sang's older brother in Hanoi has a daughter, Quyen, who's been studying at a university in America. She came to visit when she was a child.

I hold the telegram in my hand and read, "Aunt Luu send someone to come meet our daughter Quyen at the station at two o'clock on _." I ask Mi, "This afternoon?" Mi nods her head.

Aunt Luu is lying with her back against the wall. She's been lying like that for the past six years. She says, "Nham, help me by going to meet Quyen at the station, okay?"

I say, "My family's harvesting the rice."

"Leave it for a while. Which plot are you harvesting?"

"Red Fetus Plot," I tell her.

Mi carries the telegram out to the fields to talk to my mother. Mi is the same age as my sister Minh, but lighter skinned. She talks a lot and demands a lot of attention. "Hey, Nham," she says. "One day will you make a bamboo picker so I can get some guavas?" You make it from fresh bamboo, with a head like a fish trap with open teeth.

I tell Minh, "You have to find the bamboo."

"I found it already. Do it tomorrow, okay?"

I calculate in my head the things I need to do and see I'm going to be busy from early morning until late at night. Mi says, "Tomorrow."

I say, "Yeah." Her house has three guava trees. One time she climbed one of them and the branch broke and she just barely missed falling.

Uncle Phung reads the telegram and says, "What's this SNN post office? What does it mean? City people are so tricky."

My mother says, "Nham, Aunt Luu asked you to go, so go. I put your new shirt in the trunk. Take it out and wear it."

I tell Mi, "Go home. I have to cut rice until noon. I'll go right after lunch."

Mi goes home alone. Her shadow sinks little by little into the field, which is rough with the stubble of the just-cut rice. I hold the sickle, gather the rice in an arc around me close to the roots, and pull sharply. I go one step to the left. Gather again. Pull sharply. Go one step to the left again. Gather again. Pull sharply again. Like that. Like that forever. The earth in the field is wet, and you can hear the tick-tack sound of tiny grasshoppers dancing.

By noon, the fields are empty. Looking out I can see only the four people in my own family still out in the fields. My mother sits at the edge, pulling thorns from her foot. Ngu, wearing a conical hat, a scarf over her face, and with her legs wrapped from the ankles to the thighs for protection, is looking dreamily toward the far row of the Dong Son mountains. Uncle Phung is collecting rice to haul home. He says, "Are you going home now?" My mouth is so dry I can't speak, so I only nod my head. The two of us, each with one load, head home. Uncle Phung goes in front, and I walk behind. The loads of rice are heavy. My feet are shaking, but I try to walk anyway. One hundred steps. Two hundred steps. One thousand steps. Two thousand steps. Like that. Like that forever. Then we get home.

Minh sets out my lunch and then hurries to carry lunches out to the field for my mother and Ngu.

Lunch is rice with boiled sweet potato leaves, salted eggplant, and stir-fried small shrimp with star fruit. I eat six bowls of rice without stopping. Now, I'm tired. Otherwise, I would eat a lot more.

I go out to the well to wash and change my clothes. I take the new shirt and put it on, but I feel self-conscious and stop. I end up putting on my father's faded shirt from the army instead. Then I walk over to Aunt Luu's house to get the bicycle. Aunt Luu says, "Take a little money." She hands me five thousand but I only take two. Two thousand is worth more than two kilos of rice. Aunt Luu asks, "Do you remember Quyen's face?" I nod, though actually I don't remember her well, but when I meet her I'll recognize her.

I ride the bicycle to the station. From my village to the station is eight or nine kilometers. It's been a long time since I've gone that far.

The dirt path follows the edge of the village past the communal house, past the lotus pond, then along the side of a ditch back toward the town seat. I'm thinking. But my ideas aren't clear.

> *I'm thinking*
> *I'm thinking about the simplicity of words*
> *Forms of expression are too powerless*

260

While exhaustion fills the earth
Shameless injustice fills the earth
Desolate fates fill the earth
How many months and years pass by?
How many lives pass by?
No word has the skill to describe it
Who will gather this morning for me?
Gather the empty light from my little sister's eyes?
Gather the gray hairs from my mother's head?
Gather the vain hopes from the heart of my
                                        brother's wife?
And gather the smell of poverty from the countryside?
I snipe at every idea
I look for a way to chase it into a cage
And I scream in the fields of my heart
Howl like a wolf
I try to harvest some part of a life
And tie it loosely with a band of words
I howl in the fields of humanity
I gather the light from the eyes of life
Which are watching the light in my own eyes
Looking into the world of consciousness
The distant and immeasurable world of consciousness
Although I understand
It means nothing, nothing, nothing, nothing,
                                        nothing at all.

The train station is empty in the afternoon. A few tired chickens stand in the courtyard. About ten people are waiting at the entrance. There's the sound of music coming from a cassette somewhere. The voice of the singer Nha Phuong slowly sings, "You passed through my life. Do you remember anything? My darling, you passed through my life. Do you remember anything?" Noodle soup sellers, refreshment sellers. Everywhere there are shops selling clothes, shoes, sugar and milk, cigarettes. Cars running back and forth.

The sky is so clear. Blazing. The whole town has sunstroke.

The train's whistle sounds hesitant and happy from far away. Someone calls, "The train's coming." The whole town is still dreamy. Then someone yells again, "The train's coming," and now the train sounds intimidating and shrill. Everybody's suddenly excited. Old women, young women, children selling things, all running back and forth. The sound of the sellers competing with each other. "Water here!" "Bread!" "Drinks!" "Bread!" "Drinks!"

I stand with my bicycle, watching. The passengers are standing and sitting in a crowd at the door of the train. This is a local stop. My countryside is anonymous. The place where I stand is anonymous.

About a dozen people file out one after another through the ticket entrance, and I recognize a few teachers from the district high school. A soldier. A few traders. A few steelworkers. A fat man wearing dark glasses which still have the sticker on them. A tall thin youth, hair as brittle as the roots of bamboo, and intense eyes. I know him. He's the poet Van Ngoc. After Ngoc comes an old couple. Quyen.

Quyen's hair hangs down. She wears a light pullover, jeans, glasses, and a bag over her shoulder. Among all the other people, Quyen's appearance is completely different.

Quyen walks through the ticket gate and looks around. She recognizes me immediately. Quyen says, "I'm Quyen. Did Aunt Luu send you to pick me up?"

"Yes," I say.

Quyen smiles. "Thank you. How are you related to Aunt Luu? What's your name?"

"I'm Nham. I'm the son of Hung," I tell her.

"Are we related by blood?"

"No."

Quyen nods her head. "Fine. Aunt Luu hired you, then?"

I look at my shadow, dark in the cement, my heart sad.

Me, it's my destiny—everywhere people always see me as someone for hire.

The afternoon passes slowly. Shadows run after each other across the ground. The afternoon empties the spirit of anyone who hopes to prove that anything has meaning.

Quyen asks, "How many sao does your family plant? One sao harvests how much rice? How much money do you make?"

I tell her, "Every sao harvests more than three noi, nearly a ta (100 kilos). Every kilo of rice sells for one thousand four hundred."

Quyen calculates. "Twenty million tons of rice for sixty million people."

I say, "Who only thinks about eating?"

Passing the lotus pond we meet Thieu the monk. Brother Thieu says hello. I say hello back. Brother Thieu says, "I remembered to set aside some hydrangeas for you."

I say, "I'd like to come by the pagoda to get them sometime." I love flowers. Teacher Quy always says, "That's the pleasure of a person who understands life."

Brother Thieu asks, "Want to take a few lotus flowers to put in a vase?" This season the pagoda's lotus pond has a lot of flowers.

I park the bike to push the boat out for Brother Thieu. The basket boat can only hold one person sitting down. The paddle splashes the water. Quyen says, "I want to go on the boat," so I call to Brother Thieu.

He rows the boat back in.

Brother Thieu carries a bunch of lotus flowers up to the bank. Quyen climbs into the boat and I push her back out.

Brother Thieu says, "Pampering people brings trouble to us." I laugh. He and I sit on the bank. The afternoon continues to pass slowly. Bright yellow sunshine. My heart is empty and wide, so empty, an empty expanse.

Quyen comes up the bank and Brother Thieu invites us to eat lotus root. "Is it good?" he asks.

"It's good," she says.

We linger a little and then head home. Brother Thieu says goodbye. Quyen says goodbye back. Quyen carries the bunch of lotus flowers. Brother Thieu looks hesitantly after us for a moment.

I go in front. Quyen walks behind. She asks me about Brother Thieu.

The Story of Brother Thieu

Brother Thieu was an orphan. In his fifteenth year someone looked at his strange physiognomy and told him, "You must go into the monkhood. There's no place in this world to hold you." Brother Thieu followed this advice, then he traveled to many different places, seeking to learn from great intellectuals, but he never came to enlightenment. Brother Thieu said, "Now Buddha is living in a place that has no Buddha." Then he said:

> *Religion without intention suits people;*
> *People without intention are suited to religion.*

Brother Thieu discovered the foundation of an old pagoda; then he mobilized the community's resources to help restore it. Inexplicably, it was called White Teeth Pagoda. Brother Thieu often read poetry. There was a verse:

> *Only one orbit of light, the mountain and river are*
>   *quiet*
> *Only one sudden sound of laughter, the earth and*
>   *heaven are frightened.*

There was another verse:

> *If you meet a swordsman, you should show him*
> *your sword*
> *If you're not a poet, don't present your poetry.*

Brother Thieu said, "Buddha teaches humanity one way of entering the monkhood practically, by trying to rediscover one's original character. Buddha is too practical, so not everyone understands."

Quyen and I get home. Aunt Luu, with her eyes full of tears, cries, "Niece! Oh, niece!"

Quyen sits on the edge of the bed and says, "My mother and father remembered the anniversary of grandfather's death, but they're busy and can't come back. They sent you and uncle a little money."

Aunt Luu says, "We don't need money. We only need feelings."

Quyen takes five million dong out of her purse and gives it to Aunt Luu. Quyen says, "I'm giving Mi a shirt."

Mi smiles shyly. "Thank you," she says.

I tell Aunt Luu, "I'm going home." Then I stuff her two thousand dong under her pillow and leave.

At home they're husking the rice. Ngu asks, "Is little Quyen pretty?"

"Yes," I tell her.

By the time dinner is over, it's dark. Outside, it's pouring. Thunder resounds in the sky. My whole family runs around pulling the rice out from under the leaks in the ceiling. By the time we've finished everything, it's already eleven o'clock. It's still raining. Suddenly I feel anxious in my heart, and I can't sit still. I say to my mother, "I want to go out to the fields to catch frogs. In a rain like this there'll be a lot of frogs."

My mother asks, "You're not afraid of the thunder and lightening, child?" I laugh. My mother doesn't understand my laugh at all. I laugh like a bandit, like a debt collector, like a devil. I laugh at my fingernails and toenails. Why are they so long and black like that?

The Rhyme for Catching Frogs

The soul of the frog has returned
I had lain on the dry ground, now I go to the
                                        field's edge
Which is only holes and burrows
No blankets, no mats, misery in a hundred forms
I pray for March to come
With one big rain I can go outside
Outside is so spacious and relaxed
In rain or sun I can always look for food
Before, I still strove to improve myself
Unsuccessful, I was humbled
I see a boy with nearly black skin
He only stands and looks without speaking
I see a boy with very black skin
One hand with a fishing rod, one with a basket
He wears a conical hat
With a scarf wrapped around his head looking pretty

He carries a fan in his hand
He carries a bamboo pipe full of bait
He carries a slender rod
With a long red line
I just sit down at the edge of the sweet potato field
He jerks his rod and breaks my jaw
Mother! Get me medicine
Get me the leaves of chili and the xuong song herb
I am in the deepest hole
At the edge of the morning glory pond next to
                                        the coconut-raft
Bamboo Shoot Boy is the son of Uncle Bamboo Tree
He catches me to take me home to dry and skin

The Green Onion Boy goes with the Flowering
Onion Boy
Add a fistful of salt, so hot, so bitter
Oh Buddha, come down to me
Gather the martyred soul of the frog and fly back
to heaven
A lifetime mixes tears and laughter
The life of a frog and the life of a person so hot, so
bitter...

The fields are empty. Only the sound of frogs croaking. The sound of toads echoing loudly, and the murmur of insects.

It rains.

It rains continuously.

I hold the flashlight, my feet treading randomly on the wet rice stubble. There are a lot of frogs, stunned by the light, and you only need to pick them up and put them in the basket. Thunder resounds in the sky. Lightning flashes. The universe opens without limits. The wind roars, sounding like thousands of birds flapping their wings over my head. Suddenly my soul is seized by a feeling of terror. Very clearly, I see a great image gliding quickly and moving violently over my head. I lie down on the ground, stupefied, gasping. I feel certain that the invisible power hovering above me understands everything absolutely, justly, clearly, defending the inherent goodness of the human soul. It has the ability to comfort and soothe each person's fate. It brings me peace.

I was right
I am at peace because I chose this form of expression
The form is difficult, mediocre, meaningless, and vain
To add luster to the value of human knowledge
In these deserted fields
The deserted fields of stupidity and defiant cruelty
Who's there?

Who plays the plaintive flute at night?
And which bright souls, which dark souls are searching
for the way?
Which faint breath
Which faint laughter
Emerges screeching out of white teeth?
Which whispers?
Meaningless groans of insects
Sounds of the cowherd's flute, which are tiny but carry
Wandering through the fields of the heart
Wandering through the fields of humanity
Which wanderer survives?
Which soulmates listen closely?
Which origins recall
Strumming musical sounds?
On this dark night who remains awake?
Who wanders through the fields of this immense and
miserable world?

Little by little the rain stops. I go around this field, around that field. The frogs have disappeared. Sometimes I can only see one salamander quickly following the canal of water. On the horizon in the direction of the Dong Son mountains, I see the flicker of a fire. I feel like I'm lost. I don't know what time it is, but suddenly I hear the crow of the roosters, the desolate crow of the roosters falling and rising in no order at all. For a long time I don't see any frogs, then suddenly I realize that somehow I've come to the place where the canal meets the Forbidden River. Alone in the sky is the morning star.

It's dawn when I return to the village. The air is clean. The village is familiar and quiet. After the rain, the landscape seems both elegant and pure.

Crossing by Aunt Nhung's house, I stand still. The house sits close to the side of the road. The thatch screen opens. Someone's shadow slips hurriedly out. Whoever it is looks in front and behind and then runs quickly and hides behind the streblus tree. A thief? I'm about to yell when I realize it's Uncle Phung. A moment later, Aunt Nhung opens the door and steps tranquilly out, wearing a nightgown. Nhung is over thirty, her body well-proportioned and beautiful.

I carry the bag of frogs down the road after Uncle Phung. When we get to a bend, he glances back and sees me. He says, "Were there many frogs?" I don't answer. Uncle Phung is a bit startled. He insists, "Why are you being like that?" I suddenly feel a gnawing sadness. I'm sad for Aunt Nhung, sad for Uncle Phung, sad for Teacher Quy. I'm sad for myself.

Uncle Phung walks away as if he doesn't care. I go home. It turns out that I only have about twenty frogs. Ngu says, "That wasn't worth the effort. So few and you were out all night."

My mother laughs, "He probably both caught frogs and slept in the fields."

Minh is preparing to go to school for the summer program. She wears blue pants and a white blouse, which are her nicest clothes, the ones she only wears on holidays. She whispers in my ear, "I know where you went, but I won't tell. You didn't go catch frogs." She laughs. I look into her eyes. She *knows*, but I have no way to suspect that in only a few hours I will have to cry for her. She *knows*, simply because it's almost like she's experienced things and understands. Until that moment, the moment when she dies, she has only four more hours to joke and understand everything completely.

My mother says, "Child, take some frogs over to Teacher Quy's so he can have them with his rice wine."

I say, "Okay." Then I go bathe.

My mother and Ngu go out to the fields to harvest peanuts, which is also my job in the mornings.

On the way to Teacher Quy's house, I go by Aunt Luu's and Quyen yells, "Hey, What's-Your-Name!"

I say, "I'm Nham. Where did Mi go?"

"Mi went to school. Wherever you're going, let me go with you."

We go to Teacher Quy's.

The Story of Teacher Quy

Teacher Quy taught elementary school, had a generous nature, and had been reading books ever since he was small. When he grew up and his parents chose a wife for him, he said to her, "Don't marry me or you'll have a miserable life."

She said, "Even miserable, I'll still marry you."

Teacher Quy said, "If you marry me, first, you can't be afraid of poverty. Second, you can't be afraid of humiliation. Third, you can't be jealous. Fourth, you have to respect decency."

She said, "If you respect decency, then the other three are easy." The couple got married and lived in harmony together. Later, Teacher Quy lost his job because he couldn't bear to follow the textbooks and taught with proverbs and popular songs instead. One time he went to Hai Phong to administer a test, and he met a pregnant prostitute who had no place to deliver her baby, so he brought her home to be his second wife. The first wife didn't say anything, even contributed money to build another house. Wife Number Two wasn't faithful and still had relationships with a lot of men, but Teacher Quy ignored it. He only said, "Whoever you sleep with, remember to get some money out of him. If there's no money, then take rice, or a pig or a duck. Don't sleep with someone for nothing." The whole village laughed at him, but Teacher Quy still ignored it. Teacher Quy often drank rice wine. Rice wine went in and poetry came out. There were a lot of poems that were pretty good.

Teacher Quy is at home by himself, lying on a hammock reading a book. Quyen and I say hello. He gets up and hurries to make tea. We sit on a bamboo bed under the shade of the pergularia trellis. The teacher asks Quyen, "Miss, if you study at a university in America, who does it benefit?"

Quyen says, "It benefits me, benefits my family, and benefits the country."

Teacher Quy smiles, "Don't think about benefit. It'll only exhaust you."

We eat taro dipped in sesame and salt. When Teacher Quy shoves a book under the mat, Quyen says, "If you do that, you'll crush the book and ruin it."

Teacher Quy laughs, "If I crush it, it's nothing. You read books to gain knowledge. Having knowledge is for living a life that has meaning."

The sunlight filters through the trellis, scattering traces of light on the ground. Teacher Quy and Quyen and I are all quiet. I want to go out into the fields. Quyen says, "Coming back this time, I really want to get to know the countryside. Wherever you go, let me go with you." I hesitate.

Teacher Quy laughs, "She's a woman. How can you refuse a woman?"

We say goodbye to Teacher Quy and go into the fields. Quyen says, "The fields are so wide. Do you know where they begin?"

> *The fields began in a place very deep in my heart*
> *Within my own flesh and blood there were fields*
> *From over here, the fields were immense and limitless*
> *From over there, the fields were limitless and immense*
> *How can I ever forget the place where my mother gave*
>   *birth to me?*
> *My mother used a thread to wrap the stem of my*
>   *umbilical cord*
> *Washed me in pond water*
> *I knew that crying was useless because everything must*
>   *wait*
> *Must wait from January to December*
> *In January plant beans, in February plant eggplants*

271

I have gone down so many wrong paths
I have passed through so many hardships, vulgarities
I must plant and harvest in this field
I must know by heart the names of so many kinds
of bugs
And the field is sometimes rainy, sometimes sunny
Some places are shallowly raked and some are deeply
ploughed
Then one day
(an inauspicious and ominous day)
A woman came and made me miserable
She taught me the custom of unfaithfulness in love
By betraying me as she would betray anyone
I silently buried my hatred at the end of the fields
In a difficult vein of the fields, shaped like the curve
of a sword
Flowers of hope withered in my hand
Work became heavier than before
I sold produce at a price too cheap
I have had several big harvests
And also failed completely several times
When the afternoon passed, twilight was quiet
I had no time to see the scars on my body
I only knew that I was wounded
Night
The stars burned candles in the sky
I covered myself with a shroud that smelled of the fields
At that moment, Oh friend, Oh my young friend
Please understand me
I tried to make the fields so fertile

I lead Quyen past the supplementary crops. She asks, "How much has the local price for agricultural products changed this year?"

"It's gone up 0.4 percent," I tell her.

"That'll kill you! Industrial products rose 2.2 percent," she says. "What's the price of fertilizer?"

I tell her, "Nitrogen increased 1.6 percent. Phosphorous increased 1.4 percent."

"Do you use electricity here?" she asks.

"No."

"The price of electricity rose 2.2 percent."

Around ten o'clock in the morning the fields get crowded with women and children. They're the main source of labor. The men around here are adventurous. They have a lot of illusions and nurse dreams of getting rich, so they often take off for the city to look for work or to do business. There are even some people who risk going as far as the central region to dig for gold or rubies. When they come back to the village, their characters have changed. They've become like wild and dangerous beasts. Uncle Phung is a person like that.

The Story of Uncle Phung

Nguyen Viet Phung, the child of a poor family, went through secondary school and then quit. Phung had a number of professions: ploughman, builder, carpenter, oxcart driver. When he was twenty, he went into the army. Three years later he came back to the village and got married. His wife is four years older than he and gave birth to four girls in three years (the third time being twins). Phung was determined to get rich, so he sold all the furniture in his house for two gold rings which he carried to the central region to dig for gold. For a year, there was no news at all, and then out of nowhere he returned, thin as the corpse of a cicada, his face swollen like a gong. He lay down on the bed, and his hard-working wife had to take care of him for the next six months. The poor family became poorer. After his battle with illness, Phung's manner changed. There was the time he stabbed someone, scaring everyone in the village. There was also the time he suddenly started crying, putting his hands together in prayer and prostrating himself before his wife and daughters. Luckily, after that, his wife's parents moved to the city to live with their son who had just returned from abroad. They gave the family the house with three sao of land, and that changed their lives. Phung's wife is resourceful, good at raising animals, and also at making and selling tofu. Every one of those four daughters endures a lot to help their mother. At home, Phung chose one room for himself, and he forbids his wife and children to enter it. Sometimes he still goes out with Nhung and a few of the local widows. Phung's wife and daughters ask, "Why do you avoid us?" Phung says, "There's nothing valuable that's close to me. My flesh is poison. Biting me is a bite that would poison a dog. I love all of you. All I want is for you to be pure."

Quyen and I pass a peck of land in the middle of the fields. At the bottom, castor-oil plants and thorny amaranth grow abundantly. There is even corn with red flowers and green leaves. Quyen asks, "Why is it called a peck of land?"

I tell her, "In the past, King Ba Vanh dug this pit as a space in which to count the number of soldiers he had, in the same way that we would measure rice."

"About how many people?"

"Twenty people would be one fighting unit and two hundred people would be one battalion."

Quyen and I reach the field where my mother and Ngu are gathering peanuts. Water fills the plot, prompting the peanut plants to rise upward from their roots.

Quyen rolls up her trousers and wanders down to collect peanuts. "It's so easy," she says.

My mother says, "You only see it from the surface. Try to calculate from the moment we first sow peanut seeds in the furrows until we harvest, then you might understand how muddy and exhausted my children and I can be."

Ngu adds, "Whoever has a full bowl of rice should remember that each grain is full of bitterness."

I step into a nest of crickets. When I turn the ground with a shovel, thousands of fat and heavy ones swarm into the air. My mother and Ngu quit gathering peanuts to catch crickets. My mother, grinning with pleasure, says "Oh, a blessing! Such abundance for our family! Oh!"

Ngu says happily, "Maybe our family will be the richest in the village!"

Around noon we see on Route 5 a group of people screaming and crying and running around. My mother falls headfirst down into the field, then calls to me, "Nham! Oh, Nham!" Ngu and I are afraid, thinking my mother has been blown over by the wind. My mother's face gets pale, and she puts her hands in front of her face like she's touching somebody, saying, "Nham! Oh, Nham! Why does your sister Minh have blood all over her face like that?"

Ngu shakes my mother, "Mother! Mother! Why are you talking like that?"

A few people suddenly separate from the crowd on Route 5 and run across the fields. Someone screams loudly and full of sorrow, "Mrs. Hung (Hung is my father's name), hurry to receive the body of your child." With his hair standing on end, Ngoc, the poet I saw at the station yesterday afternoon, runs in the lead. He doesn't speak clearly. I only hear him vaguely, only hear enough to know that my little sister Minh and Aunt Luu's daughter Mi were cycling through the three-way intersection on their way home from school when a truck carrying electric poles hit and killed them.

My mother writhes in the peanut field, smearing herself with mud. The crickets rise up off the ground, fly for a moment, and then drop back down to bury their heads in the mud. Ngu stands silently, her eyes confused and full of fear, looking off in the direction of the Dong Son mountains as if she can't understand why the heavens suddenly became so cruel.

Ngoc, Quyen, and I run out to the road. Tears are streaming down my face. Minh was just thirteen years old.

Mi was just thirteen years old. I hadn't even had a chance to make the guava picker for Mi yet. And my little sister Minh, a child so generous that her whole life she wore only patched clothes and always set aside for me the most delicious things to eat.

The truck carrying three electric poles lies turned over by the edge of the road. People are using a jack to raise the wheel of the truck, looking for a way to pull out the bodies of Minh and Mi. Minh lies on her side, Mi on her stomach, pressed against each other, with the crumpled bicycle next to them.

I put my hand to my mouth to keep from crying out. I loved them so much. Swarms of flies cluster around their noses. I don't know where Ngoc got the handful of incense he's now holding in front of the faces of the two girls. The smoke lingers in one place, unable to rise.

I won't say anything else about the deaths of Minh and Mi. In the afternoon we have to have the funeral for my sister and my cousin. It's like every other funeral in the village, with lots of tears, lots of condolences. One of the village youths and I carry Aunt Luu on a stretcher out to the end of the fields and then later carry her back. Quyen follows. Ngoc wrote a poem about the whole thing. I don't understand how he could write a poem during such a brutal time as this.

> *"The Funeral of the Virgins in the Fields"*
>   *by the poet Bui Van Ngoc*

> *I follow the funeral of the virgins into the fields*
> *White death, completely white death*
> *White butterflies, white flowers*
> *White souls, white lives*
> *Oh, I follow the funeral of the virgins into the fields*
> *I dig a grave, 1.8 meters long, 0.7 meters wide*
> *I dig a grave, 1.5 meters deep*
> *Oh, I bury these spirits that were just beginning*

Oh, here is an offering for the earth
Completely pure virgins, completely white death
White butterflies, white flowers
White spirits, white lives
Oh, I attach to my chest this pure white poem
I break off a green branch to cover my eyes
The breeze flutters, the spirit flutters away
The spirit flies away, over the fields of humanity
I follow the funeral of the virgins into the field
On a day like that, not a special day
On a day like that, a normal day
Oh, I am lost in the crowd, in the masses, in the hearts,
   in the grief, in the desolation, in my homeland...

The next afternoon, I take Quyen to the station. Aunt Luu kept trying to get Quyen to stay, but she still insisted on leaving. We follow the dirt road that runs along the edge of the village, pass the lotus pond, then go along the edge of the ditch back toward the town seat. When we come to the lotus pond, we sit down to rest. Quyen says, "I've only been here three days, but it seems like so long!"

In the afternoon the district station is empty. There are only about ten people standing in the yard waiting for the train. In the emptiness you can hear sounds coming from a cassette somewhere. The train arrives. One by one the passengers get on the train. Some teachers from the district high school. A soldier. A few traders. A teenager wearing clear glasses, carrying a suitcase. Two old couples. Quyen.

Quyen says, "Hey! What's-Your-Name! I'm leaving! Thanks for coming to the station with me!"

I stand in the station yard for a long time. The train disappears. I have a feeling I'll never see Quyen again.

I pass through the ticket gate and go back to the village. Looking from the side, you can only see a small green spot in the yellow fields, and vaguely in the distance the outline of the Dong Son mountains. I have so many remembrances there.

Will tomorrow be sunny or rainy? Actually, rain or sunshine are both meaningless to me now. I am Nham. Tomorrow I will be seventeen years old. Is that the most beautiful time in a person's life or not?

Translated by Dana Sachs and Nguyen Van Khang

The Water Nymph

"What kind of love is this
With his borrowed illusion, he sets off..."
—from an ancient song

Story One

No doubt many still remember the summer storm of
1956. It was during that storm, on Noi Holm in the Cai River,
that lightning beheaded a great and ancient mango tree.
Someone, I'm not sure who, said they saw a pair of tightly
entwined water serpents thrashing about, muddying the entire
stretch of river. When the rain stopped, a newborn infant lay
at the foot of the mango tree.

That infant was a water nymph, left behind by the
serpents. The people of our region called the infant Me Ca,
Great Mother. I don't know who raised Me Ca, but I heard
through the grapevine that the guardian of Tia Shrine took
her home. Another rumor said that Mrs. Mong from the
market adopted her. Yet another rumor had it that the sisters
from the convent took Me Ca and gave her the confirmation
name of Johanna Phuong Thi Doan.

The story of Me Ca followed me throughout my youth.
One time, my mother came home from Xuoi Market and told
me how Me Ca had saved the lives of both Mr. Hoi and his
daughter over in Doai Ha Village. Mr. Hoi had been building
a house and took his eight-year-old daughter along when he
went out to dig sand. His tunnel caved in, burying both father
and daughter. Me Ca, who was swimming in the river nearby,
saw them. She transformed herself into an otter and, with
some concerted digging, saved their lives.

One time, the well-digger Mr. Tu Chung told me about
how he had dug up an ancient bronze drum. Officials from
the district branch of the Office of Culture visited him and

asked to take the drum. But when they started back across the river, the sky suddenly crashed with thunder and lightning and the wind rose to whip the water into layer upon layer of waves. Me Ca, who was swimming in the river, yelled, "Throw down the drum." The boat rolled and tossed, almost capsizing, so the officials had no choice but to throw the drum to Me Ca. She sat on top of the drum and beat out a fast rhythm. And then the thunder quieted and the rain stopped. Me Ca clasped the drum to her body and dove out of sight to the bottom of the river.

The stories about Me Ca were all muddled up, half truth and half fiction. My youth was a somber time, full of work— backbreaking work, all of it—so I had no time to worry about other people's business.

My family tilled the fields, dug laterite, and, on the side, stripped bamboo for weaving hats. It goes without saying that farming is hardly easy work. At fourteen, I was the lead plowman of our cooperative. The foreman of the plowing team would stand outside my gate at four o'clock in the morning, calling: "Hey Chuong, do the field out at Ma Nguy Mound today, you hear?" And so I would spring out of bed, toss down a bowl of cold rice and head out while the sky was still dark. I could hear the tiny rustles of field rats running through the cornfields that edge the holm. Half awake and half asleep, my feet stumbling over each other, I pointed myself towards the halo of electric light that hovered above the town and drove my water buffalo in that direction. That's where the Ma Nguy Mound was. It was the worst field in the area, with poor soil leaching a snowy white dirt, and the occasional buried rock. I plowed without a break until noon. When I saw that the sun was directly overhead, I unharnessed the water buffalo and went home.

My mother would say, "Chuong, Mr. Nhieu told me that that we shorted him eighty pieces of laterite this month. You and your father delivered only four hundred odd pieces the other day." I would shoulder my spade and climb Say Hill.

The laterite found in Say Hill is such that you could usually dig only six layers before the seam ran out and you hit earth. And you could only dig on sunny days. On rainy days everything would be covered with sticky, dull red mud and the laterite would crumble. In one afternoon of focused labor, I could dig twenty pieces. Mr. Nhieu passed by and praised me. "Good professional job there. Back in the old days when I dug laterite, damned if I didn't cut off my big toe." He extended his foot, clad in rubber thongs, for me to see the disfigurement. Mr. Nhieu's feet were like those of the ancient Vietnamese; the big toe was not straight but rather splayed out at an angle. I am certain no shoe would fit those feet.

In the evening, I would sit and strip bamboo. We bought the bamboo from the river raftsmen, then peeled it, chopped off the joints, and cut it into small pieces which were boiled in a cooking-pot. Afterwards it had to be steamed in sulfur, spread out to dry, and finally tied into bundles that were stored under the eaves of the house. When the time came to cut them into strips, they were soaked for several days and then out came the stripping-knife. Stripping bamboo had to be done with the utmost care; the knife used was specially made by the blacksmith and had a paper-thin blade that could cut your hand before you knew it. First the inner and outer layers of the bamboo were separated, then thin, even strips were removed and given to children hired to do the weaving. Each roll of woven bamboo was twenty meters long. We sold them to people who had sewing machines to make hats. My mother said, "There isn't much money in this business, but it's year-round work to keep the children out of trouble." My younger brothers and sisters all knew how to weave by the time they were four years old. Their little hands flew lickety-split all day long, and wherever they went they carried a bundle of bamboo strips tucked under one arm.

When the rooster crowed the third watch, I would finally go to bed. The day had been filled with hard work, so sleep came quickly. And through some very small breach, the image of Me Ca slipped into my dreams. But it didn't happen often; perhaps not even once a year.

One day Mr. Hai Thin, who was then the director of the cooperative, told me, "Chuong, my boy, all the other young men of our village have left for the army, and you are the honest sort. I was thinking of putting you to work as a bookkeeper, but you haven't got the education for it. Oh well, you can work on the oversight committee or be a watchman instead."

I asked, "What does the oversight committee do? What does a watchman do?"

Mr. Hai Thin said, "The oversight committee watches to see if we leaders skim off anything and then tells Mr. Phuong, the village secretary, about it. A watchman, well, that Noi Holm bunch keeps coming over to steal the sugarcane from the cooperative's field. You take a gun out there, and if you see anyone stealing, fire a warning shot in the air to scare them off."

"I won't do the oversight committee," I told him. "There's nothing good in being a snitch. I'll be a watchman."

The sugarcane field ran along the river and was several score hectares wide, not easy to patrol. I built a lean-to, climbed in, and lay down to read. But reading eluded me. I slipped into sleep without knowing it. Once, I dreamt that I was plowing. I plowed the entire Ma Nguy Mound field and then continued on to the town, just kept plowing and plowing, and the townspeople had to grab each other and flee. Once I dreamt that I was digging laterite and I cut off my big toe, but a moment later the toe grew back by itself, and I cut it off again, and so on scores of times, and each time the pain was terrible. And then one time I dreamt I was stripping bamboo and my knife sliced off all five of my fingers, so that when I ate I had to plunge my face into the bowl like a dog. In general, that's what my dreams were like, all about my everyday work, nothing special. This was because I had a poor imagination. Afterwards, when I grew older and wiser,

I understood this, but at the time I was only sixteen. What did I know?

One evening—I remember that it was the month of July and the moon was very bright—I went on patrol around the sugarcane field. The light of the moon illuminated everything in stark detail. I could even see the roots of the sugarcane bristling like mangrove from each joint. The rows of sugarcane cast long, inky shadows upon the sand, which had been dried to silky smoothness by the wind. Occasionally, the wind gusted and murmured in the sugarcane, sending a chill through my body. Later, I heard the sound of sugarcane toppling. I ran out of the lean-to. The sight of canes strewn helter-skelter on the sand stung me. My anger rose, and I fired a warning shot into the air. Five or six naked children came tumbling headlong out of the sugarcane. A girl of about twelve, who appeared to be their leader, was pulling a cane behind her as she ran. "Stop right there!" I yelled. They made a panic-stricken dive for the water and began to paddle like crazy in the direction of Noi Holm.

I threw down my gun, stripped off my clothes, and jumped into the river after them. I was determined to catch one of the children. If I could catch one of them, it would lead to the apprehension of the rest. That was how the Security Police usually did things.

The girl with the sugarcane struck off in a different direction than the others. She was kicking up great sprays of water as though she did not know how to swim, and heading upstream, slowing her progress. I swam after her. She turned to look at me and stuck out her tongue mischievously. I swam to head her off; she splashed water in my face. I dove and estimated the distance to her feet, intending to grab her; she shook me off. On and on we went. She swam ahead, but always made sure the distance between us was not too great.

After almost half an hour I still had not been able to catch her. I suddenly realized that my adversary was an expert swimmer and that catching her would be no easy task. This little girl had lured me away so the others might escape. Now she taunted me as she swam. Furious, I kicked and stroked with all my strength, trying to reach her. She let fly a peal of brittle laughter and swam swiftly out to the middle of the river. "Go on back," she said to me. "If you don't, your gun will be stolen, and you'll be in real trouble then!" I was startled, for I realized she was right. Then she said, "There's no way to catch me, Boy! No one can catch Me Ca!"

I panicked, feeling the hair along the nape of my neck stand on end. Could it be that this was the water nymph? My face was drenched from the splashing, but, for a fleeting moment, I caught a glimpse of the length of a supple, naked back, lustrous with water, frolicking before me in the light of the moon—a frightening sight, but very beautiful. Then suddenly it all disappeared, and I was alone in the middle of the vast river, as though nothing had happened. The river continued on as it always had, the same as yesterday, the day before, or five hundred years before. I felt ashamed. Here I was in the middle of the night, swimming naked in the river, searching high and low, and for what? What were a few pieces of sugarcane worth, really? During harvest, the cooperative regularly threw away whole piles of cane. Or, during the rainy season, it was common for a flood to destroy whole hectares. I felt suddenly sad. I floated, letting myself drift with the current until I was pushed to shore. As it turned out, they hadn't even taken much, just a few canes. I sat down and broke off a piece of sugarcane to eat. It was tasteless.

I threw away the cane and returned to the lean-to, where I tossed and turned until morning. I tried to remember Me Ca's face but couldn't. When I closed my eyes, all I saw were the faces of people I knew: Mrs. Hai Khoi's face, big and round with a nose like a warty orange peel; or Miss Vinh's face, long and pale as a water buffalo's testicles; or Mrs. Hy's face, red as a boiled shrimp; or Mr. Du with his broad, horsy jaw bones. Not a one worthy of being called a human face. They were animal faces all, common and vulgar—if not shifty and deceitful, then at least wrinkled up with misery. I found a shard of broken mirror and took a cautious look at my face. The shard was too small, I couldn't see my entire face, just a pair of eyes staring numbly back at me from the glass, like the eyes of one of those wooden temple figurines.

At the end of that year, I resigned from my post as watchman and transferred to the irrigation unit. "Farming first, woodworking second," as they say. The work of cutting up and moving earth was grueling, but I had the strength of youth and so worked briskly, hardly feeling it. Before I knew it, three years had passed, over one thousand days. If you figured the total amount of earth I had moved, it probably added up to a small mountain. But then, in all of my home region there are no mountains. It is a flat region, made up of stunted fields. The fields are criss-crossed with irrigation ditches as far as the eye can see, and still the earth is dry and cracked.

1975. That was a year to observe and remember. In my home region, a huge festival was held. There were boat races on the river, wrestling competitions, and the provincial drama troupe came to stage a performance. The wrestlers from Doai Ha village thoroughly trounced all the other wrestlers in the region. As bold and reckless as the Noi Holm locals were, all four of the wrestlers chosen by our village to compete were eliminated in the first round. After defeating Noi Holm, Doai Ha was riding high. The wrestler named Thi beat the drum and bellowed his challenge: "If no one steps up soon, I'll just take the prize home to Doai Ha now!" The young men of my village were livid. They urged me to step up. I must confess that I wasn't a very good wrestler, but I was strong, and I had a grip like a pair of pliers. I don't know if it was due to my inner mental powers or my external strength, but when I squeezed, even bricks would shatter into pieces.

I stripped down to a pair of brown shorts. A great laugh went up from the crowd. There were some long-winded, confusing explanations, which boiled down to the fact that if

I wanted to take the prize I would have to beat five different opponents. The young men of my village would not agree to this, and a shrill argument broke out. In the end it was agreed that I would have to beat two other wrestlers in preliminary bouts before I could go up against Thi, the wrestler with the most points.

A wrestler named Tien entered the ring. I charged him immediately. Tien was quite strong and tried to trip me. But over one thousand days of slurping through mud with loads of earth on my shoulders had tempered my legs; once I planted them they were as sturdy as fenceposts. Tien feinted this way and that, but still I stood, immovable. I grabbed his shoulders with my hands and started squeezing. After about three minutes he went limp, his face grew sallow, and he collapsed. The referee declared me the winner.

Then it was the turn of a wrestler named Nhieu. Nhieu was small and nimble. He jumped back and forth like a sparrow, slippery and very skilled. After just a few moves, I knew that Nhieu intended to trick me. He would wait until I was off-balance, then swoop down to grab me and throw me with his shoulder. Once I had worked this out, I turned my body sideways to him and stood with my weight balanced precariously on my forward leg. Nhieu stooped down and slid his head between my legs, intending to straighten up and throw me. A very cunning move. But I switched my weight to my back leg, clapped my knees together, grabbed his ribs, and began squeezing with all my strength. Nhieu writhed like a great snake. After a moment, when I felt the squirming stop, I set him down on his back and delivered a final blow to his belly. The cheering was thunderous. Someone stuffed a peeled piece of sugarcane in my hand. People crowded around me, fanning my face with their shirts as though I were a boxer in one of those Western boxing matches.

The drum sounded again. Thi, a large man with eyes like a boiled pig, entered the ring and performed a short series of moves, beautifully executed. The crowd oohed appreciatively.

Glowering, I entered. Thi stood before me and scowled. "If you value your life, boy, you'll give up now!"

"You wish!" I retorted.

"Son of a bitch!" Thi cursed. "Watch your nose, I'm going to pound it bloody!" And he threw himself at me, his knees raised dangerously.

Over ten minutes passed and Thi had not thrown me. He shifted tactics. He began to sneak illegal blows at me with his elbows and knees. The fight escalated. The referee should have called foul, but, being from Doai Ha himself, pretended to be blind. I was furious. Between fending off Thi's blows I asked, "What's this? Are you wrestling or fighting?"

"You son of a bitch!" said Thi. "I'm fighting you to your fucking death!" The drum beat faster, more urgently. Everyone was cheering and yelling, but no one stepped forward to stop the bout. Many were goading Thi on, hollering, "Beat him, beat him to death, damn it!" A surge of anger welled up in me. My vision blurred, my ears rang. I tasted the saltiness of blood on my lips. Thi leapt at me, both legs raised in a double kick. I dodged him and seized the opportunity to snag one of his ankles. Thi tried to pull free, but my hands were like iron pincers. Thi thrashed about on the ground. The crowd roared, "He's down, he's down!" The referee told me that my hold was illegal. Stone silent, I brushed him aside, stepped up to the awards table, and grabbed the prize for myself. Someone clapped me on the shoulders. "Brilliant! A real hooligan!" I didn't understand the meaning of the word 'hooligan,' but no doubt it was meant as a compliment.

I left the wrestling ring and stopped by a stall to buy a packet of candy for my younger brothers and sisters and a comb for my mother, then headed home by way of a shortcut across the fields and holm. It was dusk by the time I reached the river. From just beyond a turn ahead, a knot of people suddenly hurtled out aggressively. The wrestlers Thi, Nhieu, and Tien were in the lead. "You'll stop if you care to live!" commanded Thi.

"What is this, a mugging?" I asked. Without a word, they rushed at me and began to beat me. I fought back with no small skill, but suffered the disadvantage of one against many, and soon lost consciousness.

When I awoke, I found myself lying on a bed of straw. My whole body ached. "Does it hurt?" my mother asked. I nodded. My mother burst into tears. "Oh Chuong, my son! Why do you always have to outdo everyone else? Handing over your body for others' entertainment—aren't you embarrassed?" I cried silently because I realized she was right. "Promise me," said my mother, "you will never do anything like this again." I loved her, so I promised, but the thought occurred to me that from then on I should carry a knife with me wherever I went.

"Who rescued me?" I asked my mother.

She smiled. "Me Ca did." I wanted to ask more, but my mother had stepped outside to pan-roast chrysanthemum leaves for my medicine.

My recovery was a quick one. This was due more to my youth than the medicine, which was nothing more than chrysanthemum leaves roasted dry and then both rubbed into my skin and taken orally. When I was able to walk, my first thought was to grab a knife and go find the wrestler Thi. But the cooperative assigned me to a training course in town. I had to report almost immediately after receiving notice, so I resigned myself to abandoning my plans for revenge.

There were thirty people in our class, which lasted for six months. Our studies included scientific socialism, history, political economics, and accounting management skills. For the first time, I was exposed to strange new words, terms, and concepts. I craved them intensely. But after a few days I came to the painful realization that I was not a good student. It was as though the words and meanings slipped through my fingers; I was not able to differentiate between the principles of paying on receipt from accounts and those of statistical tables, just as I could not grasp the concepts of idealism and materialism. To me, dialectics meant to press forward no matter what the obstacles, sort of like my dream about plowing the field at Ma Nguy Mound. As for the rule of negation, I felt that it was like that despicable beating I had suffered at the hands of Thi and his gang. I hated them, that became the rule, and so I had to wreak revenge, to beat him worse than he had beaten me. When I studied history, I constantly muddled the different periods. My teachers were very frustrated with me, and told me I had no aptitude for learning.

No one in the class liked me. I lost merit points for the whole class. I was the odd one out. My clothes were different. Everyone else in the class dressed in the latest town fashions, which were very attractive. I liked their clothes but had no money, so I resigned myself to wearing my old brown work pants and blue shirt. As for meals, I cooked mine alone while the others ate communally. There were limits on how much you could eat in a group, and I ate eight or nine bowls of rice in one sitting, so how could I abide by their limits?

In class, I sat in a corner where I was free to doze off. My teachers gave up on me. They no longer tormented me, and on every test they gave me a straight average score of five points.

When the course was drawing to an end, the administration unexpectedly assigned Miss Phuong to our class as an accounting teacher. Miss Phuong had just returned from studying overseas. She was lively and outgoing, and wore jeans with her tee-shirt tucked in and a purse slung over her shoulder. She looked like a movie star.

As Miss Phuong was handing back our tests one day, she suddenly asked, "Who is Chuong?"

"That's me, Ma'am." I replied respectfully. The whole class burst into laughter, for Miss Phuong was quite young, barely as old as I was.

Miss Phuong suppressed a smile and told me, "I don't understand your essay. You have a truly mysterious method of accounting." Another guffaw from the class. Miss Phuong said, "Meet me after school. We'll go over the laws of economics again."

When the afternoon session was finished, I went in search of Miss Phuong. I was told that she had just taken off on her motorcycle in the direction of the river. Dejected, I shouldered my bag containing my books, money, and papers, and went for a walk.

After wandering aimlessly for a while, I somehow ended up at the river. I suddenly noticed Miss Phuong sitting alone beside her motorcycle. Around her, the scenery looked exactly like that of my village: a river in front and sugarcane fields behind it.

As I approached I saw that Miss Phuong was crying, her face buried in her hands and her shoulders shaking. I stammered out a greeting. Miss Phuong started and looked up. Seeing me, she fumed, "Go away! You and all the other goddamned men!" Shocked, I could only stare at her stupidly, my feet riveted to the spot. She grabbed her sandal and threw it at my face. It had a high heel and was put together with nails; I wasn't able to duck in time and immediately felt blood running down my face, blood running everywhere. I sat down, my head spinning. Miss Phuong ran over to me and knelt down, pulling my hands away from my face, frightened. "Are you all right? Oh God, I must have been out of my mind!"

I went down to the river and splashed water on the wound to wash it. Miss Phuong fussed over me like a mother hen, apologizing all the time. I showed her the scars on my shoulders and arms from the beating Thi's gang had given me. "It's nothing, Miss." I told her. "A little cut like that's hardly worth noticing."

Miss Phuong said, "I'm so sorry. I've just had too many rotten things happen to me. I couldn't help myself."

Miss Phuong got out some bread and bananas and pressed them on me. She said, "Forgive me. I loved, and I was betrayed. I couldn't stand it. You wouldn't understand unless you've loved too."

"I never have," I told her. "But I think that anyone who would betray love is a very bad person indeed."

Miss Phuong smiled painfully. "You don't understand at all. The traitor in this case is a good person. It's just that he didn't have the courage to sacrifice." She was sitting with her arms wrapped around her knees. She looked so tiny and sad, yet beautiful too. A feeling of compassion welled up in me, as one might feel toward a younger sister. She said, "Actually, that's not it. It's only proper that he didn't want to sacrifice anything for me. Don't you think I'm ugly?"

I shook my head, thinking that whoever might have the opportunity to love Miss Phuong would surely know true happiness. I told her, "Of course not! You're very beautiful."

Miss Phuong smiled. She picked up my bag and patted it. "What do you have in here?"

"Books, money, my ID card, and my Youth League card," I replied awkwardly. Miss Phuong said, "Chuong, if you loved someone, would you have the courage to make a sacrifice for that person?" I was embarrassed and did not know how to answer. She continued. "It's like this: suppose I loved you, would you dare to throw this bag into the river?" I nodded. "Throw it, then," she told me. I stood up, grasped the bag and launched it into the middle of the river. It sank like a stone. Miss Phuong was startled, the blood draining from her face. "And do you dare to tear down that fence over there?" Without a word, I walked to the fence surrounding the sugarcane field and proceeded to snap the barbed wire and uproot and bend the iron posts; then I threw it all at her feet.

"Come here," Miss Phuong said. She put her arms around my neck and kissed me on the lips. I went numb. Miss Phuong told me that she was delighted. "Can you believe it? It turns out I was miserable just because of one selfish man. In fact, it's nothing!" She mounted her motorcycle and, as she took off, turned around to say, "Be sure you forget everything you've learned about those damned laws of economics, you hear!"

I felt stunned. The unexpected kiss had made me dizzy. Elation swept over me. Just as I was, I waded into the river and swam to the other side, then swam back. By now, the moon shone brilliantly, and I felt that life was very beautiful indeed.

Two days later the course ended. Miss Phuong never did return; I heard that she had gone to Hanoi on business. Despondent, I packed my things, said my goodbyes, and returned to my village.

Upon my return, I was appointed chief of the accounting unit. But after a month, Mr. Hai Thin told me, "Sending you to class was nothing but a waste of good rice." I didn't mind it when they fired me. I returned to my usual work, the work I had done for the past ten years: plowing in the morning, digging laterite in the afternoon, and stripping bamboo in the evening. The work was hard, but did not ease my longing for Miss Phuong.

Once, I found an excuse to make the trip to town and stopped by the school to visit Miss Phuong. There was nobody left who recognized me. The duty staff asked me, "Which Phuong do you want to see? There are a lot of Phuongs at this school: Phuong Thi Tran, Phuong Thi Quach, Phuong Thi Le. Then there's one young woman who is about your age, but she's left the school. She used to live in the convent. Her confirmation name is Johanna Phuong Thi Doan." I gave a start, shocked. I was remembering the old fairy tale about Me Ca.

The duty staff didn't know anything else, and since it was summer vacation the school was deserted. I wandered through town, not knowing who to ask. Finally the idea occurred to me that I could go to the convent.

The Mother Superior received me. She was an older woman with a pair of distressingly melancholy eyes. She said, "Johanna Phuong Thi Doan lived in this convent from the time she was six until she was twelve. Her parents sent her to me to raise."

This surprised me. "Then why do people say that Johanna Phuong Thi Doan is Me Ca, the water nymph?"

"Johanna Phuong Thi Doan's parents live in Hanoi," said the Mother Superior. "She is the daughter of a Mr. Ngoc Huu Doan, a fish sauce merchant, who remarried."

Bewildered and disappointed, I turned to leave. The Mother Superior said, "I don't know about your Me Ca, but Johanna Phuong Thi Doan is the Lord's daughter. Mr. Ngoc Huu Doan thought he could use the Lord's house as though it were a daycare center, but the Lord wasn't angry. The Lord is all-forgiving and all-compassionate."

I spent that night sitting on the sidewalk outside the wall of the convent. The traffic on the streets was so noisy I couldn't sleep. Early the next morning, I made my way back along the dike towards the Tia Shrine.

The Tia Shrine is built right on the river, perched precariously atop a carefully constructed stone embankment. The guardian of the shrine was an old fisherman, about sixty years old, named Kiem. He had made the shrine his home. I stepped into the shrine and saw fish spread everywhere to dry; the floor of the courtyard was covered, and there were even fish hanging from the two cross-beams. Mr. Kiem gave me a snack of rice wine and roast fish. "I've been guardian of this shrine for more than forty years," he told me. "I live alone, except for the turtle I keep for company." He showed me a turtle lying underneath the bed, tethered by a string. I asked him about Me Ca. He said, "I don't know. But I remember the storm. Lightning lopped off the top the mango tree over on Noi Holm. You should go there to see what you can find out."

I visited with Mr. Kiem throughout the morning, helping

him patch some leaks in the roof of the shrine. At noon I took my leave and followed a shortcut across the fields towards Noi Holm.

The path to Noi Holm went by Doai Ha village, so I asked for the house of Mr. Hoi, the man who I'd heard had been saved, along with his daughter, by Me Ca. Mr. Hoi was old and senile. He said, "Digging sand. Dug a tunnel. Caved in. So heavy, so much blood..." No matter what I asked, he always answered the same.

Mr. Hoi's son told me, "He can't remember anything, you know. He's been deaf for three or four years now." Disappointed, I said goodbye to both father and son and left.

I swam across the river and reached Noi Holm. The ancient mango that had been struck by lightning so many years ago was now a dried-out carcass. Children had built a fire in its roots to create a deep, inky black hollow. There was a makeshift hut nearby, built to watch over some fishing nets set in the river. I stopped and peered in, then shuddered as I realized that an old man lay on a pile of straw in the dimness. Sensing me, the old man asked, "Is that Thi?" He sat up. I was horrified, for he resembled nothing so much as a demon, with his hair and whiskers bristling in every direction and a pair of murky, clouded eyes. I guessed he was paralyzed. His legs were withered and covered with stiff hairs like a pig's. I greeted him and was astounded to find that he was unusually clear-minded and articulate. After a few minutes of conversation, I learned that he was the father of the wrestler Thi from Doai Ha village. He had been paralyzed for many years, and so could do nothing but lie in one spot and watch the nets.

After chatting for a while, I asked the old man about the story of Me Ca. He laughed so hard that he held his belly and pitched back and forth, which seen together with his lifeless legs created a truly dreadful sight. I had never seen such a terrifying person. The old man told me, "See that beat-up basket over there? The water serpents did their love-making in that basket." And he laughed again. I stared, aghast. "Back then I wasn't paralyzed yet," the old man continued. "I made up the story of Me Ca. Everyone believed it. That's Me Ca's grave over there. If you want to see what she looks like, you can dig her up and take a peek." He was pointing at a mound of earth near the roots of the mango tree. I took a spade from the tent, went out to the mound, and started digging in the way that people do when excavating the graves of their ancestors for ceremonial reburial. When I had dug about a meter down, I pulled from the hole a shapeless chunk of rotted wood. For a very long time, I sat beside that chunk of wood. The demonic old man had left off his laughing, and by now he was probably sleeping in the hut.

Before me, the river flowed fervently on. Rivers flow to the ocean. Oceans are limitless. I had never known the ocean, and I had lived half my life already. Time was also flowing fervently on. In only a few more years it would be the year 2000.

I stood up and went home. Tomorrow I will go to the ocean. In the ocean, there are no water nymphs.

Story Two

When I left my mother to go to the ocean, do you suppose I knew where it lay? Not in the slightest!

My mother said, "Oh, Chuong, are you really going to abandon your mother? Abandon your little brothers and sisters?" Without a word in reply, I shot out through the gate at a near run. I knew that if I stopped at that moment I would never leave. I would return to the work of the previous ten years and continue on with it until the end of my days: plowing in the morning, digging laterite in the afternoon, stripping bamboo in the evening. I would drag out my life like this; like my father, like Mr. Nhieu, like Mr. Hai Thin, like all the meek, haggard peasants of my homeland.

I walked. I faced the rising sun and walked. I carried nothing but a razor-sharp knife that I had taken the trouble to have specially made all the way over in Doai Ha village. The knife had been forged from an automotive leaf spring; it tapered to a sharp point, and the steel had an azure sheen to it.

The thought of Me Ca, of Johanna Phuong Thi Doan, haunted me. Water nymph, if only I can find you and see you, then my life will have no regrets. For some reason I believe that you are there, so far away, in the ocean...

I passed through countless villages, hiring myself out as I went to earn money for food. These rural villages through which I passed were uniformly alike in their humdrum desolation. All around me, the same crops: rice, corn, sweet potato, and a few all-too-familiar greens. All around me, the same work: plowing, planting, transplanting, harvesting.

In the mornings I would find my way to the entrance of the nearest village and there I would stand, sometimes under a mangrove tree or in a merchant's ramshackle stall, at other times in a gritty little streetside market. There were many people like me, both men and women. They were all country folk, some drifters in search of work, others poverty-stricken locals. From the first cockcrow, these markets of human flesh gathered. The bosses thrust torches in our faces to illuminate us, then pinched each person's arms and legs. They asked, "Do you know how to do this? Or that?" Then we would agree on a price, generally nothing more than a pittance for a full day's work. If you figured it in rice, it came to about two and a half kilos to three kilos a day for a digger, and even less for a plowman, only 1.2 to 1.8 kilos. I usually hired myself out for fieldwork: planting, transplanting, harvesting, fertilizing. I didn't like to work indoors. The atmosphere out in the fields was fresher, with the free sky above my head and no burdensome need to deal with other people. The bosses who hired us were themselves barely making ends meet. They had to work day and night, and sometimes skipped a meal in order to pay us our wages.

The resentful, stagnant atmosphere of these country villages left me numb with emptiness and bitterness. Life was a constant, frantic search for food. Prejudices and tradition weighed heavily upon these folk. I saw countless people ruined by the old patriarchal practices. I also saw misconceptions about gender and morality destroy the beauty on so many young women's faces. Young men were a rarity. The only people working in the fields were old men, women, and children who didn't even go to school.

When the field work tapered off in March, I could no longer find regular work. Many days I went hungry. I walked on along the dike, surrounded by a silvery fog. Tiny suspended droplets of water stretched out in front of me, to my right, to my left, behind. Wind whistled past my ear. *"Hunger and cold are equal miseries."* The ancients who came up with that saying certainly knew what they were talking about. Once, I saw the body of an old beggar, dead from starvation, lying beside the dike. A shapeless dread welled up in me. I began to think of death, something I had never considered before. Hunger. Cold. Loneliness whipped against my face like a stiff wind. An anxious restlessness, somehow connected to Me Ca the water nymph, gnawed painfully at my heart. Who are you, my lady? Are you beautiful or homely? Where are you, in which corner of the horizon?

I began to imagine her. She came to me as a brilliant apparition. I could see every feature of her face with an intense clarity, down to her refined, courageous eyebrows. I saw immediately that her skin was burned dark, her manner cold. She is not beautiful. The distance between us is the distance between two free objects, at once antagonistic and enveloping. Neither she nor I will ever recognize the ownership of another, yet at the same time we desire to possess each other. She desires me and I desire her. She wants to enfold me into herself, as I do her, yet both she and I struggle to find release from such attachments. We yearn for freedom, yet it is at the very moment of freedom that we will lose each other. In order to have her, I have no choice but to live the life of a man sentenced to hard labor and exile. I have to wring myself out, even to my death. My lady's soul subsisted on a truly barbarous food: every bit of the freshness and liveliness in my life. In my imagination, I saw her ripping into my corpse with her delicate, sharp-nailed hands, chewing each bite of flesh, and then using her tapered tongue to lick the drops of oozing blood.

Such thoughts did not occur to me, however, while I was wandering with my hunger and thirst along the road. I would only come to understand them much later. At the time that I describe here, I was still a dullard, full of preconceptions and misunderstanding. I was a slow-witted peasant boy with a heart brimming with petty humanistic sentiments, at once idealistic, metaphysical, and thoroughly mediocre. I had not yet learned to scorn myself, or to scorn learning. I did not know how to love myself. My attachments to home and my sympathy for others of my village were wrapped in romantic, mythic colors, yet they were nothing more than a kind of low culture that could only impede me. I had not yet become enlightened as to my own individual existence, much less the existence of the human herd.

At the end of July, I agreed to make bricks for an old Son Tay woman. She was eighty years old and had a son in the army who was stationed in Cambodia. She also had a forty-two-year-old daughter named Thoi, married to a man in a distant village, who only occasionally returned to visit her mother for an afternoon of quick, cursory cleaning before leaving again. The old woman lived alone amidst an abandoned garden about one-tenth of a hectare in size. Her house was a mud-walled hut, roofed with straw, that would, with luck, last two rainy seasons before collapsing. Her son, whose name was The, commanded a company of army

engineers and had not yet married. The old woman let me
see the letters he wrote to her from Kompong Som. His
writing was fast and fluid, and the words were clearly those
of a dutiful son:

> *Dear Ma, I'm asking you to take it easy on yourself, if*
> *only to relieve me of my misery. I promise you that I*
> *will get home on leave next year. I'll build a house and*
> *get married. Go ahead and pick out one of the village*
> *girls for me. It doesn't matter if her complexion is*
> *pocked or if she is a widow, as long as she will love*
> *me. I'll only have ten days to accomplish everything,*
> *but when it's done you will be able to rest easy when*
> *you reach the Land of the Yellow River. As for me, I'm*
> *in good health and well-liked by everyone here. I*
> *always think of you, Ma. My missing you is like a thorn*
> *stabbing in my gut...*

I dug dirt and made the bricks right there in the garden.
We agreed on five hao for each unbaked brick I made. The
old woman would provide me with three meals a day, so once
the cost of the food was deducted, my actual wage would be
only three and a half hao. The old woman had told me, "All I
want is to fire six thousand bricks for him. It'll take him four
thousand bricks to build the house, and he'll have two
thousand left over for a kitchen. As you figure it, if I hire you
to do the whole job, from making the bricks to taking them
out of the kiln, do you think you can finish before the winter
solstice?"

"Yes," I said.

"I'm no good at planning," the old woman told me.
"What am I doing anyway, hiring someone in the middle of
the rainy season? What a mess! But I just kept putting it off
before. It's the fault of that Thoi. I told her to sell my earrings
for me, but she kept lying and saying she couldn't sell them.
It's fortunate that I met you and you've taken pity on me.

You're a hired hand, but I know you will work for me as though I were family. It's fate, I suppose, that I'll be able to leave behind something worthwhile for my son."

My eyes stung. I wanted to let out a cry that would rip the sky. I wanted to break our contract and return to the road. To my dismay, the rain kept coming down in sheets. After shaping each batch of several hundred bricks, I had to lug them to a sheltered area. I was always hungry. But there was no other work. I was forced to accept this accursed job, a job that might very well leave me empty-handed.

I won't go into detail describing the actual work I did. The old woman rose every morning at dawn and went out to glean the last of the sweet potato greens, spinach, and manh cong in the garden to put in the crab-paste soup. This would usually be served along with tiny pan-fried shrimp and crabs, or a mixture of salt and sesame seeds. The rice was cooked in an earthen pot. The old woman turned out to be very skilled at steaming rice; it was always just the right texture, never crushed or burned or dry, and it never had uncooked grains in it. All of her resolve was focused on those six thousand bricks. I wished I could focus my resolve on some concrete material goal like she did. If only I could be like that, if only I could be fulfilled like that.

By October I had finished making an even six thousand bricks and was beginning preparations to fire them, all at the same time, in two temporary kilns built like those used during wartime. The towering pile of unbaked bricks was quite a sight to see. The old woman stood, her tiny, frail shape almost disappearing among them, and sobbed great, bilious sobs. I said, "If I bake these in the kilns right here, the starfruit and banana trees in the orchard will die, ma'am."

"If they die, they die," she told me.

I said, "If we run out of firewood, I'll have to pull down the house for wood."

"So go ahead!" she said. "Next year my son will have a new house."

I fired up the two kilns on the day of the winter solstice, when the cold pierced all the way to one's gut. Our meal that day included a bottle of rice wine and a boiled pig's foot dipped in sauce. I drank half the bottle of wine, let fly a curse, and started to pull down the straw roof of the house to kindle the fire. The old woman lay in her hammock with an old felt blanket pulled over her. She was ill. I had to pull down half of the roof before I could get the fires going. The two kilns roared to life with brilliant red flame. It was as hot as the inside of an incinerator. As cold as the weather was, I had to strip down to my shorts, and even then I was bathed in sweat. The kilns burned for three days and three nights. The trees in the orchard were reduced to ashes. The old woman died on the third day. She died peacefully, without leaving any last words. I held her body in my arms and walked around and around the two brick ovens like a sleepwalker. Six thousand bricks. That meant that the old woman owed me two hundred ten thousand dong.

Thoi, the old woman's daughter, came the next morning with a gaggle of children in tow. They were all wearing white funeral scarves. Thoi felt around on her mother's body and found the pair of gold earrings, which she gave me as payment for my labor. I tucked them into my shirt and left while they were making a coffin. The plaintive sound of wailing echoed behind my back. I had spent nearly half a year working there. The ocean was still so far away...

At daybreak, I knocked on the door of a jewelry shop in the town of H. No doubt I presented quite a frightening sight. My hair had not been cut for six months, my clothes—the same ones I'd left home in—were now threadbare and ripped, and my only possession was a sharp knife.

I held out the earrings and offered them for sale. The store owner was barefoot. He knelt before me as though he were making an offering and said, "What are you doing with a pair of earrings like these, young man? These are just children's toys, sold everywhere in the market. Please, I've just opened for the morning, have mercy on me."

I plopped down on the ceramic tile floor. The owner pulled some jewelry from the display cases and explained to me the difference between 24K and 18K gold, between 70 percent and 100 percent purity, and how to recognize copper, platinum, and sapphires. He might as well have been speaking Greek for all I understood. The owner led me out to the street, to a small-goods vendor, and showed me the gold earrings and rings that are made for children's amusement. The earrings that I had received in payment from the old woman looked exactly the same as these toys. You could even break them into little pieces.

I said goodbye to this kindly but timid jewelry store owner and left. I stood at a three-way intersection in the road. Thick, soupy fog and silent emptiness enveloped me. I pulled out my knife and decided that I would stab to death the first person who passed in order to get a thousand dong for a bowl of noodles. I was hungry. I was as hungry as a chimpanzee. I was as hungry as a wild pig. I was as hungry as a beast in hell. I had been hungry for half a year. For half a year I had been eating nothing but the same sweet potato greens, spinach, and manh cong; a diet very conducive to anemia.

I stood for a long time. The fog gradually melted away, and I saw a group of young and old women carrying baskets on shoulder poles and heading toward me. A woman's voice, very sour, raised a brittle giggle. "Hey Phuong, there's someone you can hire to carry your baskets to the market." When they came abreast of me, the group stopped. Dumbfounded, I recognized the face of the girl named Phuong. It was the face that had haunted me in countless dreams, that same face, with its explicit, resolute features, at once unaffected and cold.

Phuong said, "Hey you, can I hire you to carry my baskets?"

"Yes," I said.

Phuong passed me the shoulder pole. She said, "You carry this rice to market for me, and I'll give you some money for a haircut." Everyone laughed, slapping my shoulders and poking my chest playfully. I shouldered the pole with its baskets and followed them as though it were something I must do, even though I had no idea why. Phuong walked beside me, swinging a red handbag made of fake leather.

It was nearing the Lunar New Year, so the market was as crowded as a temple on a festival day. It took no time at all for Phuong to sell all of her stock. She said to me, "Let's go get some crab noodle soup. Then if you wait for me to buy some things, you can carry my baskets home for me. Okay?" I nodded and followed Phuong into a crab noodle shop. In two good slurps I had finished off my entire bowl of noodles. Phuong burst out laughing and ordered another bowl. She asked me, "How many days have you gone hungry?"

As I answered, I was surprised to feel my eyes fill with tears. "I've been hungry for six months," I said. Around us, conversation suddenly died and everyone turned silently to stare at me. I doubt that any of them believed what I had said. Phuong did not say a word, but she abandoned her half-eaten bowl of noodles and sat there, watching me eat. When I finished, she asked me, "Would you like some rice pudding?" I nodded. She ordered a half-basket of rice pudding for me. In all my life, I have never had such a delicious meal.

I shouldered the baskets filled with Phuong's purchases and followed her home. She had only bought whitewash and paint, I didn't know what for. Phuong's house was situated in an area of fields and island-dotted rivers which looked exactly like my own home region. The only difference was that here there was a Catholic cathedral. Phuong lived with her father and a blind aunt whose real name I never learned. I just heard everyone call her Maria. Phuong had two younger sisters, one named Thuy and the other Lien. When she brought me home, Phuong told everyone, "I picked up this stray at the three-way intersection. He looks like an honest laborer, not some itinerant thief."

Phuong's father asked, "Well, young man, what's your name? Are you involved in any thievery?"

I replied, "I'm Chuong. I'm not a thief."

Phuong's father laughed. "I know that. You've got the face of a robber baron, not a thief. With earlobes like that, and a nose as straight as that, you are clearly not mediocre. So what brought you drifting here to our shores? Boredom?"

I said, "It's my fate."

Maria felt my face with her hands and cried out, "Dear Jesus! Lord above! Where's the human being? I don't feel any flesh at all. There's nothing here but earth and dirt."

I stayed on at Phuong's house. They offered to take me in for one month. Phuong's father was the leader of the local parish. My job was to repaint, with both whitewash and paint, the entire cathedral. The most difficult part of the job would be to repaint the statue of Our Lord which stood on the bell tower roof. The statue was a two-meter-tall image of Jesus Christ wearing a red robe, his arms spread wide and his feet planted on a globe. It was fastened to the highest point of the bell tower roof. There was no level place nearby on which one could build a scaffold. In order to repaint the statue, my only option would be to fasten a rope around my waist and then secure the rope to the statue. My job contract did not include insurance. Phuong's father told me, "Our parish will provide you three meals a day, and if you die, we'll bury you. When you finish we'll pay you two hundred thousand dong." Remembering my compensation for making bricks for the old Son Tay woman, I gave a tearful smile.

Phuong said to me, "You should think twice about this job. That statue is two hundred years old. The mortar might have rotted. What if you climbed up there and died for it?"

I said, "The Lord will be with me. If not, then there is no Lord."

It took me nearly a month to paint the cathedral. First, I

scraped off the old layers of whitewash. Then, I put on two new layers of whitewash and finished it off with a coat of yellow lime. Thuy and Lien were my assistants. Phuong's father supervised the work. He told me, "My boy, my only regret is that you're not the religious type. I've got three daughters, so if you were, I'd give you all three in marriage." My face flushed a sudden, hot red. I gave a painful laugh. What did he think I was, a dog in search of a bitch? My heart already belonged to her, to Me Ca, to the water nymph...

After finishing with the whitewash and repainting all of the cathedral's windows and doors, I began preparations for painting the statue of Our Lord. On the day before I was to climb the bell tower roof, Phuong boiled up some medicinal mint in a large kettle and told me to bathe in it. Everyone in Phuong's household was particularly solicitous of me. They knew that come the next day I might no longer be among the living. Phuong's father seemed anxious. In the middle of the night, he woke me up, brewed a pot of strong green tea, and invited me to drink. "Chuong, my boy," he said, "perhaps you should just forget about it and not do the statue after all. Somehow, I keep worrying about it."

I said, "Don't worry about me. That's what the job is."

The old man sighed. "Yes, that's what it is, all right. If anything untoward should happen, will you bear resentment against me?"

"No," I said.

He thought for a moment and then asked hesitantly, "Chuong, do you want to leave any last words?"

I smiled. "There are sixty million people in our country, and fifty-eight million would only laugh in the face of any last words I might leave."

"I understand," said the old man. "Go on to sleep then."

I slept. In fact, I wasn't worried in the least. Ever since the day I left home, I had very rarely thought about myself. My desires had lifted me away from the earth. My thoughts were in no way involved with life or my own continued existence. Of what importance was it whether I lived today as an animal or as an emperor? My heart was withered, stunted. I knew only too well about the feelings that Phuong, the parish leader's daughter, had for me. I knew that Thuy and Lien had feelings for me also. I knew it all. I had no right to bind my life to theirs, for, if I did, in the end I would live no differently than Mr. Nhieu, than Mr. Hai Thin, than all the other meek, haggard peasants of my own village or of this parish. The best I could hope for would be a house of grass thatch with four loving hearts under its roof. The Miss Phuong that I met in my accounting class so long ago and Phuong the parish leader's daughter were both nothing more than small fragments of my lady, the water nymph, the one I longed to meet.

The next morning, I climbed to the bell tower roof. I carried with me a rope tied in a noose, which I tossed around Jesus Christ's neck to secure it. I tied the other end of the rope around my waist and set about my work, swinging back and forth as I painted. The entire parish huddled below and held their collective breath as they followed my progress. It needed only a small slip, a snap of the rope, or a loss of balance and I would plummet thirty-two meters to the stone-paved courtyard.

I lost myself in my work. I had no idea how much time passed. There was a bird's nest in the sleeve of Jesus Christ's robe. The wisps of straw in the nest looked like spun threads of pure gold.

By the end of the day I had finished repainting the statue. A feeling of elation swept over me, leaving me breathless. At the last minute, without even knowing why I did it, I gave into the rash temptation to sign my name on Our Lord's broad, serene forehead. Feeling with my fingers into his flowing locks, I used my knife with the pointed blade to carve my name. For this act, I would subsequently pay a very high price, one which I could never have fathomed beforehand.

I stood on the statue's shoulders and gazed into the distance. The ocean's waters rose before me, as taut as a stretched thread. I heard the heavy, panting sound of the waves. In one corner of the ocean, I saw a halo of shimmering rays. I don't know why, but I thought that this must be the water nymph's home.

I descended to the cathedral courtyard amidst the cheers of the entire parish. I was dizzy and utterly exhausted. I lay down on the stone steps and fainted. My soul felt as light as a wisp of smoke. It skimmed above the cathedral's balconies, above the grass and straw roofs, above the small alleys and the banana groves. My soul flew above the dry, cracked fields. I didn't even wake when the crowd carried me home.

After resting for a few days, I took to the road again. I was wearing a new suit made from cloth dyed brown from tree bark and carrying my knife with the pointed blade. Phuong's entire family was sorry to see me go and followed me to see me off. The parish leader, old Maria, and little Thuy and Lien accompanied me all the way to the end of the banana grove before stopping. Maria placed a chain with a crucifix around my neck and made a sign on my chest. Phuong continued to walk with me a distance farther. She said to me, "Chuong, so you are really leaving?"

I nodded and said, "You go ahead and go home now. Remember to pray for me."

Phuong laid her head on my chest and sobbed. "Go on then, go. May your feet be firm and the rocks soft. I can't hold you. I'm asking you to go easy on yourself, if only to relieve me of my misery."

I hurried away from her, nearly running. Before me was a river. Rivers flow to the ocean. Oceans are limitless. I had never known the ocean, and I had lived half my life already. Time was also flowing fervently on. In only a few more years it would be the year 2000.

I continued on my way. Before me, who knew what

surprises awaited? Who are you, my water nymph? Where are you, my water nymph? What kind of love is this, my water nymph? Let me set out with my borrowed illusion...

Story Three

> *I wander the land of the dispossessed, left with only myself*
> *In these stranger's lands, even the smoke is bitter*
> *In these stranger's lands, even the wine is sour.*
> —Nguyen Binh

Since I left the parish by the river and set out again, several long years have passed in what seems but a moment. I have experienced countless events, met countless people, met them and then left them. Countless joys and sorrows, also bitterness and delight. Ah, but why is it that even the delights I have tasted seem so bland? Yet, there have been delights.

I have loved, and been loved. I have also fled many times. "Chuong! This isn't it. This still isn't it!"

I have lived in many places, worked many jobs. I have also abandoned all of it many times. "Chuong! This isn't it. This still isn't it!"

I remember when I was ten years old, when the village was abuzz with stories about Me Ca. I often walked along the beach by the river in the morning and secretly wished to see visions. Fog spread itself along the surface of the river. When the sun rose, the fog melted, dispersed, and drifted upward like smoke, like a cloud. The river's surface bared itself, sleepy and somewhat self-conscious. Waves washed against the beach, carrying with them the corpses of countless mayflies, pushing them up to my feet. This was the first time the sensation of permanence and impermanence came stealing in to probe my soul. I didn't know it then, and I never paid any attention to it. I was still so young! Back then, loss and absurdity, as well as the awareness of the passage of time, did not cause me any anxiety.

I walk along the sandy beach of a river. I see a cavity in the sand right at the edge of the water. I imagine that the water nymph rested here the night before. She lies on her side, curled up, her knees drawn to her chin. She talks with the waves, and the waves envelop her. She whispers secrets to the waves. She says, "Ah waves! Enough now, enough jesting, enough silliness."

I walk. The time in which I am living is a time of hardship and suffering. The war is over and people have begun to build their lives anew. The old wounds are gradually closing up under a layer of tender skin. People busy themselves in the search for work, the search for hope. An endless wave of people flows from the countryside into the city, enough to form a whole new class of drifters. I walk among these people with a heart anxious and fearful of my fate, that same fate I share with the few farmers who have either sunk to the lowest reaches of poverty or who suffer the most ambitious flights of fancy. Is there any value in the things we have left behind? The tranquil river of our home, the stand of bamboo at the entrance to the village, the moss-covered wall built of laterite, the dark shape of one's mother printed desolately against the afternoon sunlight. Ah, the devil take it! I vomit on such memories. There's no money in them, nor are they likely to bring me cheer. Here, there is no hope.

I walk. I want to see what lies ahead.

I walk. How I crave love, as a man in the desert craves water! There, a confusion of desires jostles for attention: happiness, tears, well-being, horizons; horizons and the distant stretch of ocean, a cozy corner of an orchard, a small house with large windows. Oh, so many things! My Me Ca, my vision of something more than a girl, more than a woman. It is a vision of the half of the world that lies above me—or, perhaps, the half that lies below—a vision of Heaven and Earth. Water nymph! Where are you? What are you doing? Why do you not come to me? You only send your envoys to me—like that sudden rainfall the other day, or that sudden moonlit night not long ago, or that sudden sweet flute-song I heard, or that sudden, hasty kiss that pierced me with sorrow and left me numb to the very depths of my heart.

Enough, enough. Exactly how disgraced and base have I become? Where? And from where? For what? But Chuong, do you think anyone besides yourself can see your loneliness and impotence? What did anyone do? And what did you do? For what kind of love?

So! I must acknowledge that within my desire to find my life there lurks a demon that has been sleeping, perhaps for many centuries. This demon is selfish, solitary, and shameful; it is skeptical of much, wary of much, self-seeking and contemptible. If it spends a few moments pondering religion and human nature, it does so only to better contrast and hone its own demonic character. It is at once foolish, wise, and nimble. It is as suspicious as Cao Cao. It understands the times. Ah! It understands the pitifully few opportunities afforded it. It searches and scours. It betrays my heart. It murders any decent and noble desire or ambition in me in order to continue its own life in this philistine body of mine. I have met it many times in the murkiness of my unconscious mind. At times I must hide my face, I must drown in my anguish, and at times I run away in humiliation and self-pity. It sits in a corner of my soul and softly sings its song, cold and taunting. It spits in disgust upon order. Well, that's to be expected! But also upon love, morality, friendship, trustworthiness, loyalty, and religion. It knows that these are but conventions, inexact and transient, things that one constructs to address certain inescapable situations while not understanding much of life. The man who builds them will find himself confused and ashamed when he is suffering angst or failure. In other words, when he has exhausted his possibilities in life. The Lord against which this demon is most vigilant and most fears is not God, but rather the Grim Reaper himself. Of this I am sure. Of this I am sure...

I walk. Yesterday it rained. Today the weather is sunny

and beautiful. Tomorrow will be sunny. I am Chuong. I walk. I want to lash out with curses. I walk. I am walking. I want to lash out!

Not long ago, I hired myself out to a family of city people. The head of the household was a rich man. They lived in a villa, and they were now building an additional wall to seclude it from the outside. I agreed to work for them along with five others, among them a young Muong woman from Hoa Binh named May.

I had been on the job for three days when May approached me at lunchtime and said, "Chuong, the mistress told me to invite you up to the house."

I stepped into the living room, a large, carpeted room with sophisticated and somewhat fussy furnishings. On the wall hung a woven image of two horses nuzzling each other. The clock on the wall ticked dubiously. I thought: if this were my home, it would have a small door and large windows, no decorations at all, and outside there would be grassy fields and woods.

After waiting for some time, a voice called out from above to invite me up. The mistress of the house was around thirty-two years old and beautiful. She was lying on a bed.

"Come in," she said. I stepped inside the room. She said, "Please sit down. My name is Phuong. And you, what is your name?"

"My name is Chuong, the son of Hung," I said.

Phuong smiled. "Sit down. Your name has no meaning to me. Take a good look, now. Am I beautiful?"

"Yes," I said.

Phuong laughed. "You are too quick to answer. You don't yet understand what is beauty and what is homeliness in a woman. You see that I am rich, and you assume I am beautiful. You see that I am educated, and you assume that I am beautiful. Not so! If I were beautiful, I would see in your eyes the unmistakable light of lust."

I smiled sadly, not knowing how to answer. Phuong said, "You are a hired hand, a peasant. Am I right?"

"Yes," I told her.

Phuong said, "That means you have nothing. You are powerless."

"I'll thank you not to insult me," I said.

"I'm not insulting you," replied Phuong. "I am merely stating a truth. You have no possessions, no personal belongings. You have no right to be proud. You shouldn't be offended at this observation. You shouldn't object."

I was silent, as I didn't understand much about rich and educated people. To me, they were inscrutable, talented yet dangerous. Well, so be it! Did my mistress want my labor? What did she want? My soul? It wasn't until some time afterward that I understood that I did have a few redeeming qualities along with the garbage. I had to pay a price for this lesson. But that was afterwards, much later .

In the end, Phuong and I understood each other. I got on the bed and lay down. Phuong said, "You are in such a hurry, so rushed! You're nothing but a helpless beast. Helpless beasts think love is just another job to be done, like plowing. Their attitude toward life is the same. But it is not so at all! Life is an ongoing process of deterioration, a process of getting yours. That's it!" I growled like a lion.

Phuong said, "Oh be quiet. Don't growl. Even lions are nothing but pitiful beasts, afraid of other lions. Relax, my father-in-law is dead and my husband is not at home." I tried to smile, but ended up grimacing. I regretted that I was so uneducated and unable to argue. I understood nothing. I felt nothing.

"All the mysteries of the universe, of society, of fame and prestige and money and art," Phuong told me, "are centered on this one thing. The highest and hugest obsession, above and beyond all other obsessions, even religion and politics, is sex. You men are rudderless because you are terrified of it. You don't dare to be passionate. The patriarchy is an obscene institution, full of violence and lies, designed primarily not to serve people but to suppress the bestial nature men direct toward one another. Do you understand?"

"No," I said. "Maybe because I'm alone," I added.

Phuong said, "You are despicable. You know it only too well even though you are alone. Because your father knew it. You are as vile as your father, your old Mr. Hung. And old Mr. Hung is as vile as the old Mr. Bears, or Mr. Wolves, or Mr. Goats, or Mr. Pigs that make up your ancestral line. You understand that order in your very bones. Don't pretend that you don't. Hidden within you is an anti-democratic, patriarchal power. You are as despicable as the thirty million men who are your contemporaries. Now put on your pants and get out of my sight."

Embarrassed, I left. I didn't much like what had happened. I went back to my place in the temporary workers' housing in the corner of the orchard. I slept. In my dream, I saw myself wandering, lost, in the middle of a dry riverbed. I walked upriver for a long time. On either side steep cliffs rose upward like a path to the sky. I saw the water nymph. She appeared in an eerie, amorphous light. She was not eloquent, only sad. "Chuong!" she said. "This is not the road to the ocean."

I stayed at Phuong's house for several long months. Phuong's husband was out of the country, and the children were in school all day. Phuong had rather strange opinions about love. "I am savoring you. I am nibbling at you," she told me, "just as people snack on food. I and thirty million other women are moaning. I am an activist for women's rights."

Phuong also told me, "You men have made arbitrary laws to suit yourselves. My husband, too. They have a wife and then they have a mistress, their 'number two.' They have their secret pleasures. You are my 'number two.' How do you like that?"

"I like it all right," I said.

Phuong said, "You have a simple and primitive nature. I like that. It's uneducated and immoral but wholesome."

Phuong introduced me to her girlfriends. They were all beautiful, mature, educated, and rich. The things they said in the bedroom were unlike anything I had ever heard when I still lived at home, or when I went to school, or when I left to make my own way in life. I began to grasp that there are many fraudulent things in life that have been prettified to have a glittering appearance.

Phuong asked me, "When they sleep with you, do the other women cry out?"

"A few," I said.

Phuong smiled. "Those cries—that is our true language in its most primitive and purest form, more noble than any lullaby or poetry or music. I've always felt that such cries are like the cries of the ape-men in their caves." I thought about that, and it made sense. But I didn't cry out.

I told Phuong and her girlfriends about my village near the river. About how my family was poor and everything around us was poor. About the flood season, and how I would swim to Noi Holm in the middle of the river to gather firewood. About how the river turned red from the clay silt. The rotted branches drifting helter-skelter. The dizzying whirlpools. The mosquito larvae contorting in their mad dance, and the beaches turned white with the corpses of countless mayflies who had died their calm, unruffled deaths. They never gave a second thought to morality. They were never eloquent.

"Is that how you like it?" asked Phuong.

I said, "I like it all right."

"To me, it has no meaning," Phuong said. "You should know that life is vast."

I didn't answer. To me, my life and the life of the peasants in my village was simple and mundane. It didn't raise many questions. We live, grow up, hundreds and thousands of generations one after the other centered only on making a living, on family, religion, home, and carnal desire. What need have we for much money, multiple houses, excessive morality and legions of heroes? The morning flies by, then noon, then afternoon. Spring flies by, then fall, then winter. Only sorrow is eternal.

"Only sorrow is eternal," I said.

Phuong said, "Perhaps. But don't be so sure." I envisioned the corpses of all those mayflies deposited on the beach by the waves. I suddenly realized that mankind has to search far back in time before finally uncovering anything with a trace of real cultural value, something that can touch us even today, like a couplet from *The Tale of Kieu*, or a Cham statue, or the trace of a fingerprint on an ancient ceramic vase. How many billion mayflies had died without leaving a trace?

"Only sensation," Phuong told me. "We women trust only our sensations, and sensation by definition is inexact and temporary. You enter this house and you get the sense that we are a rich and happy family. But in fifty more years, people will tear this house down. It does not belong to culture! I don't know how to transmit sensation into history, but if I did I would make it an unending stream of rapture. At least that way history would be less cruel and vulgar than it is in reality."

I had very little time to reflect upon such abstruse matters. Compared to others, I had nothing. I had no money, no prestige, no family to care for and worry about, no friends. I didn't even have legal papers. I was a zero. I was happy alone, sad alone, daydreamed alone. I had only the water nymph waiting for me.

"That's why you are a happy man," Phuong told me. "It's when people grudgingly consent to ownership that they become bound to the thing that they own. It is a kind of invisible slavery that turns the earth into hell. I am living in that hell, the hell of civilization, law, family, and school. As for you, it is you who are in heaven."

I smiled inwardly. I was remembering everything I had

experienced in life. I remembered the gaggle of naked children sitting on the riverbank, sheltering in the stands of sugarcane. We had sublime conversations about the Russians and Americans making atomic bombs, about how Mrs. Mencius disciplined her son, about the time they caught a whale, but when they finally got it onto the shore, there was nothing left but a skeleton. Such are children's tales, earth-shaking tales.

Phuong said, "Chuong! What are you thinking?"

I said, "In a house with a ceramic tile floor, it's really hard to move around."

Phuong said, "My husband says the same thing. He reproaches me, says I don't know how to walk in the house, that my movements are not vivacious, that I take each step as if I am counting them."

Phuong spoke as if she were on a stage. I was remembering the watchman's lean-to I built while guarding the sugarcane in my home village. On a clear, still moonlit night, how I sat with my chin in my hands and my eyes fastened on the distant stars. Unseen eyes somewhere in the profound space of the infinite heavens were following me. Of this I was certain, and it moved me. Afterwards I would ascribe this feeling to her, to Me Ca, to the water nymph, to the woman who was still waiting for me in some distant place, always half a globe away. I knew that she still had hope, and this knowledge was my final refuge against the desolate solitude of my heart. I had lived through many ordinary moments: fighting a gang of thugs, working without pay for the poor, swapping insolent banter with hooligans. Still, those formless eyes followed me, never leaving me. Still she whispered to me in the night. "Chuong," she said, "this still isn't the way to the ocean."

Phuong told me, "Perhaps in the previous generation my father and older brothers were as you are now. They gave us so much, material things in particular, but there is one thing they never gave us: a vibrant civilization."

"What is a vibrant civilization?" I asked.

Phuong said, "I've thought about that a lot, but maybe I only need one word to express my conclusion: pleasure!"

I lay still, without replying. I didn't really understand the things that Phuong told me. What is it that makes people hunger for life? I asked Phuong this. She answered, "Good food, adulation, and sex. If you can think of anything more, that's up to you."

The time I spent in Phuong's house wore me down. I was completely drained. I had to service up to three of her high-class friends every day. My vision blurred and I suffered dizziness. It was even more exhausting than the dirt-digging I had done in the old days. But most frightening of all were the things that those women poured into my soul. Bile, all of it. How could life be so filled with chains and slavery?

Several days after Phuong's husband returned home, I was abruptly fired. That evening I lay in my corner of the temporary housing. My whole body screamed in pain; my back ached as though bent to breaking and my throat was dry. In the middle of the night, I heard the door creak and May entered, carrying a bowl of hot rice porridge for me.

"Chuong! Are you running a fever?" she asked.

"No," I told her.

May said, "Chuong, I have to go to the master tonight. I can't refuse because the amount of money he's offered me is tremendous. I don't want to save my virginity for anyone else. I want you. You must help me." May reached out and unbuttoned the top button of my shirt. In the murky darkness, she turned away and I glimpsed a naked back wriggling before me, catching the light of the moonlight and looking at once frightening and beautiful. I suddenly thought of Me Ca, the water nymph. My heart was shot through with a sensation of pain and longing.

May gave several soft cries. To me, they seemed to be sobs echoing from some impossibly far place, sobs brought to me from the desert. My tears mingled with hers, one wetness staining two faces.

May pulled away from me in dismay. "Chuong! You're impotent?" I buried my face and cried noiselessly in shame. She stood up and said, "I understand. Such is my fate. Don't be sad. Don't cry anymore. Those people in the house up there, they always have it all. Chuong, I'm asking you to go easy on yourself, if only to relieve me of my misery."

She slipped away and ran out to the courtyard. I felt the roof above me collapse onto my head, the very heavens collapse upon my head. All was destroyed, left in ruins.

Early the next morning, I left the city. There was nobody for me to say goodbye to.

I continued, on and on. Before me, the river flowed fervently. Rivers flow to the ocean. Oceans are limitless. I had never known the ocean. I had never known the ocean and I had lived half my life already. In only a few more years it would be the year 2000.

Water nymph! Where are you? In what place? For what? Because of what? Let me set out with my borrowed illusion...

Water nymph! Where are you? In what place? For what? Because of what? Let me set out with my borrowed illusion...

Translated by Rosemary Nguyen

The Woodcutters

Sawing wood, stealing lumber,
Whoever is stronger
Can eat the king's rice;
Whoever loses the game
Can go home and suck breasts.
—Lullaby

Several years ago, I traveled with a group of woodcutters up to the mountains to earn some money. There were five of us, led by my cousin Buong. Buong was a well-known gangster. He used to be a commando in the navy. In 1975, he got involved in a case of stealing some nitrogenous fertilizers in our district and was put in jail for three years. After Buong got out of jail, he did not look for work. Instead, he opened a dog meat restaurant. He went bankrupt within a year. During the year that he ran his restaurant, many families in my village lost their dogs mysteriously. One family even kept their dog in a cage, and put the cage in a locked room, but the dog still disappeared. The People's Committee of the village suspected that Buong was responsible for these thefts, but they didn't have enough evidence to arrest him. Afterwards, he lost money gambling, got depressed, and burned down his restaurant. Buong then became a tree-trader. He tried to buy every longan, jackfruit and sapodilla tree, as well as every other kind of fruit tree in the village, even if their flowers were just beginning to bloom. He was in this business for two years, then turned to trading up the river. He eventually formed a group of woodcutters who traveled with him into the forest. He told us that up in the mountains sawing was a profession full of potential.

There were twin brothers in our group, Bien and Bieng, seventeen years old, both as strong as working buffalos. Buong and I shared the same family name, Dang. Bien and

Bieng came from the Hoangs. I didn't know how we were related, but Bien and Bieng called Buong "Uncle" and called me "Little Uncle." Bien and Bieng were the sons of Hai Dung, who taught martial arts in my village. He belonged to the Thieu Lam Hong Gia School. I was his disciple for two years. Bien and Bieng were younger than I. In our group, apart from the four of us, there was also Little Dinh, Buong's second son. Dinh was fourteen years old. He went along to cook for us.

I was a young and healthy man. I had finished my last year at the university. Since I failed the final graduation exams, I had no choice but to stay home and wait for a year to take the exams again. I had many brothers and sisters— my parents gave birth to nine children—who all worked the rice fields. They were simple and honest. I was the most troublesome in the family.

Buong said to my parents, "Ngoc [Ngoc is my name] has the blood of a wanderer. The Tu Vi Star lies in his Mobility Quadrant, aided by the Ta Phu and Huu Bat Stars. If he goes out, he will get help from others. If he stays home, he will have a poisonous life and die. If you love him, let him go with me to the forest."

"I'm just afraid that he'll spoil your work," my father said.

"If he does, I'll beat the hell out of him," Buong snorted. "Wanderers have their own rules. If he goes with me, you'll save food for your family and earn some money at the same time. I'll return him to you in one piece within a year. Is that okay?"

"You ask him," my father said.

"Come with me, okay?" Buong asked. "If you stay home with your mother, you'll never become wise."

"Okay," I said. "But if you beat me, I'll hit you back."

"All right," Buong sneered. "As cousins, we should behave kindly toward one another."

Ten days after celebrating the Lunar New Year, we set

off. Buong's wife made some food for us before we left. We were very enthusiastic, despite the fact that there was not much food: a plate of boiled stuffed pork intestine, a plate of salted greens, two bowls of potato soup cooked with chicken necks and wings, and a plate of chicken bones. Buong's wife saved the chicken meat for Buong's father, who was sick in the hospital.

"Have sympathy," Buong said. "I wanted to deploy our troop in a stately manner, but I'm too poor. This very same day of next year, I promise to treat each of you to an entire stewed chicken."

After we finished our meal, we set out toward the road. Each of us had a rucksack full of rice and clothes. Little Dinh carried pots, pans, plates, and bowls. Our equipment included two sets of saws, several jumpers, several saw files, and nothing else.

Buong's wife brought their other three children to see us off. "Enough," Buong said. "The mother of my children should go home. Guard your pussy safely. I'll be back in a year."

"Go to the devil!" Buong's wife retorted, half laughing, half crying. "The water's very poisonous up there. Don't bathe at night or you might catch marsh fever."

"Yes, I'll remember that," Buong said. "What a pain! Who would take a cold bath at midnight anyway? Go home now. Darling, keep your love for me in your heart. Please don't flirt with any bastards."

"Say goodbye to your father, children," Buong's wife told her three kids.

"Goodbye, father," all three of them chirped.

"All right, all right! Goodbye to you, gentlemen and madame. Eat and sleep in peace. Your father must leave your mother behind and endure hardship on the road."

"Dinh, my boy," the mother said. "When you cook rice, please remember to fill the water up to about one finger-joint and a half. That should be enough."

"I'll remember that, Mother. At home, please don't beat little Tin. I hid my savings of several hundred behind the mirror. You can spend it, Mother."

"Enough, you sentimentalists," Buong cut in. "If you keep going on like this, the literature of our country will melt into water pretty soon."

We went to the bus station in Hanoi, looking for the bus departing for the Northwest. Buong seemed very experienced. It was the first time that Bien, Bieng, and Little Dinh had gone to such a faraway place, and thus everything was strange to them.

"Be careful," Buong warned us. "In Hanoi, thieves are as numerous as sea slugs. If they steal our saws, we will surely become beggars."

The road to the Northwest had many hills and slopes. Bien and Bieng got carsick and vomited their bile out. After two entire days on the bus, I was also completely exhausted.

After we got out of the bus, we ate a quick simple meal and rested one night in the town of H. The next day, we followed Buong deep into a mountainous area that belonged to the Dawn Production Unit, Collective Farm X. On both sides of the road were vast fields of corn and cotton. Sky-high limestone mountains stood one after another. Walking along the base of the mountains, we seemed so small, so lonely, so daring, so helpless, and even meaningless. White mountain flowers bloomed in abundance, a white color that stirred the heart and made us anxious. White flowers, were you this white a thousand years ago?

"The bastard who gave this wretched remote place its name, Dawn, is a vile cheater," Buong said. "The title is significant. They named regions of malignant spirits and poisonous water Future, Dawn, New Establishment, Solidarity, and Self-Strengthening. Such deceptive names! Likewise, in restaurants named 'For The Common People' and 'Politeness,' customers are charged cut-throat prices. Chinese herb-sellers even name their abortion doses

'Rejuvenation' and 'Savior.' The literature of our country is truly rich!"

We laughed and chatted as we walked. When it was about to get dark, we happened upon a couple pushing a cart of firewood. The wife held the cart's shafts, while her husband pushed it from behind. The husband wore glasses and had an intellectual look. The wife, slender and light-skinned, looked very pretty. Buong teased them, "Thach Sanh chops firewood in the forest. His princess hauls the wood home without rest."

"If you pity this princess, then give her a hand," the wife retorted. "This princess doesn't need poetry."

"Well done!" Buong laughed. "Bieng, give her a hand. Excuse me, where are you going at this late hour, working so hard?"

"Back to the Dawn Production Unit," the wife replied. "And where are you going to cut wood?"

"We don't know yet," Buong said. "We don't even know where we'll sleep tonight."

"Why don't you come to our house?" the husband offered generously. "Our place is pretty big, and there are only the two of us."

Bieng took the cart's shafts, and we all pushed it. On the way to their house, the husband told us that his name was Chinh and his wife was Thuc. Chinh was a medical doctor at the collective farm and Thuc was a secondary-school teacher. The couple had a house in the area of the Dawn Production Unit. They had been married for more than a year and did not have any children yet. They were both from Ha Nam Ninh Province.

After dinner, we chatted at leisure.

"A big white seraya tree fell down in Ta Khoang," Chinh said. "Mr. Thuyet, the vice director of the collective farm, asked for its timber to build his house. If you ask him, you'll get the job."

"Forget it," Thuc said. "Make timber for that old guy

323

from the Fourth Region and you'll eat iron shit. That old guy is very stingy."

"Do dogs and horses get to choose their owners?" Buong asked. "Older sister, if you have pity on animals like us, please show us the way to that Mr. Thuyet's."

"All right then," Thuc said. "It's only a few houses from here."

Buong followed Thuc. They came back a little while later.

"Tomorrow our troop will go to Ta Khoang," Buong told us.

"I admire Buong," Thuc told her husband. "He's really humble. Chinh, do you know anyone besides that old guy who would pay people to make lumber in the forest at the same cheap rate as he'd pay workers on the collective farm? Workers on the collective farm have their subsidized rice portion. You guys are freelance workers. Where will you get food to eat?"

"I'm not humble at all. I just have no other choice but to accept the work. Sawing wood and stealing lumber, you know."

"People from the Fourth Region are terrible," Thuc said. "It must be the poor land that makes them frighteningly stingy. During the entire time we were there the head of that household did not even offer any of us a sip of hot tea."

"You're full of prejudice," Chinh said. "One should only consider the origin and homeland of ordinary people. It's not so important to consider that of able men."

"An able man, that Thuyet?" Thuc sneered.

"Whoever he might be, he is now the vice director of the collective farm," Chinh said. "Don't hold him in such contempt."

"That's you," Thuc protested. "You always consider decorum important."

"That guy truly is an able man, Older Sister," Buong said. "He talked to me as if he were talking to a Mr. Zero. It's one way of reaching enlightenment. Don't you see that he didn't let me say anything back at all?"

"What kind of a religion is that, then?" Thuc laughed.

"There are many religions in our country," Buong said. "In the South, one weird religion even worships both Quan Cong and Victor Hugo."

"Then I know what religion Thuyet follows," Thuc said.

"So do I," Buong said and smiled.

The next morning, we woke up very early. We cooked and ate our breakfast, then got ready to go see Thuyet. Before we left, Thuc said, "I saw that you cooked soup with nothing in it. Take this bag of MSG for some taste." At first, Buong refused to take it. "If you have no respect for us, then next time don't even stop by our place," Thuc told him.

Buong had no choice but to accept the gift. "We must repay this good deed," he sighed.

"It's hard to deal with this woodcutter," Chinh laughed. "If you're over-prudent like that, you'll grow old very soon."

We met Thuyet at the end of the alley. I shuddered when I saw his face: a dark-skinned face, as gray as the color of a scrotum, his eyebrows thick, his projecting teeth yellow as a dog's. "It will be several kilometers of walking," he said. He immediately led the way and did not utter another word during the rest of the trip.

The giant tree had fallen during a storm. It lay across an empty stream. It was almost thirty meters in length and about four people's embrace in width. "Can you do it?" asked Thuyet.

"It sets my teeth on edge," Buong said. Noting Thuyet's look of irritation, he added, "This place is so far from your house."

"There are only bears and monkeys here," Thuyet said. "You'll have to make your own shelter. I'll send someone to bring the mats and blankets over this afternoon. Self-sufficiency, self-strength, and diligence, okay? I've written down the sizes and the cubic centimeters for you here."

Thuyet gave Buong a piece of paper covered with

writing. Buong gave it to me. "What if the wolves eat us up?" Buong asked.

"There aren't any wolves around here," Thuyet said. "You only need to worry about snakes. Be careful with the deep-green snakes. One of their bites will kill you."

"Thank you very much for your advice," Buong sneered. "So, you'll send food over every how many days?"

"It depends," Thuyet replied. "But don't worry. I'll provide stuff regularly. I'm leaving now."

"You do that. Please give my thanks to your wife and your children," Buong said.

Thuyet left, leaving the five of us in the middle of a wild forest. Buong cursed, "Damned life! How vile it is. Don't you see how life is, my children?"

"That guy Thuyet, he looked horrible," I said.

"Let's get to work, guys," Buong ordered. "Bien and Bieng, prepare the saws. Ngoc and I will make a shack. Little Dinh, explore around here to see whether there is any water at all."

We began to work. Buong cut down some bamboo trees and very quickly made some thatch. Bien and Bieng cut down the top of the tree and made some planks for our beds. We finished everything by early evening.

While Little Dinh was cooking, a girl came, carrying two round baskets on a pole. Her name was Quy. She was seventeen years old and Thuyet's oldest daughter. With light and healthy skin, she looked very pretty. Buong asked her, "Hey, babe, my little queen, what have you brought for us?"

"Uncle," Quy replied. "My father told me to bring you two heavy cotton blankets, five kilograms of pork, one bottle of fish sauce and twenty kilograms of rice."

"Good," Buong said. "Did you bring us an oil lamp?"

"Oh no, I forgot it," Quy said. "Why do you need lamps in the middle of the forest, anyway?"

"What kind of thought is that? Don't you know the

saying, 'One needs lamps when alive and drums when dead'?"

"All right, I'll come back tomorrow, then. I'm leaving now."

"Why go? Sleep here with us. I'll ask Ngoc to tell you some detective stories," Buong said.

"Go to hell! I have to go now. It's getting dark."

"Ngoc, see the little girl off."

I followed the girl. I asked her, "So, your name is Quy, right? It's a nice name."

"What's nice about it?" Quy smiled. "Girls named Quy often have a difficult life. Someone told me that my name is very mediocre."

"There is something strange in that name. When I was at the university, all girls named Quy were insipid and unfaithful."

"You were at the university? So why did you become a woodcutter, then?" Quy asked in surprise.

Imitating Buong's way of talking, I smiled and said to Quy, "It's because of love. Love is always messy. People only regret it when they lose it."

"That sounds very interesting, but I don't understand you at all."

"Of course, you don't understand anything at all," I told her. An anger without reason suddenly seized my heart, making my mouth bitterly dry. "There's only me. The rest are them." I uttered these words between clenched teeth. Quy was surprised and frightened. We said goodbye like two strangers. And we truly were strangers. Hey, strangers, among the million I'll meet in my life, who has the blood of my blood? The flesh of my flesh? Who would live for me and die for me? Anyone at all? Who would be my emperor? My subject? Who would be my confidant? My hope? My hell?

I returned to the shack. We ate in the dark. "How was it?" Buong asked. "Did you get a chance to kiss Thuyet's daughter at all? Why do you look as gloomy as a monkey?"

"Don't joke like that." I was angry with him.

"Enough, Mr. Young Intellectual," Buong said. "You guys always worry about morality, but that only benefits politics. It doesn't benefit women at all."

I found the rice completely tasteless. I even bit into pieces of grit. It was simple. When I was at the university, I had been in love and suffered its pain. I'll tell that story another time.

At night, it was foggy and cold. We kindled a fire and huddled under the blankets. I couldn't sleep. At midnight, we could hear from somewhere on the mountain the sound of a deer barking as if in pain. Buong woke up and asked me, "Hey, brat, are you homesick?"

"No," I said. "The deer sounds so pained. Do you think it lost its mother?"

"Don't be so sentimental," Buong told me. "Life is full of hardship. We must exhaust ourselves working for food. To be sentimental will make you weak. We have a lot of heavy work tomorrow. If you can't sleep just because of the sound of a deer, it's counter-productive. I brought you along to work, not to dream."

"The deer is barking all night long," I sighed. "I wonder when it will find its mother. Go ahead and sleep. Ignore me. I won't let it affect our work tomorrow."

"Monkey!" Buong got angry. "Such pointless sensitivity will destroy your life. How could it be a deer looking for its mother? Listen kid, it's just a decadent female deer looking for its mate. Unfortunately, that mate merely seduced it and now it's off fooling around. The female deer got infected with his disease. It's as simple as that. Always. All cries at night are the cries of decadent lust. Maternal love never screams out loud like that. Maternal love is a kind of teardrop running inward. It either breaks one's heart into pieces or becomes part of the blood, forcing the body to work and produce a concrete and practical product. It's never frivolous."

I fell into a sleep full of vague dreams. I knew that Buong

did not have the ability to explain life. No one could explain it, this boundless and inexhaustible life. Whenever it encountered the darkness of hunger and poverty, it would bark loudly.

The next morning, after breakfast, we began to work. Bien and Bieng paired up. So did Buong and I. We used the saw to cut the tree into logs of different lengths, as Thuyet required. The wood of the white seraya tree was very hard and brittle. It was easy to cut it horizontally, but extremely difficult to make lumber vertically. The trunk was big and we had no choice but to make the lumber in the Thanh Hoa style, meaning we put it on the ground to cut without propping it up on anything. The sap of the tree stung our eyes, making all four of us teary.

"The Ocean King used this wood to make his castle under the water. It's so hard to saw," said Buong. "Devil, we must owe that chap Thuyet ten thousand pieces of gold from our previous lives."

Based on Thuyet's written instructions, we made lumber for house-pillars at 40cm x 40cm x 320cm. That did not include what we'd need to make planks and rafters. "What kind of a house is that Thuyet going to make that needs so many pillars?" Buong wondered. "A house-on-stilts, perhaps?"

At noon, a worker from the collective farm looking for firewood came by. Buong chatted with him and complained that we had to make thirty-six giant house-pillars. The worker laughed. "Even a five-room house would only need twelve pillars at most," he said. "That guy Thuyet is so cunning. He must be selling the rest of them to drivers from the lowlands. Those guys love house-pillars made from white seraya wood."

"Listen, brother, if you get those drivers here, we'll sell them some lumber directly, without Thuyet knowing about it. Is that possible?" Buong asked.

"Sure, but is there anything in it for me?"

"Of course. My name is Dang Xuan Buong. What's yours?"

"Tran Quang Hanh."

"You have such a beautiful name. Please don't sully it."

"All right," the worker laughed. "The trucks will come in four days."

We waited for Quy that whole day, but she did not show up. "That little bitch, she only lies," Buong said. "Guys, don't place your trust in women. They are very cruel in their innocence and purity. They provoke in you hopes, desires, and longings; we will become emaciated up to the day we close our eyes forever."

Quy came the next day. She brought us two cabbages and an oil lamp. "Wow," she said. "You work really fast. So much lumber already. I must tell my father to come and see it tomorrow."

"Don't tell him to come. We're only crazy about you," said Buong. "If your old man comes here, we'll go on a slowdown strike. Manual labor, my little girl, can't be mobilized by politics. It can only be mobilized by money and women: the vitamins of life. Capitalism is so cruel. It uses money and women to exploit the surplus value. It exhausts the wealth and energy of the proletariat. Down with rotten capitalism!"

Before Quy left, Buong told me, "Ngoc, write a letter on my behalf. Quy, please post it for me."

"Go ahead and write your letter," Quy said.

Buong dictated and I wrote the following letter:

"The Northwest forest, dated ____
Respectfully to Mr. Hai Dung [the father of Bien and Bieng], *Old Dieu* [my father] *and the mother of Little Dinh* [Buong's wife],
This is Buong. On behalf of the woodcutters' group, I inform you that we have found jobs, pretty

*well-paid ones. Everybody is fine. The mountain people
are all kind and very helpful to us. Next week I'll send
some money home. The mother of Little Dinh should
divide it into five. Bien and Bieng's family should get
three, Old Dieu's family gets one, and our family gets
one. The medicine for my old man should not be
excessive. You can't cure the disease of being old. The
most important thing is to provide clothes and food for
the kids. I feel sorry for you and the children for not
having a decent house to live in. Therefore, I am
determined to face dangers in the forest. Thanks to
heaven's good direction, I should succeed in two years.
I ask you, the mother of Little Dinh, to observe filial
piety and love properly. Everything else in life is
ephemeral. Short on writing but long on love.*

Signed,

Dang Xuan Buong"

"Your letter sounds very interesting," Quy said.

"It is only demagoguery, my babe," Buong laughed. "When a hero is far from home, the most important thing is to have a stable rear."

We invited Quy to stay for dinner, but she declined. "We make you work so hard," Buong said to Quy. "Sit down, girl. I'll tell them to wrestle so you can have some fun."

Buong told us to strip to our shorts. He made four ballots. Anyone who got a ballot with an X had to wrestle. Bieng and I got the marks. "Great," Buong laughed. "I was only worried that Bien and Bieng would both got the X marks. If the twin brothers wrestled, it would be like, 'When you make a fire of beanstalks to boil beans, the beans cry: "We come from the same roots. How can you have the heart to burn us?"'[6] Now go ahead and wrestle. The winner will not have to work this afternoon."

---

6. This verse comes from the famous Chinese poet-prince Cao Zhi, who lived during the Three Kingdoms Period.

Bieng and I entered the "ring." Bieng was younger, but bigger. He weighed sixty-two kilos. Both Bieng and I had studied with Hai Dung and thus we were very familiar with each other's style of fighting. Bieng was very hot-tempered. Once he got angry, he did not care about anyone, including his brother and relatives. I knew that. Therefore, when I entered the "ring," I smiled like buds and flowers and was very gentle, forcing him to act the same way. After about three minutes, I was able to lure Bieng into my rhythms using harmless tricks. I raised my feet. Bieng also raised his feet. I raised my hands. Bieng also raised his hands. Buong, Quy, Bien, and Little Dinh clapped their hands and cheered noisily. I gave an upper strike. Bieng also gave an upper strike. I gave a lower strike. Bieng also gave a lower strike. I thought to myself, "It must be his fate to eat the dirt; it's not my fault." I crouched down, gathered inner force and suddenly grabbed Bieng's ankles and squeezed them hard. Bieng lost his balance and fell down, hurt. I rushed upon him, pressed my knee on his bladder, my elbow on his neck and choked him. Everybody clapped and cheered. Bieng sat up and shook his head, "Little Uncle, you're mean. I thought we were playing for fun, but it became a real fight."

I patted Bieng's shoulder and smiled, "I'm sorry. Your father taught me that extra trick. That's why you didn't know about it."

Quy seemed to like it. Her cheeks were rosy. Buong said, "Now, it's my turn." He jumped onto the grass and performed the Snake Fight, a famous exercise of the Vinh Xuan martial arts sect. It looked beautiful and had many unpredictable changes. We watched him, holding our collective breath. Our hearts leapt from the intensity. I had seen many people performing martial arts but rarely someone who poured his whole heart into his performance like that. We were enchanted. Only when Buong stopped and made his ending kowtow did we let out sighs of relief.

The sun was blazing that afternoon. I asked Buong, "So, am I free?"

"No," Buong was firm.

"Didn't you say the winner could take the afternoon off?"

Buong pulled me away so that Bien and Bieng could not hear our conversation. "Hey, get rid of your roughneck tricks. You lured Bieng into a game for fun and defeated him for real. Your way of wrestling is the way of an intellectual. It can only fool Quy, not me."

I laughed. "Have you heard the saying, 'The revolutionary only concentrates on the ultimate goal'?"

"Don't lure me into the politics of ideology, you scoundrel," Buong said.

"You know Bieng," I said. "He's so strong. If he broke my arm, would you feel sorry for me?"

"You are by nature a politically intellectual roughneck. How disgusting. Get the fuck out of here."

"But you were a criminal yourself—an actual roughneck. How come you can't tolerate me?"

"You're free," Buong spat in my face. "If necessary, I'll borrow money for you to go home first thing tomorrow morning."

I lay face-down on the grass. The wind blew, drying the spit on my face. My hands were calloused and oozed blood. My feet were chapped. I had not bathed or washed for an entire week. My skin and flesh were dirty and itchy. I suddenly felt so sorry for myself. A dreadful pity seized my heart. I cried out loudly, like a dog. I turned round and round amid the thatch, full of sharp rocks and thorns. I closed my eyes, trying to imagine the face of the girl I once loved. She was small, with a round face and thick eyebrows. She had a beauty-mark on her nape, about four centimeters from her right ear. Every feature of her face appeared very clearly: her lips, her nose, her profile. She did not understand that I could give her something even more than love. (And is there really such a thing as love?) She had lost my respect and pity.

Forever. And ever. Nothing could redeem them. I was full of hatred, hatred for all the transience of the conditions of my era. Every dogma of morality was simple, stupid, uproarious, shallow, and even wicked. And the utmost cruelty of it all lay in the fact that all of these dogmas were correct. Because they were necessary. They were the chains we had to wear around our necks in order to maintain a consistent image of each other. If not, there would be ruin.

I went deep into the forest to find some water for a bath. The stream was dry. White butterflies scattered and flicked among small caves. After walking up the stream for a long time, I found a pool. I stripped and went into the water naked, like a buffalo. The water was deep green and a little sticky because there were too many rotten leaves at the bottom. I didn't dare to bathe for a long time because I was afraid of getting sick, of catching marsh fever. It would be a waste to die at the age of twenty-one. I had to live, despite the fact that life was horrible, vile, full of evil and hardship.

I returned to the shack. Buong was sawing a piece of timber with Little Dinh. Buong stood on a high log. Little Dinh squatted down. The boy tried hard and sweat soaked his shirt. He looked very pitiful. I went over to Little Dinh and quietly took the saw from his hand. Buong and I did not say anything to each other. We sawed one log after another in silence, until it got really dark.

When we were about to stop and I was standing with my feet near the lumber, the saw handle suddenly hit my chest. I cried out and fell down. I wasn't sure whether Buong did it on purpose or if it was only an accident, but he did let the saw blade cut through the wood and into one of my toes. The joint of my left toe was cut and the white bone poked through. Blood spurted out. It hurt so much that my jaw dropped open, jerking as if I were having a seizure. Sweat covered my face while my body turned horribly cold. I writhed on the ground. Bien and Bieng had to lie on me to force me to stay still. Buong went pale. He used a piece of rubber to tie my foot to stop the bleeding. He hurried Little Dinh to mix some salt and hot water to clean my wound. I was numb with pain. My teeth chattered despite my efforts to stop them. Not until midnight did I doze off. I completely lost my energy.

I was feverish for three days. My foot swelled up. The wound was horrible: the saw had cut through two thirds of the toe. The rest of the toe blackened, probably rotten. Buong ground some antibiotic tetracycline to cover my wound. Although I washed it with salt water, it still had a yellow discharge.

On the afternoon of the third day, the worker from the collective farm, Tran Quang Hanh, guided a four-ton truck to our shack. Buong sold twelve house-pillars and several pieces of lumber that were 2.20m x 60cm x 8cm. The truck driver paid fairly. Buong paid the guide twenty thousand dong and told him, "You deserve the beauty of your name."

Chinh and Thuc passed by our shack on their way to gather firewood. Seeing my foot swollen, Thuc felt sorry for me. "You are so cruel," she said, pointing at Buong. "You left his foot like this without any treatment?"

Buong looked down and started crying. "What could I do, Older Sister?"

Chinh examined my wound. "We must get rid of the rotten part," he said. "If we leave it like this for long, you will get gangrene and die. Unfortunately, I didn't bring any medical equipment with me."

Buong wiped away his tears and asked, "Could we chop it off with a large kitchen knife?"

"Yes," Chinh said. "But what about medicine?"

"Let me go home and get some," Thuc said. She briskly set off.

"Take the bag hanging on the wall," Chinh called to his wife. "And remember to bring the syringe kit."

"Dinh!" Buong called his son. "Follow Aunt Thuc."

Chinh ordered Bieng to boil the water to sterilize the knife and clean my wound. "You woodcutters are real risk-takers," Chinh said. "You equate human life with that of a mosquito."

Thuc and Little Dinh came back about an hour later. Thuc brought a chicken from her house. She told Bien and Bieng to cook some chicken porridge for me.

Buong told me to put my foot on a log. "Stay calm," he said. "I'm going to cut it off." To Chinh, he said, "Please hold the knife and put it right here. I will hit this pestle on it. That should do."

Thuc covered her face, "Horrible! This is too scary."

"This is the first time I've practiced medicine in this way," Chinh said, laughing.

Chinh put the knife blade on my wounded toe. Buong struck the pestle on the back of the blade. Thump! I jumped in pain. "I wasn't ready," Chinh said. "The knife blade wasn't on the right joint."

"Enough! Enough!" I said. "It hurts too much. I'll die if you do it again."

Thuc snatched the pestle from Buong's hand. "Get out of here," she said. "Are you planning to kill him or what?" And to Chinh, she said, "Tell me when you're ready."

"I'm ready now," Chinh told his wife. "Strike it!"

Thuc swung the pestle. Thump. The rotten flesh from my toe flew off. I bit into my hand, my eyes dazzled. Chinh gave me a shot and bandaged my foot. "It's all right now," he said. "It will be better in a few days."

Buong took the rotten piece of flesh and threw it into the fire. "I wish that all of his roughneck qualities could be burned like this piece of flesh," he said.

Thuc fed me some porridge and a piece of ginseng she got from Chinh's medical bag. Buong said, "You're lucky, Ngoc. Nobody's ever taken care of me as well as she's taking care of you."

Thuc said, "Let me cut off your foot first, then I'll take care of you."

"My wife is very hard on me, but she's very generous to others," Chinh said with a smile.

"Women are strange," Buong said. "They torment anything that belongs to them. They only value love brought over by the wind. Therefore, the most miserable thing for a man is to become a woman's possession."

"Yes, that's true," Chinh said.

"So why do you live with me then?" Thuc said. "Do you want a divorce?"

"You are so thin-skinned," Chinh laughed.

Chinh and Thuc were about to leave. Buong told Bien and Bieng to put two bundles of timber into Chinh's cart. "We present you with a bed. They belong to humankind. If good people like us don't take them, we would be letting only bad people enjoy good fortune. That would be truly sad."

Thuc declined firmly. "It's not possible. This wood belongs to Thuyet already."

"Yesterday we sold half of it to a truckdriver. Who cares?" Buong said.

"You woodcutters are real risk-takers," Chinh laughed. "You would even sell Heaven without any paperwork. What if Thuyet questions you?"

"Please don't worry," Buong said. "We have our answers. He paid us so cheaply. If we only sawed wood without stealing lumber, how could we survive?"

"No matter what, I won't take it," Thuc said.

Buong called Bien, Bieng, and Little Dinh over. "You boys kneel down and kowtow to them four times," Buong said. "If they still refuse, knock your heads on the rock and kill yourselves. They don't consider us human beings."

The woodcutters knelt down and put their hands together to kowtow. Little Dinh also knelt face down.

"Enough, enough," Thuc said through her tears. "Why are you doing that? I will take one bundle of timber, then."

Buong was extremely happy. He held Thuc's hand and shook it vigorously. "So you are sympathetic to us, Older

Sister," Buong said. "You don't consider us animals! Our lots are humble. We have no treasures at all. It would be miserable if we owed debts of compassion and charity."

Bien and Bieng helped push the cart for Chinh and Thuc all the way to the edge of the forest.

Several days later, my foot got much better and I could make lumber again. Buong was very happy. "Today Thuyet will come," Buong said. "The guy promised a feast. Our life is refreshed."

Thuyet and Quy came to see us that afternoon. The feast turned out to be only two packs of cigarettes and one kilogram of shrimp paste. "This shrimp paste is export quality," Thuyet said. "My friend from the Hai Phong Export Trade Company brought it to me."

"I know," Buong said. "This shrimp paste will be exported to Japan, right?"

"I'm not sure," Thuyet said. "But European people are addicted to our country's shrimp paste."

Thuyet examined the wood. "I thought this tree would make a lot of lumber," he complained. "It turned out to be quite little."

"You see," Buong said. "The tree was half-empty inside. This amount is pretty good, considering. To make a house, you'll need at least two more trees."

"I've thought about it," Thuyet said. "This tree will produce pillars and lumber only. As for rafters and other parts, I'll need a clausena tree. I also want to make some planks, but I'm out of money now."

"You can do it if you really want to," Buong said.

"After this job, you can cut down a clausena tree for me. That tree grows in a rather steep place and very far from here."

"Money can do anything," Buong said.

"There are two owners of the tree," Thuyet said. "I'm the secondary one. The main owner is a Mr. Song of the Thai community in Vuoc village. He'll come here tomorrow."

Thuyet got out a piece of paper and a pen to make his calculations. "Now I will pay your labor," he said. "Based on our agreement, for cutting down this tree and making lumber, I had to provide 50 kg of rice, 10 kg of meat and this amount of money. But you did not make enough lumber, so I will deduct this amount. Two heavy cotton blankets cost this amount of money. I can sell them to you if you want."

"So, you're only paying one third of the money we agreed on?" Buong asked.

"I could also deduct the bundle of timber you sold to Thuc and her husband," Thuyet said. "But they gave it back to me, so I won't do that."

"I did not sell them that bundle of lumber," Buong said. "I offered it to them as a gift. Why did you take it back?"

"You acted as if it were yours," Thuyet said. "I could have ordered the collective farm's guard to arrest Thuc and her husband for violating my private ownership rights."

"Enough. It wasn't the fault of Thuc or her husband," Buong said. "Go ahead and calculate your payment. If you don't pay as we've agreed, I'll use this knife on you. You can joke with anyone else, but not with Dang Xuan Buong."

"Hey, do you want to show off your roughneck ways? Each land has its own customs and habits. The customs and habits around here are not like yours. For your information, one wave of my hand and you'll be finished. Do you want to continue to work in peace or not?"

"Wow," Buong said. "How aggressive!"

A clap of thunder suddenly roared through the high, blue, and sunny sky. We were chilled. Thuyet lit a cigarette. "Do you give up?" he asked Buong with a smile.

"I do," Buong replied, shaking his head in defeat.

"Take the money," Thuyet said. "I will send a truck in for the wood tomorrow." Turning to Quy, he said, "You go home first, daughter. I have to go to Uncle Song's house in Vuoc village."

Quy and Thuyet left. Buong counted the money.

"According to the original plan, we need to get this much money," he said. "Working for Thuyet, we lost seventy percent. Luckily, I was flexible and sold twelve pillars and seven bundles of lumber. We got this amount of money for that. Compared to the original plan, we gained two hundred twenty percent. Life is great! That's what I would call economical accounting." A moment later, he added, "We'll take a break this afternoon. Little Dinh and I will go to the post office tomorrow morning to send the money home. If Song comes here, Ngoc can represent us."

We wanted to go and take a bath. "I have something else to do," Buong said. "Go ahead and eat dinner without me." He then looked around and took off. I found his behavior suspicious, so I decided to follow him.

Buong walked very fast in the direction of the collective farm. He chose the short cut, not the main path, which made me even more suspicious. When he got to the cotton field, he crawled into it and then got out a little while later. He looked completely different, with leaves and branches tied around himself. He only wore a pair of shorts. When he got to the turn near the edge of the forest, he crawled into a bush and stayed there. "What the hell is this guy going to do?" I wondered. I squeezed my hands together, knowing that something bad would happen.

In fact, Quy came out from the forest a little while later. The sunset covered the scenery with a dim and indescribably sad light. Quy held a stick in her hand, tapping on the trees on both sides of the path. I did not like Quy's confident and carefree appearance. It was stupid. Yes, stupid. The girl I once loved was just the same. She thought that confidence and freedom were good for her. No, not a hundred percent of the time, not ten thousand percent of the time. For women, confidence and freedom lead to unforeseen danger; they even bear the possibility of misfortune and dishonor. As for myself, the dignity of a woman lies in her dependence on me. Forever. Always like that. Because I am a man. Me. No one can change that. When Quy passed by Buong's hiding place, he jumped up. I heard Quy scream. Buong covered her mouth and carried her into a thicket. I understood what was going on. Anger seized my heart. I dropped to the ground, unable to breath. I got up and dashed to the thicket. Quy's pants were off, her two naked legs waving frantically in the air. I pulled Buong up and hit him in the face very hard. Buong was shocked to see me. We jumped onto each other like two animals.

The patch of land where we fought was very small, surrounded by thorn bushes. We could not move forward or backward. We held each other's hands to guard ourselves. We must have looked very funny.

After maintaining our guard for a while, Buong shrieked, "Bastard, if you want to fight, let's go out there. What can we do in this thorny thicket?" Then he released his hand and jumped out into an empty space.

I jumped after him. He stepped back and told Quy in a sad voice, "Little brat, put your pants on. If you like to watch a fight, then stay and watch. We'll fight because of you." Then Buong stood there and poked his nose, as if the fight between us was certain, yet meaningless and of no value.

I was a little embarrassed. Buong smiled and encouraged me, "How about that? Move forward! Offer your victory at the feet of Miss Dulcinea in the village of Toledo."

I got mad. Suddenly I thought of the first love of my life. I loved that girl despite the fact that she was so frivolous, deceptive, and immoral. I knew for sure I would have no other love after her. None of the women I would ever meet could make me happy or cause me pain. I struck Buong with all the anger and pain from the bottom of my heart.

Buong probably didn't expect that I would suddenly become so brutal and cruel. My thrust was so powerful and wicked that if I had managed to hit him, my rival would have died or at least become disabled for the rest of his life. Buong shouted and jumped away to avoid the blow.

We fought fiercely. My martial arts skills were from the Thieu Lam Hong Gia School, while Buong's came from the Vinh Xuan. When Buong was in the army, he also studied with several other groups, and therefore his methods changed unpredictably. He hit me constantly. Perhaps he didn't want to knock me out. He purposefully moved in a circle to make me gradually lose my energy. We were both exhausted after almost an hour and released each other.

Night fell. The moon lit up the entire mountain and forest. Buong and I lay on the grass, breathing heavily. A little while later, he sat up. "Don't you see how stupid we are? Two men fighting because of a woman. It's nonsense." As he continued, his voice sounded lost. "Ngoc, don't be so miserable. Do you know why the elders call that part of a woman a butterfly? Because it has wings that flutter. It's Heaven's blessing. Wherever it stops, that person can have it. Sometimes one even has to catch it."

I sat up and vomited blood. "You bastard," I told Buong, my voice trembling. "The girl is still very young."

"You don't understand anything," Buong said. "Who will think of the age of a butterfly? A young girl and an old woman are the same."

"You are so mean and cruel," I said.

Buong sneered, "My little boy, isn't Jesus Christ mean and cruel? Isn't Buddha mean and cruel?"

"The nobility of human beings seems to lie in their limits," I said.

"That's right," Buong said. "Didn't you see when Quy had her clothes stripped off?" he asked. "The way she closed her thighs—she was absolutely noble in her spirit."

It was foggy and cold. We walked back to the shack, our faces bruised. "Your blows were truly cruel, right on the face," Buong said. "That means your martial arts skill is not at a high level. High-level fighters are different. When their enemies attack, they find a way to harmonize their enemies' energies with their own. Of course, it must be done skillfully. High-level fighters lead their rivals in circles. A circle is the most perfect form in our existence. Instead of using power to solve conflicts, a high-level fighter forces his enemy to understand that only gentleness, flexibility, politeness, compassion, harmony, and peace—" he paused before continuing, "—can complete the relationships among human beings and the relationships between each individual and the entire world. The technique may be brutal, but the strategy must be conciliatory. To be more precise, the strategy must be stable and balanced. Those are the theories of high-level fighters."

I smiled quietly in the darkness. I knew Buong. Whenever he explained about life in general, he was always wise and tried to hold his dignity high. But his real life was like dog shit: too stinky to sniff at.

The next morning, we moved to the new place for sawing. Song from the Thai community was sixty-two years old. He had an honest face. "The work is really hard," he said. "Can you stand it?"

"Every road leads to Hell anyway," Buong answered.

The yellow clausena tree stood precariously halfway up the mountain, leaning toward the abyss. The main job was to cut the tree down without letting it fall into the chasm. It took us half a day to figure out the best solution, which was to cut off the branches and tie the tree to a rope on one side and, on the other, to dig out the ground around it to make a flat surface for the safe landing of the tree. It took us ten days to cut the tree down. Song was very pleased and invited us to his village for a treat. "I'll stay here to tend to our belongings," Buong said. Bien, Bieng, Little Dinh and I followed Song to Vuoc village. The village, which lay on the big road, contained about fifty houses on stilts. Everyone in the village was nice and friendly. We drank liquor at Song's house and didn't return until the afternoon. When we got back to our shack, we were frightened to see that our blankets, mosquito nets, and clothes were all over the place while Buong was nowhere to be seen. We went to search for him. When we went to the brink of the abyss, Little Dinh's sharp eyes discovered that the bushes around it were smashed as if someone had rolled on them. Bien, Bieng, and I took our big knives and found our way down.

The abyss was more than a hundred meters deep. A dry stream lay at its bottom. Noises from downstream sounded like someone fighting. We guessed it was Buong.

Then, in a narrow part of the stream, we found him fighting fiercely with a giant bear. The bear stood on its two back legs, trying to attack Buong and producing horrible roars. Buong held a short bamboo stick, trying to fend off the bear. Leaning on a rock, he tried to push the bear away so that it could not force him into a life-threatening position. The bamboo stick bent over against the bear's chest because the bear was so strong. Buong seemed weakened. One of his shoulders was covered with blood. His face was covered with sweat.

Bien, Bieng and I all joined in the fight. Bieng stabbed the bear's shoulder. The bear turned and rushed at us. The four of us stood in a circle at the bottom of the stream. The bear went crazy, desperately looking for an escape. Bien, Bieng, and I only had our short-bladed knives. Buong's weapon was only a bamboo stick. The bear was very strong, about two hundred kilograms. It became even fiercer after it was wounded. Its slaps were frightening. Luckily, none of us was hit.

Bieng was very smart. He pretended to attack in front of the bear so that the three of us could stab it from its back and its two sides. When the bear knelt down once, I stabbed my knife deep into its nape. The bear fell down. Bieng rushed in and stabbed his knife into the bear's heart. The bear roared its last horrible roar. Blood spilled out from the two corners of its mouth. Bien stabbed a few more times on the bear's two sides. After several last movements, the bear died.

We were completely exhausted. Our hands and feet trembled. Buong looked pale, his smile was like a cry. Later, I witnessed many victorious smiles in many different cases, and those smiles always looked like cries. I always felt frightened and moved by them.

Buong used one of our knives to cut the bear's chest open and get its gallbladder. As big as four fingers, it was very watery. Buong was pleased. He used a thread to tie it to his neck.

That evening, we packed our belongings and carried the bear back to Thuc's house on the farm.

We knocked on her door at two o'clock in the morning. Her neighbors gathered around as if it were a festival. "I admire you woodcutters," Chinh said. "You knocked down such an impressive bear."

"Can we skin this bear and make a party for everybody here, Sister Thuc?" Buong asked.

"Nothing could be better," Thuc said. "There are ten households in this hamlet. It would be a great honor for my house if everybody came."

Everybody gathered to cook the bear. Its meat tasted good. Thuc cooked a pot of porridge. She threw into the pot all of the bear's bones and its four legs. "One bowl of this porridge is worth one hundred grams of ointment made from tiger bones," Chinh remarked.

Thuyet also joined the party. He brought a ten-liter can of rice alcohol. "This afternoon when I went to the New Establishment Unit," Thuyet said, "for some reason, I brought this can of alcohol back. It was truly predestined. I usually scold people who invite me to drink alcohol."

"Please, sir," Buong said. "Please don't scold bribers. They are sincere but stupid. A high-level man must feel pity for them."

Everybody merrily drank the liquor. Buong got more and more excited. "I was sitting in the shack when the bear came," he recalled. "Frightened, I grabbed the stick and continuously hit it."

"Weren't you scared?" Thuc asked.

"Of course, I was. But then I thought, to hell with it. Life is so boring. To live or to die is the same. If I tried, I might be able to kill the brutal animal. It was a miracle. Not everyone could do it." Everybody laughed.

Thuyet's younger brother Khang, from Hanoi, was also at the party. He jokingly said to Buong, "So, when you accomplish some humanitarian act or do a good deed, it's only because you're tired of life. Is that right?"

"Sir, are you serious or are you mocking me?" Buong snapped.

"I am serious," Khang replied with a smile.

"Let me ask you, sir. What do you do for a living?" Buong asked with a serious face.

"I teach aesthetics in Hanoi."

"And you call that a profession?" Buong asked. "According to me, the study of beauty is formless and does not truly exist. Your speciality is actually to cheat people. I once read a book by a guy named Chernobyl.[7] He wrote, 'Beauty is life.' That statement contained in itself a good laugh. You teach aesthetics, so don't you recognize the humor?"

"I'm sorry," Khang replied. "I am not equipped with knowledge similar to yours."

"Mr. Khang, please go home and suck your mother's breast," Buong said.

"Enough, enough, Buong," Thuc said. "Please respect the saying, 'Live and let live.'"

"I'll follow your advice," Buong replied to Thuc with a smile.

Song arrived. Everybody invited him to drink. He smiled

---

7. Buong made a mistake. The author's name was Chernyshevsky.

and asked, "So will you continue to make lumber for me or, now that you've killed a bear, will you stop working?"

"We helped you get the tree down. That should be enough," Buong said. "As for making lumber, you're a worker yourself, so we know you can handle it."

"That's right," Song said.

"I know a place where they need lumber to make a shrine for worshipping a spirit," Thuc said. "After you finish your meal, I'll tell you where."

"We are sincere at heart," Buong said. "It would be great luck to make lumber for the spirits. How could we repay such love?"

"Love is repaid by love," Thuc said. "If a person lives in accordance with the creator and is truly sincere, even if that person lives in mud, then that person should not be afraid of being an unworthy human being."

"Ngoc," Buong said. "Please write that sentence down. Its form is unclear, but it seems to have some content."

After the meal we went to sleep. In my sleep, I dreamed that the five of us woodcutters were walking on a seven-hued rainbow. Heaven's crystal messengers came out to welcome us in their blue and red clothes. One messenger looked very much like Quy. My family and relatives stood on the two sides of the road. I was very surprised to see her, the woman I once fell in love with. She ran to me with open arms. She put her head on my chest and cried, "Ngoc, my darling, after so much pain and shame, I came to understand that you are the only one. The rest are them." I smiled and took her small hands off mine. "Please don't be so extreme," I told her. "It's not true at all. I am only as small and insignificant as a grain of sand. I would probably bring nothing good to you. Please continue on your predestined road." I pushed her away and was frightened by my own heart's indifference.

We continued to walk on the seven-hued rainbow. White mountain flowers bloomed in abundance, a white color that stirred the heart and made it anxious. White flowers, will you be this white a thousand years from now?

We continued to walk, forever. I knew for sure that ahead of us was the sky's gate, Heaven's Gate...

* * *

After that trip, my fate turned in a different direction. I no longer went off to make lumber. I got a different job.

Translated by Nguyen Nguyet Cam

THE TRANSLATORS:

Linh Dinh is the author of a collection of stories, *Fake House* (Seven Stories Press, 2000), and three chapbooks of poems, *Drunkard Boxing* (Singing Horse Press, 1998), *A Small Triumph Over Lassitude* (Leroy Press, 2001), and *A Glass of Water* (Skanky Possum Press, 2001). He is also the editor of the anthologies *Night, Again: Contemporary Fiction from Vietnam* (Seven Stories Press, 1996) and *Three Vietnamese Poets* (Tinfish, 2001).

Nguyen Nguyet Cam earned a B.A. in English Language and Literature from the University of Hanoi and an M.A. in Asian Studies from the University of California, Berkeley, where she currently teaches advanced Vietnamese language and literature. Her translations of E.B. White's *Charlotte's Web* and *The Trumpet of the Swan* have been published by the Kim Dong Publishing House in Hanoi. She is the co-translator (with Peter Zinoman) of *Dumb Luck*, a novel by Vu Trong Phung.

Nguyen Qui Duc is the author of *Where The Ashes Are: The Odyssey of a Vietnamese Family* (Addison-Wesley, 1994) and the editor (with John Balaban) of *Vietnam: A Traveller's Literary Companion* (Whereabouts Press, 1995). He is also the translator of the novella "Behind the Red Mist" in the collection of stories *Behind the Red Mist* (Curbstone Press, 1996) by the novelist Ho Anh Thai, and a collection of poetry by Huu Thinh, *The Time Tree* (Curbstone Press, 2003). He lives in San Francisco where he hosts a National Public Radio program devoted to Asia.

Nguyen Van Khang is a professor of philology and the director of the Department of Sociolinguistics at the Institute of Linguistics in Hanoi. He is also the general secretary of the Hanoi Society of Linguistics. His publications include

Introduction to Sociolinguistics in Vietnam, *Vietnamese Slang*, and *Conversational Vietnamese Within the Family*. He has also co-authored numerous dictionaries, including *The Dictionary of Vietnamese*, *The Dictionary of Vietnamese Idioms*, *The Dictionary of Vietnamese Homophones*, *The Dictionary of Sino-Vietnamese Everyday Usage*, and *The Vietnamese-Muong Dictionary*. He lives in Hanoi.

Birgit Hussfeld is a social anthropologist specializing in Vietnam. After having worked in Vietnam for several years, she now lives in the Ukraine. She has curated exhibitions on contemporary Vietnamese art and Vietnamese political posters. Her translations from the Vietnamese have appeared in *Manoa* and *Rowohlt Literaturmagazin*. Her articles—mainly on Vietnamese arts and culture—have been published in various exhibition catalogs as well as in magazines and newspapers.

Viviane Lowe lived and worked in Hanoi for several years in the early 1990s. She studied Vietnamese in Hanoi and at the Australian National University, where she received an MA in Anthropology in 1996. She has translated several short stories and articles from Vietnamese. She now lives in Switzerland and works as a freelance editor and translator.

Rosemary Nguyen's love affair with the Vietnamese language began with a stint as an English as a Second Language teacher in the Hong Kong boat people camps in 1987 and continued during a year of study at the University of Hanoi in 1990. In 1992, she launched a career as a full-time freelance translator and interpreter. She is the translator of *Literature News* (Yale University Council on Southeast Asia Studies, 1997), an anthology of Vietnamese short stories originally printed in the Vietnam Writer's Union newspaper, *Bao Van Nghe*. Her translations of Vietnamese fiction have also been published in *The Viet Nam Forum* and *Virtual Lotus:*

Modern Fiction of Southeast Asia. She currently resides in Seattle, Washington, with her husband and daughter.

Courtney Norris is a consultant in the field of agricultural development, specializing in Vietnam. She recently co-authored a textbook with Bac Hoai Tran entitled *Sinh Hoat Bang Anh Ngu* (Living With English) for Vietnamese learners of English. She lives in San Francisco and is currently researching a book on Vietnamese silk weaving.

Dana Sachs is the author of *The House on Dream Street: Memoir of an American Woman in Vietnam* (Algonquin Books of Chapel Hill, 2000). She has translated a wide range of contemporary Vietnamese fiction, including, with Bac Hoai Tran, *The Stars, The Earth, The River: Short Fiction by Le Minh Khue* (Curbstone Press, 1997). With her sister, filmmaker Lynne Sachs, she made the award-winning documentary about Vietnam, *Which Way is East?* She lives in Wilmington, North Carolina, with her husband and two sons.

Peter Saidel lived in Vietnam in the 1990s. He then earned his M.A. in writing from the Columbia University School of the Arts, before returning to Asia as news and politics editor at the *Far Eastern Economic Review* in Hong Kong.

Bac Hoai Tran received his master's degree in English with a concentration in linguistics from San Francisco State University in 1999. He has been teaching Vietnamese at the University of California at Berkeley since 1992. He is the author of the textbooks *Anh Ngu Bao Chi* (1993) and *Conversational Vietnamese* (First Edition 1996, Second Edition 1999). He and Dana Sachs are the translators of *The Stars, The Earth, The River: Short Fiction by Le Minh Khue* (1997). Some of their translations of Vietnamese short stories have also appeared in the anthologies *The Other Side of*

Heaven (1995), *Vietnam: A Traveler's Literary Companion* (1996), *Night, Again* (1996), *North Viet Nam Now* (1996), and in *Behind the Red Mist* (1998). He is a co-author of the textbook *Living With English* (2001). He has been the Vietnamese language coordinator for SEASSI (Southeast Asian Studies Summer Institute) at the University of Wisconsin-Madison.

Peter Zinoman is currently an associate professor of Southeast Asian History at the University of California, Berkeley. He is the author of *The Colonial Bastille: A History of Imprisonment in Vietnam, 1862-1940* (University of California Press, 2001). He has published translations of several works of modern Vietnamese fiction including (with Nguyen Nguyet Cam) *Dumb Luck*, a novel by Vu Trong Phung (University of Michigan Press, 2002).

Voices from Viet Nam
a series of contemporary fiction
edited by
Le Minh Khue, Ho Anh Thai, Wayne Karlin.

#1: *The Stars, the Earth, the River*, short fiction by Le Minh Khue, translated by Bac Hoai Tran & Dana Sachs; paperback, ISBN 1-880684-47-0, $14.95.

#2: *Behind the Red Mist*, short fiction by Ho Anh Thai, translated by Nguyen Qui Duc, et al; paperback, ISBN 1-880684-54-3, $14.95.

#3: *Against the Flood*, a novel by Ma Van Khang, translated by Phan Thanh Hao & Wayne Karlin; paperback, ISBN 1-880684-67-5, $15.95.

#4: *Past Continuous*, a novel by Nguyen Khai, translated by Phan Thanh Hao & Wayne Karlin; paperback, ISBN 1-880684-78-0, $15.95.

#5: *Crossing the River*, short fiction by Nguyen Huy Thiep, edited by Nguyen Nguyet Cam & Dana Sachs, translated by Bac Hoai Tran, et al.; paperback, ISBN 1-880684-92-6, $15.95.

CURBSTONE PRESS, INC.

is a non-profit publishing house dedicated to literature that reflects a commitment to social change, with an emphasis on contemporary writing from Latino, Latin American and Vietnamese cultures. Curbstone presents writers who give voice to the unheard in a language that goes beyond denunciation to celebrate, honor and teach. Curbstone builds bridges between its writers and the public – from inner-city to rural areas, colleges to community centers, children to adults. Curbstone seeks out the highest aesthetic expression of the dedication to human rights and intercultural understanding: poetry, testimonies, novels, stories, and children's books.

This mission requires more than just producing books. It requires ensuring that as many people as possible learn about these books and read them. To achieve this, a large portion of Curbstone's schedule is dedicated to arranging tours and programs for its authors, working with public school and university teachers to enrich curricula, reaching out to underserved audiences by donating books and conducting readings and community programs, and promoting discussion in the media. It is only through these combined efforts that literature can truly make a difference.

Curbstone Press, like all non-profit presses, depends on the support of individuals, foundations, and government agencies to bring you, the reader, works of literary merit and social significance which might not find a place in profit-driven publishing channels, and to bring the authors and their books into communities across the country. Our sincere thanks to the many individuals, foundations, and government agencies who support this endeavor: J. Walton Bissell Foundation, Connecticut Commission on the Arts, Connecticut Humanities Council, Daphne Seybolt Culpeper Foundation, Fisher Foundation, Greater Hartford Arts Council, Hartford Courant Foundation, J. M. Kaplan Fund, Eric Mathieu King Fund, John D. and Catherine T. MacArthur Foundation, National Endowment for the Arts, Open Society Institute, Puffin Foundation, and the Woodrow Wilson National Fellowship Foundation.

Please help to support Curbstone's efforts to present the diverse voices and views that make our culture richer. Tax-deductible donations can be made by check or credit card to:
Curbstone Press, 321 Jackson Street, Willimantic, CT 06226
phone: (860) 423-5110   fax: (860) 423-9242
www.curbstone.org

IF YOU WOULD LIKE TO BE A MAJOR SPONSOR OF A CURBSTONE BOOK, PLEASE CONTACT US.